PERSPECTIVES ON ARGUMENTATION
Essays in Honor of Wayne Brockriede

Edited by

Robert Trapp
Willamette University

Janice Schuetz
The University of New Mexico

WAVELAND
PRESS, INC.
Prospect Heights, Illinois

For information about this book, write or call:
Waveland Press, Inc.
P.O. Box 400
Prospect Heights, Illinois 60070
(708) 634-0081

Preface

The goal of this book is to explore a variety of perspectives and situations in which teachers and learners can find arguments. The book is dedicated to Wayne Brockriede (1922-1985) whose career focused on teaching and learning about argument. To his colleagues, Brockriede was both a gentleman and a scholar. He began his career in 1947 teaching speech at Miami University; he later taught at Carthage College, Universities of Illinois, Oklahoma, and Colorado. He ended his career at California State University in Fullerton. Brockriede's roles included director of forensics, department chair, editor of several journals, and president of the Speech Communication Association.

Although Brockriede thought of himself as a mediocre or average teacher, his friends and colleagues considered him to be an outstanding teacher, scholar, and mentor who contributed a great deal to their own teaching and research about argumentation. Schuetz (1986) noted: "In a few cases, outstanding teachers model the philosophy and theoretical principles that they advocate in their scholarship. Wayne Brockriede was such a teacher" (p. 357). He displayed his talents as teacher and scholar by applying the values of the human sciences to his professional activities and by treating persons as reasoners who actively choose their responses to arguments, peoples, and contexts.

The collection of chapters in this book allow the authors to share collectively with their own students of argumentation the ideas Brockriede held and those ideas he generated in others' scholarship. The chapters in this volume demonstrate the important role that reasoning plays in personal, social, philosophical and technical communities. The chapters also emphasize the great variety of unique places where students can search for and find arguments. We hope that students will see the broad range of human behavior in which argument plays a central role.

Contents

Part IV   Arguing in Philosophical
and Technical Communities   175

Part V   Arguing in Non-traditional Places   241

Part VI   The Future of Argumentation   285

Part I

Argumentation
Perspectives and Places

> Perspectivism recognizes that everything is related to everything else. A perspectivist view is a way of focusing on one picture at a time without violating the integrity of the view under scrutiny (Brockriede, 1985a, p. 153).

Wayne Brockriede promoted perspectivism as a useful approach for understanding argument and claimed that argument could be found in a variety places including the traditional as well as the nontraditional. For this reason, we have chosen "perspectives" as the key word in the title of the book and "perspectives and places" as key words in this introductory section. The first section of the book explains different perspectives on argument and different places where argument can be found.

In the first chapter, Brockriede deals with the concepts of perspectives and places. First, he concludes that argument is a *perspective* that can be brought to bear on communication situations when persons share to some degree each of these six characteristics: an inferential leap, a perceived rationale, a choice among disputed claims, regulation of uncertainty, risk of confrontation, and a shared frame of reference. Second, he asks us to look for argument "in such relatively exotic places as the aesthetic experience, the interpersonal transaction, and the reporting of research studies" (1975, p. 179). Many of the subsequent chapters in the book refer to his conception of argumentative perspectives and places.

In the second chapter, Joseph W. Wenzel uses the concept of perspective to explain the historical tradition out of which modern conceptions of argument

1

evolved. In so doing, Wenzel clearly aligns himself with Brockriede and other perspectivists.

Perspectivists make several different assumptions about how argumentation can be studied. First, argumentation, like any other aspect of human communication, involves a complex interaction of people, language, contexts, and communities. This interaction contributes to the products, processes, and procedures of argumentation. Thus, we are unable to understand the arguments we engage in, hear, and read without knowing something about the people who create them, the language in which they are created, the contexts in which they occur, and the communities for whom they are designed.

Second, those who study argumentation can grasp its complexity by studying one set of features at a time. This approach places the student of argumentation in a role analogous to a photographer. At first the camera focuses on the argument. Next, the camera zooms in to get different views—the people who create the argument, the relationships between the arguers, the way arguers use language and evidence, and the rules and procedures of the community who respond to the argumentation.

Finally, we who study argumentation need to identify our perspectives so others will know what feature of argument we are investigating and the implications of our investigation. To do this, we need to explain our perspectives by identifying assumptions, defining parameters, noting limitations of our points of view, and acknowledging that other perspectives may be just as legitimate as the one we have adopted.

Wenzel describes three specific perspectives on the study of argument. First, Wenzel explains argument from the perspective of rhetoric by focusing on the *process* of arguing persuasively. Second, from the perspective of dialectic, he views arguments as *procedures* for regulating discussion and organizing argumentative interactions. Third, from the perspective of logic, he explores arguments as linguistic *products* and applies evaluative standards to distinguish sound from unsound arguments.

Not only can we study argument from a variety of perspectives, but we can find it in a variety of places as well. One way we can conceptualize the places in which argument occurs is to envision different argument communities. In the various essays that comprise this volume, we will travel to different places where arguments occur and will visit with various communities of arguers. We have organized our itinerary around Raymie E. McKerrow's conception of argument communities.

In the third chapter, McKerrow describes several argument communities that share a set of rules for communication that authorize and guide common expectations among arguers. He identifies four types of communities—personal, social, technical, and philosophical. McKerrow claims that these communities differ from one another according to the authorities considered to be legitimate, the relevance of the expected content, and the justifiability of commitments to the beliefs of arguers within each of the communities.

As the book develops, a variety of authors taking different perspectives will examine argument occurring in diverse places. Expect to find important variations on argument as it is practiced in different places and as it is viewed from different perspectives.

Chapter One

Where Is Argument?

Wayne Brockriede

Before looking for the clues that may lead to the discovery of where "argument" is, perhaps I should state some of my biases so you may be less surprised if I don't go instantly to where you presume I could find the culprit without difficulty. My principal bias is a humanistic point of view that denies an interest in logical systems, in messages, in reasoning, in evidence, or in propositions—*unless these things involve human activity rather directly*. One of the most famous cliches during the past fifteen years in the study of communication, originated by I know not whom but popularized by David K. Berlo (1960, pp. 174-175), is that meanings are not in words but in people. Arguments are not in statements but in people. Hence, a first clue on the whereabouts of argument: people will find arguments in the vicinity of people.

Second, argument is not a "thing" to be looked for but a concept people use, a perspective they take. Human activity does not usefully constitute an argument until some person perceives what is happening as an argument. Although defining the term on this basis is not as neat as speaking of necessary and sufficient conditions, seeing argument as a human activity encourages persons to take into account the conceptual choices of the relevant people. Hence, a second clue: only people can find and label and use an argument.

Variations of this chapter were first presented as lectures at Ohio State University and Michigan State University and as a convention paper at the Speech Communication Association, 1974.

4

Third, because arguments are in people and are what people see them to be, the idea of argument is an open concept. Seeing it as an open concept is consistent with the ideas that arguers are people, that people change, and that the filtering concepts people use when they make perceptions also change. Hence, a third clue: the location of argument may change, and so may the road map.

Fourth, because argument is a human process, a way of seeing, an open concept, it is potentially everywhere. During the past four years some undergraduate students at the University of Colorado have found argument lurking in some strange places. We asked them specifically to look for it beyond the traditional habitats of the law courts (where textbook writers tend to find their doctrine) or the legislative assemblies (where teachers typically want students to imagine presenting their arguments). We asked them to look in such relatively exotic places as the aesthetic experience, the interpersonal transaction, and the construction of scientific theory or the reporting of research studies. I've read some interesting papers by students who have applied an argumentative perspective to a novel by Camus, to a symphony by Bernstein, to marriage and divorce, to Zen Buddhism, and to Thomas S. Kuhn's *Structure of Scientific Revolutions* (1970). Throughout the reading of the arguments of such papers, I have been able to maintain my bias that ''argument'' has not been stretched out of shape, that it constitutes a frame of reference that can be related potentially to any kind of human endeavor (although, obviously, the idea of argument is not the only perspective that can be applied to a novel or a symphony). And until someone disabuses me of this eccentricity, I'm stuck with this fourth clue: the perspective of argument may pop up unexpectedly and usefully in a person's head at any time.

Fifth, but even though I appear to have constructed the idea of argument out of elasticity, I do not wish to argue that all communication is usefully called an argument. At this moment I see six characteristics that may help a person decide whether argument is a useful perspective to take in studying a communicative act. These characteristics, taken as six ways of looking at the same gestalt, define argument as *a process whereby people reason their way from one set of problematic ideas to the choice of another.*

The six characteristics of my construct of argument imply three primary dimensions. First, argument falls squarely into the realm of the problematic. What people argue about are nontrivial enough to pose a problem, but they are not likely easily to resolve the problem and so the issue remains somewhat problematic for a significant period of time. Second, each of the six characteristics of argument is a function of the variable logic of more or less and not a function of the categorical logic of yes or no. That is, each characteristic, and the construct as a whole, lies within the midrange of the more-or-less continuum. If an argument is not problematic enough or if any characteristic is too minimal—no argument. Too much of a problematic character or too much of any of the characteristics—no argument. Third, as my preliminary biases imply, argument is based on the perceptions and choices of people (see Brockriede 1974 & Darnell & Brockriede 1975).

Characteristic One.—an inferential leap from existing beliefs to the adoption of a new belief or to the reinforcement of an old one. One way to explain what I mean by an inferential leap is to contrast an argument of the sort I am talking about with a syllogism, the most famous member of the analytic family. Because its conclusion is entailed by the premises, no inferential leap is needed: nothing is stated in the conclusion of a syllogism that is not stated in the premises. As long as people stay within the closed system of a syllogism, nothing is problematic. To question a definition or a premise, people must leave that closed system by leaping inferentially into problematic uncertainty, and by doing so, they may then make the kind of argument I am delineating in this paper. To function as an argument an inferential leap occupies the midrange of the more-or-less continuum. A person has little to argue about if the conclusion does not extend beyond the materials of an argument or extends only slightly; but one may be unable to make a convincing argument if the leap is too large, perhaps perceived as suicidal.

Characteristic Two.—a perceived rationale to support that leap. An arguer must perceive some rationale that establishes that the claim leaped to is worthy at least of being entertained. The weakest acceptable rationale may justify saying that the claim leaped to deserves entertainment "for the sake of argument." A stronger rationale may justify a person's taking a claim seriously—with the hope that after further thought it may be accepted. A still stronger rationale may convince someone to accept a claim tentatively until a better alternative comes along. If a rationale is too slender to justify a leap, the result is a quibble rather than an argument; but a rationale can also be so strong that the conclusion entailed removes the activity from the realm of the problematic and hence from the world of argument. If the perceived rationale occupies either polar region, it fails to justify the label of argument because the claim either appears ridiculous (not worth arguing about) or too risky to entertain.

Characteristic Three.—a choice among two or more competing claims. When people quibble or play the analytic game, they do not make arguments because they cannot see a situation as yielding more than one legitimate claim. The right to choose is a human characteristic, but people are not free to choose without constraints. They are limited by what they know, what they believe, what they value. They are limited by how they relate to other people and to situations. They are limited by cause and by chance. But within such constraints people who argue have some choice but not too much. If they have too little choice, if a belief is entailed by formal logic or required by their status as true believers, they need not argue; but if they have too much choice, if they have to deal with choice overload, then argument may not be very productive.

Characteristic Four. — a regulation of uncertainty. Because arguers make inferential leaps that take claims beyond a rationale on which they are based, because they choose from among disputed options, they cannot reach certainty. If certainty existed, people need not engage in what I am defining as argument. When uncertainty is high, a need for argument is also high, especially if people are uncertain about something important to them. Usually arguers want to reduce uncertainty, but sometimes they may need to employ a strategy of confrontation to increase uncertainty enough to get the attention of others. Only then may such people be receptive to arguments designed to reduce uncertainty. If people have too little uncertainty to regulate, then they have no problems to solve and argument is not needed. But if the regulation of uncertainty is too difficult, if people have too much trouble reducing or escalating the degree of uncertainty, then they may be unable or unwilling to argue.

Characteristic Five. — a willingness to risk confrontation of a claim with peers. In his evolutionary theory of knowing, Donald K. Darnell argues that scientists and other kinds of people gain knowledge by taking an imaginative leap from an accumulated and consolidated body of information on a subject and then by undergoing the risk of confronting self and others with the claim that results, a risk that may lead to the disconfirmation or modification of the claim (Darnell & Brockriede, 1975). Arguers cannot regulate uncertainty very much until their claim meets these tests of confrontation. A person confronting self has no public risk (unless someone overhears one self arguing aloud with another self), but the private risk is that an important claim or an important part of a self may have to be discarded. When two persons engage in mutual confrontation so they can share a rational choice, they share the risks of what that confrontation may do to change their ideas, their selves, and their relationship with one another. If the leap is too little, the rationale too minimal, the choice too slender, the problem of uncertainty-reduction too minuscule, then the potential risk of disconfirmation after confrontation probably is not enough to justify calling the behavior argument. But if these characteristics are too overwhelming, the risk may be too great and a person may be unwilling to subject an idea through argument to confrontation and almost certain disconfirmation.

Characteristic Six. — a frame of reference shared optimally. The emergence of this characteristic is consistent with the idea that argument is an open concept. Until the spring of 1974 I knew of only five characteristics of argument, those I have just discussed. Then while working on a doctoral dissertation, one of my advisees, Karen Rasmussen (1974), wrote a chapter on argument that added this sixth characteristic. She argued that arguers must share to an optimal degree elements of one another's world views or frames of reference. This idea squares with a position Peter A. Schouls (1969) took in contending that professional philosophers (and, one may presume, others as well) cannot argue with one another very effectively if their presuppositions share too little or are virtually irreconcilable; but argument is pointless if two persons share too much. It also squares with Kenneth Burke's doctrine of identification, which implies that polar extremes are empty categories — that the uniqueness of individuals makes for at least some divisiveness (which occasionally makes argument necessary), but on the other hand individuals are consubstantial in sharing at least a few properties (which occasionally makes argument possible) (Burke, 1950).

So this is my argument about where argument may be discovered: among people, by people, in changing forms potentially everywhere, but especially where six characteristics are joined. I have contended that argument deals with the problematic and ignores the trivial or the certain, that it depends on the perceptions and choices of people who will decide whether viewing an activity as an argument is appropriate, and that it lies in the midrange of the more-or-less continuum of a variable logic and not a categorical logic.

I argue that what I have done in writing this essay is an illustration of my construct of argument. I have made some inferential leaps. I have presented what I perceive to be a rationale for supporting those leaps. I have made some choices. I may have succeeded in regulating some uncertainties. I have presumed throughout that our frames of reference overlap at some points but not at too many. I now invite your confrontation.

Chapter Two

Three Perspectives
on Argument
Rhetoric, Dialectic, Logic

Joseph W. Wenzel

The purpose of this essay is to explain three different ways of thinking about argumentation. It should be emphasized from the start that separating the perspectives of rhetoric, dialectic, and logic is not intended to classify different types of argument. All arguments can be regarded as rhetorical, dialectical and logical phenomena; why that is the case should be clear after you have read this chapter. The point of this essay is to explore different ways of understanding any case of human communication when argument seems to be involved. The perspectives, therefore, should be understood as different points of view. Like the plans for a building, showing front, side and top views, the three perspectives discussed here reveal different aspects of any instance of argumentation. As a first general statement, we may say that rhetoric helps us to understand and evaluate arguing as a natural process of persuasive communication; dialectic helps us to understand and evaluate argumentation as a cooperative method for making critical decisions; and logic helps us to understand and evaluate arguments as products people create when they argue.

Mr. Wenzel is in the Speech Communication Department at the University of Illinois at Urbana-Champaign.

Most of this chapter is devoted to elaborating those general descriptions, but it begins with some recent history of the field of argumentation to show how the idea of perspectives emerged from a concern for conceptualizing argumentation. Next, the perspectives of rhetoric, dialectic, and logic will be discussed in some detail. By the end of the chapter you should understand how these three viewpoints contribute to a theory of argumentation.

Perspectivism in the Study of Argument

When Wayne Brockriede (1975) wrote the preceding essay, "Where is Argument?" the field of argumentation studies was expanding to take account of the occurrence of arguments in new places. Whereas before scholars had usually studied argumentation in public settings, in well-structured formats like debate and discussion, in fields like politics and law, now they were beginning to examine arguments in less public and less formal settings. As Brockriede reported, his students were looking for argument "in such relatively exotic places as the aesthetic experience, the interpersonal transaction, and the construction of scientific theory" (p. 179). As a result of such extensions, older ways of thinking about argument were being challenged and new conceptions were being tried out (Cox & Willard, 1982; Trapp, 1981).

At least until the 1960s, the dominant conception of argument among communication scholars was one borrowed from the field of logic. Arguments were thought of as logical constructions, little units that speakers and writers built into their discourses and that critics could take out for evaluation. Think of the syllogism as an example of this conception of argument. Although speakers and writers seldom produced formal syllogisms, it was commonly supposed that one could reconstruct arguments in a way that allowed them to be evaluated by the rules of the syllogism (and/or other related formal constructs). So, if a speaker said something such as, "A vote for my opponent is a vote for higher taxes," a critic would restate the argument in formal terms:

> You should not vote for a person who will cause your taxes to be raised.
>
> My opponent is a person who will cause your taxes to be raised.
>
> Therefore, you should not vote for my opponent.

In other words, the idea of an argument was a very restricted one, an image of argument-as-product, a kind of "thing" to be manipulated by speakers and critics. In order to count as argument, language had to fit some predetermined, logical form. This "applied formalism" came under attack from several quarters in the 1960s and 1970s (Cox & Willard, 1982, pp. xxii-xxv).

As new approaches to the study of argumentation were being developed, it became increasingly clear that some of them had little to do with the conception of argument-as-product. One alternative view developed around the idea of argument-as-process focusing on interactions between people by which they try to manage disagreements. These alternatives gave rise to a lively and useful academic debate. Nevertheless, as Zarefsky (1980a) pointed out, there was a danger of scholars getting bogged down in definitional disputes, e.g., whether argument-as-product or argument-as-process should be taken as the more important construct. Zarefsky suggested, instead, that critics and theorists acknowledge multiple conceptions of argument and adopt a hermeneutic stance, regarding argument as a point of view, a perspective that may be useful in explaining some aspects of human communication.

Clearly, Zarefsky was on the same wave length as Brockriede who wrote, "Argument is not a 'thing' to be looked for but a concept people use, a perspective they take. Human activity does not usefully constitute an argument until some person perceives what is happening as an argument" (1975, p. 179). Elsewhere, Brockriede (1985a) explained perspectivism as "a strategy of emphasis" (p. 153). It means attending to an object or a phenomenon from one point of view at a time so as to highlight some feature in the foreground of our understanding while allowing other features to recede into the background. It allows us to shift our viewpoint as our purposes and interests require. So, for example, in considering the purchase of an automobile, we may take in turn the perspectives of cost (Can we afford it?), of safety (Are the brakes sound?), and of utility (Will it hold the whole family plus the camping equipment?), etc.

Thus, perspectivism emerged from a lively debate about how to study argumentation. As a response to that question, perspectivism has much to recommend it. First, it acknowledges the legitimacy of multiple approaches to the study of argument. There is no need to choose between a "process" or "product" orientation, for each one is valuable at different times for different purposes. Second, once we begin to see how different research traditions are grounded in different perspectives, we can appreciate how each kind of research produces unique results, how it differs from other approaches, but also how different perspectives relate to one another. Third, recognizing that there are so many possible perspectives enables one to admit to limitations: not everyone can study argumentation in every way. So, in choosing which perspectives to employ, we take a stand on what questions we consider important in the study of argumentation.

Brockriede extended the perspectival approach a step further in articulating the three perspectives on argument featured here. To the conceptions of argument as rhetorical *process* and logical *product*, he added the notion of argumentation as dialectical *method* (1980, pp. 128-134; 1982, p. 139; Ehninger & Brockriede, 1978, pp. 224-227). Working independently, but about the same time, Wenzel (1980) essayed a detailed analysis of the three perspectives, using similar key terms: rhetorical *process*, dialectical *procedure*, logical *product*. Both writers operated from a certain intellectual tradition that gave their thinking a distinctly normative cast, and we should note here both the values and the limits of that orientation.

The perspectives of rhetoric, dialectic and logic are grounded in the tradition of Western humanism. The study of rhetoric, dialectic and logic emerged in the ancient Greek city-states concurrent with the emergence of democratic government. Although never perfectly realized, perhaps, the Greeks fashioned a civic ideal of free persons, freely communicating, to serve the common good. Upon that ideal rest the interests that motivate rhetoric, dialectic and logic: the interest in adapting speech to audiences and situations; the interest in cooperative methods for decision-making; and the interest in devising standards for rational judgment. Given those original motives, it was natural that the three subjects developed, first, as normative or prescriptive studies. That is to say, they aim to establish norms for effective speaking, critical discussion, and sound judgment; and their role in education has been to teach people how to do a better job of communicating, discussing, and deciding. The particular normative stance of each perspective can be seen in the answers each gives to the question. "What is a good argument?" The rhetorician would say something like, "Good arguing consists in the production of discourse (in speech or writing) that effectively helps members of a social group solve problems or make decisions." The dialectician might say, "Good argumentation consists in the systematic organization of interaction (e.g., a debate, discussion, trial, or the like) so as to produce the best possible decisions." The logician might say, "A good argument is one in which a clearly stated claim is supported by acceptable, relevant and sufficient evidence."

Of course, rhetoric, dialectic and logic have descriptive and theoretical dimensions as well, but the kinds are of theories they develop are typically colored by their normative interests. Finally, you should not expect these perspectives to reveal everything you might want to understand about argumentation; there are many other approaches, some of which are represented in other chapters of this book. Nevertheless, rhetoric, dialectic and logic are central to the study of argumentation. They will help you understand how it works and how to argue better.

Main Elements of Each Perspective

The remainder of this chapter discusses the three perspectives in detail. Each perspective helps us to think about argument in a particular way just because it takes a special slant on certain dimensions or elements of argumentation. Taking up those elements one at a time, we will see how each one is considered differently within the perspectives of rhetoric, dialectic and logic. We will also see that various elements assume differential importance in each perspective. For example, rhetoric is especially concerned with the verbal artistry used to create arguments whereas logic is uniquely concerned with standards of validity. I use the term "elements" here—for lack of a better word—to name a set of analytic categories or topics:

   the practical and theoretical purposes relevant to each perspective;
   the general scope and focus of each perspective;
   conceptions of the argumentative situation or context in each one;
   the resources employed or examined within each perspective;
   standards of evaluation applied in each perspective;
   the roles of arguers envisioned in each perspective.

The following sections take those elements one at a time to show how each one is understood when we think about argument rhetorically, dialectically, or logically.

Purposes

I said before that rhetoric, dialectic and logic originated in Greece to meet certain practical needs of people who were learning how to manage democratic government. In this section, therefore, let us first consider the practical purposes associated with the three subjects and then briefly note how their theoretical purposes follow.

The purpose of rhetoric is persuasion, but stating it that simply risks misunderstanding by evoking all the negative connotations that have been associated with both rhetoric and persuasion. In the worst conceptions of rhetoric, persuasion is thought to be a matter of verbal trickery by which one person gains unfair advantage over others. In a monologic fashion, a clever speaker manipulates the opinions of a passive audience without much regard for truth. That was Plato's view of rhetoric as taught by the early Greek sophists, and his critique echoes through the centuries. Plato was unfair to the sophists, however, and wrong about the essential nature of rhetoric. He took the worst possible scenario for the use of rhetorical skill and assumed that was the whole story. Other classical rhetorical theorists painted quite a different picture of rhetoric, however, because they understood how it contributed to the processes of decision-making in a democratic society.

Pervading most classical theories is the assumption that rhetoric is applied in decision-making situations where people have to make a choice between alternatives and where there may be good reasons on both sides. In Aristotle's theory, for example, the two most important arenas for rhetorical argumentation were the courtroom and the legislative assembly. These situations are inherently dialectical in the sense that they encourage the critical testing of positions one against the other in the give and take of debate. The tacit assumption is that the better arguments will win out in such a contest. One important implication of this controversial setting is that the speaker cannot simply use rhetorical skill to hoodwink an audience; rather, in the face of real or potential opposition, the speaker must apply rhetoric to make the best possible case. In a recent essay, Braet (1987) shows how classical theories of rhetoric based on these assumptions about controversial situations are sensitive to the rationality of argumentation as well as to effectiveness. The speaker's task is not merely to win a personal victory, but to offer good reasons on which to base decisions.

A further implication, then, is that the speaker's personal motive—to persuade the audience to adopt a particular position—is conditioned by the larger purposes of the society—to make decisions for the common good. That is why Aristotle, Isocrates, Cicero, and a host of other theorists portrayed rhetoric as an adjunct to politics. Democratic government requires the exercise of human judgment to choose among alternatives and that judgment requires skilled advocates to articulate the various options in public deliberation. To sum up then, we want to regard the practical purpose of rhetoric as helping speakers marshall all the available means of persuasion to help people in social groups make wise decisions. That constructive task, and not mere success, is the standard by which to judge rhetorical action.

The notion of one speaker serving as a check on another brings us to the dialectical perspective and its practical purposes. Of all the meanings of the term "dialectic," the one I employ here takes dialectic to be a method, a system, or a procedure for regulating discussions among people. The ultimate object of such regulation is to produce good decisions. It is presumed in most theorizing about dialectic that decisions will be better to the degree that the discussion is candid, comprehensive and critical. The simplest form of dialectic is that depicted in Plato's dialogues, where two people alternate in the roles of speaker and interlocutor, critically testing one another's opinions in an effort to arrive at the true answer to some philosophical question. Of course a dialectical encounter might stop short of a decision but still serve the purpose of critically testing and clarifying positions. As Aristotle wrote of the method, "the ability to raise searching difficulties on both sides of a subject will make us detect more easily the truth and error about the several points that arise" (Topics, 101a, 35).

To characterize the outcome of dialectic in the last paragraph, I used the words "true" and "truth," but those are tricky concepts. For Plato, truth referred to perfect knowledge that existed only in some divine mind, and dialectic was, at best, a means of discovering as much truth as was humanly possible. Aristotle saw dialectic as a method to apply to any question on which we could not reason our way to the answer by means of strict, formal, deductive logic; the outcome of dialectical discussions, therefore, allowed us to come as close to certainty as the subject matter permitted. The sophist Protagoras expressed another version of the dialectical idea in relation to knowledge and truth. He believed that there was no absolute truth about the kind of subjects the Greeks discussed in their political and legal forums. To questions about government, law, justice and morality, he said, there are no "true" answers, there are only "better" answers. Furthermore, because there are two sides to every question, the way to discover which is the better answer is through vigorous debate. So, even before Plato and Aristotle wrote systematically about dialectic, Protagoras combined a dialectical perspective with a rhetorical system to teach critical decision-making.

Logic is also concerned with decision-making, but on what we might call a micro-level. The practical purpose of logic is to apply appropriate criteria to judge the merits of particular arguments. Rhetoric, dialectic and logic are functionally related. In decision-making situations, people produce persuasive discourse to advocate one choice or another. Often, they organize their discourse into formats designed to facilitate comparison and criticism. And, mustering whatever logical insights they have, people evaluate specific units of argument within the discourse.

So far, we have been considering the practical purposes that guide the three perspectives. But, rhetoric, dialectic and logic have theoretical purposes as well. Since ancient times, scholars have not only tried to teach how to produce effective discourse, organize critical discussions, and pass judgment on arguments; they have also sought theoretical grounding for their prescriptive advice. Consequently, there are many different theories within each domain, and it is impossible in a brief essay to give a systematic account of them. Nevertheless, it is possible to characterize theoretical objectives generally by noting what each type of theory is about. As a theoretical study, rhetoric is about how people influence one another through language and other symbolic modes of expression. Applied to argument, then, rhetoric helps to explain how arguments are made and interpreted by people. Dialectical theory is about the rationale for principles and procedures used to organize argumentative interactions for critical purposes. Logical theory is about the standards and criteria used to distinguish sound arguments from unsound ones. Discussion of the remaining elements will inevitably lead into matters of both practical and theoretical interest.

Scope and Focus

Argumentation consists of a set of complex activities that people engage in together for the sake of making decisions, solving problems, and generally managing disagreements. Each of the perspectives takes certain of those activities within its scope and focuses on them in distinctive ways. The notions of argument as *process, procedure* and *product* will prove helpful in sorting out these differences.

The rhetorical perspective directs our attention to the occurrence of arguing among people as a natural communication process. Arguing as a natural process includes the many different ways that people try to manage their disagreements, and these can be studied from many different angles in communication research. The particular focus of the rhetorical perspective is on the symbolic means (primarily language) by which people try to influence one another's beliefs, values and actions. Rhetoric, Burke (1950) said, is *"rooted in an essential function of language itself, . . . the use of language as a symbolic means of inducing cooperation in beings that by nature respond to symbols*" (p. 43). In other words, arguing as a rhetorical phenomenon is a natural activity because of human nature. We influence one another for the sake of agreement and cooperation, and we do so chiefly through symbolic appeals.

In contrast to the process sense of argument which stresses natural speech, the dialectical perspective calls up a procedural or methodological sense of argument. Think about "parliamentary procedure" or "courtroom procedure" as examples of this viewpoint. Decision-making bodies adopt procedures in order to exercise some deliberate control over the way their members argue. In other words, the dialectical perspective considers all the methods people and institutions use in order to bring the natural processes of arguing under deliberate control. They make rules, set limits, create forums, and organize formats for debate and discussion. On the simplest level, the dialectical perspective may come into play whenever we apply critical concepts like fairness, honesty, and the like to ordinary natural interactions. Suppose two friends are quarreling and one of them happens to be loud, aggressive and domineering to the point that the other doesn't get a chance to speak. Suppose now a third party steps in saying, "That's not fair. And besides, you'll never settle your differences if you don't try to see both sides of the issue." The third party is implicitly expressing a dialectical principle: provide opportunity to hear both sides of a dispute. This perspective is one we all understand on at least a rough-and-ready level, for we all care about making good decisions (at least some of the time). We realize, further, that good decisions require clear thinking about alternatives, and clear thinking is promoted by orderly procedures. Thus, the dialectical perspective embraces all methodological, procedural approaches to organizing argumentative discussions. The focus of this perspective which we will elaborate later, is on rules, standards, attitudes and behaviors that promote critical decision-making.

Logic is concerned with arguments as products. Think of an argument as a commodity: someone makes it and offers it to someone else. The person to whom it is offered has a choice: to "buy" it or not. Just as we evaluate products offered to us in the commercial marketplace, we also evaluate the arguments and appeals offered to us in the so-called marketplace of ideas. This is where logic enters the field of argumentation, to help us evaluate arguments as intellectual constructions offered for acceptance. Logic, in its theoretical form, is the study of the standards by which to evaluate arguments. In its practical form, logic involves the application of those standards to judge specific arguments; it is a method of criticism. The ultimate question in a particular case is: Shall we accept this claim on the basis of the reasons put forward in support of it?

The logician thinks of an argument as a particular kind of thing to be evaluated. An argument may be described as a set of statements consisting of premises and conclusion, or as a claim and support for the claim. But, arguments do not always appear in such tidy forms in natural language. When people engage in the natural (rhetorical) process of arguing, they express themselves in many different ways—sometimes clearly; sometimes not; sometimes at great length; sometimes in a few words; sometimes in a figure of speech; sometimes in precise, literal statements. So, a first step in the use of logic is to restate an argument in a way that facilitates criticism. Logical critics try to recast an argument into some "standard form." The syllogism is one such standard form; Toulmin's well-known diagram is another; still others are featured in current textbooks on informal logic. The purposes of such a restatement of an argument are (1) to make clear what the critic thinks the arguer intended to be taken as claim and support; and (2) to allow for careful evaluation.

Here we should note some important distinctions. One might say that anytime a speaker (or writer) tries to persuade a listener (or reader), there are at least three versions of an argument present. First, there is the version of the argument that exists in the mind of the speaker. Inasmuch as this version partakes of all the speaker's experiences, emotions and cognitions relevant to the topic, it could not possibly be expressed in full; we can never say all that we think and feel about an issue. Second, there is the version of the argument that is overtly expressed in speech or writing, or in some other symbolic form. This version is the object of rhetorical study for, as we said before, rhetoric is concerned with all the ways that people go about making arguments. Still a third version of the argument is the one that comes into being in the mind of the listener, for the listener has to interpret what was said, very often reconstructing the original message into her/his own terms, and connecting the meaning thus constituted with her/his own experiences, beliefs, and values.

Notice that logic hasn't even entered the picture yet. So far all we've mentioned are psychological processes of reasoning and interpretation and rhetorical processes of expression. Sometimes logic is confused with those processes, for example, when we speak of someone "thinking logically," or "speaking logically," but those are secondary meanings of "logical." As a method of criticism, logic is best understood as a perspective that comes into play after an argument has been expressed (Toulmin, 1958, pp. 3-8). It is a retrospective viewpoint which is activated when someone adopts a critical stance and "lays out" an argument for inspection and evaluation. In such a case, a fourth version of "the" argument is created. Such versions of arguments, reconstructed for purposes of examination, become the subject matter for logical evaluation. So, the special concerns of the logical perspective are with techniques for representing an argument in a form amenable to criticism and with standards for evaluation.

3 — Situation

The notion of situation is construed differently in the three perspectives. Rhetorical situations, as suggested before, are natural occurrences. People find themselves in situations where it seems that persuading others will serve some purpose—solve a problem, bring about a happier state of affairs, or just enhance their relationships. We usually tend to think of argumentation occurring in more or less formal and public situations (e.g., courtrooms, legislatures, and political campaigns), but arguments, as Brockriede observed, are potentially everywhere. Moreover, although many (perhaps most) arguments are created by deliberate intention of speakers and writers, on the other hand, arguments can also be construed into existence by the interpretations of listeners and readers even where none was intended. As Burke (1950) wrote, "Wherever there is persuasion, there is rhetoric. And wherever there is 'meaning' there is persuasion" (p. 172). Another contemporary theorist put the point this way: "The more holistic view of human nature toward which the communication discipline seems to be moving invites us to regard 'argument' as simply any act of conjoining symbolic structures (propositional or otherwise) to produce new structures" (Willard, 1976, p. 317). So, rhetorical situations feature argument emerging, at least potentially, in all media of human communication and in every kind of social situation where people talk.

In contrast to natural rhetorical situations, dialectical situations are consciously planned or designed. Whenever people have sought to improve their decision making, it seems, they have found it useful to bring rhetorical action under some sort of deliberate control. What characterizes dialectical situations more than anything else is the existence of procedural rules to control a discussion. These may vary from the strict rules of a criminal court to the customary politeness of conversational arguments. Dialectical situations are often institutionalized by the creation of specific forums, e.g., courtrooms, legislatures, and the regular meetings of learned societies. In Western civilization, at least, the creation and maintenance of dialectical situations seems to be a common characteristic of all disciplined inquiry.

There will be more to say later on about the requirements for successful dialectic, the kind of rules and attitudes that sustain the situations. Before leaving the topic, however, it is important to note that dialectical situations are simultaneously rhetorical situations. People who engage in systematic dialogue must function as communicators, exchanging messages to make arguments. And, we might add, rhetorical situations always have the potential for being transformed into dialectical situations; when anyone speaks (or writes a book, for that matter) it is always possible for an opponent to arise, challenge, and initiate a debate.

Because rhetorical and dialectical activities involve people making arguments, they naturally give rise to logical activity. Frequently, someone extracts particular sets of statements from the on-going talk, treats them as argument-products, and evaluates them. Arguers themselves may do this in the course of their exchanges, or someone else might enter the scene as a critic. The criticism need not be close to the original communication in space or time; witness the way scholars often critique the arguments of ancient texts. One might be inclined, therefore, to say a logical situation is just any case of someone identifying, restating, and evaluating an argument. As a parallel to what I have said about rhetorical and dialectical situations, that seems all right, but there is a distinctly different notion of "situating" argument that will reveal more about the logical perspective.

To employ another useful, albeit ambiguous term, consider how "context" influences the way we evaluate arguments from any perspective. Arguments can be evaluated in light of their rhetorical contexts: Is this discourse a fitting response to the situation? They can be evaluated in light of dialectical contexts: Is the manner of arguing conducive to the critical purposes of the discussion? What then is the context for logical evaluation? The answer has three parts.

First, in the tradition of formal deductive logic, it seems that logicians situated any instance of real argument in a universe of possible forms in order to test for validity. If a real argument corresponded to one of the predetermined valid forms, it was said to be valid. So, the familiar example of the syllogism— "All men are mortal; Socrates is a man; therefore, Socrates is mortal."—is valid because it conforms to the abstract ideal— "If all A is B, and C is an A, then C must be B." Modern logicians have noted problems with the standard of validity itself, but those problems are beyond the scope of this chapter. (See Blair & Johnson, 1987a, pp. 41-42.) In any case, a knowledge of correct forms of inference is bound to be of some use in argument evaluation. But that cannot be the whole story because arguments have substance as well as form.

Second, therefore, we need some method for evaluating the merits of premises as the substantive content of an argument. In his elaboration of a more sophisticated approach to the substance of arguments, Toulmin (1958) introduced the concept of argument fields. Although that concept is variously employed by scholars of argumentation, one useful interpretation by Burleson (1979) answers our question about the substantive context for evaluation:

> Toulmin's notion of field-dependence is a particularly useful and insightful way of conceptualizing context. Properly understood, the Toulmin diagram leads critics and theorists to consider what may be termed the *substantive context* of an argument. . . .
>
> This context is a locus of ideas and relationships among ideas shared among members of a community. A consideration of this context dictates concern with issues such as: What constitute believable and relevant data and backings? What kinds of claims legitimately can be put forth? What factors determine the extent to which claims must be qualified? What types of warrants are permissible? Obviously, this list could be extended to encompass a variety of similar issues (p. 146).

The third part of the answer calls attention to a feature of Toulmin's model that seems not to have been fully appreciated by those who have used it (see

Toulmin, 1989). The parts of the Toulmin model serve to indicate the *different kinds* of substantive considerations that may be relevant in assessing the worth of a claim. In that sense, the model is a functional analysis: the parts show how different statements may have to be brought forth by an arguer, each statement doing a different job, to meet the demands of a critical interlocutor. Thus, data (grounds, evidence) answer the question: What information do you have to go on? Warrants answer the question: Why is it legitimate to base a claim of this kind on data of that kind? And so on through all the parts of the model (Toulmin, 1958, pp. 97-107). So, in the end, substantive evaluation is bound up with a functional understanding of how language works to secure claims. In summary, logical evaluation requires the re-situation of an argument in a context where it can be evaluated with respect to form, substance and function.

Resources

Another way to flesh out the account of the three perspectives is to examine the resources available in each domain. By resources, I merely mean the kinds of knowledge, methods, and the like, that can be deployed in each perspective. Given the normative purposes of rhetoric, dialectic and logic, we might ask with respect to each one: what guidelines does it provide to help people argue effectively, or discuss and debate critically, or judge rationally? In addition, we might ask what resources are available to critics and theorists for evaluating the complex of activities that constitute argumentation. The answers to these questions could encompass all theories of rhetoric, dialectic and logic, but that is clearly impossible in this chapter. So, what follows is intended as a representative sampling of the existing store of knowledge in the three domains.

Let us consider the resources of rhetoric, first, from the standpoint of the arguer. Rhetoric was first conceived as "the art of speaking persuasively." It follows that any body of knowledge, precepts, insights, and so forth, that help people communicate effectively can be regarded as part of the practical resources of rhetoric. The classical rhetorical theories evolved a system for presenting such information in an organized fashion. They grouped the various tasks of the speaker under five main heads:

> *Invention* included all the operations by which speakers analyzed their situation, audience and subject; surveyed the relevant sources of evidence and other supporting materials; and constructed appropriate persuasive appeals.
>
> *Disposition* included all aspects of what we now call organization: putting the parts of the speech together cogently to promote clarity and/or strategically to maximize persuasive effect.
>
> *Style* included attention to all the facets of language use: choice and arrangement of words to produce desired effects; qualities of clarity, appropriateness and impressiveness; figures of speech.

Memory considered techniques for keeping the whole plan and the substance of the speech in mind during delivery.

Delivery attended to all aspects of expression, vocal and physical.

These five canons, as they were called, systematically laid out principles for doing all that a speaker had to do from initial preparation to delivery of the speech. The canon of invention dealt specifically with argumentation. Under that head were found methods for analyzing the issues in a controversy, types of arguments, sources of evidence, and all sorts of general advice on how to marshall the materials to prove one's case. As a student of argumentation, you probably have learned, or soon will learn, techniques of analysis, research, briefing, case construction, and presentation that trace back to the classics.

Of the many other approaches to rhetorical theory in modern times, the work of Perelman and Olbrechts-Tyteca (1969) is noteworthy in the present context because they equate rhetoric with a theory of argumentation. The object of such a theory, they write, "is the study of the discursive techniques allowing us *to induce or to increase the mind's adherence to the thesis presented for its assent*" (p. 4). In a wide-ranging analysis, they show how argumentative effects are achieved by virtually any discourse features, from the placement of arguments to the use of figures of speech.

Perelman and Olbrechts-Tyteca's analyses of arguments in all kinds of discourse, including literary texts, points up another way in which rhetoric serves as a resource in argumentation. All arguments are not made up of clearly stated support for clearly stated claims. Rather, argumentative "moves" may be subtly woven into the internal dynamics of a text. Consider, for example, the way women and minorities are often stereotyped in fiction by attributing certain actions to them. Although we may not usually think of such literary constructions as arguments, it is entirely appropriate to note how such portrayals imply claims and to question their validity. As a critical study of how language works to produce effects on people, rhetoric is sensitive to such semi-concealed appeals. Consequently, the study of rhetorical criticism yields insight into how arguments get made in ways that are not always obvious on the surface.

Within the dialectical perspective, the chief resources of interest are designs or plans for conducting critical discussions. The term "discussion" is used here generically to include all kinds of communicative interactions, ranging from simple conversation to formal debate. Any of these interactions is "dialectical" to the degree that it is motivated by the desire to examine a question critically by means of orderly procedures. A conception of what constitutes a critical discussion may function both as a guide to practice and as a set of criteria for evaluating a given instance of interaction. So, on one hand, faith in debate as a critical method may lead someone to say, "Let's debate the question following these rules . . . ." Or, an understanding of discussion methods might be used as a basis for criticism, as when someone says, "That staff meeting was not very well conducted because the chair kept cutting people off before they had a chance to develop ideas."

As a student of argumentation, you are presumably already familiar with debate as a method of critical discussion. A well-planned debate is presumed to be a critical method because it follows certain rules and principles. Ehninger and Brockriede (1978) illustrate this point nicely when they characterize debate as implementing six directives:

1. Enter the competing views into full and fair competition to assess their relative worth.

2. Let this competition consist of two phases. First, set forth each view in its own right, together with the most convincing supporting proofs. Second, test each view by seeing how well it withstands the strongest attacks an informed opponent levels against it.

3. Delay a decision until both sides have been presented and subjected to testing.

4. Let the decision be rendered not by the contending parties themselves but by an external adjudicating agency.

5. Let this agency weigh the competing arguments and produce a decision critically.

6. Let the participants agree in advance to abide by such a decision (p. 13).

Note that this is a design for a particular kind of debate, one very similar to trial procedures in American courts. We could design debates with other features, using for example, a legislative body wherein the debaters are also the decision makers. And, of course, there are other methods and models of critical discussion procedures, including Socratic dialogue, parliamentary rules of order, and the like. In any case, Ehninger and Brockriede's first three directives above seem to capture very well the central idea of the dialectical perspective on argumentation as a critical method. It is critical because ideas that can stand up to informed and systematic criticism are presumed to be good ones.

In contemporary argumentation studies, one well developed theory within the dialectical perspective is that of van Eemeren and Grootendorst (1984). Their pragma-dialectical theory treats argumentation as a complex of speech acts that function in a regulated discussion between people who are attempting to resolve a difference about an expressed opinion. They employ speech act theory to explain the pragmatics of argumentative language use and to characterize the kinds of speech acts that play a role in rational discussions. After describing the stages through which a discussion must pass to achieve resolution, they consider the various kinds of speech acts that are dialectically relevant to each discussion stage. On that foundation, they develop a "Code of Conduct for Rational Discussants," consisting of specific rules for the types of speech acts that may legitimately be performed by each discussant in each stage of the discussion. Van Eemeren and Grootendorst (1984) explain their objectives as follows:

> The rules . . . are designed to further the resolution of disputes about expressed opinions by means of argumentative discussions. In other words, they are intended to enable language users to conduct themselves as rational discussants, and they are also calculated to prevent anything that might hinder or obstruct the resolution of a dispute. (p. 151)

Van Eemeren and Grootendorst, thus, contribute to the dialectical perspective a well developed design of critical procedures, one that is grounded, moreover, in a fully articulated philosophical and theoretical position (van Eemeren, 1987a).

In addition to its utility as a guide to practice, the pragma-dialectical theory of these Dutch scholars can be applied to analysis and criticism of argumentative discussions. This application, which they call "normative reconstruction," consists of a set of "dialectical transformations" by which the actual language of a dispute is translated into standardized representations of the dialectical moves that may take place in a rational discussion. This allows an analytic, functional representation of what arguers did in the dispute, stated in terms of the possible "moves" in a rational discussion. On that basis, a critic can assess how well the arguers' performance measured up to the ideal model posited in the Code of Conduct (van Eemeren, 1986). Although on a larger scale, dialectical reconstruction seems similar to the step in logical criticism whereby an argument is put into some standard form to facilitate criticism.

Turning to the logical perspective, there is probably less need to describe the available resources. Presumably, you have some general idea of what logic is about. The aspect of logic stressed in this chapter is its application as a method of criticism which, in turn, entails some idea of how to identify arguments, a method for reconstructing arguments in a form that facilitates criticism, and the critical standards themselves. There appear to be two main variants of these tools in the current literature. One version is associated with the philosophical logicians who make up what has come to be called the informal logic movement. Realizing that formal deductive logic does not provide the best foundation for analysis and criticism of argumentation as a human communicative practice, informal logicians have been working out new methods of criticism (Blair & Johnson, 1980, 1987b). A second variant of informal or practical logic is that based on the work of Stephen Toulmin (1958; Toulmin, Rieke & Janik, 1984). Toulmin's approach to modeling and criticizing arguments has had its greatest impact among teachers of argumentation in the communication field. In argumentation classes you will no doubt study one of these approaches.

Standards and Roles

Against the background of what has been said so far, it should be possible to state concisely what kind of standards we have in mind when thinking about argument from each perspective and also how we conceive the roles of arguers striving to meet those standards. I will treat those topics together in a frankly normative attitude. What do we expect of arguers, at their best, functioning rhetorically, dialectically, and logically?

Against the conception of rhetoric as "mere" persuasion for personal advantage, I have offered a conception of rhetoric as an art and science to serve the highest human purposes. Never mind for a moment the assertions of rhetoric's defenders, and consider examples of speakers and writers. Perhaps every age has its demagogues, its Hitlers and Joe McCarthys, proving that rhetoric can be debased. But, for every one of those, we can find other men and women who used the power of language for noble purposes, e.g., Susan B. Anthony, Winston Churchill, Franklin Roosevelt, John Kennedy, Barbara Jordan, and Martin Luther King, Jr. Speakers like these embody the idea of rhetoric as an art by which to articulate the highest values and aspirations of a people. Each of those speakers met the challenge of producing arguments to cope with specific problems and situations, but they did more. They combined wisdom and eloquence to give their audiences words to live by. Although not every speaker will rise to that level of eloquence, we can still expect the arguer-as-rhetor to function as a responsible agent of social improvement.

In the case of dialectic, we have stressed norms based on dialectical rules and principles. We might sum those up by saying that good argumentation-as-procedure should measure up to the "four Cs." Good dialectical argumentation depends on the arguers being *cooperative* in following appropriate rules and committing themselves to the common purpose of sound decision-making. Good argumentation is *comprehensive* in dealing with a subject as thoroughly as possible. Good argumentation is *candid* in making ideas clear and getting them out in the open for examination. Finally, sound argumentation is *critical* in its commitment to basing decisions on the most rigorous testing of positions that circumstances allow.

Rules and principles alone, however, will not guarantee critical argumentative discussions. The arguers must bring to the situation attitudes of the right kind and must behave accordingly. Although this necessary element of sound argumentation has not been analyzed thoroughly by theorists, several have commented in a helpful way. Johnstone (1982) stresses bilaterality as a condition in which "each interlocutor speaks as if the others were capable of propagating a message fully as credible as his own. He treats his hearers with respect rather than as merely means to the end of their own credulity" (p. 99). In a similar vein, Ehninger (1970) wrote of argument as a "person-risking" enterprise in which the arguer, while seeking to change another's mind, accepts the possibility of being changed as well. Brockriede (1972) wrote metaphorically of "arguers as lovers," motivated by a regard for others as equal partners in the search for the best mutual understanding. So, the ideal role of arguers in the dialectical frame includes several personal qualities as well as adherence to principles. They should be rhetorically competent and "dialectically astute" (Blair & Johnson, 1987a), but those skills must be guided by appropriate attitudes. Ehninger (1970) summed up this point nicely, noting that the arguer "must play the role of a restrained partisan— must stand poised between the desire to maintain his present view and a willingness to accept the judgment which a critical examination of that view yields" (p. 104).

The standards relevant to the logical perspective have been touched on, at least in a general way. I suggested earlier that in weighing the merits of a particular argument, the logical critic has to be attentive to formal, substantive, and functional criteria: Is the argument coherent? Are the premises acceptable, relevant and sufficient? Do the premises provide all the functionally relevant information? The logical critic must be well trained in the application of such criteria—and something more.

In performing logical evaluation, the critic must also be rhetorically and dialectically astute. This is a fact not so widely recognized. Rhetoric enters, first, in the analysis of arguments, simply to figure out what's going on. Because the symbolic resources by which we can make arguments are virtually infinite, arguments can be made in the most subtle and obscure ways. If you are inclined to doubt this point, try figuring out the arguments in John Donne's poetry (Sloane, 1985). Rhetorical analysis is helpful in unpacking the subtle (and not so subtle) moves within argumentative texts and, therefore, rhetorical analysis is a necessary adjunct to logical reconstruction (Wenzel, 1987b). Rhetoric, in other words, helps us to see what arguments are being made and by what symbolic means.

Second, rhetorical and dialectical abilities may enter into logical evaluation when logical critics disagree. When one expresses a critical judgment about a particular argument, one takes a position that might very well be challenged by another critic who sees the merits of the argument differently. Let us suppose the two critics are equally intelligent, informed, and well-trained in logic. What are we to make of their disagreement, and how can we expect it to be resolved? Let us recognize that logical evaluations of particular arguments are just additional instances of human judgment. And all such judgments depend, in the end, on the quality of reasons we can bring forward to support them. So, the answer seems to be, first, that our opposing critics must go to work rhetorically, each fashioning the strongest and most appealing reasons for their evaluation. Second, supposing they are both committed to critical decision-making, they will very likely enter into a dialectical interaction to test the quality of one another's arguments. If ever they reach agreement, it will be another symbolic construction, a way of speaking in answer to the original question that both find appropriate.

The final moral of this essay should now be clear: human judgment depends upon argumentation, and argumentation depends equally upon the resources of rhetoric, dialectic and logic. It should not be surprising, therefore, that since antiquity those domains of action and inquiry have been central to the study of argumentation. Your further study of the specialized subject matter in each area is bound to be rewarding.

Chapter Three

Argument Communities

Raymie E. McKerrow

In his discussion of philosophical argument, Brutain (1979) observes that "the very problem of the typology of argumentation is one of the important questions in the theory of argumentation" (p. 77). There are various responses to this problem, depending on whether one focuses on argument as act, on the arguer as person or on the context in which the argument occurs. From an "argument as act" approach, Wenzel (1979, and this volume) distinguishes argument in terms of its dialectical, rhetorical, and logical dimensions. Considered dialectically, argument is perceived as a procedure that follows rules for "right conduct"; considered rhetorically, argument is seen in terms of the process involved in arguing with others; in its logical mode, argument is understood as a specific product which is developed in accordance with certain criteria. From the "arguer as person" perspective, argument is seen in terms of its interpersonal dimensions, as an "encounter" in which social actors engage when confronted by challenges to individual beliefs or actions (Willard, 1983). Perceived in terms of context, argument is discussed in terms of the "audience" to whom it is addressed or in terms of the "community," "field" or "sphere" in which it takes place. In taking this latter perspective,

Mr. McKerrow is in the Speech Communication Department at the University of Maine, Orono.

I will discuss the nature of argument perceived in terms of "community" and its cognate terms. As part of this analysis, a "model" of argument from a community perspective will be elaborated. With this as a basis, I will then describe the nature of argument in four communities: personal, social, philosophical, and technical.

A Community Perspective

A "community" is generally thought of as a collective group of people interacting in a space-time continuum. What makes a group a community rather than a simple collection of individuals? As van Eemeren (1988), following Hynes (1988), suggests "a collection of people should be called a community if they . . . share a set of rules for verbal or non-verbal behavior which are authorized and guided by the uniting rationale for their common aspirations, and which are observed in the display of their communal interactions" (p. 3). The space which a community embraces may be a specific geographic locale, as in the locution "I am from the community of. . . ." or may denote a broad expanse, unencumbered by clear boundaries, as in the locution, "I am a member of the gay community." Communities exist in time—they may range from relatively stable groups to those which come into being for singular purposes and disband when those goals are achieved. Within whatever space-time continuum a given community exists, the dimensions of "rule," "authorization," and "observance" suffice as essential conditions for the creation of argumentative communication. That is, communities are typified by the specific rules which govern argumentative behavior, by social practices which determine who may speak with what authority, and by their own "display" of these rules and social practices in response to challenges from within or outside the community.

Communities are both real and imaginary "products" of our personal and social environment. They are "real" when we can ascribe specific geographic boundaries to them—they occupy a designated space, often one that has been arbitrarily determined by a legislative body. A religious collective such as the Hutterites constitutes a real community to the extent that one can "see" who is and is not a member; individuals display through dress and actions their allegiance to the group. A Masonic order exists in real terms to its members by virtue of specific signs or emblems which are worn in public, demonstrating membership in a select society. A gay community is real to its members by virtue of cues that are, for the most part, invisible to the "straight" community.

Communities also are imaginary creations of our own making. The concept of "nation," for example, is an imaginary one: [*I*]*magined* because the members of even the smallest nation will never know most of their fellow-members, meet them, or even hear of them, yet in the minds of each lives the image of their communion'' (Anderson, 1983, p. 15). The reality of a community is muted by the extent to which you can or cannot literally see or contact each member; hence one creates an image of community that suffices in those instances where boundaries are indistinct, and members are not always everywhere present. For example, the concept of ''nationhood,'' often projected as ''nationalism'' in argumentative discourse, is not identical with the boundaries of a state—there may be nations or nationalistic arguments within single states or crossing the boundaries of states (consider the arguments of the PLO for example, or those of the Quebec Separatists [Charland, 1987, McKerrow, 1988]). Even though a Masonic order is real to its members, its reality is partly the result of the same imaginary construct which creates the sense of belonging to a nation. The same may be said for members of a gay community, or any other group that identifies itself as a collective joined together in a communal enterprise.

Communities are composed of individuals who ascribe to the rules either as a matter of choice, a matter of conditioning, or as a result of an edict from others in positions of authority. If you participate in a community as a matter of choice, there is a conscious ascription to the communicative rules. You follow the community standards because you prefer that to other choices or at least because you are willing to accede to the norms for behavior. One can also be conditioned to a community's standards. As Therborn (1980, pp. 16-17) notes, members of a community are simultaneously subjected to the dictates of the community, and through appropriate training or socialization to those rules, become qualified to enact the rules. Finally, one can also be an involuntary member of a community. The inmates of a prison come to mind as the most logical example. Those least noticed as ''imprisoned'' within a community, as belonging without choice, are those who are victims of social or sexual abuse, those who lack empowerment to change or alter their own condition, by virtue of having their voices silenced through community standards governing who may speak and with what authority.

There is, in any community, an ineluctable tension among all of these parameters. A community is neither locked into a special time or space, nor is it simply real or only imaginary. Its members may, at different times, be conditioned, free, or imprisoned. However they are constituted, and whatever their dimensions or parameters at a given point, one common feature which all communities share, and which serves to distinguish them, is the discourse in which they engage. Discourse—language aimed at members or at outsiders—constitutes the community by presenting it with those symbols by which it identifies itself. As Castoriadis has said of institutions, communities ''cannot be reduced to the symbolic but they can exist only in the symbolic'' (1987, p. 117). They are creatures of language. More specifically, argument is a central vehicle for the creation of those symbols which sustain a community. For those imprisoned by virtue of community standards, argument is a means of obtaining freedom—it is a way of expressing one's dissatisfaction, and of managing (sometimes within the rules, and sometimes in overt protest) a change in the social practices which legitimated the absence of power among those abused. For those who participate in a spirit of free choice, and for those conditioned by and qualified within the community, argument is an orderly or rational means of dispute resolution (van Eemeren, 1988, p. 3).

Given these general features, communities of discourse or "argument communities" can be delineated in terms of the following model:

Argument Communities

Lifeworld: Space/Time, Real/Imaginary, Free/Conditioned/Forced

Primary	**Generic**	**Secondary**
Personal		
		Religion
	Nation	
Social		
		Law
	State	
Technical		
		Medicine
	Class	
Philosophical		
		Business

Judgment: Legitimacy, Justifiability, Authority, Teleology

As this model suggests, communities can be further subdivided in terms of the primary context in which one argues (personal, social, philosophical, technical) or secondary (law, business, medicine, religion, science, etc.). The former are primary in the sense that they function as "home bases" from which argument emanates. When argument takes place in a secondary community or field, it always does so with some dimensions of a primary context in mind. Further complicating the "community mosaic" is the tripartite group of nation, state, and class. These function as generic traits that an individual carries into an argument. While they may not always be the focal point, or even a clearly explicit part of the argument, allegiance to nation, state, or class (or protest directed toward) is never entirely removed from the mosaic. The categories are permeable; that is, one may move within the personal to social or social to technical community, may integrate arguments from law and religion, and may incorporate symbols that reflect allegiance to a nation or class within or across any single community. It should be clear, then, that a person may spend time in only one or in a multiplicity of communities at any one moment.

The final element of the model is the application of general standards of judgment, directed at argument within or across communities. Adapted from Goodnight's (1988) discussion of argument within communities, they function as guarantors of an argument's probative value. Legitimacy refers to the rightfulness with which an argument is put forward—is it promoted by someone with legitimate authority to stake out a position? It also may refer to the relevance an argument has within a particular context—is it an argument that one might expect, given the community from which it emanates? Justifiability concerns the rationale put forward—is it one which others can commit to belief or action? While the rationale may be "wrong" in some ultimate sense, its articulation at a particular moment needs to be seen as a sufficient or adequate basis for acceptance. The authority standard focuses attention on the force the argument has in compelling response or compliance. Though an argument may be legitimate and justifiable on other grounds, if spoken by one without power to enact its sanctions or its rewards, it may well fail to move people to belief or action. Finally, an argument has a teleological end, a purpose or reason for being. Within communities, that purpose must be seen as advancing the issue being deliberated; at the very least, the motive or grounds for arguing must be sanctioned by the community (Rowland, 1982).

The communities identified above share a common feature: they each reflect the intuitive notion that people argue differently in different situations. The "standards of judgment" referred to above determine the appropriateness or potency of arguments as they are advanced within any one of the communities. Not all of the decisions that are reached in applying these standards will be compatible with one another. Arguments that are legitimate or justifiable in one community may not be in the terms of another community. When one is arguing across two communities in which the standards are incommensurable or are "out of sync" with one another, a person will have to select one set of standards as the guide or face a contradiction that cannot be easily resolved. Chaos, more than the orderly progress of an idea through the rational application of standards of judgment, may be more the norm than the exception in argumentative encounters that involve multiple communities. To keep the potential confusions to a minimum, the following discussion of four "primary" communities will concentrate on argument within each, rather than approach the issue from the perspective afforded by multiple involvement.

① Argument in the Personal Community

Whatever else it may be, argument is inherently the property of individuals. It is, as Willard observes, "a kind of interaction in which two or more people maintain what they construe to be incompatible positions" (1983, p. 21, italicized in original). Within this community, people argue in private, or if overheard, without necessarily intending to direct their conversation to others.

Using the label "personal sphere" rather than community, Goodnight's (1987c) description of the nature of argument in this context is appropriate:

> The consequences of a conversation always pertain to the interlocutors who share time together, even though the discussion sometimes has repercussions beyond the relationship. External constraints may impinge on the ability to continue talking, but conversation takes its own time in coming to terms with whatever meaning is created between people. Social norms may govern the initial relationship, but communication becomes more private as a relationship progresses or idiosyncratic as it decays. The meaning of language in a conversation, its valence and weight, remains uniquely accessible to those engaged in dialogue (pp. 428-29).

Within this community, individuals are free to select their own standards for what constitutes appropriate communication, for what will serve as a criteria for reasonableness or adequacy in an argument. The resultant standards will, in many cases, bear resemblance to those drawn from other communities and also will reflect individual taste or discernment. The final choices will represent mutual agreement on criteria, or the progress of an argument will be restricted by conflict over the standards of judgment. In its most extreme form of free choice, there is no "community" beyond two individuals, each with the same freedom to ignore all standards other than those agreed upon with a participant in an interchange of competing claims or "points of view" (van Eemeren, 1987b). While the standards selected may appear ludicrous to an outsider, they nonetheless remain as an authoritative force for those agreeing to their existence.

Within this community, the principal motive for engaging in argumentative behavior is to manage (with a view to minimizing) disagreements (Jacobs & Jackson, 1982, p. 224). Thus, arguing with others has a functional role — it serves to resolve conflicts or problems that arise, even if the "stimulus" was not one which sought to create a disagreement (pp. 224-28). A simple request of another person, for example, may be responded to in a variety of ways, ranging from passive agreement to a violent outburst or physical action. Argumentative behavior expands the nature of the disagreement from a simple request-response scenario to a series of interchanges which, hopefully, end in a resolution of the dispute.

In following this "expansionist" tendency, argument does not generally proceed whimsically or arbitrarily. Rather, as Jacobs (1987) notes, "conversational argument is conducted through a procedural mechanism that enables participants to *locally manage* the issue of who speaks when for how long" (p. 231). The act of arguing thus has a formal dimension — it follows socially derived rules for turn taking, interrupting, etc. (Jacobs & Jackson, 1982, pp. 228-32). The reference to "local" management is in keeping with the freedom that each has to negotiate with another person what the precise rules will be. In some interchanges interruption will be tolerated, even expected, while in others it will be a sign of irresponsibility. Because each person is intimately involved in the selection of the mechanism, or in their own adaptation to social rules for acceptable argument, arguing in the personal community assumes the greatest potential for being risk-bearing. In the personal community, the "immediacy of risk depends on adherence to three preconditions for the conduct of argumentative discourse: (1) The arguers agree to 'hear each other out'; (2) They agree on the standards of judgment by which their claims will be evaluated; and (3) They agree to accept the other's position if their own proves to be indefensible" (McKerrow, 1977, p. 140). If a person enters into an argument intent on remaining steadfast, one or more of these preconditions will not be addressed, and risk-of-self will be lessened.

The nature of risk assessment is implicit in Jackson's (1987) assertion that the orientation of argument within this community is toward the "propriety or acceptability of *acts*" rather than simply toward the probity of claims (p. 218). An individual's motives or reasons for arguing may be more crucial in determining one's response than the content of the argument itself. In a study which supports the general premise that argument is aimed at disagreement resolution or "repair," Benoit (1987) highlighted several reasons for continuing or not continuing an argument:

> A content analysis of the reasons for choosing to repair indicate such a preference when 1) the relationship is serious, 2) the blame for wrongdoing is accepted or shared, 3) a desire to reinstate understanding and trust exists with a corresponding lack of desire to create enemies or produce animosity, 4) the offense is perceived as serious, or 5) the offense is perceived as trivial and easily resolved. A similar analysis of the reasons given not to repair include 1) the issue is not important enough to exert the effort, 2) the other is perceived at fault, 3) avoiding the issue is easier, 4) the offense is perceived as serious enough to terminate the relationship, and 5) the relationship is not perceived as serious (p. 148).

These reasons function as "felicity conditions" which help determine which issues and actions (including non-response) are relevant and which are irrelevant to the dispute (see Jackson, 1987, p. 219). Thus, the focus of argument may be on the claim, or on the evidence, or on "matters of rights, obligations, desires, intentions expectations, understandings, feelings, and relationships" (Jackson, 1987, p. 218). In any of these instances the individual's sense of how rules should be applied and her or his involvement with others in negotiating how they will be used in particular resolutions of disputes is of paramount importance.

Argument in the Social Community

The use of "social" refers explicitly to the "collective" and "societal" nature of argument addressed to persons inhabiting the "public sphere"

(Goodnight, 1982, 1987c). As Goodnight observes, "the language of public address emanates from a community tradition of deciding and discussing priorities, constraining and protecting habituated prejudgments, and indulging and confronting common problems. While public discourse makes open and common collective preference, it also provides an arena where interests conduct controversy and openly struggle for power" (1987c, p. 429). Letters to the editors of local newspapers about the actions of town officials and arguments raised at meetings of local school boards or zoning commissions typify a dimension of discourse within the social community. Advocacy by politicians on behalf of proposals for change and the support of a President for a Cabinet nominee under fire also typify argument addressed to this community. Social arguments are audience oriented: the construction of reasons on behalf of claims owe their existence to one's analysis of an identifiable audience. To quote Mannheim's (1936) discussion of collective or social thought, social argument "constitutes a complex which cannot be readily detached either from the psychological roots of the emotional and vital impulses which underlie it or from the situation in which it arises and which it seeks to solve" (p. 2). Although argument in this context may appear far removed from such "impulses," it ultimately is reducible to a prevailing ideology — the values and beliefs of individuals within the social community.

Argument may be addressed to members of a social community with a view to maintaining the authority of those in power; it also may create or constitute a new community — a particularized "public" which becomes a new agent for social change. Between the poles of maintenance and creation, argument mediates the perceived needs of the members of the social community — it functions to solve problems, to promote social cohesion, or to alter the relations of power between those who currently speak for the community and others who seek a voice in public affairs. When used for maintenance, it involves and uses as its motivating force the accepted modes of thinking within the community to promote socially defined ends. When engaged in protest, or in the creation of a new collective, it seeks to alter the accepted modes of thinking or to apply them in new ways to problems or relations of power.

The arguments of those in positions of power are aimed at fostering support for political actions. In this instance, social argument which incorporates visions of a "Cold War" or "Detente" is premised on a leader's understanding of America's mission in the world and of our emotional involvement with and sense of obligation to honor that mission. In identifying with the collective consciousness of the audience, such argument may be relatively innocuous or it may be irresponsible. Nixon's November 3, 1969 speech on Vietnam, as Newman (1970) and Campbell (1972) assert, is an example of irresponsible social argument. Designed to appeal to America's sense of honor on the battlefield, it effected a division within the populace by pitting an "old" consciousness adhering to a "peace with honor" motif with a "new" one that perceived little honor to be gained from continued involvement in the war effort. In so doing, the social argument sought to preserve a prevailing community ideology with one that was struggling to emerge.

Social argument that attempts to create a new public—a new community with different values or altered applications of old values—was typified in the protest argument revolving around our participation in the Vietnam conflict. Changing allegiance from "peace with honor" or "peace" itself involved the assertion of symbols which would, if accepted, alter support for an administration's policies in conducting the war effort. As another example, Charland's (1987) study of the creation of the Quebec separatist movement illustrates the manner in which social argument is constitutive. In this case, "supporters of Quebec's political sovereignty addressed and so attempted to call into being a *peuple quebecois* that would legitimate the constitution of a sovereign Quebec state" (p. 134). Although the attempt ended in failure, the arguments addressed did achieve a sizeable impact on the community and forced subsequent administrative arguments to take into account the concerns of this nascent collective.

Just as communities exist in space and time, argument can alter or affect these variables with respect to how a public perceives a problem. Space refers both to the degree to which an argument may occupy the public agenda and the degree to which individuals are brought into the specific "collective" that participates in the argument. Those pointing to a need to address the needs of the homeless, for example, expand the nature of the public space allotted to "who counts" in the consideration of the issues. To the extent that feminists are successful in advancing their issues, their claims emerge as critical controversies in the public's attention to the problems of equality and opportunity. In transcending the personal lives of individuals, argument also affects the sense of urgency with which issues will be taken up by the community. The arguments concerning the effects of acid rain and the disposal of hazardous waste, for example, are more "timely" now than they were a decade ago as they disrupt our complacent attitude toward how long we have to address these issues. The fragility of planet Earth is brought into sharp relief in the arguments focused on the necessity for a public response to ecological concerns. As Goodnight (1987c) notes, "the public sphere is made available by public space, the locations of common meetings and discussion where the discourse of community is held open to all who have a say in the matter of common urgency, and by public time, the temporal structures and processes that uphold traditions of collective decision making, alternatively disrupting and preserving private and social temporal patterns" (p. 431).

The nature of argument in this context may be characterized as less formal than that employed in other communities. While the basic element of "reason plus claim" is the same across different contexts, the standards governing the relationship between reason and claim—what constitutes an acceptable argument—differ radically. Where argument in the personal community focused attention on the propriety of the act and entailed consideration of substantive issues unrelated to the actual content of the claim advanced, argument in this community is generally focused on the proposition or on the motive of the arguer. In both communities, argument forms such as "ad hominem" (argument against the person) and "ad populum" (argument premised on popular support) may be highly appropriate (see McGee, 1975, 1978). An argument "against the person" attaches value to one's motives for acting and assesses the personal intent and expertise of the person advocating the ideas. Argument which uses popular support as a rationale for an idea's acceptance may be highly relevant to the future of the community; ideas with support are not necessarily correct, but their strength of appeal functions as a legitimating force for acceptance. The bumper sticker that advises "eat sheep; 10,000 coyotes can't be wrong," is a tongue-in-cheek recognition of the force of popular will. In using argument forms which are less rigorous than might be employed in other contexts, the beliefs and values which function as social truths are maintained or altered through recourse to argumentation.

③ Argument in the Technical Community

Specialized vocabulary provides the substance for argument within the technical community. Where argument in the personal and social community may make use of special terms or special meanings for more commonly used words, argument in the technical domain requires a language that precisely names the objects under discussion. One's knowledge of the issues under discussion is measured, in part, by the ease with which the language of the specialty is employed. Fields such as law, medicine, or the "hard sciences" are excellent examples of communities which depend on one's knowledge of the vocabulary in constructing and evaluating arguments. Having the requisite knowledge makes one an "insider"—a member of a community composed of those "in the know." The obvious corollary is that those "outside" the community cannot appreciate the issues being discussed, as they cannot be presumed to understand or to follow the merits of arguments phrased in highly technical language.

When members of the social community defer to the judgments of the "experts"—the members of a specific technical community—there is a corresponding loss of control or power over the direction of decisions that may affect their lives. To the extent that the judgments of the technical community supercede or overshadow the social community's ability to engage in public deliberation about issues, there is a corresponding diminution of the "public sphere" (Goodnight, 1982). Farrell and Goodnight (1981) provide a case study of this phenomenon in their examination of the arguments following the nuclear crisis at Three Mile Island. In convincing fashion, they illustrate the manner in which technical argument solidified its dominant position in the aftermath of the crisis and, thereby, restricted the role of the "public" or social community as the arbiter of their own destiny. In part, the experts relied on reassurance, attempting to place a technical issue in more common terms (e.g., "The radiation level is what people would get if they played golf in the sunshine" p. 283). As Farrell and Goodnight observe "in attempting to reassure prematurely, those who employed such language assumed, or rather hoped, that the chain reaction of faulty system relays, turbine trips, and exposed fuel rods [explained in saying "Plutonium has taken up residence in the building"] had been terminated quietly in the technical sphere, even as their ramifications were being hidden from the social sphere" (p. 283). Deference to those in authority, to those who presumably know the dangers and have the public's safety uppermost in their minds, may be a faulty decision, especially if, as the Task Force which evaluated the crisis concluded, there was greater attention paid to protecting "the image of the nuclear industry" than to the "potential significance of the breakdown" (p. 299).

Even when technical domains enter the public arena with the avowed purpose of taking testimony, of learning what is on the public's mind, the process may privilege the ultimate authority of "those in the know." As Wallinger (1985) points out in his study of utility rate hearings, "utility regulation appears to be a forum of argument that partially preempts the public domain, even though legally required to solicit public participation in the deliberation" (p. 497). To the extent that public officers see such hearings as serving to "gather comments for the record," and "allow cathartic public expression" and to "educate the public about the powers and procedures" of the particular agency conducting the hearing, little if any impact on actual decision-making may occur (p. 505). Such hearings function instead to legitimize their own authority within the technical domain rather than to consider seriously the public interest.

In emphasizing the potential for dominance by the technical domain, there is an implicit norm being asserted that "is democratic/egalitarian: to hold experts accountable to the 'will of the people,' and thereby to promote the art of public deliberation in communities of equals" (Lake & Keough, 1985, p. 485). In the interaction between communities, there must be an appropriate balance of power such that the interests of each can be heard, and the public's will served. As Lake and Keough's (1985) study of arbitration hearings indicates, the disjunction between social and technical communities need not always be negative or adversarial: "social knowledge need not oppose technical knowledge, but in fact may inform it; . . . technical knowledge need not oppose social knowledge, but in fact may articulate it within the constraints of particular fields; . . . [and] neither the technical nor the social spheres are 'whole cloths,' but instead often are manifested in combinations or patterns" (p. 492). Individuals exist simultaneously in personal, social and technical communities, and draw their arguments from a mixture of concerns relevant to each. While there always will be the potential for separation of the respective interests of the communities, there is too the potential for their integration in the arguments between individuals.

④ Argument in the Philosophical Community

Argument within this community functions as the moral conscience of the people. From Perelman's perspective, the role of the philosopher is that of "the systematic study of value judgments" (1980, p. 58) with a view to conveying "a reasonable vision of the world" (1982b, p. 293). In presenting the "reasoned vision" to the community, the philosopher does not pretend to have absolute knowledge of what should be the actions of the members. Rather, in Perelman's (1980) view, "the criteria, the values, and the norms of a philosophy do not constitute absolute and impersonal values and truths. They express the convictions and aspirations of a free but reasonable [person], engaged in a creative, personal, and historically situated effort" (p. 74).

The form of argument receives the greatest attention in this community. Hare's (1975) discussion of the nature of philosophizing epitomizes the manner in which a philosopher attempts to reach a "reasoned vision":

> Philosophical arguments, conducted in the way that I have described, have the same sort of objectivity that chess games have. If you are beaten at chess, you are beaten, and it is not concealed by any show of words; and in a philosophical discussion of this sort, provided that an unambiguously stated thesis is put forward, objective refutation is possible. Indeed, the whole object of our philosophical training is to teach us to put our theses in a form in which they can be submitted to this test. . . . [W]e prefer professional competence to a superficial brilliance (p. 733).

Rescher (1985) affirms the rational process which philosophy undertakes in its analysis of values: "Philosophizing is a work of reason; we want our problem resolutions to be backed by good reasons—reasons whose bearing will doubtless not be absolute and definitive but will, at any rate, be as compelling as is possible in the circumstances. Reasoning and argumentation are thus the lifeblood of philosophy" (p. 39). In this context, philosophically powerful arguments are distinguishable from those which might be acceptable in the personal or social communities. As Ryle (1954) puts the distinction: "On the whole, Plato is rhetorically more efficient than Aristotle, but we can distinguish the question whether a certain argument of Aristotle is more or less powerful than a corresponding argument of Plato from the question whether the presentation of the one is more or less persuasive than the other" (p. 151). Power, in Ryle's sense, derives from the "boundary setting" function of arguments in this community. They aim not at a collective conscience nor even at an individual person, but instead at what the community regards as an appropriate form or manner of inferring one idea from another. The community defines what will constitute acceptable or reasonable "moves" within the process of advancing reasons—what will satisfy the advancement of unambiguous theses for dispute.

As one illustration, the concern for "words" among linguistic philosophers is exemplified in a discussion of pleasure. Plato suggests that the enjoyment we derive from eating is the same as that which we obtain from drinking: we are merely moving from one "state" to another. Aristotle objects to the equivalency implicit in Plato's analysis: if enjoying were a process of moving from state to state, a person could begin a process but not complete it, as in starting a meal and not finishing it. Enjoyment, however, exists for a finite time. It cannot be fractionalized, hence you cannot equate dining with enjoying. In this fashion, Aristotle effectively (and objectively) refutes Plato. His concern is not for a cultural analysis of the nature of eating, nor is he concerned with the motives or expertise of Plato as a person. Instead, his concern is focused solely on the implications derived from the words, arranged in a particular order. While this perspective is only one of many that philosophers may engage in, it identifies a common feature of argument in this community: "arguments are effective as weapons only if they are logically cogent, and if they are so they reveal connexions, the disclosure of which is not the less necessary to the discovery of truth for being also handy in the discomfiture of opponents" (Ryle, 1971, p. 196). While argument in this community also is concerned with problems, its disposition of those is directed at the "issue" rather than at the individual or the social context.

While the focus is on ideas rather than persons, there is still the sense that "philosophy is a matter of publicly accessible inquiry" (Rescher, 1985, p. 33). While two philosophers may radically disagree to the extent that their competing visions seem incommensurable, it is not the case that one philosopher cannot imagine the position of the other—"in general, philosophers fail to agree not because they do not *understand* each other's views but because they *reject* them" (Rescher, 1985, p. 33). One approach to the position of another is *ad hominem* argument—attacks directed at the internal consistency of the individual's position. The attack is toward the person in the narrow sense that one is dealing with another's development of an idea. The focus of the attack is on the logical parameters of the argument rather than the opponent's motives or expertise as an arguer. The second approach is *ad rem*: an attack on a philosophical position by proposing a counter position. The argument is advanced against an opponent's claim irrespective of the internal consistency of the opponent's overall position. In either case, the arguers agree to express themselves in accordance with the linguistic conventions of the community; the risk that is engendered by each is premised on rigid standards of what constitutes an acceptable reason for changing one's position. While limiting their domain to logical inquiry, philosophers engaged in disagreement resolution are not simply functioning as disembodied automatic response mechanisms, charging and counter charging in accordance with the dictates of an inexorably controlling logic. As Johnstone (1978) affirms, the practice of rhetoric is part of being human:

> It has long been acknowledged that one person can use rhetoric to call the attention of another to conditions of which he had been unconscious. It is no more than a natural extension of the use of the term to apply it to situations in which the person makes himself [or herself] attend to data. This reflexive rhetoric must occur wherever consciousness occurs. If philosophers are conscious, they must engage in rhetoric that is at least self-directed (pp. 58-59).

The constraints on this self-reflexivity function as they do in other communities; what differs are the specific senses of judgment which are employed. In this community, argument serves to evoke an awareness of the other's position in a manner which clarifies the nature of the dispute, and allows a dialogue to ensue that is marked by deliberateness and a strict adherence to clarity of language and consistency of argumentative form. Only in this way can the results of such disputes be confidently and comfortably communicated to the other communities as "reasonable visions" by which persons should live.

Conclusion

The focus of this essay has been on four communities designated in the model as "primary." The designation serves to underscore the pervasive influence of these communities on the arguments that may be used or directed at the other communities or fields within the model. Thus, arguments addressed to the "nation" or to a specific "class" will have, depending on the issue, elements of one or more of the "communities" inscribed in the language choices or the values implicit in the positions advanced. Arguments within specific fields such as law or medicine may reflect the language of a technical community but will have vestiges of other communities implied or explicit in the language used. Given the fact that an individual may inhabit more than one community at any moment, the potential choices for which arguments will dominate will depend on the specific issue being discussed and the judgment of the person about the effectiveness of arguments drawn from any one of the communities. If nothing else, the model serves to highlight the necessary complexity of our arguments with one another, whether they deal with mundane issues or with concerns of international significance.

Part II

Arguing in the Personal Community

One does not pursue the art of being human by coercing others through superior power or by manipulating them by charm or deceit to gain adherence to propositions from powerless or naive individuals. Instead, one seeks a dialogic acceptance of others as persons and develops a bilateral relationship by equalizing opportunities to express attitudes and intentions and by enhancing everyone's capacity for arguing (Brockriede, 1986, p. 64).

This section of the book focuses on how persons in personal communities resolve disagreement and achieve understanding. The authors of the next four chapters analyze interpersonal arguments to determine the strategies and effects of a variety of argumentative approaches for negotiating disagreements. These chapters identify how persons start and end disagreements, how issues change, what rules participants apply, the nature of the relationships between arguers, the effects arguments have on relationships, and the strategies used to increase or reduce the disagreements. Scholars find interpersonal arguments in a variety of places—among friends, within families, within marital dyads, between coworkers, and between romantic partners.

Argumentation theory has traditionally been a normative field. That is to say, argumentation theorists have tried to develop standards that separate good arguments from bad ones. Some theorists whose interests primarily lie in the personal community continue to take normative approaches, but others take descriptive perspectives. A theorist with a descriptive perspective describes the way argument actually occurs while a theorist whose perspective is normative prescribes how arguments should occur in the ideal. Both descriptive and normative views are exemplified in this section. Chapters 4-6 exemplify descriptive perspectives on argument in the personal community while chapter 7 clearly takes a normative view.

In Chapter 4 Robert Trapp develops a model that describes interpersonal arguments as a series of episodes. An argument episode begins with perceived incompatibility between participants; this incompatibility leads to confrontation; the confrontation leads to the inventing and editing of arguments by arguers and, eventually, to the actual process of arguing. Interpersonal arguments have consequences that include argument resolution, positive or negative effects on relationships and self-concepts, conflict escalation or de-escalation, or, possibly, even physical violence. This overview describes the general qualities of arguments occurring in interpersonal relationships.

In Chapter 5, Pamela J. Benoit and William L. Benoit look closely at the unique qualities of the arguments and identify strategies of the arguers. Benoit and Benoit describe interpersonal arguments from the point of view of the subjects who themselves participated in interpersonal argumentation. The chapter explains how often arguments occur, with whom arguments are transacted, how persons get into arguments, and how persons get out of arguments. The authors emphasize that arguers in personal communities must find ways of establishing cooperation so that their relationships are not entirely chaotic. Additionally, this chapter identifies some potential strategies arguers can use to stabilize relationships.

Chapter 6 focuses on arguments between marriage partners. The author, Daniel J. Canary, reviews existing literature in the social sciences to determine how couples within marital dyads resolve disagreements. The marital dyad is one type of relational category within the broader classification of personal communities. Canary describes marital dyads according to goals, motives, topics, and power and control. He also describes the arguers themselves and suggests how their personality characteristics, relationship histories, and the type of relationships provide clues about the type of argumentation that will take place between married couples. Finally, Canary describes a system (Conversational Argument Coding Scheme) that he and his colleagues have developed for the study of interpersonal argument.

In the final chapter in this section, Frans H. van Eemeren and Rob Grootendorst look at interpersonal arguments as speech acts. This chapter provides an excellent summary of the argumentation research program being conducted at the University of Amsterdam in The Netherlands including their book-length treatment of argumentation and speech acts. They identify how the speech acts of assertives, directives, commissives, and usage declaratives occur when persons try to reach agreement about the acceptability or unacceptability of the standpoint toward an issue. They also describe how critics of interpersonal arguments should reconstruct personal conversations so arguments can be analyzed using van Eemeren and Grootendorst's ideal system.

Chapter Four

Arguments in Interpersonal Relationships

Robert Trapp

Husband: Will you help me plant the trees this afternoon?
Wife: No, I could help you tomorrow.
Husband: But I need help today!
Wife: I have to clean the house.
Husband: The house is clean.
Wife: No, you see, that's the difference between men and women.

This example of an argument between a husband and wife sounds familiar to most of us. Their exchange demonstrates the focus of this chapter: argument as an ordinary, everyday concept.

In ordinary language, the term "argument" has different meanings; Daniel J. O'Keefe (1975) reminds us of two of them. First, in everyday talk the term "argument" is used in sentences such as "Her argument about capital punishment is persuasive" or "He argued that the economy is in terrible shape." O'Keefe calls this sense of the term "argument₁." Second, the term "argument" can be used to describe a particular kind of interaction. "Yesterday Dan and I had an argument about the competence of one of our employees" or "Susan and Bill argued about which computer they should buy." O'Keefe called this "argument₂." In the first sense of the term, a person "makes an argument." In the second sense, people are "having arguments." Although these are interdependent senses of argument, the term "argument" is used in both of these ways.

Mr. Trapp is in the Speech Communication Department at Willamette University in Salem, Oregon.

In this chapter, we are concerned primarily with the second sense of argument. For the sake of simplicity, we will use the term "argument" to refer to O'Keefe's argument$_2$.

While doing research on arguments in interpersonal relationships, Nancy Hoff and I noticed that "argument" contained two subtly different meanings. When someone says "my husband and I had an argument," she can be referring either to a single argument episode or to a serial argument composed of several argument episodes. An argument episode is a communication event that occurs at a definite moment in time and has a clear beginning and ending. A serial argument, on the other hand, occurs and recurs at several times and contains many different argument episodes. Its beginning may be difficult to identify, and it frequently has no end.

Thus, "My husband and I are having an argument" could refer to a particular interaction that occurred at that very moment. Its meaning could be construed as "Please don't interrupt me now. My husband and I are having an argument." The wife's statement may refer, however, to an argument that has been going on for several months and even for years: "I just can't believe it. My husband and I are still having an argument about keeping on a budget." In the first case, "argument" refers to an argument episode; in the second it refers to a serial argument.

In this chapter, we will examine a model of an argument episode and a model of a serial argument. Finally, I will discuss how the content of argument episodes and serial episodes reflects upon relational issues.

A model is a representation of a thing. Since it can never be the thing itself, it will always be imperfect. In developing and revising the models of argument episodes and serial arguments, we have struggled with the trade-off between accuracy and simplicity. When accuracy is the goal, models become less simple; but when simplicity is reached, accuracy is sacrificed. Although the models I present are far from perfect, at this time they represent my best attempts to model argument episodes and serial arguments.

A. Argument Episodes

According to this model (Figure One), an argument episode begins with the perception of incompatibilities. The episode is enacted by one participant deciding to confront the other, inventing and editing argument strategies, and arguing. The goal of an argument is to resolve the perceived incompatibility. [1] While argument episodes may never be resolved, they always have consequences. The potential consequences range from conflict escalation or de-escalation, to conflict resolution, to self-concept damage or improvement, to relational improvement or dissolution, and/or to physical violence.

Figure 1
Argument Episode

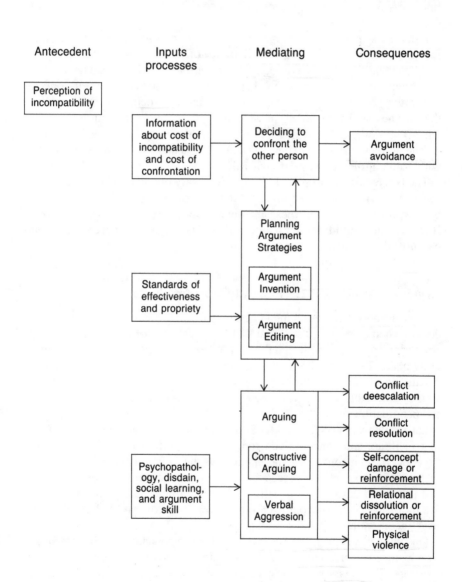

The Antecedents of Arguments

Argument episodes begin when one or both participants perceive some kind of incompatibility. Sources of incompatibility range from attitudes to values to behaviors. People can have incompatible attitudes on issues like abortion, find parts of their value systems to be incompatible, or can behave in ways that create incompatibilities.

Individuals perceive incompatibilities in terms of self-focused, partner-focused, and relation-focused conflicts (Roloff, 1987). When the perception of incompatibility is self-focused, a wife, for instance, believes that her husband is behaving toward her in ways that are inconsistent with her self-concept. When the perception of incompatibility is partner-focused, a wife believes that her husband is behaving in ways that are inconsistent with her view of what is appropriate behavior for him. When the perception of incompatibility is relation-focused, the wife believes that her husband's behavior is inconsistent with some agreed-upon relational rules.

The perception of incompatibility is a necessary but an insufficient condition for the occurrence of an argument. Many people perceive minor incompatibilities almost daily, but these incompatibilities are not serious enough to stimulate the individuals to go any further. Only when the perceived incompatibility is of sufficient magnitude are the participants motivated to begin the process of arguing.

Argument Processes: Deciding to Confront the Other

Once arguers perceive an incompatibility of sufficient magnitude, they must decide whether or not to confront their partners. As long as the cost of confrontation appears to outweigh the cost of continued incompatibility, arguing is avoided. Persons who avoid arguing may do so simply by avoiding a discussion of the incompatibility; they also may talk about it in covert ways, so they can avoid confronting their partners and deny the very existence of an incompatibility.

Sara E. Newell and Randall K. Stutman (1982) discovered seven elements that facilitate and constrain confrontation. These factors include perceived urgency of confrontation, the nature of the relationship, the perceived responsibility to confront, perceptions of the other, resources, appropriateness, and perceived outcomes. Newell and Stutman found that relational partners are more likely to confront each other over an incompatible behavior than over incompatible ideas.

One thing that Newell and Stutman's study does not address is the role played by a history of confrontation. A history of productive arguing will probably facilitate confrontation. If a husband and wife have a relationship that encourages productive argument, they are more likely to continue to confront one another before incompatibilities become insurmountable. On the other hand, if a couple has a history of arguments that are counter-productive, they may avoid confronting one another. Thus, argumentative history may be facilitating or constraining.

In summary, the first process involved in an argument is the decision to confront the other. If the decision is negative, the consequence is argument avoidance. If the decision is positive, the next step involves planning argument strategies.

Argument Processes: Planning Argument Strategies

Once arguers decide to confront each other, they need to develop the content of the arguments they will make and the strategies they will use. They must invent and edit the arguments and strategies they think will be most effective and appropriate in the situation. Since people can develop their arguments and strategies without *conscious* reflection, this process is frequently unconscious or mindless. When the stakes are high or the situation is novel, conscious attention is more likely to be paid to inventing and editing arguments and strategies.

Dale Hample and Judith M. Dallinger (1987) show how developing arguments and argument strategies involve the interconnected cognitive activities of inventing and judging potential arguments. These processes usually involve selecting a single argument and then applying internal judgment standards to decide whether or not that argument will be perceived as effective or appropriate. If the argument passes minimal standards for effectiveness and appropriateness, the argument is used. If not, another argument is invented and the same standards reapplied. The inventing and editing of arguments continues until an acceptable argument has been selected, after which time no further possibilities are considered.

Research by Hample and Dallinger (1987) reveals four categories of editing standards: effectiveness, principled objection, person-centered rationales, and discourse competence. When an effectiveness standard is used to reject a potential argument, the arguer believes that the argument would not work. A principled objection standard can be used by an arguer who refuses to use a particular strategy for an ethical or moral reason. Person-centered standards can be used to edit an argument that might endanger the arguers' relationship. Finally, discourse competence standards can be used to reject arguments that are false or easily refuted. People use these four categories of editorial standards to judge the effectiveness and appropriateness of potential arguments.

In summary, the process of developing arguments and argument strategies consists of an invention phase and a judgment phase. Arguers invent potential arguments and judge them according to their internal standards of judgment. Having selected arguments and argumentative strategies, arguers are ready to proceed to the next phase of the argument episode.

Argument Processes: Arguing

The clearest and most easily recognizable example of people arguing "*occurs when two or more parties intentionally engage in disagreement over incompatible goals and are unable to resolve these differences*" (Trapp, 1986, p. 23). One of the most important aspects of this characterization is that people are frequently unable to resolve their incompatibilities. Many people do not possess the skills needed to resolve important incompatibilities with significant partners. Thus, their arguing frequently is unproductive or counterproductive. Argumentative encounters would be much more productive if arguers developed those skills encompassed in the concept of argumentative competence. Those skills can be grouped into two broad categories called effectiveness and appropriateness (Trapp, Yingling, & Wanner, 1987).

Effective arguers use effective persuasive tactics, make clear connections, push arguments to a clear conclusion, are logical, provide support for arguments, and explain things clearly (Trapp, Yingling, & Wanner, 1987). Argumentative effectiveness parallels what Dominic Infante (1988) has called "arguing constructively." Arguing constructively "includes the ability to recognize controversial issues in communication situations, to present and defend positions on the issues, and to attack the positions which other people take" (p. 7).

But competence involves more than effectiveness; it involves appropriateness as well. The appropriate arguer learns to avoid the kinds of tactics that are frequently associated with arguing—being obnoxious, arrogant and overbearing; insulting or poking fun at others; belittling opponents; trying to prevent others from expressing their points of view, and directing arguments against the other person rather than the other person's position (Trapp, Yingling, and Wanner, 1987). In general, the appropriate arguer avoids behaviors which are not suitable to the situation or the relationship.

The appropriate arguer avoids what Infante (1988) calls "verbal aggression." Infante defines verbal aggressiveness as "the inclination to attack the self-concepts of individuals instead of, or in addition to, their positions on particular issues" (p. 7). An arguer who resorts to personal attacks on another person rather than confining those attacks to the other person's position on the issue is being verbally aggressive and, hence, inappropriate as an arguer.

So the actual process of arguing constructively involves disagreeing with someone's position on an issue, articulating the reasons for your position on that issue, and refuting their position on the issue. This is all done in an attempt to resolve the incompatibility.

Unfortunately, many arguers are unable to use these skills to resolve incompatibilities because these arguers are not as competent as they might be. They become frustrated when they are unable to resolve incompatibilities with their relational partners. They blame each other for their lack of success, and they focus their arguments on each other rather than on the issues that underlie the incompatibility. When this happens, constructive arguing escalates to verbal aggression. A few of the most common forms of verbal aggression include character attacks, competence attacks, personal appearance attacks, insults, teasing, ridicule, profanity, and threats (Infante, 1988, p. 21).

What causes potentially constructive arguments to escalate into verbal aggression? Infante (1988) believes that psychopathology, disdain, social learning and argumentative skill deficiency are among the causes (p. 25). Psychopathology, a mental disorder, is quite rare as a cause. Even disdain, or hatred of the other person, is not a frequent cause of verbal aggression. Social learning is perhaps more prevalent than psychopathology or hatred. Some people grow up in environments where verbal aggression is rewarded. Others, on the other hand, are taught that personal attacks are inappropriate. But Infante believes that the most serious cause of verbal aggression is argumentative skill deficiency.

When arguers are deficient in the skills of arguing, constructive strategies fail them. When they are unsuccessful in developing arguments to support their positions or in refuting opposing positions, they may think that they have no alternative but to attack the other person.

This analysis of the causes of verbal aggression is particularly optimistic because it holds forth the hope that the problem can be alleviated by teaching the skills of argumentation. The kinds of issues that are addressed in this volume may help people to become more adept at arguing constructively and to avoid verbal aggression. The kinds of skills that are taught in courses in argumentation and debate, persuasion, and conflict management can help people learn to become more competent arguers; those skills can help arguers to be effective in getting others to understand (and perhaps even to accept) their points of view while at the same time avoiding verbal aggression and other inappropriate argument strategies.

The Consequences of Arguments

Argument episodes result in a variety of consequences. The consequences I will discuss are conflict escalation or de-escalation, conflict resolution, self-concept damage or reinforcement, relational dissolution or reinforcement, and physical violence. These are not mutually exclusive consequences; one or several of them can result from an argument.

While the goal of an argument is usually to resolve an incompatibility, a more frequent consequence is conflict de-escalation. Paradoxically, a consequence of argument involves pressures to discontinue the argument, at least temporarily. As I have said earlier, arguments can spiral out of control and turn into verbal aggression. When arguments heat up, arguers need to find ways to cool down. De-escalation is the only way that arguers can stop the spiral toward verbal aggression and return to constructive arguing.

Specialists in interpersonal conflict suggest different ways of breaking out of destructive spirals (See Hocker & Wilmot, 1985, pp. 157-8; Peterson et al., 1983, pp. 377-88; Robert, 1982 and Wilmot, 1979, pp. 128-9). For instance, Joyce Hocker and William Wilmot (1985) suggest changing the other party, changing conflict conditions (for example, changing the perception of incompatible goals), and changing your own behavior (pp. 157-58). De-escalation has to occur before arguments can be resolved.

If people argue constructively, incompatibilities can be resolved (at least temporarily) by consensus, compromise, understanding, or capitulation. A consensus occurs when parties reach a solution that is preferred by both of them—when they arrive at a win/win rather than a win/lose solution to the problem. Arguers can also resolve the problem by compromise—by allowing each party to win something and lose something in order to meet the demands of the relationship. Another way an argument episode can be resolved is through understanding. This means that the partners may not resolve the incompatibility, but they may learn to understand each other's position in a way that will allow them to "agree to disagree." Another way that the argument can be resolved is through capitulation. One person just gives up. She or he decides to switch rather than to fight. This is not a constructive way to resolve an argument because it leaves the initial incompatibility unresolved.

Another consequence of arguments involves changed self-concepts. When the style of arguing is verbal aggression, self-concept damage is likely. When arguers attack another person rather than the issue, that person may be able to fend off the blow by saying something such as "Oh, she really didn't mean that. She only said it in a fit of anger." But when verbal aggression is repeated over and over again, the receiver becomes less and less able to defend against it. Some of the blows begin to take a toll resulting in serious damage to the person's self-concept. On the other hand, by arguing constructively, both parties can maintain or perhaps even strengthen their self-concepts.

In addition to their effect on self-concepts, arguments also have relational consequences. Infante (1988) reports a variety of studies that show the positive effects that constructive arguing can have for a variety of interpersonal relationships. He reports that constructive arguing can improve different types of relationships from marriages to the work place (p. 9).

A potential consequence of verbal aggression is deterioration or termination of relationships. Continued personal attacks make people less interested in working on a relationship. When partners lose their motivation to work on a relationship, the relationship deteriorates. When verbal aggression becomes commonplace, some people simply decide they have had enough; they start looking for a way to end the relationship.

These effects are very serious, but an even more serious consequence of an argument involves escalation into physical violence. Infante cites research by Gelles (1974) and by Toch (1969) which indicates that physical violence is usually preceded by verbal aggression. Thus while we must realize that many factors combine to cause child and spouse abuse, in some cases failure to argue constructively could be a major contributing factor.

So an argument episode begins when one or both relational partners perceive an incompatibility that is important enough to cause them to confront each other. Then arguers plan argument strategies and begin the process of arguing. The consequences of the argument can be positive or negative depending, among other things, on whether the predominant style is constructive arguing or verbal aggression.

This has been a relatively simple explanation of an argument episode. Having already described an argument episode, the move to serial argument is easy.

β. Serial Arguments

A serial argument is a series of argument episodes that are related to one another in some way. These episodes are quite frequent occurrences in many relationships. The consequences of an argument episode can be thought of as stopping places in the process. In order to develop into a serial argument, people simply move from those stopping places back to the antecedents and start the process over again. This movement is indicated by the dotted lines on Figure Two. In the next few paragraphs I will explain how people move from these stopping places to the antecedents as they enact serial arguments.

The first consequence of an argument is conflict de-escalation. This is an important consequence when the style of argument includes verbal aggression. In order to accomplish anything positive, verbal aggression needs to de-escalate so constructive arguing can begin. In other words, after the argument heats up, the arguers need to simmer down (Willard, 1979a). But they do not stay in this cooled-down state perpetually. Something else happens to remind them of their perceived incompatibility with each other so they decide to confront their partner, and the argument starts again.

Arguers loop back through the process of serial arguments even when the consequences of an argument include conflict resolution. Arguers may be strongly committed to the resolution, or their commitment may be weak. Perhaps two people come to a resolution that sounds good at the time, but after more time passes, one or both of them begin to question some aspects of it. When their commitment weakens, other events may be perceived as involving incompatibilities, and they loop back to the beginning of the argument sequence. For example, a wife expects her husband to do the dishes after she prepares a meal. She may agree to a compromise that she will do the dishes every other night. If her commitment to that compromise is weak, however, she may feel the need to confront him again because she believes she is doing an unfair amount of the housework.

Figure 2
Serial Argument

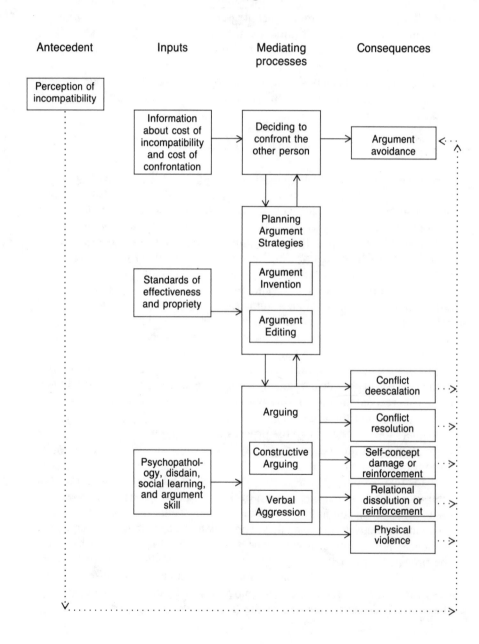

Self-concept consequences also allow arguers to loop back into a new episode. Let us say, for instance, a person's self-concept is improved due to some positive outcome of the argument. That improvement may further motivate the person to continue to seek a resolution to the conflict; that motivation may, in turn, lead her to return to the argument once an incompatibility is perceived. On the other hand, if a person's self-concept is damaged by the argument, she may begin to notice that the ways she is treated by her partner seem incompatible with her ideal self-concept. The need to narrow the gap between her real and ideal self-concept may motivate her to reenter the realm of argument.

Relational damage or reinforcement can motivate people to loop back through the process of argument. If an argument reinforces a relationship, the arguers may be motivated to continue that kind of behavior. They will come to see constructive arguing as a positive way to work out their difficulties. If a verbally aggressive argument damages a relationship, the partners will feel motivated to continue the argument only as long as they remain committed to the relationship and as long as the issue about which they are arguing is important to them. Verbally aggressive arguments may damage the relationship to the point of relational dissolution. Such arguments may mean a permanent end to the argument if it means that the relationship is forever ended and the parties do not see each other again.

Physical violence, another potential consequence of argument, is rarely confined to one argument session. That aggression breeds aggression is particularly true in regard to physical violence. Physical violence is frequently followed by some kind of temporary de-escalation. Persons who are prone to physical violence, however, seem to cycle back through the argument in increasingly negative ways until someone is killed or seriously hurt or until third-party intervention solves the problem of physical violence.

Thus, a serial argument happens when people engage each other in an argument episode, come to a temporary stopping place as a consequence of that argument, and loop back through the process of argument episodes again and again. Although I have not specified many of the details of this process of reversal, I believe that the nature of the consequence will influence the direction that future episodes will take. If the consequences are completely negative, future argument episodes are more likely to be negative. If the consequences are positive, future argument episodes are likely to be more constructive.

Relational Dimensions of Serial Arguments

Interpersonal communication specialists have observed that communication has relational as well as content dimensions (Watzlawick, Beavin, & Jackson, 1967). In other words, although a message always carries some content, it also carries a message about the relationship. It communicates something about how the partners see themselves, each other, and how they see their relationship.

Arguments are no exception; in fact, the way people argue carries important messages about their self-concepts, how they see each other, and how they see their relationship. Every argument episode is about some content, but in its shadow is a larger relational issue. For example, the content of an argument episode may be about who should take out the garbage or do the dishes. But in the shadow of that content may be a relational argument that involves how the arguers see themselves, each other, and their relationship in terms of gender roles.

In any particular relationship, several argument episodes centering around different topics at the content level all may be processing the same issue at the relationship level. In a recent undergraduate course, one of my students, Mike Lash, wrote an insightful essay where he analyzed a serial argument between himself and a female friend. He claimed that his friend wanted him to be a different kind of person although he was comfortable with himself as he was.

Lash illustrated this serial argument through three argument episodes. In the first, Lash and his friend argued about whether or not he should wear his red leather pants when they went on a date. He liked himself in his red leather pants but she thought they were inappropriate. In a second episode, they argued about whether he was a "mama's baby." In the third episode, they argued directly about whether or not she liked him as he was or wanted to change him.

According to Lash's analysis, the content dimensions of the first two episodes were different from the relational dimensions. In the third episode, the relational issues were also the content issues. These three examples illustrate how different argument episodes with different content can converge to create a serial argument that unites different content episodes at the relationship level.

This chapter shows how the concepts of argument episodes and serial arguments can be united to explain some important aspects of interpersonal relationships. Hopefully, these models are broad enough that they incorporate aspects of communication theory and interpersonal communication with concepts traditionally reserved for the domain of argumentation. By uniting ideas from fields of study that are traditionally separate, perhaps we can get a broader view of the human condition, in this case how people argue with significant others.

Notes

[1] Although generally the goal of an argument is the resolution of incompatibility, some arguers perpetuate argument to continue a communication pattern to which they are accustomed. If the argument should end, they create another. Their goal is to generate argument, not eliminate incompatibility.

Chapter Five

To Argue or Not to Argue

Pamela J. Benoit and William L. Benoit

How Real People Get In and Out of Interpersonal Arguments

> Nancy: . . . Well I can't believe you went to dinner and left the
> kids in a hotel.
> Elliot: (pause) Are we done with this *argument*?
> Nancy: (pause) Yes. I guess.
> (February 28, 1989 episode of *thirtysomething*, emphasis added)

Jones who lives in Kansas City, allegedly shot and killed Tarrus Cross, 22, of 216 Lincoln Drive, during an *argument* the two men had early Sunday morning. The men were squabbling over a woman during a party celebrating the wedding of a local couple.

(*Columbia Daily Tribune*, February 28, 1989, p. A1, emphasis added)

I had an *argument* with my girlfriend about whether she was having a good time at a dance. She's never bothered to tell me she didn't like to go to dances. I got mad at her and she got mad at me. It didn't get anywhere. Our feelings were too strong. I think the same feelings about an issue can be discussed without *arguing*.

(Excerpt from a student diary, emphasis added)

Ms. Benoit and Mr. Benoit are in the Department of Communication at the University of Missouri at Columbia.

Each of these examples refers to having an *argument*. The references highlight one sense in which we use this term: Arguments are recognizable events. They are a type of interaction that requires at least two participants. They have boundaries marked by openings and closings that distinguish them from other forms of interaction. They are known to produce consequences that are sometimes severe. This chapter begins by briefly summarizing findings about interpersonal argument and then develops a more elaborate description of two important parts of arguments: 1) the ways arguers report they get into arguments and, 2) the ways they report they get out of arguments.

Findings about Interpersonal Arguments

What is an argument?

One way to define an argument is to describe the generic characteristics of this event (Brockriede, 1975; 1982). This suggests that it is possible to find a set of characteristics that commonly appear in arguments. Each particular instance of argument may not have all the characteristics, but interactions with more of these features are most likely to be classified as arguments. Perhaps another example of generic characteristics would make this idea more concrete. Westerns are a particular genre of movie and a set of characteristics is commonly identified with them (e.g., they take place in the western United States, there is a hero and villain, the hero will face difficulties but will defeat the villain). When more of these features are present, audiences are more likely to see the movie as a western. A particular movie may not show the hero as beating the bad guy, but if a number of other features that are associated with westerns are present, the movie will still be classified as a western.

So what are the features of arguments? One is that arguments involve a relationship of opposition between participants. This opposition occurs when one person impedes the satisfaction of the wants of the other. If your friend really wants to see *Psycho* and you refuse to go, you've overtly blocked satisfaction of a known want and an argument may be the result. The most easily recognized cases of argument also appear to be between two or more persons who intentionally disagree over incompatible goals and are unable to reach a resolution (Trapp, 1986). Arguments involve competing claims and a willingness to risk confrontation (Brockriede, 1975).

We began this chapter with some examples of events labeled as arguments by real people. Each of the examples demonstrates overt disagreement. Nancy and Elliot disagree about whether he has mismanaged the children. The two men disagree about the appropriateness of directing attention toward a particular woman. A boyfriend and girlfriend dispute the obligation to disclose relevant information. These examples also illustrate the failure to resolve the issue prompting the disagreement. Even in the first example there seems to be agreement to stop arguing but no attempt to resolve the issue.

Disagreement, or a relationship of opposition, can be expressed in many different forms of interaction. Consider a sample of terms that connote types of interactional events: discussion, negotiation, altercation, argument, squabble, quarrel, fight, row. Each of these events involves the overt expression of disagreement, but there are variations in the characteristics of conversations we would label as a "discussion," "argument," or "fight."

Thus, in defining what is meant by argument, some theorists contrast arguments with other disagreement-centered events. People believe that arguments should solve problems, while fights are less likely to have this result (Willard, 1979a). By asking individuals to recall instances of arguments and discussions and to account for why they choose one label over another, we can describe perceived attributes of arguments and discussions. Five characteristics are attributed to arguments. They: 1) express overt disagreement 2) are accompanied by increased volume and a negative tone 3) involve the use of irrational beliefs and the display of emotional reactions 4) are one-sided, for interactants argue their own position and are unwilling to listen to or understand an alternative perspective, and 5) have potentially negative consequences for the relationship (Benoit, 1982; Martin & Scheerhorn, 1985). Discussions, on the other hand usually have three different things in common. They: 1) involve the expression of multiple perspectives, 2) are more likely to result in a resolution of the disagreement, and 3) demonstrate a respect for alternative perspectives by listening to each other and attempting to understand the other's perspective (Benoit, 1982).

So, the differences in the ways in which we use the terms "fight," "argument," and "discussion" vary along a competition-cooperation continuum. In competition, it is important to reach individual goals, and the desired outcome is to win. In cooperation, the goals of both interactants are maximized and the desired outcome is to reach an acceptable solution. Fights are even more competitive than arguments, and so the behavior associated with them are more extreme. Arguments may result in problem solving but are still essentially competitive in nature. This competition explains behaviors typically associated with arguments like increases in volume, negative tone of voice, and the release of emotional reactions. Discussions are cooperative events and thus are most likely to solve the problem. This collaboration encourages behavior like expressing views and empathizing with a partner's perspective.

When someone says they are having an argument, they are referring to a particular kind of interactional event. Defining what is meant by an "argument" helps us to understand the meaning we share about the nature of this activity. Choosing this term rather than "discussion" or "fight" to describe what we are doing will affect our interactions. If I believe I'm having an argument, I produce behavior typically identified with this event and I

won't be surprised when my partner does the same. I also have certain
expectations about the probability of reaching a solution and the potential impact
on the relationship.

How often do arguments occur?

Disagreements are commonplace in relationships. When college students
are asked to keep a diary of their arguments, they report that they participate
 in about seven arguments per week and that each of these interactions lasts
an average of three minutes. Most are likely to have argued with the other
person before (86%), and many have argued about the very same topic before
(41%) (Benoit & Benoit, 1987). People in long term relationships often repeat
arguments from their past (Trapp & Hoff, 1985). This is probably because
arguments usually don't resolve the issue and reoccurrence of the topic fuels
another round of arguing. Romantic partners may argue repeatedly about the
amount of time they should spend together, while roommates recreate
arguments about whose turn it is to do the dishes.

With whom are arguments transacted?

College students argue most with romantic partners, roommates, and friends.
They rarely argue with subordinates, teachers, relatives, or co-workers (Benoit
& Benoit, 1987). This is probably because college students (while they are
in school) spend more time with romantic partners, roommates, and friends
and the opportunity for disagreement increases. In addition, those who write
about interpersonal communication indicate that arguments are more likely
to occur in developed relationships (Altman & Taylor, 1973). For example,
roommates are bound to have some history of arguing with each other, have
information to adapt to each other, and know the relationship can withstand
an argument. Arguments with instructors are riskier since information is scarce
and the effect on the relationship is more difficult to predict.

What goals motivate arguments?

Many theorists (Burke, 1978; O'Keefe, 1988) agree that human beings are
purposeful, that they interact to achieve goals. When interactants argue, they
have expectations of reaching particular goals and make inferences about what
their partners hope to achieve as well. When individuals are asked about their
most important goal in an argument, 36% indicate that they want their partners
to understand their view, 18% are interested in having their partners admit
the reasonableness of an alternative view, and 10% want to convince their
partners that they are right. When these individuals are asked to assess their
partners' goals in the argument, they make inferences that are very similar
to their own objectives. Partners are seen as wanting the other to understand
their views (22%), attempting to convince the other that they are right (17%),

getting the other to admit error (16%), and inducing guilt in the other (16%) (Benoit, 1982).

This perception of goals in arguments is consistent with the definition of argument as a competitive event. In competitions, there are winners and losers. To avoid losing, you need to get your partner to understand the legitimacy of an alternative perspective. Often arguers believe that they are right and their partner is wrong. The goal becomes convincing their partner to see it his/her way. In general, arguers assume that the goals motivating their behavior are similar to the goals directing their partners' behaviors.

What are the outcomes of arguments?

Given the way that people define the event, the argument, and the goals they perceive as directing their own and their partners' behavior, what are the likely outcomes from arguments? As individuals kept diaries of actual arguments, they were asked to evaluate whether things got better, worse, or remained the same after an argument. Over half of those reporting indicate that there is no change for themselves (52%), their partner (61%), or the relationship (70%) (Benoit & Benoit, 1987). Since arguments are not usually expected to resolve the issue that created the disagreement, this is not surprising.

Whether or not people perceive that things are better or worse after an argument depends on who won or lost. Individuals feel most satisfied with the outcome of an argument when their partner gives in and they can declare a clear victory (Benoit, 1982). But, according to the diary accounts of arguments, this does not happen very often. Individuals report that they are the winners of arguments in only 23% of the cases reported; usually neither wins or both manage to claim victory (60%) (Benoit & Benoit, 1987). Arguers often experience frustration after engaging in an argument "that ends up going nowhere." These kinds of arguments are also likely to regenerate the seeds of disagreement again and again in relationships.

Summary

So, when real people talk about having an argument, they are making references to their shared meanings about a kind of interactional event. This event has a number of characteristics that are commonly recognized: overt disagreement, inability to resolve the issue, increased volume and negative tone, irrational beliefs and emotional displays, a one-sided perspective, and the possibility of negative consequences for the relationship. Arguments are a common event in relationships and for college students they occur most often between romantic partners, friends, and roommates. Arguers want their partners to understand their views, acknowledge its legitimacy, and admit the error of their ways. They expect that their partners are attempting to reach the same kinds of goals. Individuals report that arguments usually do not change things for themselves, their partners, or the relationship. This may occur because solutions are difficult to reach in arguments. Thus, arguments are viewed as competitions and both goals and behaviors are consistent with this perspective.

Getting Into Arguments

Most of our conversational activity is cooperative; analysts have documented a preference for agreement in discourse (Jackson & Jacobs, 1980; Pomerantz, 1984). As people talk, they are creating images of themselves. In cooperative discourse these identities are reaffirmed by their partners. This identity is known as a person's face (Brown & Levinson, 1978). In maintaining the other's face, a person has agreed to allow the other freedom of action and to be considerate of his or her wants. If a person protects the face of another, he or she can feel assured that his or her own face in turn will be maintained by the other.

But, of course, arguments are competitive rather than cooperative events. Their very nature, involving the expression of disagreement and casting interactional partners into a relationship of opposition, changes the understanding about face. Individuals are not likely to assist their partners when their partners impede or ignore their wants. In arguments, interactants direct their energy toward protecting their own face and attacking the face of their partner to gain an advantage in the competition.

Conversations can be thought of as a stream of activity. Interactants contribute by exchanging remarks. Some of these turns are loosely organized, while others are recognized as discrete interactional events. Interactional events are composed of sequences of talk, a series of related turns (McLaughlin, 1984). These sequences are distinguishable from the stream of conversational activity by boundaries that mark the beginning and end. Since arguments are interactional events, there are conventional or standard ways for getting in and out of arguments. These ways are clearly related to the issue of face. Real people get into arguments by exchanging remarks that threaten the face of their partner. These turns violate the norm of cooperation regarding face. A person attacks the other's face in hopes of winning and protects his or her own face to avoid losing. Real people get out of arguments by terminating the talk or by re-establishing the norm of cooperation regarding face. When the competition is no longer overt or is removed, interactants can return to other forms of interactional activity. Thus, arguments have boundaries that separate them from other kinds of interactional events.

To examine these boundaries, we asked college students to recount who said what in recent arguments with a parent, friend, roommate, or romantic partner. Then, we examined the beginnings and endings of each of these instances, found similarities, and developed a description of each of the types of openings and closings. The most common ways interactants say they actually get into arguments include insults, accusations, commands, and refusals of requests.

Insult

Many arguers report they get into arguments when their partners insult them or when they insult their partners. An insult derogates the person or a valued third party (e.g., the partner's girlfriend or mother) and overtly attacks the face of the other. Individuals want to be treated with respect and to be valued by the other. An insult shows that these wants will not be observed. The person's qualities or disposition are treated with disrespect.

In the following example, a romantic couple is celebrating an anniversary when Brad gets into an argument by insulting Lisa:

> Brad: I don't like your dress.
> Lisa: Why not? (bitterly)
> Brad: It makes you look like a clown.
> Lisa: Go to hell!

Appearance is an important part of Lisa's identity or face and Brad is particularly remiss in failing to show appreciation on the occasion of their anniversary. The insult generates a negative response from Lisa. By her tone she lets Brad know immediately that an argument has started.   *She started it.?*

In the second example, friends who also happen to work together get into an argument when one of them assails the other's disposition:

> Joe: You are certainly grumpy. Why?
> Mary: Because everyone including you is taking over my job
> and pushing their noses into my personal life.

Joe may have been trying to show concern for Mary rather than trying to hurt her by remarking that she was grumpy. This highlights the interpretation we do when we talk to each other. Speakers generally try to convey their intentions by what they say and hearers make inferences about the best interpretation of the speaker's remarks. In this case, if Joe had meant to show concern, he could have asked "Are you feeling all right?" which would have been less likely to threaten Mary's face. Of course, how Mary reacts will be determined by her interpretation of Joe's statement, not necessarily by how Joe meant the statement. Mary perceives that she has been insulted and that the norm of cooperation regarding face is no longer being observed by Joe. Accordingly, she lashes out at Joe and protects her own face by arguing that she is not responsible for any grumpiness.

Accusation

Arguers also report that accusations get them into arguments. Accusations find error and assign blame to the behavior of a partner. An individual's face is attacked when his or her actions are considered unacceptable because an individual's identity is created through their behavior. An accusation calls for a justification of the actions and such a confrontation is not a cooperative exchange. This competition justifies attacking the face of the other. We think our partner has done something wrong and deserves to be reprimanded. Chris and Kim are arguing about whether he shows an appropriate amount of affection:

> Kim: You never show me any affection.
>
> Chris: I think I do. You're just too mushy.
>
> Kim: Your way of showing affection to me is by making fun of me.
>
> Chris: Maybe. But I still care for you and you know how I feel.
>
> Kim: I still like to hear it.
>
> Chris: It's okay in private but you always want to be kissy face in public.

She accuses him of failing to give her enough affection. She sees him as being at fault. He disagrees and assigns fault to her for being "too mushy." They disagree about the kind of behavior that is appropriate in this relationship. Both arguers attack the face of their partner by locating the blame squarely on the other.

In another example, romantic partners tangle over the failure to be on time for a date. Meg believes Greg made a commitment to pick her up and he failed to arrive at the appointed time:

> Meg: Do you know what time it is? It's 11:15 and you said you would be here at 10:30.
>
> Greg: I said I would come over as soon as possible. Don't put me on a time schedule.
>
> Meg: Why can't I ever depend on you? Nothing's changed. You are the same as always.

generalizing

Greg's actions are criticized and he responds by justifying his behavior. He argues that he did not make a commitment for a particular time and is therefore not to blame. Notice that in defending his actions, he also attacks Meg's face by accusing her of putting him on a time schedule. Both people find error and assign blame to their partner. Cooperation in maintaining each other's face is abandoned by both people in favor of protecting their own face and attacking the other.

Most accusations and counter-accusations are based on disagreements over expectations concerning the relationship. Chris and Kim have different ideas about the appropriate amount of affection as well as the place where affection should be displayed. Meg and Greg disagree about whether you can expect punctuality for dates and whether this is an indication of dependability. We have a lot of expectations (often implicit) about how our partners are supposed to behave. In romantic relationships, we expect similarity, supportiveness, openness, loyalty, shared time, and romance (Baxter, 1986). When our expectations aren't met, we feel justified in using an accusation that may get us into an argument.

Command

Interactants report they often find themselves in an argument when they have issued a command to their partner or a partner has attempted to order them around. A command directs the other's behavior and is perceived by the recipient as threatening personal freedom. Thus, a command impedes the face wants of a partner. We expect others not to impinge on our freedom to act and not to order us to do things that we do not want to do.

In this first example, a boyfriend commands his girlfriend to stop seeing an ex-boyfriend. The command has the force of an order. It indicates that the issue is not negotiable and the partner should simply comply:

> Jay: You are never to see him again!
> Michelle: Why?
> Jay: Because I can't handle it.
> Michelle: He's just a friend.
> Jay: It's him or me, bottom line.

Jay's pronouncement is not accepted without question. Michelle offers reasons for rejecting the command and the argument escalates as Jay forces a choice between himself and her ex-boyfriend. This example illustrates the one-sided perspective that individuals have as they argue. Both Jay and Michelle concentrate on their own views and do not acknowledge the other's perspective.

The next example occurs between roommates. This argument is about a recurrent problem between roommates, cleaning the apartment:

> Joan: Clean up this mess.
> Julie: When I'm good and ready.
> Joan: You're a pig. If I'd known . . .
> Julie: And you're a saint? (sarcastic)

In many of our interpersonal relationships, we expect to be treated as equals. When partners command us to do something they are telling us that they have the right to order us around. Bosses or parents may have this right, but roommates, friends, and romantic partners usually feel that they are equals. In the argument between Joan and Julie, the disagreement is not just about cleaning the apartment but also about whether Joan can tell Julie what she must do. Julie's face has been threatened, for Joan has certainly ignored Julie's desire to be free to determine her own behavior.

Refusal of a request

When we ask others to do some action, we expect that they will agree to the request. Usually they agree to the request because of the preference for agreement in conversation. So, we are surprised when a request is met with a refusal. Refusals are most likely to get interactants into an argument when there is no apparent or acceptable reason for failing to honor the request. The request is made because the partner has some want that can be satisfied by the other. In refusing to do so, the partner has hurt the other's face by failing to show consideration for their wants.

Two friends get into an argument when a request to cook dinner is refused:

> Mark: Aren't you going to cook dinner for me?
> Sally: No.
> Mark: But you said yesterday you would!
> Sally: I changed my mind because I have too much to do.
> Mark: (silence)

Mark believes the request will be accepted since Sally has promised earlier that she would cook dinner for him. She offers a reason for her refusal but Mark's silence (instead of accepting her reason) is a clear indication that he doesn't think her reason is a good one. From Mark's perspective, Sally refused his request even though she promised and thus failed to show consideration for his wants. Sally believes that her refusal is justified and Mark should understand her needs.

In this next example, a boyfriend requests confirmation of weekend plans with his girlfriend. He is surprised by her refusal:

> Steve: Well, am I still coming up?
> Teresa: Well, there's this party that I'm invited to and I really want to go with Lynda.
> Steve: But I thought I was coming up! I was all prepared to.
> Teresa: I know but Lynda wants me to go and I guess I really want to.
> Steve: But I thought you wanted to see me! What am I going to do now? (accusing)

Steve expects that his request will be accepted. The plans were made earlier and there was no indication they would be changed. Teresa refuses the request to visit and offers a reason—she wants to go to a party with a friend. Not only has Steve's face been damaged by her refusal, but her reason threatens his self-worth. She is choosing to go to a party with Lynda rather than to spend time with Steve. This face threat causes him to disagree to protect his own face.

Summary

Arguments are set apart from other interactional events. The norm in interactions is a preference for agreement and collaboration in maintaining face. Arguments involve the overt expression of disagreement and explicit attacks on the face of the partner. This analysis of how interactants become involved in arguments indicates that insults, accusations, commands, and refusals of requests all threaten the face of the partner and thus often foment arguments.

Getting Out of Arguments

Relationships can be described as alternating cycles of harmony and disharmony (Feldman, 1979). During some periods of time, partners get along beautifully and in other periods of time, conflict emerges. These periods alternate when a saturation point is reached. In other words, people who argue will eventually feel compelled to stop and/or make up. Since arguments attack the face of the partner and thus abandon the cooperative maintenance of face, damage is done that may need to be repaired. Arguers may choose to get out of arguments by terminating the interaction or re-establishing the norm of cooperation regarding face. When individuals were asked how they might react to hypothetical arguments, they indicated that they would choose to repair in more than half of the arguments. Repairs are more likely when the relationship is serious, when the blame is accepted or shared, when there is a desire to reinstate understanding and trust, or when the face attack is perceived as having been trivial or easily resolved. In contrast, interactants choose not to repair when the issue is not important enough to exert the effort, the partner is perceived as at fault, avoiding the issue is easier than confronting it, the face attack has been serious enough to terminate the relationship, or the relationship is not perceived as serious (Benoit, 1987).

The next section of this chapter describes the ways that arguers get out of arguments: physical or psychological disengagements, agreements, apologies, and restoring the relationship. We first describe a strategy that ends the argument but does not repair face damage; we then describe several strategies that attend to the face of the partner.

Physical or Psychological Disengagement

It takes two to argue. If one person disengages from the argument by physically or psychologically exiting the situation, the argument cannot continue. Getting out of arguments in this way does not repair the face damage done to the partner. Rather, it signals a refusal to continue the argument, which can be interpreted as a refusal of even the small amount of cooperation necessary to continue a conversation.

Physical disengagement distances the individuals so that further interaction is prevented at that time. This may involve leaving the locale or hanging up the phone. Usually, the departure is abrupt and unexpected by the partner. In this example, roommates argue about cutting classes, and Goldie gets out of the argument by leaving the room:

> Sheila: What time did you get up?
>
> Goldie: 2:30 (Laughs)
>
> Sheila: I don't think that's very funny.
>
> Goldie: You're not my mother.
>
> Sheila: No, but I care.
>
> Goldie: Your priorities aren't necessarily mine.
>
> Sheila: If you skip every class, how do you expect to pass?
>
> Goldie: (leaves the room, slamming the door)

Getting out of an argument by a physical disengagement may be interpreted as an overt refusal to listen to the partner any longer. The person who leaves may perceive that this signals their contempt (i.e., I don't have to listen to this), while the partner may perceive that it indicates closed-mindedness about the issue or a loss (i.e., they couldn't stand to hear the truth, so they had to leave). Whatever the interpretation, physical disengagement does not smooth over the face concerns generated by an argument.

Psychological disengagement does not involve the actual removal of participants from the same environment, but the effect is the same. It is accomplished by silence. Silence prevents further interaction since conversation requires two participants. The person who chooses silence may be attempting to show stern disapproval (i.e., the silent treatment) but the partner may read silence as an inability to respond (i.e., silence means consent). Of course, silence cannot repair the norm of cooperation regarding face since the interactants aren't even speaking. Joan and Renee are roommates and their argument is about the appropriate purpose of a gift:

> Joan: I didn't give you that shirt to wear. I gave it to you
>   to sleep in.
>
> Renee: It's my shirt now. I can wear it the way I want to.
>   What's the big deal anyway? Why does it matter when
>   and where or even **if** I wear it?
>
> Joan: (Silence)

Joan's silence is particularly noticeable because Renee asks her a question. If she had been cooperating, Joan would have answered. Her silence deliberately snubs her roommate. While the silence prevents the continuation of the argument at this time, it signals another attack on the partner's face rather than reestablishing the norm of cooperation regarding face.

Physical and psychological disengagement get people out of arguments. The person chooses not to repair the face damage, perhaps because the issue is not worth the effort, the partner is considered at fault, avoiding the issue is easier, the face attack has terminated the relationship, or the relationship is not serious enough to warrant concern about the other's face. In some cases, physical or psychological disengagement simply postpones the argument until another time. Leaving the situation and silence stop the argument but do not resolve the issue or repair the face damage.

Agreement

Disagreement is the impetus for an argument and so agreement is a means for getting out of an argument. An argument cannot continue without a disagreement. Agreement indicates a change of heart, an acceptance of the partner's point of view. If the agreement is sincere, resolution of the problem is accomplished. At the same time, agreement repairs the face of the partner by validating their position, indicating that their ideas are to be respected.

In this first example, roommates disagree about the importance of keeping the apartment clean:

> Bob: Hey, do you ever think of doing the dishes while you sit here watching television?
>
> Mike: No, that is probably the last thing on my mind.
>
> Bob: Well, Bill [the other roommate] and I have been talking. And we feel that you haven't been doing enough around the apartment for the last six weeks. Don't you think you could at least clean up after yourself?
>
> Mike: Yeah, I guess I could.
>
> Bob: Well, we hope you do.

These roommates disagree about the priority of doing the dishes and other cleaning tasks, yet the argument terminates when Mike (somewhat reluctantly) agrees to accept more responsibility for keeping the apartment clean, thus eliminating the source of disagreement.

The next example involves an argument between two resident assistants in the dorm. The disagreement is about who should break up a party and whether they have sufficient justification for acting:

> Shelley: There is a party going on in room 217 and they are drinking so since you're on duty you bust them.
>
> Julie: I didn't hear any noise not even a stereo. If they are drinking they are doing it maturely and responsibly. Besides how do you know they are drinking?
>
> Shelley: I heard a quarter bouncing off of a table a couple of times and you don't play "quarters" with water.

Julie: I don't think that is justification for busting the party.

Shelley: But I know they are underage and drinking.

Julie: Why don't you go bust the party? Think first why we have this job. Is it to be the police and bust everybody or is it to promote maturity and personal growth? If you feel it's best we bust them then I will.

Shelley: Well, you're right. I'll forget it. Thanks.

One interesting feature of this argument is that both people move toward agreement in the end; the norm of cooperation regarding face is quite evident. Julie agrees to accept Shelley's command, while Shelley agrees that there is no justification for busting the party.

Apology

Arguers report that arguments frequently end when one or both people apologize. An apology acknowledges fault, injury, or insult. It expresses regret and asks for forgiveness. Apologies indicate that face attacks were wrong and that the arguers are willing to re-establish the norm of cooperation. Apologies repair the threat to face.

A friend is accused of putting another friend down and apologizes to right the injury to face:

Cori: Why do you constantly put me down?

Josh: I don't put you down.

Cori: Then what would you call it?

Josh: I have no idea what you're talking about.

Cori: You make me feel terrible. You make fun of the way I talk, the way I spell, who I go out with, my class, and my job. How would you feel if I did that to you?

Josh: I'm sorry. I didn't know you took it so personally.

Cori: How was I supposed to take it?

Josh: I was only joking around when I said those things.

Cori: Well, after so many, I begin to wonder.

Josh: I'm sorry. I won't do it anymore.

Notice that Cori does not immediately accept the apology. She rejects Josh's attempt to share the fault (i.e., that she is also to blame for taking his comments too personally), renewing her view that he is the only one at fault. His next apology is accepted because he acknowledges the fault and promises not to put her down again.

In another example, friends argue about their behavior with a third party:

Lilly: I can't believe you were talking to that guy, what a creep.

>   Deb: He was a nice guy and easy to talk to. Besides if you hadn't been such a bitch to him he would've been a little nicer to you.
>
>   Lilly: It was like he was only interested in you and didn't want to talk to us.
>
>   Deb: Lilly let's just drop it. You know how I feel and you were wrong. I guess I was also wrong. I shouldn't have gotten all over your case like that. I hope this doesn't create tension between us.
>
>   Lilly: I'm sorry—I was wrong.
>
>   Deb: Let's just forget it and have a good time.
>
>   Lilly: Okay (with a smile).

Lilly accuses Deb of being nice to someone she feels is a creep. Deb accuses Lilly of mistreating this third party. Both end up apologizing. Deb apologizes for criticizing her friend, and Lilly apologizes for her behavior with the third party. The apologies restore the norm of cooperation.

Restoring the Relationship

Arguers indicate that they get out of arguments by explicitly commenting on the importance of their relationship. This makes the issue that they are arguing about seem trivial in comparison. Restoring the relationship attends to the partner's face by emphasizing the values and the wants of the partner. The disagreement is a minor concern compared to their relationship.

A romantic couple crosses wires about plans for the weekend. Andy comes home to find that his girlfriend has other commitments:

>   Andy: I come home and you leave. I thought you'd want to spend some time together. What's wrong? Are you dating someone else?
>
>   Brooke: No. I told you I have to go help at the church.
>
>   Andy: I understand that. But you knew I was coming home to see you. Couldn't you have made plans for the next weekend when I wouldn't be around?
>
>   Brooke: Don't get so upset. I had to go. You know how I feel about you.
>
>   Andy: Okay. I know but. . .
>
>   Brooke: Don't be upset. Let's have a good time tonight.
>
>   Andy: Okay. It's nice to be home.
>
>   Brooke: It's nice to have you here.

Brooke makes several comments intended to reassure Andy that this disagreement does not reflect on their relationship. Although she cannot spend more time with him, she still cares about him. In the end, they both refocus on how they enjoy being together rather than on the dispute about plans for the remainder of the weekend.

In the next interaction, friends argue over money but the friendship is perceived as more important than the disagreement:

> Vicky: I know I said I'd pay you back on Friday but I also owe my mom some money. So I can't.
>
> Jean: I was counting on having that money on Friday. I'm tired of you walking all over me.
>
> Vicky: I didn't realize I was doing that. I know you've really helped me out of some jams and I appreciate it. I'll get the money to you. Still friends?
>
> Jean: Of course.

Jean perceives that Vicky is taking advantage of the friendship by reneging on her promise to pay back the loan. When Vicky sees that the dispute may affect their friendship, she is quick to emphasize the value she has for her friend and works to restore their relationship. Restoring the relationship reinstates the norm of cooperation regarding face by clarifying that the partner is valued and that all consideration will be given to their wants.

Summary

Arguers say that they get out of arguments by terminating the talk (physically or psychologically) or by repairing the norm of cooperation regarding face. By agreeing, apologizing, or restoring the relationship, arguers attend explicitly to the partner's face. In many instances, some combination of these strategies is used at the end of the argument. People may apologize and agree. Or, they may affirm the relationship and apologize for having caused disharmony. When these strategies occur, the argument ends and other forms of interaction can follow. However, even strategies that repair the norm of cooperation regarding face do not always resolve the issue that caused the dispute. This accounts for the feeling that arguments generally do not improve the situation for self, other, or the relationship. *Do arguments really end? Residue of weakened trust, appeal?*

Conclusion

In this chapter, we have described one way of talking about arguments, but it is not the only perspective. Others are represented in this book. We are describing what people mean when they say they are having an argument. Real people shared meaning about this interactional event. Arguments can be characterized by overt disagreement, an inability to resolve the issue, increased volume and negative tone, irrational beliefs and emotional displays, and the possibility of negative consequences for the relationship. So why do people argue so much? At certain times in all relationships, a person's wants come into conflict with his or her partner's wants. Arguments are expressions of this frustration. The examples provided throughout this chapter suggest that people will argue about almost anything.

Given that arguments are inevitable, what practical advice can be given to the arguer? We cannot discuss this topic in detail but will offer some brief suggestions. First, in long term relationships, sometimes arguers can renegotiate the meaning of an argument for that relationship. Counselors suggest that couples need ways of expressing their frustration and train them to use a "Vesuvius" or "haircuts" (McKay, Davis, & Fanning, 1983). A Vesuvius is named after the volcano and is used to release steam. In this kind of argument, one person expresses emotional frustrations and the partner is trained to be supportive rather than defensive. If the listener can keep from feeling that his or her face is threatened while their partner blows off steam, the conversation may not erupt into an argument. In a haircut, one person clips their partner about the ears by criticizing them, while the partner is trained to give positive responses. Again, if the listener can keep from being upset that his or her face has been attacked by the criticism, an argument may be avoided. If partners can agree that these techniques are not to be interpreted as face attacks, they can be used to reduce frustrations over unmet wants without endangering the relationship. Of course, recommending these techniques is easier than executing them.

Second, interactants can choose to argue or not to argue. If they want to avoid arguments, they should try not to insult, accuse, command, or refuse the requests of their partners. For example, try to phrase a command as a request because a request is less likely to attack the face of your partner than a demand. Of course, one difficulty is that even if you believe that you have steered clear of these kinds of comments, that does not mean that your partner will not think that you have used one of them and attacked his or her face. In addition, when you feel you have been wronged, you may have difficulty restraining a natural impulse to fight back by attacking the partner's face and protecting your own. A useful technique in this situation is to call a time-out. Sometimes postponing the disagreement to a specified later time will allow you to discuss the issue calmly and to avoid an argument.

If you do find yourself in an argument, you can get out in several ways. Arguers report that this is done by physical/psychological departure, agreement, apology, and restoring the relationship. The particular choice of strategy will depend on the situation. A physical/psychological departure does not solve the problem, but may give you some satisfaction in refusing to talk to your partner. With agreement, you have to admit that your partner was right. With apology, you have to admit that you were at fault in some way. Restoring the relationship places the emphasis on the relationship and minimizes the importance of the disagreement, without giving in about the issue. Some issues, however, are too important to the future of the relationship to be treated in this way.

Relationships would be boring and too predictable if they were always characterized by harmony. Arguments have a way of spicing things up. Making up after an argument can be better than continuing a period of harmony. Relationships would be chaotic if they were always characterized by disharmony. There must be ways of reestablishing the norm of cooperation regarding face so that interaction forms other than argument can also be accomplished.

Chapter Six

Marital Arguments

Daniel J. Canary

> He would not admit that the difficulties with his wife had their origin
> in the rarefied air of the house, but blamed them on the very nature of
> matrimony; an absurd invention that could exist only by the infinite grace
> of God. . . . He would say: "The problem with marriage is that it ends
> every night after making love, and it must be rebuilt every morning before
> breakfast."
> Gabriel Garcia Marquez (from *Love in the Time of Cholera*, p. 209).

People use argument to advocate their ideas or to comment on the process
of arguing (Jackson & Jacobs, 1980). Several episodes elicit advocacy and
commentary in marital interactions. One episode occurs when partners express
their conflicting goals. A second episode occurs when one or both want to
discuss a problem area (e.g., household responsibilities). Moreover, the
problem may indicate trouble with the relationship itself. A third episode is
when partners jointly construct a position (e.g., preparing an excuse for being
late to a party). This may also involve one of the partners talking through
ideas and relying on the other to clarify issues. These episodes reveal that
interpersonal argument functions to support ideas offered by goal-directed
persons (see also Jacobs & Jackson, 1983).

There is little research on marital argument; how arguments between married
persons arise, progress, and affect the relationship has not been studied
systematically. However, much research has focused on marital communication
and conflict. We can glean from the conflict literature relevant information
concerning marital arguments. In addition, several recent advances in the study

Mr. Canary is in the Department of Speech Communication at California State University,
Fullerton. He wishes to thank Joyce Flocken for comments she made on an earlier version
of this chapter.

73

of interpersonal argument can inform us about the nature of marital arguments (see Benoit & Benoit, 1987; Meyers & Seibold, 1987; Trapp, Hoff, & Chandler, 1987). By drawing on research in marital conflict and in interpersonal argument, this essay identifies the following factors that affect marital arguments: (1) characteristics of the individual, (2) relationship properties, and (3) marital communication taxonomies and patterns.

A. Individual Factors

1) Goals

Individuals are goal-directed. At a very abstract level, people have instrumental goals, which refer to obtaining assistance or resources; relational goals, which refer to maintaining relational expectations; and face goals, which refer to upholding the dignity of self and other (Clark & Delia, 1979). Research suggests that people are motivated most by instrumental goals, and relational and face needs constrain these instrumental goals (Dillard, Sergin, & Hardin, 1989). One study found that people are most cooperative in pursuing goals that involve changing their relationships but are competitive in goals that involve protecting themselves from a violation of a right (Canary, Cunningham, & Cody, 1988). Put simply, each person's goal affects the way he or she argues.

2) Topics

What do marital couples argue about? Zietlow and Sillars (1988) found the following topics to be the most salient for their Midwest participants: (1) irritability, (2) lack of communication, (3) lack of affection, (4) money, (5) criticism of the partner, (6) leisure time activities, (7) housing arrangements, and (8) household responsibilities. Gottman (1979) reported the following problem areas: (1) sharing events of the day, (2) money, (3) in-laws, (4) sex, (5) decision to have children, and (6) how to discipline children. Felmlee, Sprecher, and Bassin (1988) found four critical issues that accelerated relational termination: (1) attractiveness of alternatives, (2) lack of time spent together, (3) dissimilarity in race, and (4) lack of support from the partner's social network.

Is marital satisfaction related to spouses' understanding the partners' views on these topics? Probably not. Sillars, Weisberg, Burgraff, and Zietlow (1989) report that accurate knowledge of marriage partners' views of various instrumental and relational issues was mostly unrelated to marital satisfaction. Instead, the association of agreement and perceived agreement with marital satisfaction was stronger than the association between understanding and marital satisfaction. In fact, these researchers found that husbands' understanding of wives' views of relational issues was negatively correlated with husbands' satisfaction. Likewise, Bochner, Krueger, and Chmielewski (1982) found that consensus regarding the spouses' perceptions about behavioral expectations and actions was unrelated to marital adjustment; they conclude that "there is no empirical basis for claiming that husbands' and/or wives' accurate perceptions of each other are a necessary condition for marital satisfaction" (p. 146). If understanding is not associated with marital satisfaction, why should we read about marital arguments? The reason is that while content may be unrelated to satisfaction, the form of the communication behavior is crucial to perceptions of the partner and to the stability of the relationship (Canary & Spitzberg, 1989; Stafford, Burgraff, & Yost, 1988).

Attribution

Each partner perceives who or what is causing the couple's problems (see Seibold & Spitzberg, 1982). Unhappy people tend to blame their partners for relational problems. Fincham (1985), for example, found that partners in distressed couples (i.e., those in counseling) attributed marital difficulties to the spouse or the relationship more than to themselves or to circumstances. Fincham (1985) also reported that distressed couples perceived a greater variety of problems, so that problems for that group were not limited to just one or two issues. Both persons may blame the spouse for their relational problems when both persons use the same "attribution style" (Doherty, 1982). Since husbands and wives may not see the "problem" in the same way, they may disagree about which issues are critical. Besides goals, issues, and attributions, an individual's locus of control affects the manner in which he or she argues.

Locus of Control

"Locus of control" refers to the manner in which persons believe that the successes and failures in areas of their lives are due to internal or external factors (see also Brenders, 1987). Internal factors include one's self-perceived ability and effort; external factors refer to the influence of other persons, chance, or the nature of the situation (Lefcourt, 1982). In some domains of their lives, people believe that their locus of control is primarily internal, while in other areas they believe that outcomes are due to external factors. Because they believe that their abilities and efforts will lead to success, persons with an internal locus of control have more confident intonation than persons with an external locus of control (Bugental, Henker, & Whalen, 1976), and they use more assertive, persistent, and rational influence tactics (Canary, Cody, & Marston, 1986; Doherty & Ryder, 1979). In addition, internality is positively associated with cooperative conflict tactics while externality is positively associated with use of topic shifting, extended denials, and sarcasm (Canary et al., 1988).

Research shows persons' goals, salient problem issues, attribution biases, and loci of control are relevant to marital arguments. Individuals decide whether or not to argue to obtain a goal or to discuss a problem area. Although understanding each other's views may be important to relational satisfaction, perceived agreement and how people argue do affect satisfaction. For example, dissatisfied couples find it especially difficult to perceive agreement due to the attribution bias of blaming the other. Still, a partner's locus of control determines the extent to which that individual works at overcoming problems in the marriage. Other factors such as gender, age, and argumentativeness may also have some influence, but the factors discussed seem to be the most salient ones. While this section has examined some individual factors, the next section focuses on relationship properties.

B.   Properties of Relationships

Understanding marital arguments requires that we examine the relational system in which these arguments take place. Argumentative behavior reflects the marital system, as well as reinforcing and changing it. Several system properties affect how married persons argue. These include the development of the relationship and the type of relationship.

1) Marital Development

In Western post-industrial societies, couples typically establish routines for interaction during courtship. These routines accompany the couple on their honeymoon and into their marriage. Research has shown that both the amount and the kinds of conflict behavior performed during courtship transfer into marriage (Kelly, Huston, & Cate, 1985; Raush et al., 1974). In addition, Gottman and Krokoff (1989) found that demonstrations of anger were negatively associated with marital satisfaction early in the marriage, but the same observations of anger were positively associated with marital satisfaction measured three years later. Whining and withdrawing were negatively associated with marital satisfaction three years later. In short, marriages are relational systems which begin in courtship and continue to develop after the wedding.

2) Marital Types

There are different types of dating relationships as well as different types of marriages. For example, Huston, Surra, Fitzgerald, and Cate (1981) identified four types of courtship: *accelerated-arrested* begins with much intensity then slows in its final approach toward marriage; *accelerated* escalates quickly and has smooth passage to marriage; *intermediate* does not escalate quickly and has some trouble when the couple is more than 80% sure they will get married; and *prolonged* refers to couples who have a slow escalation toward intimacy and a rocky path toward marriage. These researchers found that *accelerated* couples moved quickly to interdependence of activities while *intermediate* and *prolonged* couples did not jointly perform activities as much. In all likelihood, these patterns of interdependence transfer into marriage and affect the problem topics for each couple.

Fitzpatrick (1988) studied how communication behavior affected differences in marital types. Over the past decade, she identified three "pure" couple types: *traditionals* share in a traditional ideology, are highly interdependent, and have conflict only over important issues; *independents* do not have traditional views and sex role expectations, are moderately interdependent, and fight over anything because they must negotiate everything; and *separates* are autonomous persons living under the same roof who occasionally show affection toward one another. Fitzpatrick also found that husbands and wives differ in their perceptions of marriage; these couples are *mixed*. These marital types appear to use very different kinds of arguments.

Traditionals are likely to use domineering messages (e.g., interruptions) during conflict but not in neutral situations (Williamson & Fitzpatrick, 1985). In addition, Whitteman and Fitzpatrick (1986) found that *traditionals* were likely to appeal to relational identification to the degree the activity is important to them, but they did not appeal to values. Appealing to the relationship or the activity is due to the couples' interdependence. *Traditionals* are unlikely to reference values outside the dyad since they already agree on a traditional ideology. During conflict, *traditionals* use cooperative, competitive, and avoidant strategies (Sillars, Pike, Jones, & Redmon, 1983). In addition, *traditionals* have the highest satisfaction scores among the couple types (Fitzpatrick & Best, 1979).

Independents, on the other hand, eschew a traditional ideology and attempt to define for themselves what marriage is. Accordingly, some issues which are "givens" for *traditional* couples must be negotiated in *independent* marriages (e.g., "Do we take the children to church?" "Who should cook tonight?"). Moreover, as their title suggests, *independents* value their personal goals as much, and probably more, than their partners' goals (Fitzpatrick, 1988). Hence, for *independents*, marital satisfaction is not the product of a smooth running system, but it is the result of obtaining personal goals with the assistance of a partner. Accordingly, Sillars et al. (1983) found that during conflict, *independents*' lack of nonverbal love and affection was positively associated with relational satisfaction. Additionally, *independents* use information gaining and giving to obtain their personal goals (Sillars et al., 1983; Whitteman & Fitzpatrick, 1986). *Independents* are also the most likely type to refute openly their partners' statements, and they reciprocate competitive statements even if the issue is a neutral one (Williamson & Fitzpatrick, 1985).

Separates' communication behaviors illustrate that they are indeed "emotionally divorced" (Fitzpatrick & Best, 1979). *Separates* are vigilant about their autonomy; that is, they guard against both information and emotion from entering the relationship. Whitteman and Fitzpatrick (1986) reported that separates used "guerilla-like" tactics to gain compliance from their partners; *separates* constrained the behavior of their spouses, were unlikely to search for information, but appealed to the partners' values and external demands. Sillars et al. (1983) noted that *separates* used "blatant" forms of avoidance (e.g., extended denials) to limit conflict although they had indicated on a questionnaire those issues were trouble spots in their marriages. Sillars et al. (1983) also found that *separates'* neutral affects were positively associated with their marital satisfaction. We can partially explain these findings by studying marital schemata.

Marital Schemata

People probably have "marital schemata," or "knowledge structures that represent the external world of marriage and provide guidelines about how to interpret incoming data" (Fitzpatrick, 1988, p. 255). Such marital schemata would very likely affect courtship and marriage, thus providing dating partners mechanisms for making and interpreting arguments. The schemata continue during marriage so that those who value interdependence over autonomy are not dissatisfied with their partners over small goal disruptions; those who value personal goals over relational goals get emotionally upset over any goal disruption; and those who define marriage as habituated autonomy simply do not need the other, so they can avoid arguing (Fitzpatrick, 1988).

The definition of marriage itself may not be of critical importance, but the fact that both persons mutually agree to the definition is critically important (see also Morton, Alexander, & Altman, 1976). Consensus about relational definition is positively associated with marital satisfaction (Fitzpatrick & Best, 1979). Thus, it may not be important to a person to be interdependent, affectionate, or involved in arguing as long as both partners agree to the same relational definition. Given my own inclination to argue, I might value an *independent* model of marriage over a *separate* model, but I would not assume that persons in *separate* marriages are argumentatively dysfunctional; using avoidance is an obvious means of maintaining autonomy (Fitzpatrick et al., 1982). Regardless of the type of relational definition, marriages and arguments in marriages are functional to the degree that they are bilateral; unilateral definitions of marriage and unilateral arguments within the marriage are dysfunctional. Empirical research indicates that unilateral control is quite dysfunctional (e.g., Bochner, Kaminski, & Fitzpatrick, 1977; Courtright, Millar, & Rogers-Millar, 1979).

In this section, I have argued that reaching a bilateral definition of marriage is much more important than imposing our personal values about marriage and argument on others. The following section examines ways of looking at marital arguments and patterns of marital arguments.

C.   # Communicating Arguments and
Patterns of Arguments

/) ## Observing Marital Arguments

Due to the overlap between conflict and argument, one can obtain an image
of how persons argue by examining conflict tactics. Several researchers have
presented schemes to observe marital conflict (e.g., Gottman, 1979; Raush
et al., 1974; Sillars, 1986; Ting-Toomey, 1983). Of these, Sillars (1986) most
clearly distinguishes conflict from other communication behaviors. His scheme
assumes that conflict tactics vary according to directness and affect. He
separates conflict behaviors into seven categories: (1) denial and equivocation,
(2) topic management, (3) noncommittal remarks, (4) irrelevant remarks,
(5) analytic remarks, (6) confrontative remarks, and (7) conciliatory remarks.
These categories represent three basic strategic orientations to conflict:
integrative—working with the partner; *distributive*—working against the
partner; and *avoidance*—working to avoid the partner (Sillars et al., 1983).
Some research findings using this scheme are reviewed later.

A second way to observe argument is to discover how couples deal with
relational problems. Rusbult (1987) identifies four basic approaches to dealing
with marital problems: *exit*, *voice*, *loyalty*, and *neglect*. *Exit* behaviors include
"formally separating" and "thinking or talking about leaving one's partner";
voice includes strategies such as "discussing problems" or "suggesting
solutions"; *loyalty* encompasses "waiting and hoping that things will improve"
and "supporting partner in face of criticism"; and *neglect* involves "ignoring
the partner" or "refusing to discuss problems." Rusbult (1987) names two
factors that predict which problem-solving method is used. The first,
investment, is the degree to which each person devotes time, energy, and
other resources to the relationship, satisfaction with the relationship, and
comparison of alternatives. The second factor is comprised of individual
elements, such as a person's age. Rusbult reports, for example, that *loyalty*
behaviors are used when the person has much invested, but there are no
attractive alternatives; the person is elderly with a low income; and the person
has a feminine sex-role orientation (p. 228). Rusbult, Johnson, and Morrow
(1986) found that persons often use *voice* to deal with mild problems. These
authors also found that relational satisfaction was negatively associated with
use of *exit* and *neglect* behaviors.

A third way to observe argument is to utilize a system that directly assesses
how individuals and couples develop their ideas. One such method of examining
interpersonal argument is the Conversational Argument Coding Scheme
(Canary, 1989), a taxonomy that has been developed in empirical examinations
of interpersonal and small group arguments. Table 1 presents the Conversational Argument Coding Scheme.

Table 1: Conversational Argument Coding Scheme

Arguables

1. **ASRT: Assertion**. Statements of belief or opinion.
2. **PROP: Proposition**. Statements that call for discussion or action.
3. **ELAB: Elaboration**. Statements that support other statements by providing evidence or clarification.
4. **AMPL: Amplification**. Explicit inferential statements.
5. **JUST: Justification**. Statements that offer norms, values, or rules of logic to support the validity of other statements.

Convergence Markers

6. **AGMT: Agreement**. Statements that indicate agreement.
7. **ACKN: Acknowledgement**. Messages that indicate recognition and/or understanding of, but not agreement to, another's point.

Promptors

8. **OBJC: Objection**. Statements that deny the truth or accuracy of another statement.
9. **CHAL: Challenge**. Messages that present a problem, question, or reservation that must be addressed to reach agreement.
10. **RESP: Response**. Statements that defend other statements that are met with objection or challenge.

Delimitors

11. **FRAM: Frame**. Messages that provide a context for and/or qualification of another statement.
12. **F/SE: Forestall/Secure**. Statements that attempt to forestall discussion by securing common ground.
13. **F/RE: Forestall/Remove**. Statements that attempt to forestall discussion by not allowing something to be discussed.

Non-Arguables

14. **NARG: Non-argument**. Statements with no argumentative function.
15. ***N:** An asterisk plus the turn number indicates that the thought is completed at that turn number (read: "See turn _____").

Five basic categories reveal how a person might make a point or help another make a point. The first category is called *arguables*, which can be further divided into "starting points" of an argument (i.e., assertions and propositions) and "supporting points" of an argument (i.e., elaborations, amplifications, and justifications). The second category is *convergence marker*, which indicates that one person understands or agrees with the partner. The third category is *promptor*, which refers to disagreements with the partner. The fourth category is *delimitor*, which refers to qualifying arguments or limiting the scope of the discussion. Finally, a general miscellaneous category refers to any dialogue that is not argument.

In a study that compared satisfied with dissatisfied married couples, Canary, Brossmann, Sillars, and LoVette (1987) found that satisfied couples had a higher proportion of *simple arguments* and a lower proportion of *compound arguments*. *Simple arguments* are those that support one point only. For example, the following is a *simple argument* (an assertion is followed by an elaboration): "I don't think we have a problem with that. We go out to movies all the time and never argue about what to watch." *Compound arguments* occur when one person attempts two or more points (as in "parallel arguments"; see Canary, Brossmann, & Seibold, 1987a) or offers more than one line of reasoning for one point (as in "extended arguments"; see Brossmann & Canary, 1990). In the following example, the wife extends the point that her husband is affectionate (turn 1.3) by adding that he is not physically affectionate (turn 1.4). She begins by agreeing with her husband that they have too little time together to show much affection.

(1)	1.1	Wife:	Yeah, it probably has.	AGMT	
	1.2		You've probably summed it up there.	ELAB	
	1.3		Because, uh, I think that you show affection in lots of ways.	F/SE	
	1.4		But you're not physically affectionate.	ELAB	(1.4)
	1.5		So I think that's the temperament I wish we could work out.	PROP	
	1.6		But we'll have to work on that a bit.	ELAB	(1.5)
	1.7		Because we have to talk, we have to talk about these more.	AMPL	(1.6)

Besides *simple* and *compound* structures, we have identified two others: *convergent* and *eroded* (Canary, Brossmann, & Seibold, 1987; Canary, Brossmann, Sillars & LoVette, 1987; see also Brossmann & Canary, 1990). *Convergent* arguments are those that are jointly constructed. For example, the following is a convergent argument. The wife offers support in 2.7 for her husband's point made in 2.2; the husband continues in 2.8 to develop a point they both understand, as evidenced by her agreement in 2.9.

(2)	2.1	Husband: Ah? Okay.	F/SE
	2.2	Actually, the only time that I think cleaning and household chores are a problem is when one of us is really overworked.	ASRT
	2.3	And we see work that needs to be done.	ELAB (2.2)
	2.4	And we feel, "I'm just too tired to do that; it's the other person's turn."	AMPL
	2.5	And we both yell at that point.	ELAB (2.4)
	2.6	Wife: Yeah.	AGMT
	2.7	Either overtired or being pressured by some event that's coming up and we want the house special clean for that situation,	ELAB (2.2)
	2.8	Husband: Or if I spent too much money and you're feeling perhaps . . .	ELAB (2.2)
	2.9	Wife: There you go, yes.	AGMT (2.8)

Eroded arguments are arguments which fall apart because the partner could not or would not complete the thought, or perhaps is not allowed to complete the thought. The following is an example of an eroded argument:

(3)	3.1	Wife: That's where our problems come in, right?	PROP
	3.2	Because I always come home . . .	*7.3
	3.3	Husband: And bitch, bitch, bitch!	ELAB (7.1)

Initially, we labeled this a *convergent* structure. But because the wife did not complete her idea, this example is better identified as an *eroded* argument. Analyses now in progress of other couples' conversations should reveal the extent to which argument structures reflect perceptions of the partner and of the relationship.

Patterns of Argument

In addition to the taxonomies used to label marital argument, researchers have identified patterns of communication behavior that married persons experience. Two patterns seem especially relevant to the study of marital arguments: stationarity and reciprocity (see Sillars, Weisberg, Burgraff, & Zietlow, 1989). Stationarity refers to the movement of interaction through phases, and reciprocity refers to how couples exchange behaviors.

Trapp, Hoff, and Chandler (1987) present a "serial" model of argument in their review of interpersonal argument research. They indicate that interpersonal arguments move through three phases: deciding to confront the partner, formulating arguments, and arguing. This model helps synthesize research on interpersonal argument, and it identifies the process that persons may undergo when faced with a problematic situation.

Gottman (1979) also offers a three-stage depiction of marital arguments. It applies only to the third phase of the serial model described by Trapp et al. Gottman observed that persons first offer a solution to a problem; second, persons state their agreement or disagreement; and third, partners exchange information concerning the proposal. Interestingly, Gottman noted that married persons do not offer reasons before agreeing or disagreeing (pp. 90-91). A few observations of married persons' arguments lead me to believe that most of the time couples do not offer reasons before they agree or disagree. There are instances, however, when couples cycle through phases in unpredictable ways. Accordingly, models of the phases of communication probably represent the norm, with some couples deviating from the predicted phases.

Examining satisfied versus dissatisfied married couples' argument sequences, Canary, Brossmann, Sillars, and LoVette (1987) found that most satisfied couples enacted phases of "primary development." Typically, satisfied couples would allow the partner to make (or they would offer themselves) supporting statements for assertions and propositions. But, dissatisfied couples often do not allow such phases to occur. Instead these couples more likely engaged in sequences of "primary refutation," wherein objections, challenges, and responses were met with similar defensive statements (Canary, Brossmann, Sillars, & LoVette, 1987). The use of primary refutations is similar to Gottman's (1982) finding that distressed couples engage in four destructive patterns, one being the proposal-counterproposal reflected in statements such as "Let's go to the beach." "No, let's go to the mountains."

Reciprocity refers to the manner in which behaviors are exchanged. There have been several relevant findings regarding reciprocity. First, research in marital conflict indicates that reciprocity may be the most important factor that determines someone's argument behavior; married persons simply mirror one another's discussion behaviors. Two studies found that the effects of reciprocity on communication behavior were stronger than the effects due to gender or Fitzpatrick's (1988) relational types (Burgraff & Sillars, 1987). Second, satisfied marriages differ from dissatisfied marriages on the basis of behaviors that are reciprocated. For example, Ting-Toomey (1983) found that high adjusted married couples enacted strings of verbal coaxing, confirming behaviors, and descriptive statements. On the other hand, low adjusted couples responded with defensiveness and confrontation to their partners' previous communication (see also Gottman, 1982). Likewise, Rusbult et al. (1986) found that reciprocation of *exit* and *neglect* problem-solving communication significantly increased relational distress. Third, research indicates that dissatisfied couples get caught in negative reciprocation for longer periods of time than do satisfied couples (Gottman, 1979; Zietlow & Sillars, 1988). Fourth, some partners in dissatisfied marriages tend to reciprocate by provoking their partner and then withdrawing, a tactic Sillars, Weisberg, Burgraff, and Zietlow (1989) refer to as "hit-and-run." Fifth, marriage partners can also take advantage of the reciprocity norm to cut off negative spirals by initiating more functional means of arguing (Krueger & Smith, 1982).

Researchers have used three schemes to examine marital conflict, problem-solving, and argument. While the first two schemes offer insights about marital conflict and problem-solving strategies, the last scheme is more relevant to the study of how arguments are offered in conversation. Finally, two interaction patterns, stationarity and reciprocity, were discussed. When arguing, couples often experience phases and they mirror one another's communication behaviors.

Conclusion

Although the study of interpersonal argument in general and marital argument in particular has a recent history, several conclusions about married couples' argument behaviors are warranted. First, actors in marriage attempt to achieve goals. Because marriages vary in their interdependence and socially defined expectations, actors should be aware that their goal pursuits are also tied to their definitions of marriage. Marriages that are defined bilaterally are more likely to be rewarding than marriages defined unilaterally (Morton et al., 1976). Moreover, argument probably looks and functions differently in different types of relationships. For example, while *independents* enjoy complaining and offering information to support their views, *separates* protect their autonomy through blatant avoidance and control of the partner. Yet, various forms of argument can be functional if the relational definition is mutually accepted.

Second, individuals' loci of control guide expectations regarding how much effort should be expended in marital arguments. Those with an internal locus of control try harder to make their marriage a success. Moreover, those who believe that their problems are the result of another person are likely to give up on the relationship by avoiding the partner or by lashing out. It appears very likely that internals cooperate more in the production of marital arguments, given their faith that their relational destiny is under their control.

Third, actors decide upon whether or not to argue, and then they decide how. As the argument episode unfolds, partners engage in phases of idea development or refutation; within each phase, partners reciprocate argument behaviors. Satisfied couples have fewer constraints due to stationarity or reciprocity than do dissatisfied couples who often engage in negative spirals. The saving feature of the reciprocity effect is that it is so powerful that married persons (and all who are in personal relationships) can use this effect to their benefit.

Chapter Seven

Analyzing Argumentative Discourse

Frans H. van Eemeren and Rob Grootendorst

In this chapter, we explain some of the basics of the pragma-dialectical approach to argumentation which was introduced in van Eemeren and Grootendorst (1984). First, we make a comparison between dialectical analysis and rhetorical analysis, which is probably more familiar to most readers. Then, we sketch an ideal model of a critical discussion that can serve as a point of departure for dialectically analyzing argumentative discourse. In this model, we distinguish the various stages through which the resolution of a difference of opinion should pass and mention the types of speech acts that can play a constructive role in each of these stages. Finally, we show what kind of pragma-dialectical transformations are to be carried out in a reconstruction of argumentative discourse which starts from this ideal model and leads to an analytic overview of the aspects of the discourse that are crucial for its evaluation.

Rhetorical Stages in Persuading an Audience

According to the rhetorical tradition, what constitutes good and successful discourse depends on the text genre. Traditionally, three genres are distinguished: forensic, deliberative and epideictic. A forensic discourse (*genus*

Mr. van Eemeren and Mr. Grootendorst are members of the Instituut voor Neerlandistiek at the University of Amsterdam, The Netherlands.

iudiciale) relates to judicial situations in which speeches are made in favor of a particular judgment. The point at issue is whether a past act is to be regarded as lawful or unlawful, just or unjust. A deliberative discourse (*genus deliberativum*) relates to political situations in which—as in a council of citizens—speeches are made for or against the desirability of a particular political measure. An epideictic discourse (*genus demonstrativum*) relates to festive or ceremonial occasions at which a person or thing is praised or condemned.

Although each of these three genres makes particular demands on the discourse, there is also a common characteristic—to persuade an audience. Hence, the general requirement that must be fulfilled is that means of persuasion must be employed which are adapted to the audience.

In order for the discourse to be effective, a judge in a court of law must be approached differently from an audience that wants only to hear something praised or condemned. A parliamentary committee requires yet another approach. Different means of persuasion must be employed in different genres. These may vary from supplying factual information, presenting evidence from witnesses or citing statutory requirements to playing on the emotions of the audience or stressing one's own reliability.

Any discourse which is to be rhetorically effective must contain four components: the *exordium*, the *narratio*, the *argumentatio*, and the *peroratio*. The *exordium* is an introduction with which the speaker or writer tries to gain the audience's sympathies and to interest them in the subject. In the *narratio*, the speaker or writer goes on to set out the subject or the course of events about which he or she wishes to speak or write. This is the preparation for the *argumentatio*, which is itself often divided into a part in which evidence is adduced for the speaker's own point of view (*confirmatio*) and a part in which the speaker tries to refute the opposite point of view (*refutatio*). The *peroratio* consists of a recapitulation and a conclusion. Sometimes the *argumentatio* is opened or closed by a digression (*digressio*). All these components can be seen in the following speech:

exordium	Hello! If you've got children you'll know me or my wife, Judy. She's sitting over there. For some time now, we've been engaged in a campaign for a safe crossing point for the little ones. You may have heard of it even if you don't have children.
narratio	Our efforts are now supported by another group. This time the initiative doesn't come from only Judy and me but from a whole club of people—parents known as the action group, "Dyer Street Play Street." We want Dyer Street to be a play street and we need your help for it.
digressio	Together, we should be able to do it. "Unity is strength," they say, and it's true. In the Smith Street area, they realized what was needed

more quickly than we did and now they've got a full-scale play park complete with monkey bars and other equipment. Even there, they say "if only we'd done it earlier."

argumentatio-
refutatio

"Why is it so important that Dyer Street should be a play street?" you may ask. "The kids can go into the park on the corner of Swan Street, can't they?" I would say to you: "Just go and take a look!" It's one great pool of mud. And it's full of dog dirt. We can't let our kids play there!

confirmatio

Dyer Street is perfect for a play street. It's too narrow for traffic anyway. Although the kids can't play there now at all, if there should be a fire, nothing can get through because of all the parked cars. And the stink! Imagine living there! Where are you supposed to go if there *is* a fire?

If Dyer Street could be turned into a play street, we parents would not have to sit and worry all the time. We would not need to wonder where the children had wandered. They can romp around as much as they like; they won't have to keep looking out for cars or bikes. We'll be able to put out nice plant boxes to prevent access by car.

peroratio

Friends, it's obvious. Closing off Dyer Street is in the best interests of the whole neighborhood. It ought to have been done long ago. So support our campaign, "Dyer Street Play Street." If we succeed, you'll never be troubled again. The people of Swan Street and Green Street will be able to take a chair out in the summer and sit in the road together, with a barbecue perhaps, in Dyer Street, while the kids are happily playing. Can you imagine it? Wouldn't that be great?

Dialectical Stages in Resolving a Dispute

A rhetorical approach to argumentative discourse concentrates on how people try to persuade their audience. A dialectical approach to argumentative discourse, whose roots are by no means less classical, concentrates on how people deal with disputes. For those who are not primarily interested in effective persuasion but in reasonable discussion of differences of opinion, this approach is more appropriate. Because the dialectical approach is not so widely known as the rhetorical, we would like to explain its main characteristics. We do so by outlining our own conception.

First of all, in our view, settling a dispute is not identical to resolving it. The main point in settling a dispute is that the difference of opinion is brought to an end. This can be achieved in a civilized or in a less civilized manner. Going for the jugular, fighting it out, or getting one's own way by intimidation or blackmail are some uncivilized tactics. Settling a dispute by more civilized means might include relying on the arbitration of an unbiased third party—umpire, referee, ombudsman or judge—who may give a considered judgment or, perhaps, may toss a coin to see who gets his or her way.

A dispute is only resolved if the parties reach an agreement on whether or not the disputed opinion—the standpoint at issue—is acceptable. This means that either one party retracts the doubts because he or she has been convinced by the other party's argumentation, or the other party withdraws the standpoint after realizing that the argumentation cannot stand up to the criticisms levelled at it. Argumentation and the critical reactions to it play a crucial role in a critical discussion aimed at resolving a dispute. That is why the notion of a critical discussion is pivotal to our dialectical approach to argumentative discourse.

In a critical discussion, the parties involved try to resolve their difference of opinion by reaching agreement about the acceptability or unacceptability of the standpoint at issue. They do so by finding out whether or not this standpoint is defensible against doubt or criticism. In order for a difference of opinion to be adequately discussed, the resolution process must pass through four stages. These stages correspond to different phases in a critical discussion.

In the first phase, the confrontation stage, a standpoint meets doubt or contradiction so that a difference of opinion arises.

In the second phase, the opening stage, the parties determine whether they have sufficient common ground (shared background knowledge, values, rules) for a fruitful discussion. Only if there is such a starting point does it make any sense to attempt to eliminate the difference of opinion by means of argumentation. If this is the case, one party makes it clear that he or she is prepared to defend the standpoint at issue, thus taking on the role of protagonist; the other party is prepared to respond critically to the standpoint and the defense, thus taking on the role of antagonist. The role of antagonist can easily coincide with the role of protagonist of another—contrary—standpoint, but to doubt a standpoint is not necessarily to adopt a standpoint of one's own.

In the third phase, the argumentation stage, the protagonist offers arguments for the purpose of overcoming doubts about the standpoint and the antagonist puts forward reactions to those arguments. If the antagonist is not yet wholly convinced of all or part of the argumentation of the protagonist, new argumentation is elicited from the protagonist, and so on. As a consequence, the protagonist's argumentation can vary from very simple to extremely complex, so that the argumentation structure of one argumentative discourse may be much more complicated than that of the next. Because of its crucial role in the resolution process, the argumentation stage is sometimes thought to be the whole critical discussion. In order to resolve the difference, however, the other stages are equally indispensable.

In the fourth phase, the concluding stage, the result of the attempt to resolve the difference of opinion is determined. Only if both parties agree on the outcome of their discussion can the dispute really be regarded as resolved.

If the protagonist has withdrawn the standpoint, the dispute has been resolved in favor of the antagonist. If the antagonist has retracted the doubt, it has been resolved in favor of the protagonist.

After the concluding stage has been completed, the discussion of the standpoint at issue is, of course, over. This does not mean that the same discussants will not embark upon a new discussion. This new discussion may relate to quite a different dispute, but it may also relate to a more or less drastically altered version of the same dispute. The discussants' roles may switch or they may be the same. In any event, the discussants then start again from the beginning.

Dialectical versus Rhetorical Stages

As the Dyer Street Play Street example shows, argumentation not only plays a part in a dialectical but also in a rhetorical perspective. In fact, the argumentation stage in the dialectical, and the *argumentatio* in the rhetorical roughly overlap. The other stages show some similarities as well. However, there are also important differences. For one, from the rhetorical perspective the speakers (or writers) can use any means of persuasion that will have the desired effect on the audience; their freedom is not limited by any sort of rules. The rhetorical objective is to win the audience over to the standpoint, whereas the dialectical objective is to resolve the dispute. More importantly, the listener (or reader) in a rhetorical perspective merely plays a passive role and does not act as antagonist. When a one-sided argumentative discourse is analyzed dialectically, it is treated as if it were part of a critical discussion. Although the role of antagonist has, in this case, not actually been fulfilled by another person, possible doubts about the standpoint or the arguments will have to be taken into consideration by the speaker (or writer).

Not only should "genuine" argumentative elements in an article or speech be included, but also elements belonging to the confrontation, opening and concluding stages. The writer or speaker must first make it clear that a difference of opinion exists or may develop (confrontation stage). The speaker or writer will then have to clarify the intent to attempt to resolve this difference of opinion by overcoming the doubts of the readers or listeners, thus assuming the role of protagonist (opening stage). And finally, the speaker or listener will have to indicate to what extent the difference of opinion has been resolved in favor of the standpoint (concluding stage).

This is how the dialectical and the rhetorical stages relate:

Dialectic	Rhetoric
A *Confrontation state* The speaker or writer establishes that a dispute exists or is about to develop.	I *Exordium* The speaker or writer attempts to gain the sympathy of the audience for the subject to be treated.

B *Opening stage*
The speaker or writer makes an attempt to resolve the dispute by defending the standpoint against antagonism and promises to do so according to certain rules.

C *Argumentation stage*
The protagonist advances argumentation to defend the disputed standpoint against doubt (or possible doubt) and other forms of antagonism relating to that standpoint or to parts or all of the argumentation in defense of it.

D *Concluding stage*
The protagonist makes it clear to what extent the dispute has been resolved in his or her favor.

II *Narratio*
The speaker or writer gives an account of the matter, in preparation for the *argumentatio*.

Digressio
Part of the *narratio* or transition to the *argumentatio* (or possibly termination of the *argumentatio*) in which the speaker or writer gives a digression if the standpoint is problematical.

III *Argumentatio*
The speaker or writer attempts to increase the credibility of the defended standpoint with the audience by advancing argumentation in which the proposition to which the standpoint refers is justified (*confirmatio*) and the opposite standpoint refuted (*refutatio*).

IV *Peroratio*
The speaker or writer recapitulates standpoints and facts.

An Ideal Model of a Critical Discussion and Argumentative Reality

The overview of the dialectical stages that can be distinguished in a critical discussion represents an ideal model which does not provide a true-to-life description of argumentative reality. Needless to say, argumentative discourse rarely, if ever, corresponds exactly to the ideal model. The ideal model indicates which speech acts contribute to the resolution of the dispute at what stages. Speech acts that do not contribute to this in a direct way—such as jokes, anecdotes and other asides—are not included in the model, although they may be among the psychological prerequisites for resolving the dispute because they help create the right atmosphere.

The ideal model fulfills a heuristic as well as a critical function. In its heuristic function, it is a tool for dealing with the interpretation problems that arise when it is not clear what kind of speech act has been performed. The ideal model gives us something to go by. In its critical function, the model provides a yardstick which enables us to establish the extent to which the actual discourse deviates from the course that would be most conducive to the resolution of the dispute.

In some institutionalized contexts, the presentation of the argumentative discourse is to a greater or lesser extent laid down in a particular formal or informal procedure. This may already create certain expectations regarding the structural organization of the discourse. When dealing with the discourse in a court of law, this effect is obvious, but many other institutions have similarly defined conventions. Knowledge of the conventions pertaining to legal proceedings, scientific and scholarly dissertations, political debates, policy documents and so on, can thus be useful supplements to the guidance provided by the ideal model.

However, not all argumentative discourse takes place in an institutionalized context in which a fixed procedure exists. Therefore, it is often unclear exactly what expectations are justified. Sometimes some light can be shed by indications from the verbal and nonverbal context. Furthermore, knowledge of the text genre involved can furnish some insight into the kind of speech acts that can and cannot be expected to occur. In one text genre, one sequence of speech acts may appear more natural than another, so we can sometimes make a reasoned guess as to the function of a particular speech act. Particular expectations may also be justified by referring to general and specific background knowledge.

In conjunction with the ideal model, these different kinds of expectations together build a framework for the interpretation of argumentative discourse that fulfills a heuristic function by suggesting that the discourse proceed in a particular manner and that certain types of speech acts may occur. Unless there is clear evidence to the contrary, it would be wise to make use of this framework in which the ideal model of a critical discussion plays a central part.

Classification of Speech Acts

In order to make the ideal dialectical model of a critical discussion pragmatically meaningful, the model must specify which speech acts at the various stages can contribute to the resolution of a dispute. A classification of the types of speech acts that can actually be performed serves here as a preliminary model.

The first type consists of the speech acts known as *assertives*. These are speech acts through which the speaker or writer states an opinion. The performance of an assertive is an attempt to bring the words into accordance with the world. The speaker or writer has made a commitment in a particular way to the acceptability of a proposition; if asked to do so by the listener or reader, he or she is obliged to provide arguments for its acceptability.

The prototype of an assertive is an assertion by which the speaker or writer guarantees the truth of the proposition being expressed: ''I assert that

Chamberlain and Roosevelt have never met.'' However, there are also assertives where the chief concern is not the truth but the speaker or writer's opinion concerning the event or state of affairs that is being expressed in the proposition. Assertives relate not only to the truth of propositions but also to acceptability in a wider sense: ''No exceptions can be made to the freedom of expression,'' ''Baudelaire is the best French poet.'' Other examples of assertives are stating, supposing, emphasizing, denying and conceding.

The second type of speech act comprises *directives*. These are speech acts through which the speaker or writer tries to get the listener or reader to do something or to refrain from doing something. A directive is an attempt to bring the world into accordance with the words by making the listener or reader do what is stated.

The prototype of a directive is an order, which requires a special position of the speaker or writer *vis-à-vis* the listener or reader. The utterance ''Come to my room'' can only be an order if the speaker is in a position of authority over the listener, otherwise it is a request or an invitation. A question is a special form of request; it is a request for a verbal act—the answer. Other examples of directives are forbidding, recommending, begging and challenging.

The third type of speech act consists of *commissives*. These are speech acts through which the speaker or writer makes a commitment *vis-à-vis* the listener or reader to do something or to refrain from doing something. A commissive, like a directive, is an attempt to bring the world into accordance with the words; unlike a directive, the speaker or writer is the person who is supposed to act in a commissive—not the listener or reader.

The prototype of a commissive is a promise by which the speaker or writer explicitly undertakes to do or not to do something: ''I promise you I won't tell your father,'' ''You can count on it—you'll have the money by the weekend'' and ''I'll be no more trouble to you.'' The speaker or writer can also make a commitment to something about which the listener or reader may be less enthusiastic: ''I swear I'll make you pay for this,'' ''I assure you that if you walk out of here now you will never set foot in this house again.'' Other commissives include accepting, rejecting, undertaking and agreeing.

The fourth type of speech act consists of *expressives*. These are speech acts through which speakers or writers express their feelings about something by thanking someone, revealing disappointment, etc. An expressive is neither an attempt to bring the world into accordance with the words nor an attempt to bring the words into accordance with the world. Rather, it is assumed that this accordance already exists; we congratulate someone on an appointment only when we believe that the person has actually been appointed.

No single speech act can be regarded as the prototypical expressive. An expression of joy might be ''I'm glad to see you're well again.'' Hope is expressed by ''I wish I could find such a nice girlfriend.'' Irritation resounds in ''I'm fed up with you hanging about all day'' and conventional cordiality in "Welcome to Amsterdam." Other expressives include commiserating, apologizing, regretting and greeting.

The fifth type of speech act consists of *declaratives*. These are speech acts through which a particular state of affairs is called into being by the speaker or writer. That is to say, the mere performance of the speech act creates a reality; the employer who addresses an employee with the words "You're fired," is not just describing a state of affairs but is actually making the words a reality.

Declaratives are performed in institutionalized contexts such as court proceedings, meetings and religious ceremonies. In all these contexts, it is clearly delineated who is authorized to perform a particular declarative and when. Consider the declaratives "I hereby open the meeting," "I hereby declare you husband and wife," and "I give notice to quit effective May 1st." Declaratives are frequently performed on occasions of great ceremony and solemnity, although appointing someone treasurer of The Darts Club also qualifies as performing a declarative too.

There is an important exception to the rule that declaratives are performed in a specific institutionalized context; this is the subtype of declaratives known as *usage declaratives*. Usage declaratives, as the term indicates, refer to linguistic usage. They are speech acts whose purpose is to facilitate or to increase the listener's or reader's comprehension of other speech acts, such as definitions, clarifications, amplifications and explications. The speaker or writer uses these speech acts to indicate exactly how a speech act that may be unclear to the listener or reader is to be interpreted.

Distribution of Speech Acts in a Critical Discussion

Assertives

In principle, all assertives can occur in a critical discussion. They can express the standpoint that is at issue, be part of the argumentation in defense of that standpoint, and be used to establish the conclusion. In establishing the conclusion, the standpoint can be upheld, and thus repeated, but it can also be retracted, so that the standpoint is negated. Someone who upholds his or her position might do so by clearly stating, "I uphold my standpoint." This speaker is committed to the same proposition in exactly the same way as in the assertive with which the standpoint was originally expressed. A speaker might retract a standpoint which is no longer supported by saying "I retract my standpoint." The speaker would no longer be committed to the proposition expressed in the assertive which first advanced the standpoint. The original commitment could also be terminated by statements, such as "I do not assert that . . ." or "I no longer assert that. . . ."

Although an assertion is the prototypical assertive, the advancing of a standpoint or of argumentation can also be accomplished by the performance of assertives such as stating, claiming, assuring, guaranteeing, supposing and opining. Our belief in a proposition expressed in a standpoint or argumentation can be very strong, as in the case of a firm assertion or statement, but it may also be fairly weak, as in a supposition.

Directives

Not all directives can occur in a critical discussion; their role must consist of either challenging the party that has advanced a standpoint to defend that standpoint or requesting argumentation to support it. A critical discussion does not contain directives such as orders and prohibitions. The party who advanced the standpoint cannot be challenged to do anything other than to provide argumentation for the standpoint—a challenge to a fight, for example, is out.

Commissives

Commissives fulfill the following roles in a critical discussion: (1) accepting or not accepting a standpoint, (2) accepting or not accepting argumentation, (3) accepting the challenge to defend a standpoint, (4) deciding to start a discussion, (5) agreeing to take on the role of protagonist or antagonist, (6) agreeing on the rules of discussion, and, if relevant, (7) deciding to begin a new discussion. Some of the required commissives can only be performed in cooperation with the other party (for example 6).

Expressives

Expressives play no part in a critical discussion. The purpose of an expressive is to express a feeling and by using this type of speech act, the speaker creates no commitments which are directly relevant to the resolution of a dispute. This does not mean that expressives cannot affect the course of the resolution process. If we wish someone luck with a shortsighted standpoint, or sigh that we are unhappy with the discussion, we are expressing our emotions. Although this may have some significance, it distracts attention from the resolution of the dispute.

Declaratives

With the exception of the usage declaratives, declaratives make no real contribution to the resolution of a dispute. They depend on the authority of the speaker or writer in a certain institutional context. At best, they can lead to a settlement and not to a resolution of a dispute. This is why, ideally, there are no declaratives in a critical discussion.

Usage declaratives, such as definitions and clarifications, which require no special institutional relationship, enhance the understanding of speech acts and can thus fulfill a useful role in a critical discussion. Usage declaratives can prevent unnecessary "verbal" disputes from arising or can prevent real disputes from terminating in spurious resolutions. They can occur at any stage of the discussion (and they can be requested at any stage). At the confrontation stage, they can unmask a counterfeit dispute; at the opening stage, they can clarify uncertainty regarding the rules of discussion; at the argumentation stage, they can prevent effects of premature acceptance or non-acceptance, and so on.

The Distribution of Speech Acts in a Critical Discussion

Stage	Role of Speech Act in Resolution
	Assertives
I	expressing a standpoint
III	advancing argumentation
IV	upholding or retracting of standpoint
IV	establishing the result
	Commissives
I	acceptance or non-acceptance, upholding of non-acceptance of standpoint
II	acceptance of challenge to defend standpoint
II	decision to start discussion; agreement on discussion rules
III	acceptance or non-acceptance of argumentation
IV	acceptance or non-acceptance, upholding of non-acceptance of standpoint
	Directives
II	challenge to defend standpoint
III	request for argumentation
I-IV	request for a usage declarative
	Usage Declaratives
I-IV	definition, precision, amplification etc.

A Pragma-Dialectical Analysis of Argumentative Discourse

When analyzing argumentative discourse, one is interpreting the discourse from a specific perspective; the interpretation takes place in terms of a theoretical framework which concentrates on certain aspects of the discourse. When analyzing argumentative discourse pragma-dialectically, the discourse is interpreted as a critical discussion consisting of speech acts aimed at resolving a difference of opinion.

What is pragma-dialectical about such an analysis? The dialectical aspect consists of the assumption that two parties attempt to resolve a difference of opinion by means of a systematic exchange of moves in a discussion. The pragmatic aspect is represented by a description of the moves in the discussion as speech acts.

It is interesting to ponder the question of when the discourse is an argumentative discussion and when it is not. We need some kind of criterion which will enable us to treat equally discourse which is explicitly presented as (part of) an argumentative discussion and discourse which is not explicitly presented as such but which, nevertheless, functions as (part of) an argumentative discussion. The most suitable criterion is whether or not the speech act of argumentation has been performed; all spoken and written discourse in which this is the case should be treated as (part of) an argumentative discussion. The use of this criterion can be justified by pointing out that, in any case, the purpose of the speech act of argumentation is to remove someone's doubt about a standpoint.

Such doubt about a standpoint may be purely imaginary, as when a speaker or writer envisions how a standpoint might be received by a skeptical listener or reader. In that case, the speaker or writer anticipates any possible doubt. We refer to this as an implicit discussion.

In ordinary discourse, much more will generally remain implicit. For example, a speaker or writer does not often state explicitly the purpose of a contribution, and new stages in the discussion are hardly ever announced explicitly. For this reason, in fact, it is easy to overlook that an indispensable stage for the resolution of the dispute has been omitted. One stage that is quite often partly or wholly absent in any clear form is the opening stage. Rules for reaching a resolution are often not explicitly mentioned, undoubtedly due partially to the fact that they are considered to be self-evident. However, this assumption of self evidence may also be a device to make it appear as if both parties have already agreed on the rules when in fact, they have not.

In practice, some of the agreements regarding the rules of discussion are often made in advance of the discussion itself. If so, the opening stage can be omitted. The rules may have been established in the distant past: the discussants may, for example, have become acquainted with the regulations during school. The same prior agreement may pertain to certain other speech acts in the opening stage. For example, someone who is defending a standpoint by advancing argumentation immediately after having expressed that standpoint, need not state explicitly that he or she accepts the challenge to defend it.

It is often not quite clear who is to be convinced of the acceptability of the protagonist's standpoint. For instance, the protagonist might address someone who has challenged the standpoint other than the true antagonist.

In the case of a political debate, the target group may consist not only of the audience in parliament but also of the television viewers who will vote for the person speaking. In a letter to the editor, the reaction expressed might be toward other readers rather than the writer of the original article. There may thus be two antagonists: the official antagonist and the listeners or readers.

A similar complication may arise out of the fact that many spoken and written texts are not straight reproductions of discussions but reports. The person reporting is not intent upon resolving a dispute by convincing someone else. For example, most newspaper items containing speeches and elements of discussions are intended solely as information for the reader. Particularly where no explicit conclusion is drawn and no explicit thesis formulated, it is sometimes difficult to distinguish reports from argumentative discourse.

Here is a fairly typical example of a newspaper report in which a dispute is fought out with an opponent who is not clearly identified.

Low Incomes for Elderly

Should a new debate spring up in the coming weeks about who is actually receiving a so-called "genuine minimum" income, the Local Authorities' Association has demonstrated that many elderly people are included. The Association has surveyed those applying for the Christmas bonus. The survey covered 114 districts and found 506,000 people applying for the bonus. Most of them were either elderly or members of ethnic minorities. The Association believes that information aimed specifically at particular sections of the community would have resulted in more applications from the elderly and foreigners. The survey showed that precisely those groups have the most difficulty finding out about and applying for the bonus.

It is not quite clear who is the antagonist here, the reader, perhaps. On the other hand, it is fairly easy to identify the dialectical stages that have to be passed through in the resolution of the dispute. The first sentence signals the confrontation stage: the dispute (or possible dispute) is introduced. As quite commonly happens, the opening stage is less clear-cut, but in the first sentence we are told that the Local Authorities' Association will act as protagonist with respect to the proposition that the elderly are among those receiving a "genuine minimum" income. The argumentation stage contains the results of the Association's survey and is located further in the future ("Should a new debate spring up in the coming weeks . . ."). The concluding stage is left unilaterally to the Association ("has demonstrated").

Even in this short text, which is far removed from the ideal model, we can still recognize a train of argument that is part of a critical discussion between the protagonist and the antagonist of a particular standpoint, despite the implicit discussions and other complications. As long as we do not allow ourselves to be confused by such elements, we should be able to identify, using the ideal model as a guidelines, the elements of a critical discussion in most other spoken and written discourse.

Transformations in a Pragma-Dialectical Analysis

To be able to analyze argumentative discourse systematically — which is a prerequisite for an adequate evaluation — we must first establish whether part or all of the discourse can be reconstructed as a critical discussion. To clarify what this normative reconstruction entails, let us look at an example:

1   Frans: Now that I've got you for a moment — have you got around to thinking about your birthday yet? Are you having people in or not?

     Rob: I was thinking of having a party, actually. Not a bad idea it seems to me. What do you think? Why don't we get straight down to it

5   and work out who I'm going to invite — I mean, am I going to ask Francisca or not?

     Frans: Francisca? Of course you'll ask her. You must!

     Rob: Actually, I don't think I ought to.

     (Enter Tjark. He joins Frans and Rob.)

10   Tjark: What's new?

     Rob: What do you mean, new? Hey, have some coffee.

     Frans: Hi, Tjark. Dropped in at the right moment again, didn't you?

     Tjark: This coffee is much too strong again. What were you talking about?

15   Rob: Whether I ought to ask Francisca to my party.

     Tjark: 'Course you must. Every time.

     Frans: You keep out of this Tjark. Let Rob decide that for himself in peace. I'd just like to know, Rob, exactly why you object to Francisca coming.

20   Tjark: She can come as far as I'm concerned!

     Frans: I'm sure your wife would like to hear that. But I just happen to be talking to Rob, if you don't mind: what's the objection to her coming? It's your birthday, so you decide.

     Rob: But you're the one who's so frightfully keen to invite her. *I* think

25   *you* should start by telling us why it's so important that she should come.

Frans: I've told you, it's your birthday, so it's up to *you* to say why she isn't welcome.

Rob: That's all very well, but I have the strong impression that *you've*
30 got some reason of your own. So you've got to say why, too.

Tjark: Are you two managing to work things out? Just invite her, will you? Stop going on about it all the time. Anybody seen Michel, by the way?

Rob: No, Michel's dropped out — the creep.

35 Frans: Do you want it to be another one of those awful drags? . . . Francisca is the nicest woman I've met in a long time.

Rob: And you wanted me to stay away, did you? I can't ask Francisca, Michel would come too!

Frans: Okay then: exit Francisca.

40 Tjark: Figured it out, have we?

Frans: Just give me a beer.

Rob: Okay, so what are we doing? Asking her?

Frans: No, no, I said you were right, didn't I? Have it your own way. Don't bother.

In this example, we happen to be dealing with an ordinary conversation. However, the points illustrated are basically the same in more formal discussions, editorial comments, policy documents, or scholarly polemics. In all these cases, we are dealing with discourse in which an attempt is undertaken to resolve a difference of opinion. In the conversation above, there is a difference of opinion between Rob on the one hand and Frans and Tjark on the other; this difference of opinion relates to whether or not Francisca should be invited to Rob's birthday party (7, 8, 16).

In a normative reconstruction of this conversation as a critical discussion, it is treated as an argumentative discussion solely aimed at resolving the difference of opinion concerning whether or not Francisca is to be invited. Language use can serve diverse goals and the resolution of a difference of opinion is naturally only one of them. There may be more than one goal at the same time, and resolving a dispute will not always be the chief of these. One form of usage, accordingly, will be closer to the ideal of a critical discussion than another, so that in one case a more comprehensive reconstruction may be necessary than in another.

A normative reconstruction in the pragma-dialectical sense does not mean that every discourse is automatically regarded *in toto* as a critical discussion. Rather, we look to see what happens if the analysis is carried out as if it were a critical discussion. How far we are justified in choosing this approach depends on various factors in the "speech event." In the example we have chosen here, at least, applying this analytical starting point presents no major problems.

Naturally, other approaches besides a pragma-dialectical one are also possible. A Freudian psychological analysis would undoubtedly be able to produce interesting results. Again, the same sort of restriction would apply: things that appear relevant from one angle remain out of sight when viewed from another. However, one approach need not necessarily preclude another. The same conversation can very well be examined and analyzed from different angles at the same time, although it is a good idea to keep the different perspectives separate.

In a pragma-dialectical analysis, a normative reconstruction entails a number of specific operations which amount to the performance of a number of pragma-dialectical transformations. The various transformations can be explained by reference to the example.

The first transformation that is needed entails selection from the descriptive representation of the text. Elements that are relevant for the process of resolution are recorded in the analysis; elements that are irrelevant for this purpose are omitted. This transformation, in other words, amounts to the removal of information that is not required for the chosen goal. For this reason, it is known as deletion.

The first thing to be done in a normative reconstruction of the discourse in the example is to leave out the passage in which greetings are exchanged and something is said about coffee (10-13). There is no connection between this passage and the resolution of the difference of opinion. The same applies to the passage in which Frans asks for a beer (41). The text does contain other passages suitable for deletion in a normative reconstruction, but these obvious cases are sufficient to give a general idea of the purpose of this transformation.

The second transformation entails a process of completion. This is partly a matter of making implicit elements explicit and partly of supplying unexpressed steps. Supplying missing elements might include assuming that someone who advances a contrary standpoint is thereby also indicating doubt about the original standpoint. Another example is the explicit statement of a premise that has been left unexpressed in the discourse. In such cases something is added that is not explicitly present. Thus, this transformation is supplementary by nature; accordingly, it is called addition.

In the example, there is an implicit premise in "Michel would come too!" (38). Here, the additional transformation means that these words are allotted the communicative function of a premise. The same applies to Frans's implicit argumentation in "Do you want it to be another one of those awful drags? . . . Francisca is the nicest woman I've met in a long time" (35-36).

Rob advances his standpoint explicitly: "Actually I don't think I ought to" (8). The indicator "I don't think" makes it clear here that we are dealing with a standpoint. Rob's standpoint is contrary to Frans's (7). Here, the addition transformation means that doubt concerning Frans's standpoint is added to

Rob's standpoint. On the basis of his contrary standpoint, Rob may be assumed to have doubts about Frans's standpoint.

In Frans's argumentation for his standpoint that Francisca ought to be invited (35-36), it is assumed that a nice woman is capable of ensuring that a party is not boring, but it is also presupposed that parties ought not to be boring and that an earlier party or parties *was* or *were* boring. Here the addition transformation means that these unexpressed premises in the argumentation are supplied.

The third transformation entails an attempt to produce a clear and uniform notation of elements fulfilling the same pragma-dialectical function. Ambiguities and vaguenesses in the discourse are replaced by unambiguous and clear standard formulations. Different formulations of the same standpoint or premise, for example, are reduced to a single (standard) formulation. The transformation of translating the literal wording into the language of pragma-dialectical theory amounts to replacing the pretheoretical formulations of colloquial speech with theoretical standard formulations, and is called substitution.

In the example, Frans and Tjark adopt a positive standpoint with respect to the proposition that Francisca must be invited, but the wording in which they cast their standpoints varies from "Of course you'll ask her. You must!" (7) and "'Course you must. Every time" (16) to "She can come as far as I'm concerned!" (20). The standard formulation of this standpoint in a normative reconstruction might look like this: "Our standpoint is that Francisca must be invited to Rob's birthday party."

Frans's pro-argumentation for this standpoint is presented indirectly in the form of a rhetorical question: "Do you want it to be another one of those awful drags?" (35-36). The same applies to the contra-argumentation put forward by Rob: "And you wanted me to stay away, did you?" (37). Here again, to improve the clarity of the analysis it would be necessary to carry out a substitution transformation by replacing the indirect argumentation with a direct standard formulation (which is rather more difficult here, as it happens, than with Frans's and Tjark's indirect standpoints).

The fourth transformation entails ordering or rearrangement. In contrast to a strictly descriptive record, a normative reconstruction need not necessarily follow the order of events in time or in presentation. In a pragma-dialectical analysis, we are concerned with clearly indicating the elements that are directly relevant to the resolution of the difference of opinion, in the order that is most suitable for the analysis. Sometimes, this means that the actual chronology can be retained, sometimes it calls for some rearrangement. The result of the rearrangement depends directly on the ideal model of a critical discussion that is taken as the starting point for the analysis. The transformation of ordering or rearranging the relevant elements is called permutation.

In the example, the confrontation stage is spread throughout various places in the text. To begin with, look at lines 7 and 8:

Frans: Francisca? Of course you'll ask her. You must!

Rob: Actually I don't think I ought to.

Here, both Frans and Rob advance standpoints: Frans a positive one and Rob a negative one. By advancing a contrary standpoint, Rob also signals that he has doubts about Frans' standpoint, while conversely Frans may be assumed to have doubts about Rob's standpoint.

The second place of confrontation is lines 16-19:

Tjark: 'Course you must. Every time.

Frans: You keep out of this, Tjark. . . . I'd just like to know, Rob, exactly why you object to Francisca coming.

Here, Tjark proves to have the same (positive) standpoint as Frans, i.e., the standpoint with which Rob disagrees. Frans invites Rob to advance arguments for his (negative) standpoint and, thereby, again shows that he does not accept that standpoint but continues to doubt it.

The third place of confrontation is in line 22:

Frans: . . . what's the objection to her coming?

Here, Frans tries again to lure Rob into the open by asking for arguments in favor of his standpoint. Thus, he still has doubts about the acceptability of Rob's (negative) standpoint that Francisca ought not to be invited.

One of the elements of the opening stage is the willingness of the parties concerned to take upon themselves the role that is appropriate to the position they adopt in the difference of opinion. If you have yourself advanced a point of view you must also, in principle, be prepared to defend it against doubt or criticism, i.e., to play the part of protagonist of the standpoint. If you refuse, the discussion grinds to a halt at the opening stage.

In the example, the opening stage actually occurs at various places. First of all, in lines 22-26:

Frans: . . . It's your birthday, so you decide.

Rob: . . . *I* think *you* should start by telling us why it's so important that she should come.

Here, Frans makes no bones about reminding Rob of his responsibility as the protagonist of the standpoint that Francisca ought not to be invited. In other words, he thinks Rob ought to take his duties as protagonist seriously. Rob then reminds Frans of his duty as the protagonist of the opposite point of view. Moreover, he believes that Frans should be the first to perform *his* duty as a protagonist by beginning with his argumentation.

The second part of the opening stage is in lines 27-28:

Frans: I've told you, it's *your* birthday, so it's up to *you* to say why she isn't welcome.

This is merely a repetition of the same remark that Frans has already made in lines 22-23.

The third part of the opening stage is in lines 29-30:

> Rob: That's all very well, but I have the strong impression that
> *you've* got some reason of your own. So you've got to say why, too.

Here, Rob reminds Frans of his responsibility as protagonist of the (positive) standpoint that Francisca ought to be invited. All these three passages must be regarded as minor skirmishes in which the parties jockey for position in the allocation of roles and the order in which they will play them. As such, all three belong to the opening stage of the discussion.

The argumentation stage is represented in lines 35-36:

> Frans: Do you want it to be another one of those awful drags? . . .
> Francisca is the nicest woman I've met for a long time.
>
> Rob: And you wanted me to stay away, did you? We can't ask
> Francisca: Michel would come too!

Here, Frans advances an (indirect) argument for his (positive) standpoint that Francisca ought to be invited; inviting her will ensure that the party is not boring and a failure. Also indirect is Rob's argumentation for his (negative) standpoint that Francisca ought not to be invited; inviting her will mean that Michel will come too, and that, it seems, is undesirable. Although the argumentation of both protagonists is not explicitly presented as such and, although it is argumentation in an indirect form in which there are also a number of unexpressed premises, it nevertheless requires no effort whatever to recognize the argumentation stage of the discussion in the passages quoted.

The concluding stage is present in lines 39 and 43-44:

> Frans: Okay then: exit Francisca. . . .
> No, no, I said you were right, didn't I? You have
> it your own way. Don't bother.

In these passages Frans leaves no doubt that he is abandoning his own (positive) standpoint and is going along with Rob's (negative) standpoint that Francisca ought not to be invited. The difference of opinion has thus been terminated in Rob's favor.

This identification of the various stages of a critical discussion in the example shows once again that we really are dealing with analytical distinctions. True, the concluding stage, as might have been expected, actually does come at the end of the conversation and it is preceded—as it ought to be—by the argumentation stage; but the confrontation and opening stages have become rather mixed up. Thus, for a normative reconstruction it is necessary to apply the permutation transformation, just as the other transformations, at various points. In this example, it was necessary only to a limited degree. Incidentally, the repetitions that occur at some stages—even if they are slightly differently worded—demonstrate the use and necessity of the deletion and substitution transformations. The implicitness and indirectness demonstrate the use and necessity of the additional transformation, especially if we look at the premises that are left unexpressed at the argumentation stage.

An Analytic Overview

Once a normative reconstruction of the argumentative discourse has been carried out, it is possible to give an analytic overview of those aspects of the discourse that are crucial for the resolution of the dispute. Here we must remember to attend to the following points:

(1) determining the points at issue,
(2) recognizing the different positions that the parties concerned adopt with respect to these points,
(3) identifying the explicit and implicit arguments that the parties adduce for their standpoints, and
(4) analyzing the structure of the argumentation of each of the parties.

Identifying the points at issue entails determining the propositions with respect to which standpoints are adopted and called into question.

Identifying the positions of the parties in the discussion amounts to determining who plays the part of the protagonist of which standpoint and who takes the role of the antagonist.

In identifying the arguments that are being advanced in an argumentative discourse in favor of a standpoint, the first difficulty is often that the arguments are not explicitly presented as such. Recognizing the implicit or even indirect argumentation as argumentation is a matter of interpretation. Sometimes there will be verbal indicators to help here (such as ''since'' or ''so''), but in other cases either the textual or the broader context will have to provide the answers.

Analyzing the structure of argumentation entails determining how the arguments put forward relate to one another in their support for the standpoint. In the simplest case, of course, a standpoint is defended by no more than one argument. Generally, however, the argumentation structure will be more complex because the speaker or writer believes that more than one single argumentation is needed to defend the standpoint. The nature of the complexity depends on the precise relationship between the component arguments.

An analytic overview of an argumentative discourse shows to which differences of opinion the text refers, the distribution of dialectical roles, the explicit, implicit, indirect and unexpressed premises which make up the argumentation, and the argumentation structure. Applied to the example, this produces the following result.

The difference of opinion relating to the question of whether or not Francisca ought to be invited to Rob's birthday party is mixed; Frans and Tjark adopt a positive standpoint, Rob a negative one. Frans and Tjark play the part of the protagonist of their own standpoint and the antagonist of Rob's standpoint. Rob by himself is the protagonist of his own standpoint and the antagonist of Frans' and Tjark's standpoint.

The argumentation for both standpoints is implicit and indirect. Furthermore, in both cases there are one or more unexpressed premises and the argumentation is compounded subordinately. After the implicit argumentation has been made explicit, the indirectness resolved and the unexpressed premises expressed, it is possible to look at the structure of Frans' (35-36) and Rob's argumentation (37-38). (The unexpressed premises are shown in parentheses.)

Frans:

Francisca should be invited to Rob's birthday party

Francisca's presence guarantees that the party won't be an awful drag	—————&—————	(Birthday parties must not be a drag)
Francisca is the nicest woman I've met in a long time	—————&—————	(Nice women prevent a party from being a drag)

Rob:

Francisca should not be invited to my birthday party

If Francisca comes, I will stay away	—————&—————	(You must be at your own birthday party)
If Francisca comes, Michel will come too	—————&—————	(Rob wishes to avoid seeing Michel)

The points that are included in an analytic overview are of direct relevance to the evaluation of the argumentative discourse. If it is unclear what standpoint is being defended, there is no way of telling whether the argumentation that has been advanced is conclusive. And if more than one standpoint is being defended in a discussion, it must be perfectly clear which language users are — singly or jointly — acting as the protagonist of which standpoint and who is the source of the various argumentations that have been advanced to defend each one. Otherwise, for example, it will be impossible to tell whether the various argumentations for the same standpoint actually constitute a coherent whole.

An adequate evaluation of the argumentative discourse is also made more difficult where implicitness or indirectness mean that arguments are overlooked or unexpressed premises fail to be noticed. A failure to have a clear picture of the structure of the argumentation can also be detrimental to its evaluation.

Part III

Arguing in the Social Community

A sociology of knowledge implies a grounding of methods in processes. Methods are shaped by a community of arguers, by a forum. . . . The very perception of things is screened by social concepts developed rhetorically (Brockriede, 1982, p. 146).

Brockriede recognized that the contexts of social communities gave important clues to the meanings and effects of arguments. Students can find the arguments of social communities in a wide variety of places—meetings of social groups, political rallies, press commentary about public disputes, international controversies, business negotiations, and the courtroom. Arguments in the social community are prominent in our everyday experience because they include nearly all forums for public controversies. Typically, public arguers adopt rhetorical perspectives, adjusting their reasons through language to the interests and values of the audiences whose adherence they seek. To analyze reasoning within the social community, scholars adopt a critical perspective that seeks to explain how arguments work to persuade or dissuade audiences or how arguments create social meanings. The chapters in this section show several different perspectives for investigating social arguments.

James F. Klumpp, in Chapter 8, establishes a rationale and a vocabulary for examining arguments in social contexts. He claims that a social perspective about argument evolved from interactionist approaches developed by Brockriede and Ehninger (1963), Scott (1967, 1976), and Habermas (1984). These approaches emphasized either a formalist perspective which focused upon how arguers can invent and criticize argumentative forms, or they emphasized a mechanistic perspective that focused on strategy and persuasive effects. Taking a social perspective is different in that it asks the student of argument to examine reasoning as a process whereby argumentation transforms and coordinates experience as it creates social meaning. Klumpp emphasizes that taking the social perspective on argument requires the student to examine the contexts of public argument according to various aspects of the material, the moral, the social, the political, the historical, and the rhetorical.

In Chapter 9, J. Anthony Blair examines both the products and processes of argument in social communities. His focus is on informal logic and the mistakes in argument that characterize reasoning in social communities. He is concerned with arguments that have wide public acceptance even though they are false. First, Blair explains the fallacies of inference in argumentive products, such as jumping to a conclusion, hasty generalizations, false inferences based on analogical reasoning, and false inferences based on authorities. Next, Blair delineates mistakes of argument that surface in the process of rational dispute resolutions, including adversary context fallacies, fallacies of language, and fallacies of unacceptable premises. The chapter provides a variety of contemporary illustrations of common mistakes in different forms of public arguments and gives clues to students about how they can create stronger arguments.

In Chapter 10, Gregg B. Walker and Malcolm O. Sillars analyze arguments by examining the values and audiences of social argument. They explain that social values are the best place to start evaluations of social arguments because value premises connect argument to audience. Walker and Sillars show how social controversies, such as the Ayatolla Khomeini's pronouncement of a death sentence on Salman Rushdie and the United States Senate's rejection of Senator John Tower for Secretary of Defense can be explained using their adaptation of Chaim Perelman's theory of values.

Adopting still a different perspective for the criticism of argument in social communities, Robert L. Scott explains in Chapter 11 that arguments are epistemic. He reasons: arguments are created from communicative interaction; therefore, interpreters of argument help create reality. To demonstrate the epistemic qualities of argumentation, Scott shows how Dwight Eisenhower's 1961 Farewell Address gave meaning and social reality to the term "military-industrial complex." Scott's analysis shows that arguers and audience supply names, constitute meanings, and thereby establish social reality.

Jane Blankenship concentrates on language as Scott does. In Chapter 12, she explains how the media interpreted arguments presented in the 1988 political campaigns of Michael Dukakis and George Bush. Blankenship notes that the press characterize political campaigns in the general metaphoric terms of warfare, games, and show business. In 1988, Bush and Quayle defined Dukakis by the terministic screens of "iceman" and "liberal." Terministic screens are linguistic terms that provide audiences with categories for interpreting what they see and hear during a campaign. Blankenship claims that the Bush and Quayle campaigns established these categories and made them the dominate interpretive frameworks of the public. Dukakis' own behavior affirmed the truth of the categories. Blankenship emphasizes that the way arguers name things contributes to the persuasiveness of the arguments they make in social communities.

One question students of argument may want to consider is whether Klumpp's chapter is fundamentally different from the other chapters in Part III. Klumpp argues for a perspective on argumentation that views argument as a social, rather than an individual perspective. The other chapters examine how individuals operate within the social community. To what extent are these different points of view?

Chapter Eight

Taking Social Argument Seriously

James F. Klumpp

Over twenty-five years ago, Wayne Brockriede and his coauthor Douglas Ehninger (1963) wrote that "debate is a co-operative rather than a competitive enterprise" (p. 19). For a form of discourse where the primary metaphors of analysts and journalists continue to this day to be military, this was an improbable, but insightful, observation. Furthermore, Ehninger and Brockriede carried this distinction through their explanation of the motive for debating: debate leads to better decisions in choosing social action. To be sure, the treatment of debate which followed this social orientation often sounded like the same old debate advice that had been with us for centuries. The orientation advised the individual debater to sift evidence, formulate positions, and argue persuasively for a position. Thus the idea of sociality surfaced to disappear once again without fundamentally changing the way we think about argument.

Since Ehninger's and Brockriede's text appeared, two other theoretical developments in argumentation have promised to provide a socially oriented theory of argument. The first was the "rhetoric as epistemic" idea introduced by Robert L. Scott (1967). From the place where Brockriede had begun, Scott moved to the position that argument about human action was "a way of knowing" distinct from other ways of knowing, particularly the way of knowing defined by the scientific method. Dominant theories of rhetoric from the Renaissance to this time had viewed discourse as merely a way to

Mr. Klumpp is in the Department of Communication Arts and Theatre at the University of Maryland, College Park.

disseminate knowledge acquired through other means. Scott argued that discourse could not only be knowledge-passive but could be knowledge-creative. Scott later elaborated his idea (1976), observing that "rhetoric aims at knowledge that is social and ethical" (p. 259). Yet, in the end, even Scott's concept of intersubjectivity rested on the individual with an awareness of the social nature of argument, rather than on a decidedly social-centered argument.

While the rhetoric as epistemic ideas were developing in this country, Jürgen Habermas (1984) was offering a critique of argumentation grounded in the continental tradition. Habermas argued that there were different sorts of rationality appropriate for different situations. The traditional technical/instrumental rationality of science has been extended beyond its domain of appropriateness into what he called the "lifeworld"—the world of socially shared belief, concepts of right and wrong, and values that guide action. Habermas writes of "the interpretive accomplishments . . . of a communication community" (p. 70), but finally his theory of argument, like those in the American tradition, become a theory of the individual arguer and what he or she takes into consideration in formulating arguments.

The developments outlined above are among the most important in theoretical work in argumentation in the last quarter-century. Together, their indictments of earlier ideas about argument compel a theory which stresses socially defined argument. Yet, all fail to take their own admonition seriously. This chapter follows some of these ideas in the direction toward which they lead but then proceeds beyond the point at which these theories return to the individual perspective. The purpose in doing so is to communicate the perspective which takes social argument seriously.

A. Who is the Arguer?

A current central question in literary theory asks, "Who is the author?" The question focuses attention on the tradition that takes an individual writer of discourse sitting alone with his or her pen to define authorship. When this assumption is altered—for instance, a text is seen as an expression of a social class, as generated by a particular society, or even as inventing itself as each discursive element constrains the next—different perspectives open on the literary act.

In the question of argument we can also ask, "Who is the arguer?" Our viewpoint on argument has always been dominated by the perspective of the isolated individual arguer. We posit an *individualistic* image of argument flowing from an individual mind toward a bringing into existence of discourse. Traditional theories of logic add to this model a restriction of strict material antecedents—that is, the arguer works with the "facts" discovered through other means to formulate argument in a social vacuum. Brockriede, Scott, and Habermas move to a second perspective that I think is best termed *interactional*. They remove the restriction of materiality on the non-social and discuss the individual arguer's awareness of a social context. Thus, invention includes assessments of social context. The ethic of such a position eventually compels the concept of argument as a "cooperative enterprise" which marks Brockriede's thought. The arguer's awareness of responsibility to the other constrains him to "walk a mile in her shoes." The image which dominates the interactional is still the individual inventor of argument. The thrust of the suggested change is merely to expand the awareness of factors in the inventional process.

Taking social argument seriously involves a much more radical departure. Suppose that argument is considered as a much broader scope than the individual as inventor. Suppose argument is considered to emerge through a social communicative process. Suppose further that even the concept of argumentative purpose is viewed more broadly: a community engages in argument to tie action to experience. The image of argument constructed in this manner places individual argument into a framework in which its meaning is derivative. Kenneth Burke (1971) uses the example of a cocktail party conversation. We arrive at a party and see a conversation occurring in a corner among four acquaintances. After acquiring the requisite drink, we walk up to the conversation and listen awhile. Soon we enter the conversation and participate for twenty minutes or so. During that time, participants in the original conversation have departed and others have joined. The cast of characters is entirely different. We leave and the conversation continues. This conversation has a life that transcends each of its participants. This is not to deny that each participant contributed. The point is that a satisfactory account of this conversation would begin with its character as socially constructed discourse and not as the sequential statements of various individuals.

So it is with social argument. We can describe the student standing to deliver a speech on abortion. There is a different story to be told when we consider society coming to terms with the moral conflict of abortion. To tell this story by identifying those who speak is not an appropriate place to *start* our account. Indeed, it may not be necessary at all to a meaningful account of the debate. The focus of description should be on the socially constructed debate with other considerations justified only when they provide insight to the central task. A community invents arguments to select courses of action and to socialize responses to the situations it confronts. To describe this community invention necessitates punctuating the arguments differently. Accounts of experience provide the community historically grounded argumentative products which compose the rationale for social action. A language to perform social argument orients the commentator toward this transformation of social experience into social response.

β. **Structuring the Study of Argument**

The initial difference in taking social argument seriously is a difference in how the student of argument treats the subject. Over the years, two traditions have dominated the study of argument. Each of these is strongest in providing answers to certain types of questions. Taking social argument seriously involves a third major approach to the study of argument.

The earliest study of argument in this century was *formal* study. Formal study best answered questions about the logical veracity of arguments. Such study involved mastering a set of forms for arguments—analogy, syllogism, generalization. The forms were then applied to textual arguments to judge the truth of inferences. This type of study separated the theory and practice of argument, with theory defined as a study of forms. Theorizing about argument proceeded analytically with the objective of evaluating which forms supported sounder inferences. Instruction in argumentation involved the memorization of the types or forms of argument, the tests the arguer applied to each type, and methods of recognizing types in practice.

To this day, argumentation textbooks use this structure to discuss single inferences. Formal study is not focused so much on arguers who invent arguments as on properly abstracting the forms of argument from text. For purposes of instruction, an arguer is posited who applies the forms to evaluate or create text, but the involvement of the individual is not important to the central study of argumentative form. Ehninger and Brockriede (1963) returned to a formal structure when they turned from the introductory chapters of their text toward providing instruction in argument. They converted the Toulmin model into a formal system of warrant types. The result eliminated the social from their instruction in argument.

The major alternative to formal study, the methods of social science, brought a *mechanistic* structure to the study of argument. This approach focused on the strategic choices made by the arguer and asked whether these were effective in persuading or convincing those who were addressed. Attacks on the formalists called for seeing how argument *really* worked. Often researchers in argument devised experiments to test the persuasiveness of forms delineated by the formalists. Invention was conceptualized as a matter of selecting from among available strategies to win an argument. Once again, theory was divorced from practice but in a different relationship. Theory was derived from generalizations about practice through the social-scientific procedures of observation, operational definition of strategies and intent, and experimental testing of effectiveness. Category systems developed to describe argument by dividing arguments into their component parts. Arguments were divided into evidence, warrants, claims; evidence into source and content; source into credibility and sincerity; credibility into trustworthiness, qualification, and dynamism, and so on. After separating the component parts, category systems tested the relationship among various parts and the ability to affect the belief of the target audience (Bettinghaus, 1972). Instruction became a matter of teaching arguers the results of research about what really worked when they wished to move their audience.

The mechanistic study of argument turned the focus away from text to the individual arguer. There was, of course, an interactional character—argument required someone to be persuaded—but the target was little more than a static element of context to be analyzed by the arguer (Clevenger, 1966). The action in the model was in the selection of strategy by the arguer who assessed the audience and then adapted to this assessment. This arguer also assessed the effectiveness of possible argument strategies.

For the individual inventor of argument seeking to deliver an effective message, the mechanistic study of argument was quite fruitful. Unfortunately, many argumentation textbooks today are hodgepodges that combine formal and mechanistic elements. Students are often confused when one chapter on argument is based in formalistic theory and another chapter on evidence is based in mechanistic assumptions. The former declares stridently the need for a commitment to formal correctness to assure the material truth of arguments and the latter promises sincerely that the best arguer is the one who can persuade the audience. Both concepts instruct on how arguments should be constructed, but they do so in dramatically different ways and with diametrically opposed values at their base. Textbooks which attempt to bridge the gap do so with a faith statement that most people are persuaded by logically sound arguments, even as others argue that experimentation shows that hearers are not rational.

The natural questions that arise in these structures lead us away from taking social argument seriously. Questions of material veracity and questions of persuasibility narrow the range of interests which social argument poses. The focus on text or the focus on the arguer, even when combined, elevates particular concerns that de-emphasize the characteristics that the social view of argument stresses.

A third viewpoint on argument takes social argument more seriously—a perspective rooted in the intellectual tradition that Stephen Pepper (1942) has identified as contextualism. If social argument is described in terms of the selection and socializing of action, argument becomes a means of organizing and focusing the community. In the face of ongoing daily events, the community argues to develop common interpretations of community experience which coordinates community action. In short, the community argues to place events into context.

The fundamental language activity in such an inquiry is *critique*. Critique has the characteristic of throwing theory and praxis together. Without argument there is no common interpretation of community experience, indeed, there is no *community* experience. Argument transforms nonsymbolic and symbolic experiences into contexts—into something that we can meaningfully call *community* experience. To argue about community experience is to argue about the relevance of various contextualizations to meaning, thus the argument is a theory about the praxis. At the same time, the praxis of experience inherently entails the meaning. Thus theory and praxis become intertwined.

In addition to separating theory from praxis, the other viewpoints for structuring the analysis of argument separate the study of argument from its instruction. Formal approaches attempt to convey forms which are then available later when the arguer has taken over from the student of argument. Mechanistic approaches convey principles of influence and a framework for assessing situations to select an abstract strategy prior to the verbalization step in the argument. When social argument is taken seriously, however, the act of arguing is a form of teaching about the prior interpretation, and, in turn, becomes the subsequent interpretation.

Can the actions of individuals in the social process be discussed in a contextualist viewpoint? Yes. From the perspective of the individual arguer, to critique interpretation—to argue—is, at the same time, to provide an alternative interpretation. Making judgments about arguments—critiquing arguments—is not accomplished through comparison with a formal ideal, through the assessment of effectiveness in creating community, nor through any other objective. Critique proceeds by elaborating the context entailed in an argument in such a way that the very interpretation that is being argued is reargued. To punctuate argument through this sequence of interpretation and reinterpretation necessitates a consciousness of the social process. Thus, a consciousness of the arguments of individual arguers is accommodated, but a contextualist instruction in individual skills presupposes the social viewpoint.

Can anything be learned for critique by analyzing arguments formally or mechanistically? Yes, but fundamental differences in perspective limit such insight. Declaring the existence of types in the strategies which contextualize community experience creates a context which influences interpretation. Making generalized statements about better and worse types isolates the theory from the rest of the context and elevates its importance on a basis other than its relevance to interpretation. To open the list to critique in terms of its relevance in context yields a contextualist rather than a formal structure. Asking which strategies for critique allow the community to interpret and to respond to experience most effectively either privileges a particular interpretation of effectiveness or begs the central premise of the question. If the value question of what the community considers effective is opened for critique, the answer will depend on context, not experimental result. Thus, both formalism and mechanism can provide meaningful context for critiquing social argument, but neither is privileged over other contextual interpretations.

To the formalist or mechanistic, the contextualist perspective seems disabling. The feeling emerges from the exclusive definition each offers for empowerment. In truth, critique is an extremely active stance. Far from eliminating the power of instruction, the perspective moves theorizing about argument to a central place in the process of social interpretation.

ℰ ⸱ The Qualities of Public Argument

The public process in which a society socializes experience and coordinates action is natural. We should not marvel at its accomplishment nor flatter ourselves by assuming the responsibility to make it happen. It is as irrepressible as communication itself. Nor is critique any more remarkable. Communication definitionally contains a quality to transform experience into something it is not. Critique turns the experience toward a new context that accomplishes the transformation. If taking social argument seriously involves the student of argument so intimately in a natural process, the burden on the vocabulary to study argument is lessened considerably. The vocabulary does not face the burden of teaching those who would reason fallaciously how to avoid the traps, nor the burden of teaching dedicated arguers how to negotiate the swamp of irrational listeners. Instead, the vocabulary must simply facilitate the socialization of experience by stimulating critique. The vocabulary that takes social argument seriously is thus a vocabulary which captures the qualities of the critique.

Viewed from this perspective, the possibilities for vocabularies to assist study are richly plural. Tracing the vocabulary of the rhetoric-as-epistemic movement reveals a terminology very different from the terminology which activates formal study of argument. A cursory reading of Habermas reveals yet another vocabulary which empowers critique. To illustrate one such vocabulary, consider the qualities of a public argument.

The Material

Obviously, public argument transforms materiality. Abortion must account for the fetus. The account may place the fetus into context as an evolving human life or as a pre-life form. The public argument turns on the context which the argument wills. The material fact of the woman's body is a central context for a particular argument on this issue, while another position finds this material fact irrelevant to the argument. Materiality is a quality invoked in interpretation.

The paragraph just concluded not only describes the social argument, it can be read as critiquing the argument that would exclude the woman's body. This merging of observation into critique is the merging of theory and praxis. We can deepen the argument. We can make it more concrete. We can talk about *Silent Scream* which treats the woman's body as if it were not there. The film is another material presence in this debate. Once again, our observation entails critique which transforms the statement of the film into a different role in social argument. Thus, critique transforms the compelling quality of material "reality" as interpretations develop which socialize our struggle with the power society grants humans to choose abortion.

Formalist theories of argument help us most directly in dealing with the material quality. Questions of material veracity are central to critique from this quality, and formal structures of argument point in that direction. Thus, this quality is the one which most often calls upon the theories of argument we traditionally learn.

2. The Moral

It is difficult to discuss the material quality of the public argument about abortion without demanding recognition of the moral quality. Assertions of fact soon exude moral quality. "Sharon is going to have a baby." The statement seems quite descriptive. Yet, the use of her name grants Sharon a moral status. The statement carries with it a sense for responsibility that emerges from the morality of parenting. Even the choice of tense—what Sharon has now is not a baby, but what she has later will be—has implication on the moral judgment.

The moral is an extremely important quality of public argument. Both formal theories of argument and mechanistic theories of argument are disabled in the face of the moral. Formalists must treat morals as principles to be applied and thus outside the domain of argumentative interest. Mechanists must either reduce morality to its effects or suggest that morality is a question different from argument—perhaps associated more with emotion than reason. Thus, the most activating dimension of public argument—the sense of human morality which permeates Habermas' life-world—is reintroduced in the contextualist study of social argument.

3. The Historical

Public argument infuses experiences with historical quality. Public argument about abortion very quickly invokes political rights: either a right to life or a right to privacy. The progressive expansion of rights is a prominent narrative in American historical myth which pervades the debate on abortion. The history of abortion prior to *Roe v. Wade* may also be invoked. The stories of backroom abortions under horrible medical conditions is a story rooted in historical quality. The debate itself with factors such as the conservative evolution of the court and the possibility of the reversal of *Roe v. Wade* becomes a historical context for the argument.

The historical is another quality which only social argument takes seriously. Formalist theories of argument by definition build on forms which are not historically located. Mechanistic theory treats an argument in an isolated moment of time and space. Questions of historical relationship are found in no debate textbooks. Social argument is different. While these arguments define the space-time moment, they do not take place in a single space/time moment. The definition of the moment performed in the transformation of context into text entails a historical dimension to the story. Any rich public argument which socializes interpretations of experiences has historical quality permeating those experiences. Whether it is a parent remembering when they were a child, a minister calling upon the historical beliefs of the church, or a veteran invoking Munich to teach a lesson about response to communism, the historical quality leaves an indelible mark on public argument.

4. The Social

To talk about socializing experience obviously entails the social quality in public argument. The terms through which experiences are to be motivated shape argument. The abortion debate may become social as the taking of human life. In this society, we consider the taking of human life to be *socially* significant in a way that praying to one's God is not. The society also uses the vocabulary of "rights" to socialize our reservation of certain powers to the individual — to the non-social. Rights are invoked by those we call pro-choice as the grounds for the socialization of abortion. The terms for the socialization of pregnancy are also critical to the debate. Do we take pregnancy to be an experience for a woman, for a family, for a community? Interpretations flow from the differences.

5. The Political

European students of rhetoric, such as Foucault, have increased awareness of the distribution of power entailed in public argument. Certainly the power of men over women and of powerful adults over the powerless unborn are qualities which mark the abortion debate. In a society in which political equality is such a central moral quality, critiques grounded in the power dimensions of particular socializations of experience are ubiquitous in public debate.

6. The Rhetorical

Public debate is often conscious of itself; that is, those engaged in public argument are conscious of their choices of language in shaping the debate. This consciousness provides a rhetorical quality to the debate. Is the symbolic representation of fetuses in *Silent Scream* a cheap tactic? Is it an attempt to bring accuracy to the debate? Is it a distortion of facts? These critiques work with the rhetorical quality of the film in a way that comments on how we are to conduct the debate.

The list could no doubt continue to be expanded with other qualities represented in public argument. The interrelationship of these qualities indicates another important characteristic of taking social argument seriously. The formalists' and mechanists' techniques of sorting argumentative statements into forms or strategies cannot be the model for working with qualities. Any social argument contains these qualities throughout its discourse. Even achieving the distinctiveness that permits us to talk consciously about these as qualities becomes difficult. Indeed, this characteristic of language keeps social debate going. Argument which socializes experience with an interpretation stressing particular qualities leaves in its wake other qualities exposed to critique. The constant reinterpretation that results marks the dynamism of social argument.

D. Learning Social Argument

Efforts to take social argument seriously too easily fall into a concern to train the individual arguer. Each of the theories mentioned make this transition differently. Ehninger and Brockriede (1963) define the social as interactive; thus, the social can become the arguer's consciousness of the other with whom he or she cooperates in the argument. Scott (1967, 1976) views the arguer as a seeker of knowledge who approaches argument with particular ethical precepts—toleration, will and responsibility—which benefit the search for knowledge. Habermas (1984) discusses social theory extensively. A great deal of this essay has been built on the obvious characteristics of social argument. An additional obvious characteristic is that individuals do participate in social argument. This last section provides some advice for students about taking social argument seriously.

A first step is to reconceptualize one's self-image as arguer. Arguers should be both more humble and more sanguine about their role in social argument. The image of the arguer as the lonely but powerful persuader who alters the course of world history does not fit the social approach. No one person can be said to be the author of the cocktail party conversation. At the same time, each of the participants constructed that conversation. Definitions of success in terms we traditionally expect from mechanistic models of argument simply are not applicable. Social argument evolves as arguers construct its interpretations. The elevating characteristic of the perspective is that each of us are participants in the major process of interpretation.

Second, social argument should be approached in a spirit of enrichment. Taking part in the social conversation means more than merely repeating the arguments already present. Imagine the poverty of contribution of a participant in the cocktail party conversation who merely repeats things already said. Certainly a student, politician, or anyone can rehearse arguments. Meaningful participation involves engaging the social argument to enrich interpretation.

Third, social argument should not be reified. Social arguments are not those which best conform to formal patterns. Nor are social arguments those which persuade masses of people. Some social arguments are better than others, but that has little to do with normal notions of hierarchies of importance in social arguments. There is no more profound social argument in America today than the effort to socialize our experience with drugs. There is, to be sure a "national" debate on this subject. The true arena of this social debate is in millions of encounters day to day when drug choices and drug use are confronted and socialized.

Finally, critique calls for responsibility and deserves respect. Arguments, if listened to carefully, reveal their own seams that open up the possibilities for critique. Turn the argument in different ways to approach it differently. Marshall the material facts to support a perspective. Trace the moral implications of a position. Social argument shapes our lives; respect for critique defines quality in our life-world.

Conclusion

In August 1985 at the Fourth Summer Conference on Argumentation in Alta, Utah, Brockriede (1985) described his many interests in argument. He talked about several projects he had underway. In that presentation and the discussion that followed, Brockriede made clear his commitment to the study of argument focused on individuals. One of the goals he set for those at the conference that day was to see argument relating to experience primarily as a process of criticism. "We argue about our experience and try to make sense of it, critically" (p. 36). As in so much of his work, Brockriede's charge captured so much of modern thinking about the powers of language. If we are to fulfill his charge, we should begin to take social argument seriously. With that move will come new perspectives on the powers which argument exercises in the human experience.

Chapter Nine

Fallacies in
Everyday Argument

J. Anthony Blair

This chapter discusses the ways fallacies occur in everyday argument and briefly considers the merits of using the concept of fallacy as a critical tool in the assessment of everyday argument.

This chapter treats "argument" as meaning both various practices involving arguing back and forth (the giving and the criticizing of reasons in support of claims—the process) and also the arguments so used (stopped in time and taken out of their places in the sequential flow for the purpose of analysis and appraisal—the products). "Everyday" argument is about topics that might concern people in any of the myriad roles they occupy in daily life that can be followed by any moderately well-educated person.

The method here is to discuss in turn the three senses of fallacy found in the dictionary. "Fallacy," it turns out, ranges over beliefs and inferences as well as arguments, and fallacious inferences figure in a major category of fallacies in arguments.

Mr. Blair is in the Department of Philosophy at the University of Windsor, Canada.

A.   # A Fallacy as a False Belief

A fallacious belief is (a) a general belief that (b) has wide currency, and (c) is false. One might say, "It is a fallacy that men have greater endurance than women," if it is falsely but widely believed that men have greater endurance than women. This sense of "fallacy" does not concern us in what follows.

B,   # A Fallacy as a Mistaken Inference

If someone reasons that since the lower 48 States are south of Canada, therefore no place in the lower 48 States is north of any place in Canada, they reason fallaciously. Their inference is fallacious. (The extreme southwestern part of Ontario hooks south of the extreme eastern part of Michigan.) What makes inferences fallacious?

1.   ## What Is an Inference?

The concept of inference is central to our discussion, but accounts of inference differ. Inference means the mental act of coming to accept one proposition on the basis of a given set of one or more other propositions.

2,   ## When Is an Inference Fallacious?

If a fallacy, in one of its senses, is a mistaken inference, then we need to know how to distinguish mistaken from correct inferences. So what are the conditions under which we are justified in accepting one proposition on the basis of a given set of other propositions? What are the criteria of rationally justified inferences? There is no single universally accepted answer to this question. Be forewarned that the author presents his own view of the matter.

The criteria of a rationally justified inference comes from the ways the set of propositions from which the inference is drawn supports the proposition inferred from it. For instance, if someone infers that,

(1) The U.S. should try to support Gorbachev.

on the basis of the evidence that

(2) Gorbachev's goals are in America's best interests.

then whether the inference is justified depends on whether (1) is supported by (2).

An inference is justified when the propositions in the role of (2) provide rational grounds for accepting propositions in the role of (1). So our question can be put this way: Under what conditions is a given set of propositions rational grounds for another given proposition?

The conditions for rational inferences will vary because there are several different ways propositions can be related, each giving rise to different criteria by which one set of propositions rationally grounds another. These variations are due in part to the differing standards appropriate to different subjects and in part to the different types of inferences used. Correspondingly, there are different types of fallacies of mistaken inference. To illustrate both these claims let us review in some detail a number of the standard types of support for inferences.

3. Logical Implication as a Criterion of Legitimate Inference

What is logical implication?   One type of relation in a set of propositions is when one of them is logically implied by the others. Suppose, for example, you are playing a game of chess and (3) is true:

> (3) You have just touched your Queen, and under the strict rules
>   of chess if you touch a piece without saying that you merely
>   intend to adjust it, you are required to play that piece.

Then (4) must also be true:

> (4) Under the strict rules of chess you must play your Queen.

(4) follows necessarily from (3), which is all that is meant by saying that (4) is logically implied by (3).

The move from (3) to (4) is an instance of a pattern that logicians have named "modus ponens." Any statements whatever that exemplify this pattern are related such that the ones in the place of (3) logically imply the one in the place of (4). Patterns having this property are called "valid forms" of implication.

By definition, then, any set of propositions that is an instance of one of these valid forms has this property that one proposition necessarily follows from the others. This relationship of logical implication guarantees that if the first set of propositions is true, then the one implied by them is also. Logical implication between propositions is always a rational ground for inferring one proposition from the set of different propositions that logically implies it.

Formal fallacies.   If logical implication is a guarantor of an inference, can we classify as fallacious all inferences not based on logical implication? No, that would follow only if there were no other kinds of inference-legitimizing relationships between propositions, and as we shall soon see there are many others. Still, if someone takes an inference to be warranted by a deductively valid form of implication when it is not, then they have made a mistake about the nature of their inference. Such mistakes have been labelled "formal fallacies" — naturally enough, since they consist of assuming that an implication has a valid form when it doesn't.

In everyday reasoning, formal fallacies of inference are rare. J. L. Mackie (1967) presents an excellent discussion of formal fallacies recommended to interested readers.

Inductive Support as a Criterion of Legitimate Inference

Inductive support and inductive fallacies. One of the other inference-legitimizing relationships besides logical implication is inductive support. In general terms, inductive support is evidence that provides grounds, varying from weak to strong, for accepting a proposition as probable. The degree of probability varies according to the degree of strength of the support. An inductive inference is fallacious when the inferred claim is accorded a higher degree of probability than the evidence warrants.

The inductive fallacy of jumping to a conclusion. "Jumping to a conclusion," a common inductive fallacy, consists of drawing an inference on the basis of only a few bits of evidence which are not sufficient grounds for accepting the proposition inferred. Most of us jump to conclusions on a regular basis. We see two people talking and we conclude they are acquaintances; we notice that one cereal box is bigger than another and we conclude that the bigger box contains more cereal; we note that one brand of jeans costs more than another and we conclude that the more expensive brand is better; and so on.

The mistake is a natural one, for at least two reasons. It is highly efficient to infer from a small amount of evidence, and the available evidence, though insufficient, is usually consistent with, or even supports, the proposition inferred.

The inductive fallacy of hasty generalization. "Hasty generalization" denotes an inference to a generalization from a number of particular instances, whereas we jump to particular conclusions from different evidence.

Hasty generalizations are a source of stereotypes, among other mischief. Consider the relationship between (5) and (6):

(5) Most Palestinians referred to on television are described as terrorists.

(6) Most Palestinians are terrorists or favor terrorism.

We need to remember that (5) is true because television tends to refer only to Palestinians in connection with terrorist acts. It is doubtful that the sample of Palestinians available for any inferences about them is representative of the Palestinian population. If so, anyone who infers (6) from (5) commits a hasty generalization in their reasoning.

Hasty generalizations from polling results. A noteworthy subtype of the hasty generalization fallacy is hasty inference from polling results.

In public-opinion polling or survey research, the incidence of an attitude, opinion, or preference measured in a small subgroup or "sample" is generalized to the larger group or "population" under study. Gallup and Harris polls, for example, generalize about national voting preferences on the basis of samples of fewer than 2,000 people. A national television commercial campaign will be tested first in one region of the country to see if sales increase there before expensive national network time slots are purchased. Inferences drawn about populations that are based on surprisingly small samples can be highly reliable if the sample is appropriately selected and the method of measurement is appropriately designed and implemented. Given the prevalence of polling in contemporary society, a prudent citizen or consumer will learn how it works. Details of the theory and practice of polling are beyond the scope of this article. But common sense can help inoculate us against some common invitations to draw hasty generalizations in this area.

For example, when a television news program interviews a few people on the street about some issue of the day, you can figure out for yourself that this tiny sample of people who happen to be on that street corner at the time the camera crew is there and who are willing to be videotaped is certainly unrepresentative of the city, let alone the country. Yet local and national news broadcasts use these interviews all the time. A radio/television phone-in show or a newspaper phone-in survey will purport to present an accurate picture of public opinion on an issue. Yet, there is no control over who chooses to phone in and so no way of knowing that the sample of views represented by the callers is representative of general public opinion in the area. Moreover, frequently the questions asked are so loaded in favor of one particular answer—e.g., "Do you support Americans being left defenseless by the legislated control of handgun sales?"—that the results are totally unreliable.

Anyone who draws an inference about public attitudes or opinions on the basis of this sort of evidence is committing a fallacy of hasty generalization.

Hasty causal generalization. We assess policies partly on the basis of whether we believe they will have the results predicted. We base such beliefs partly on our knowledge of causal operations in the world. The best evidence for any general causal explanation will consist of a number of elements including the following: (a) A high correlation between the supposed causes and their supposed effects; (b) a hypothesis supported by evidence explaining the former as a cause or the cause of the latter; (c) evidence eliminating alternative hypotheses; (d) an account of the mechanism of causation.

For example, evidence that steroid use combined with exercise causes muscle-mass buildup is supplied by the following combination. Evidence that steroid-using athletes have a significantly greater increase in their muscle mass than non-users—a correlation. Evidence that the difference is not due to such other factors as more intensive weight-training programs among steroid-users—an alternative hypothesis ruled out. Details of the chemistry of steroids and their likely interaction with muscle and other body tissue—the mechanism of causation.

This sketch is skeletal and general: the particular evidentiary requirements for causal explanations in any given field can only be understood after a close study of that field. You can see in general how an inference to a causal claim can be based on incomplete evidence. Such inferences are a species of hasty generalization.

One typical sort of hasty causal generalization is an inference from mere correlations to causes. For example, the high correlation between owning a handgun and being involved in a shooting has been taken to be evidence that handgun ownership is a contributing cause of violence. More evidence is needed because the correlation could be equally consistent with some other factor causing both. Marginal economic status could cause a sense of vulnerability and insecurity leading people to buy handguns for protection. That same economic status could also independently cause family and other social tensions leading to violence in which people use their handguns. Without the handguns, they might use knives or bats but be no less violent (if less lethally so).

Inferences Based on Analogical Reasoning

Reasoning by analogy plays a large role in ethical, legal and political life. Judgments about fairness are a good example. Consider the following set of propositions:

(7) Prof. Hardcase gave Frank an A- on his essay for, she said, the originality and thoroughness of his arguments.

(8) Freda's essay was similar to or better than Frank's when it came to the originality and thoroughness of its arguments.

(9) Prof. Hardcase should have given Freda at least an A- on her essay — and not the C+ she gave her.

The first two propositions provide good grounds for the third — other things being equal. Fairness requires that similar cases be treated similarly. The two essays, according to (7) and (8), were similar with respect to the stated grading criteria. Unless Freda's essay has some other feature that should lead to a lower grade (was it poorly organized? Was it handed in a week late?), then her essay should have received a grade similar to Frank's.

You can see that fallacious inferences involving analogical reasoning of this sort (sometimes called a *priori* analogy) occur when someone infers that two cases should be treated similarly, but the evidence shows that they are not similar in the respect(s) that bears on what treatment they should receive.

In a letter to the newspaper someone once reasoned that just as the costs of highway maintenance are paid for by those who use the highways through a tax on gasoline, so too should the social costs of alcohol abuse be paid for by those who drink alcohol through a higher tax on alcohol. I think this reasoning is fallacious since the two cases are not similar in the respect needed. Highway users do pay for highway upkeep in approximate proportion to the wear and tear they cause, since the amount of gas used (and gas tax paid) corresponds roughly to the mileage travelled (admittedly, city-only drivers add a considerable distorting factor). But alcohol users are not responsible for the social costs of alcohol abuse in proportion to the amount of alcohol they buy. It is only alcohol abusers who are responsible for these costs. So a tax added to the price of alcohol will not charge buyers in rough approximation to the proportion of their contribution to the social costs of drinking. This sort of mistaken inference is called the fallacy of "faulty analogy."

A priori analogical support for a claim is different from logical implication, and it is also different from inductive support. Moreover, there are other types of grounding for inferences and of corresponding fallacies, other than these three.

Inferences Based on Reliable Sources

Almost everything we believe or accept is based on the testimony of other people. We accept propositions because we consider them to come from reliable sources. For instance, we treat dictionaries as authoritative on questions such as how words are spelled and what their meanings are in current speech and literature. We treat our textbooks and reference books as authoritative so far as they supply us with information. We believe, more or less, what we see, hear and read in the media — that is where we get our information about current events. We even take the word of strangers for such information as the time of day, the directions to downtown, and when the next bus is due.

In general, such reasoning has this form:

(10) X says P, and

(11) X is a reliable source about such things as P, or there is no reason not to think so,

hence,

(12) other things being equal, we may presume P.

For example:

(13) According to the van Dale English-Dutch dictionary, the Dutch term for "to infer" is "conclusies trekken" — literally, to draw a conclusion.

(14) Some Dutch scholars I know recommend the van Dale dictionary as the best English-Dutch dictionary.

(15) Those scholars were trained as linguists, speak and write English, and translate much of their work into English.

(16) The Dutch for "to infer" is "conclusies trekken."

Here (13), (14) and (15) provide ample grounds for (16), so to infer (16) from the previous three propositions is justified.

The qualifications of a reliable source will vary enormously, according to both the subject matter and also the importance of being right. If the proposition in question is a claim about biochemistry and a life depends on your being right, you may need to find someone with a Ph.D. in biochemistry to verify it. If you want to know which way to downtown and if it doesn't matter whether you have to drive around a bit to find it, then almost anyone standing at an intersection might be a reliable enough source.

The fallacy of drawing an inference from an unreliable source is called *ad verecundiam* or "improper/illegitimate appeal to authority." The point is that in drawing such an inference, one is relying on the authoritativeness of some source; when that reliance is misplaced, the inference is fallacious. Examples include renting from Hertz because Arnie and O.J. back it although they haven't compared service and prices, plus they get paid so they have a conflict of interest; taking massive doses of vitamin C when a cold is coming on because Dr. Linus Pauling recommends it although the question of its efficacy doesn't belong to his expertise, moreover nutritionists disagree about its value; treating what you are now reading as beyond question because it is in a book even though theorists disagree on many of the points here discussed, moreover the best you can get from anyone in philosophy is thoughtful opinion.

We have examined in some detail a variety of ways inferences can go wrong and so be fallacious. The mental act of coming to accept one proposition on the basis of others is justified when the latter provide adequate grounds for the former. We briefly looked at some of the main ways propositions can be rationally grounded: logical implication, inductive support of various sorts, analogical support and support from a reliable source. In each case, a fallacy is a mistaken inference in the sense that it is an inference drawn from a set of propositions that do not supply either the appropriate kind of support, or enough of it, to justify accepting the proposition inferred.

C   A Fallacy as a Mistake in an Argument

Our sense of argument is the one people have in mind when they say things like, "What are your arguments for postponing the test—or do you have any?" or "Both sides delivered their arguments to the judge, who reserved judgment," or "Aquinas presented five arguments for the existence of God." Contrast the sense of argument found in examples such as: "They had a terrible argument; she threw a pot at him and he walked out" or "The children don't get along: they argue interminably." In the latter examples, the reference is to quarrels and bickering. We will restrict ourselves to the first sense: arguments as the reasons given in support of claims.

How Fallacies Occur in Arguments

In presenting an argument, one invites the person who is addressed to accept the argument's conclusion on the basis of the reasons or evidence produced in support of it (the premises). That means one invites the person to infer that conclusion from those premises.

In this way, our whole discussion of fallacious inferences applies to fallacious arguments. Any argument whose premises do not supply adequate justification for an inference to the conclusion is inviting a fallacious inference, and an argument that invites a fallacious inference is a fallacious argument.

Look at it this way. When we present an argument to someone, we (typically) just restate the propositions that led us to draw our inference; we invite the person we are addressing to draw the same inference. For example, you infer that a test should be postponed based on the fact that it was scheduled on an important religious holiday and your belief that students should not be forced to chose between academic and religious obligations. You then present the argument that the test should be postponed because—and you give the same reasons. The reasoning in both cases is identical. If it is sound in the first case, it will be sound in the second; if the first is fallacious, so is the second.

It follows that all types of fallacious inference also qualify as types of fallacious argument—formal fallacies, inductive fallacies (jumping to a conclusion and hasty generalization in its various forms), faulty analogy and illegitimate appeal to authority. So one answer to the question, "What makes an argument fallacious?" is: "It invites a fallacious inference."

Other Kinds of Fallacious Arguments

Their invited inferences are not the only feature of arguments that can go awry and produce fallacies. The practice of argument has other rational aspects, and the failures to honor them are also fittingly termed fallacies.

The suggestion has been made by the Amsterdam theorists van Eemeren and Grootendorst (1984 and Chapter 7 of this book) that argument be conceived as a rational procedure for settling disagreements. Such a procedure will be defined by rules, rules which have as their justification the claim that following them is necessary for the realization of the end or objective of the practice— rational dispute resolution. Any violation of these rules will, then, impede the achievement of that goal and can be condemned or judged improper on that basis. Van Eemeren and Grootendorst (1987) think that all the traditional fallacies can be accounted for in this manner. This conception is a useful organizing principle for the fallacies connected with argument.

A rational dispute-resolving procedure would obviously have to include a rule that the inferences invited by arguments should be well-grounded (for otherwise agreement would not be rational). Hence, all the fallacies of inference that are fallacies of argument will also be counted as fallacies on the Amsterdam conception.

Rational dispute resolution is a social, communicative procedure as well as a logical one; moreover it takes place always in a context in which meanings and background assumptions are shared. Thus there will be further rules designed to take these features into account. Let us examine some of the fallacies associated with violations of these other rules.

Adversary Context Fallacies

When two parties are contending in argument, they often have interests at stake which they do not want to give up, so each tries to "defeat" the other and to "win" the argument. Yet the fact that they are bothering to engage in argument commits them to certain rules. For instance, they should address the issue at hand—the point over which there is a controversy. And they should, in criticizing their opponent's viewpoints and arguments, actually address the positions that the opponent holds. If these conditions are not met, the discussion will be irrelevant to the disagreement. Sometimes the heat of the disputation and other times calculated obfuscation produce violations of such rules. Several well-known fallacies can be identified here.

One is "red herring" or *ignoratio elenchi*—missing the point. The remark of a spokesman for a doll company serves as an example. One of the dolls had the head attached with a large, easily-exposed spike. A consumer group was lobbying for regulations to outlaw such potentially dangerous toys. The spokesman commented, "All the legislation in the world isn't going to protect children against the normal hazards of life." His comment was true, but also totally beside the point, since an easily-exposed spike in a child's toy is not a normal hazard of life.

Another well-known fallacy in this group is the abusive *ad hominem* attack—a personal attack intended to discredit the opponent without refuting the opponent's position or arguments. Mr. Bush labelling Mr. Dukakis a "liberal" played this role in the 1988 presidential campaign. By painting Dukakis as a liberal, Bush succeeded in discrediting him among voters for whom a liberal is an anathema but did not prove Dukakis's policies defective or inferior to Republican policies.

The "two wrongs make a right" or *tu quoque*—you too—fallacy is another way of avoiding the issue by counterattacking. Accused of cheating on a test, a student defended herself by saying, "Others cheat and get away with it." So they may, but that fact does not legitimize cheating. Certainly it is unfair to non-cheaters that some cheat and get away with it; but that is a reason for steps to stop cheating, not for cheating.

Yet another adversary context fallacy is "straw man"—attacking a misrepresentation of one's opponent's position. Opponents of the women's movement who attack it for trying to destroy the family are using a straw man argument, since equality for women and the ending of male domination throughout society are not inconsistent with family life. The women's movement is trying to destroy the patriarchal family, but that is a different matter. The women's movement does not hold, or imply, the position criticized—that the family should be abolished.

These adversary context fallacies—and there are others—share the feature that they block or try to avoid coming to grips with the opponent's point of view to show that it is flawed or mistaken. Thus these moves impede or avoid the resolution of the disagreement which they ostensibly address.

4) Fallacies of Language

Given the social, communicative character of the ideal of rational dispute resolution, those who engage in it are obliged to avoid using language in ways that interfere with communication or obfuscate the activity. The use of terms that are vague or ambiguous in the context, or of value-laden language can violate this injunction.

When a cereal company tries to persuade us to buy one of its products because it is "natural," should we find that reason compelling? We respond favorably to what is natural, so the term conveys positive value to us. Yet in this context it is vague. Without further specification, we don't know if it means there are no chemical additives, no sugar added, no other food types besides the grain of the cereal included, or none of the above. The cereal company's information is not precise enough to make a reasoned judgment; yet, the positive value attached to the term "natural" invites us to draw an unwarranted inference.

When Canadian Prime Minister Pierre Trudeau stated that we should rely on our consciences to decide whether to disobey a law we consider unjust and face the consequences, he was criticized. "Trudeau is confused about the relation between law and conscience," the critic wrote, "because there can be no conscience without law. We think a certain law violates our conscience only because we think there is another law on the same subject which should be followed." There is confusion here due to the ambiguity of the word "law" in the discussion. Trudeau used "law" in the sense of legislation. The critic was using both that sense of law and also "law" in the sense of "moral principle" and was switching back and forth between the two senses. It may be true that there can be no conscience without moral principles, but Trudeau did not deny that. It may also be true that we think a certain piece of legislation violates our conscience only because we think there is a higher moral principle against obeying that legislation, but Trudeau did not deny that either. By failing to recognize the ambiguity in the word "law" in this context, the critic made up a dispute where no disagreement existed.

Following the Amsterdam approach to fallacies, we can say that in these two examples, two fallacies occurred. The use of "natural" was a fallacy of vague and loaded language. The confusion over "law" was a fallacy of ambiguity. In both cases the failure to be precise with language interfered with the rational assessment of a position.

5) Unacceptable Premises

If someone argues that capital punishment is immoral and should be abolished because it is nothing but legalized murder, the arguer commits an interesting fallacy called "begging the question." Here is how it works. The reasoning is that because capital punishment is legalized murder, it is immoral. But we will not permit the description, "legalized murder," unless we already agree that capital punishment is immoral. If we think it is not, we won't agree to call it legalized murder. So the arguer "begs" us to accept as a premise the very "question" or position we need to be convinced of. The argument spins its wheels.

Begging the question is perhaps the most dramatic form of the fallacy of basing one's arguments on propositions that one's interlocutor or audience cannot or will not accept. If they do not accept that capital punishment is immoral, then they cannot accept a premise that presupposes that capital punishment is immoral. The rule violated here is that one's premises may only be propositions that one's interlocutor is willing to, or can be (rationally) persuaded to accept, and moreover that would be acceptable to a reasonable, accurately informed person. The point behind this rule is that disagreements can be resolved only by working from points of common agreement, and such resolutions will be rational only if these are reasonable points to accept.

Whether a premise is acceptable will quite often itself be a matter of dispute. Consider the argument that no man can be a total feminist because only someone who knows what it feels like to be discriminated against as a woman can be a total feminist, and obviously no man can have that experience. I am uneasy about the first premise. Is having all the experiences of discrimination that a woman can have really necessary for being a total feminist? What seem needed are imagination, empathy, and appreciation of the myriad ways of power's exercise—all of which are accessible to men and women who have not experienced discrimination as a woman. But some might dispute my claims.

Arguers must be willing to answer their interlocutors' actual, likely, or possible reasonable objections to their premises. The failure to do so would prevent the rational resolution of disagreements and on that basis can be judged a fallacy of argumentation.

If an argument is a set of reasons offered to try to convince someone to accept a position, then when such an offer amounts to an invitation to draw a mistaken inference, it also amounts to a bad or fallacious argument. One class of fallacious arguments, therefore, will be invitations to fallacious inferences. In addition, however, there will be moves in argumentation that violate the rules which specify the conditions for the rational resolution of disagreements. These will include, among others, the adversary context fallacies, the fallacies of language, and fallacies of unacceptable premises.

D. Fallacy as a Critical Tool of Argument Appraisal

Let's turn briefly, and lastly, to the second question of this chapter: is fallacy a useful tool for the critical appraisal of everyday arguments? I think it is, if it is used correctly, but not otherwise. Here are my reasons.

You might have noticed that in the discussion of the examples of different fallacies, it was necessary to assume that you already understood a lot of the relevant background information and that you understood the topic that the inference or argument was concerned with. I suspect that where you found my allegations of fallacy the least compelling, I had sketched only a thumbnail case. Identifying a mistaken inference requires knowing the standards of solid grounding for inferences in the field in question. Recognizing when an argumentative move undercuts the rational resolution of a disagreement requires knowing the issues and positions relevant to that disagreement. All of this shows that in order to be in a position to recognize a fallacy and to make a solid case that it has been committed, one needs a solid understanding of the subject matter and its appropriate standards of reasoning. Simply knowing a set of general descriptions of fallacies will be of little use. The incorrect way to use fallacies as a critical tool, then, consists of treating such a set of descriptions as sufficient for argument appraisal.

On the other hand, an understanding of the various fallacies—the identifiable patterns of mistaken inference and bad argument—can serve to alert us to the presence of fallacious reasoning or arguments particularly as they are refined in considerable detail in the literature, and not merely as they have been briefly outlined above. Moreover, it can serve to refine our appreciation of the standards of good argumentation.

A final warning, identifying fallacious arguments is not similar to finding milk gone bad. The mere presence of a fallacy is rarely a sufficient reason to discard an argument. Spotting a fallacy is more like finding a small leak or a bit of dry rot in a boat. It shows where the argument needs repair and indicates how the repair is best made. Properly used, then, fallacies can contribute positively to the ongoing challenges of avoiding persuasion by bad arguments, strengthening weak arguments and constructing solid arguments.

Chapter Ten

Where Is Argument?
Perelman's Theory of Values

Gregg B. Walker
and Malcolm O. Sillars

In early 1989, two quite different kinds of arguments dominated the news reports. On the international scene, Iran's Ayatollah Khomeini, symbolic leader of Shiite Muslims, called for the death of author Salman Rushdie because his book, *Satanic Verses*, represented slander against the prophet Mohammed. To slander the prophet and, therefore, Allah, who had chosen him to bring the *Koran* to humanity, was an attack on the value system which Allah represents. Death, because of the seriousness of the offense to that system of values, was a reasonable sentence. The response, particularly in western Europe and the United States, by authors, civil libertarians and political leaders was a counter argument based on a western democratic defense of a value system featuring freedom of thought, speech and the press.

Concurrently on the American domestic scene, the United States Senate considered and rejected President George Bush's nomination of former Texas Senator John Tower for Secretary of Defense. Those critical of Tower argued that his alleged drinking problem and "womanizing," together with his close ties to the defense industry he would be supervising as Secretary of Defense,

Mr. Walker is in the Department of Speech at Oregon State University, Corvallis and Mr. Sillars is in the Department of Communication at the University of Utah, Salt Lake City.

rendered him unqualified to serve in so vital a role. Those championing the Tower nomination stressed that his experience made him the most competent person to hold the position.

The arguments surrounding the *Satanic Verses* conflict and the Tower nomination featured contrasting uses of values. In the former case, Shiite Muslims and western liberals developed arguments based on a basic value clash between God and Freedom. In the latter case, Tower opponents and advocates proved opposite claims while arguing from the same value warrant of competence.

These were not the only issues Americans heard argued in early 1989; there were questions of abortion, deficit reduction, acid rain, minimum wage, drug control, and a host of others. But, these two quite different issues illustrate (as would the others upon further explanation) the centrality of values to public argument. When people argue, attempting to gain adherence from an audience, they appeal to, employ, and interpret values.

Many people, including us, have made such a claim (Ehninger, 1968, 1970; Eubanks & Baker, 1962; Fisher, 1978; Rieke & Sillars, 1984; Sillars, 1973, 1985; Sillars & Ganer, 1982; Steele, 1962; Wallace, 1963; Walker, 1984; Wenzel, 1977) What has not been done is to illustrate how the arguer develops arguments and the critic of argumentation analyzes arguments from this value-centered perspective. Such a value-centered understanding of argumentation is provided by an examination of, and extension from, the writings of the Belgian Philosopher, Chaim Perelman.

In his keynote address at the third AFA/SCA Summer Conference on Argumentation, Brockriede (1983), in celebrating a "renaissance in the study of argument," cited Perelman as a major actor in that renaissance, remarking that Perelman's ideas have endured as "a major force" in argumentation theory and practice" (p. 17). Because much of Perelman's writings are intended for philosophers rather than students of argumentation, some adaptation is necessary, but we believe this is quite possible without doing injustice to Perelman's ideas. Most important, Perelman's comprehensive theory of values should guide students of public argumentation to locate, understand, criticize and employ values in argument.

Where Is Argument?

Argument, explains Wayne Brockriede (1975), is "a process whereby people reason their way from one set of problematic ideas to the choice of another" (p. 180). In public argument the purpose of the argument is "to elicit or increase the adherence of the members of the audience to theses that are presented for their consent" (Perelman, 1982, p. 9).

There are "six characteristics that may help a person decide whether argument is a useful perspective to take in studying a communicative act," notes Brockriede (1975). They are (1) "an inferential leap from existing beliefs to the adoption of a new belief or to the reinforcement of an old one"; (2) "a perceived rationale to support that leap"; (3) "a choice among two or more competing claims"; (4) "a regulation of uncertainty"; (5) "a willingness to risk confrontation of a claim with peers"; and (6) "a frame of reference shared optimally" (pp. 180-82).

Beginning with the idea that argument is a "process" rather than a thing and that it aims to get adherence on problematic ideas, these six characteristics lay a foundation for saying what is and what is not argumentation. Any message is communicated but not all messages are arguments. These important distinguishing characteristics of argumentation clearly imply value choices.

For instance, consider Brockriede's initial characteristic of an argument as "an inferential leap from existing beliefs to the adoption of a new belief or to the reinforcement of an old one" (p. 180). If one is to convince others that John Tower is the most competent person for the position of Secretary of Defense that belief, appearing as a claim about a specific person in a specific situation, depends upon the word "competent." Competence is a value, "a type of belief, centrally located within one's total belief system, about how one ought or ought not to behave, or about some end state of existence worth or not worth attaining" (Rokeach, 1970, p. 124).

Brockriede also notes that an argument offers "a perceived rationale to support that [inferential] leap." Argumentation emphasizes a rhetorical process in which arguers persuade through justifications and reasons for their points of view. The reasons appear in the form of support for, and criticism of, a claim as arguers attempt to gain adherence and reach agreement. Reason-giving, comprising part of a "perceived rationale," may make explicit value statements as in the case of "competence" in the claim about Tower mentioned above. Even when the explicit statements do not appear, as with the claim "*Satanic Verses* is a slander against the prophet Mohammed," there are values of truth, faith, and God, at least, implied in the statement. So, "any argument involves reasoning and any reasoning can be driven back to a value orientation" (Sillars & Ganer, p. 195).

Each of the other four characteristics of argument also imply that values reside at the center of their rationale. Where there is a choice, there are value decisions to make. The regulation of uncertainty is achieved by adherence to values. When confrontation occurs, there is a difference in values which confront. Finally, the frame of reference which people share can be defined as the values to which a society or community adheres.

Where Are Values In Argument?

Writing in *The New Rhetoric*, Perelman and his colleague Madame Olbrechts-Tyteca (1969) contend that "values enter, at some stage or other, into every argument" (p. 75). This leads us to inquire, "where do values enter and what do they do?"

Argumentation is a decision-making process in which arguers give reasons. "Fundamental to this reason-giving activity are the values held by the persons receiving the arguments." These values are arranged in "receiver-oriented systems." These audience value systems "provide a basis for finding the issues." Furthermore, values may function as claims, grounds, backing and especially warrants. They "are essential supports in any argument situation" (Rieke & Sillars, 1984, p. 107). "Social values," Sillars & Ganer (1982) observe, "are the best starting point for evaluating public argumentation" (p. 185). They occur as the basis of common ground so essential to the resolution of argumentative disputes (p. 189). Values serve as premises which link the argument and the audience (pp. 194-96).

This analysis suggests that values are important to argumentation in a variety of ways. First, values help arguers select claims and locate important issues. Second, values can serve as any part of an argument, including the claim, the grounds, or the warrant. They appear as the reasons for positions taken and decisions advocated. Third, values provide potential or actual common ground between arguers. They link arguments with audience. Fourth, values offer critics a means for scrutinizing public argument.

So, values are fundamental to argument and are found in all parts of the argumentation process. Still missing, though, are the conceptual tools for analyzing issues from a value perspective. Perelman provides these with his comprehensive and interactive system for understanding how values are structured, evaluated and related to audiences.

Where Do Arguments Start?

An understanding of argumentation begins, for Perelman, with its starting points. These appear in two separate groups of three. All depend for their power on the audience addressed but they have different levels of probability. Facts, truths, and presumptions are a part of what Perelman has identified as "reality." That is, they depend upon audience adherence but the adherence is so strong that no reasonable person doubts them (Perelman & Olbrechts-Tyteca, 1969, pp. 67-74). For example, no one doubts that George Bush is president of the United States (a fact), that the earth revolves around the sun (a truth), or that a person is innocent until proven guilty (a presumption). These claims usually do not need proving; therefore, they are not arguments. Rather they serve as grounds or warrants for proving argumentative claims. For instance, the argumentation of those who favored John Tower's nomination included the claim that charges about his excessive use of alcohol were based on lies, innuendo and unsupported claims. So, the argument went, he should be confirmed because of a presumption of innocence unless there was substantial proof of guilt.

As soon as someone contests a claim, it requires support. Consequently, there are no facts or truths in the commonly used sense of these terms. Even "facts" may require affirmation. For Perelman, as these become argumentative subjects they become openly value-oriented. Note that the definition of argument we began with in all six of its characteristics implies or states that a choice must be available. The third characteristic explicitly states: "a choice among two or more competing claims." The statement, "George Bush is president of the United States" is accepted as a fact. There is no choice, no competing claim; hence, there is no argument. However, the statement might serve as support as in the argument "John Tower should be confirmed as Secretary of Defense because he is George Bush's choice and the president has a right to choose his own cabinet."

When a fact, truth, or presumption becomes argumentative, and therefore value-oriented, it becomes one of the second group of three starting points that comprise key concepts in Perelman's theory of values: (1) values, (2) hierarchies, (3) loci.

What Is The Framework Of Values?

When Perelman published his first treatise on justice in 1945, he concluded that the value underlying justice was not subject to reason (1963, pp. 56-7). Dissatisfied with this conclusion, Perelman inquired: "Is there a logic of value judgments that makes it possible for us to reason about values instead of making them depend solely on irrational choices, based on passion, prejudice, and myth?" (1979, p. 8). Perelman answered his own question by developing a nonformal "logic" of practical reasoning, which enlarged "the domain of reason to encompass a rhetorical rationalism that allows for a pluralism of values and a multiplicity of ways of being reasonable" (Dearin, 1969, p. 214).

Perelman's theory of practical reasoning—his "new rhetoric"—emphasizes a pluralism wherein people use argument as a means of justifying claims and choosing among claims. He clarifies:

> To admit the possibility of a rational or reasonable justification is at the same time to recognize the practical use of reason. It means that we are no longer limiting reason to a purely theoretical usage (for example, the discovery of truth or error), as Hume wished. To reason is not merely to verify and demonstrate, but also to deliberate, to criticize, and to justify, and to give reasons for and against—in a word, to argue (1980, p. 59).

This theory of practical reasoning features values at the center of the deliberations, criticisms, justifications, and reasons which comprise the argumentative process. Values in argumentation may be understood alone, hierarchically, or as loci.

Values

Perelman draws his definition of values from Louis Lavelle: "The word 'value' applies whenever we deal with 'a break with indifference or with the equality of things, wherever one thing must be put before or above another, wherever a thing is judged superior and its merit is to be preferred'" (1982a, p. 26). "Often, positive or negative values indicate a favorable or unfavorable attitude to what is esteemed or disparaged, without comparison to another object," explains Perelman, noting that "What is described by the terms 'good,' 'just,' 'beautiful,' 'true,' or 'real' is valued, and what is described as 'bad,' 'unjust,' 'ugly,' 'false,' or 'apparent' is devalued" (1982a, p. 26).

In various writings, Perelman identifies a variety of value types. Universal values transcend any particular situation or audience. They are the objects of agreement of the universal audience, a hypothetical group of hearers competent and reasonable with respect to the issues under consideration (Perelman, 1968, p. 31; 1982, p. 17). Referring to universal values as "instruments of persuasion," Perelman (1982a) quotes sociologist Eugene DuPreel: "Spiritual tools totally separated from the material they mold, prior to the moment of using them, and remaining whole after they are used— ready, as before, to be used again" (p. 27).

Thus, for instance, justice, freedom, truth, nature, faith, honesty, are all universal values when viewed in their pure forms. "Do you believe humans deserve justice?" is a question which generates a virtually universal "yes" response in western culture. Universal values, "such as the true, the good, the beautiful, and the just," perform a critical role in argumentation, Perelman (1982a) contends, "because they allow us to present specific values, those upon which specific groups reach agreement, as more determined aspects of these universal values" (pp. 26-27). When values held by an arguer's universal audience become transformed into the specific values of a particular audience, adherence through argument becomes possible.

A recent Public Broadcasting Service (PBS) special, "To What End?" illustrates the universal value—specific value relationship. "To What End?" examines four diverse long-range policies the United States government could advance in order to maintain national security while reducing the risk of nuclear war. The policy options all promote "peace," a universal value. Yet each policy manifests "peace" in ways that emphasize quite different specific values. The first policy, "peace through strength," stresses military superiority, power, and toughness. The second, arms control, regards superiority as impossible to achieve. It features the specific values of negotiation, agreement, and interdependence. Strategic defense, the third option, prizes technology and science and devalues security via treaties. The fourth policy, disarmament, advocates military reduction and unilateral action.

All four options, while cherishing peace, also treasure national security. The latter may also seem to sustain universal agreement and point to a universal value. But Perelman (1982a) surmises that universal values "are the object of universal agreement as long as they remain undetermined. When one tries to make them precise, applying them to a situation or to a concrete action, disagreements and the opposition of specific groups are not long in coming" (p. 27). National security is determined or tied to particular situations and actions and is therefore not universal but specific to a particular group of claims. These specific values are what involve the arguer and the critic of arguments. The policies of the United States government on national security, the right of an author to blaspheme someone's prophet, the fitness of a person to hold public office: these all deal with the specific values that make a claim reasonable.

All the examples of universal values we have used appear as single words (e.g., "peace," "justice," "competence," "freedom," "truth"). While universal values can be expressed as single words and perhaps even as a sentence which identifies their universal character (e.g., "Honesty is a universal value," "Freedom is good"), as soon as the word becomes applied to a situation it loses its universal status. Therefore, it makes sense to say that public argumentation never uses universal values. Still, the concept of universal values serves an important purpose. It reminds us that there is a universal respect for freedom even though there is no similar respect for freedom to run a stop sign. Universal values comprise a repository of adherence on which the arguer draws. Specific values, such as national security and freedom defined in a specific context like freedom from foreign domination, are the material one sees in public argumentation.

These specific values come in two forms: abstract and concrete. Like universal values, abstract values surmount a particular context. Perelman (1982a) posits that abstract virtues are "rules" valid for everyone and for all occasions, such as justice, truthfulness, [and] love of humanity . . ." (p. 28). These examples imply that a specific value may also appear as a universal value. Values such as "justice" and "love of humanity," though, are abstract rather than universal to the degree that they are controversial, arguable, and involve choice when applied to a specific situation.

In contrast, concrete values refer to particular people, groups, institutions, or objects—anything considered a unique entity. Security and freedom are abstract values, while the Flag, The Presidency, and The Church are concrete values. Abstract and concrete values reflect respectively the intangible and the tangible. Enlisting for military service, for example, seems a tangible manifestation of the abstract values of loyalty and duty.

Perelman surmises that argumentation cannot exist without abstract or concrete values. Either can take precedence. "Argumentation is based," he and Olbrechts-Tyteca (1969) explain, "according to the circumstances, now on abstract values, now on concrete values: it is sometimes difficult to perceive the role played by each" (p. 77).

The controversy over Salman Rushdie's *Satanic Verses* provides an interesting example of this interaction of abstract and concrete values. The issue did not involve blasphemy or who was a prophet. Rather, it concerned the appropriateness of the death sentence for Rushdie, the demand that the book not be published or sold, and that existing copies be burned. Economic profit was not an issue, although ironically the Ayatollah Khomeini probably made Rushdie a tidy sum by his pronouncement. Those who opposed the sentence and ban appealed to the abstract value of freedom—freedom of speech and press. Those who supported the Rushdie sentence appealed, perhaps, to the ultimate concrete value—God, and additional concrete values of the prophet and the *Koran*. Linked to these concrete values were abstract values of reverence, truth, and honesty. While, at the same time, the opponents' abstract value of freedom was linked to concrete values of the western legal tradition, the Constitution of the United States and the credibility of authors such as Susan Sontag and Henry Miller.

As a side point, we might note that Perelman (1982a) observes that abstract values are associated mostly with change and reform while concrete values are associated with preserving the status quo (p. 28). Such a view is intriguing but overshadowed for our purposes by the realization that abstract and concrete interact with one another.

Hierarchies

The interaction of values in an argument demonstrates that a value does not exist alone. Arguers will relate a value to other values and achieve adherence more from accepted value associations than through a particular, isolated value. Argument occurs via different value arrangements. "While not denying the possibility of a direct confrontation of values, a modern system of analysis should assist the arguer to select the potential value hierarchies in each issue which will seem most reasonable to the audience" (Sillars, 1973, p. 302).

Perelman's theory of values accentuates hierarchies. Value hierarchies are, Perelman and Olbrechts-Tyteca (1969) clarify, "more important to the structure of an argument than the actual values" (p. 81). A hierarchy exists when an organizing principle orders values. For example, our concern for fellow humans may accord charity and compassion greater importance than equality and justice when deciding whether or not to give aid to Ethiopia. While we may dislike Ethiopia's Marxist form of government and abhor its treatment of its citizens, we act in favor of more important hierarchical values. Our ordering promotes value comparisons, influencing our decision.

Arguers generate reasons for the claims they advance. Value hierarchies provide a key to analyzing salient values and value conflicts in the predispositions of their audiences. These hierarchies lead an arguer to understand how an audience will "weigh" a value or give it importance. "A particular audience is characterized less by which values it accepts than by the way it grades them,'' Perelman and Olbrechts-Tyteca (1969) explain, "the audience admits principles by which values can be graded" (p. 81). They note that studying values in isolation, independent of their practical use in argument, "may neglect the question of their hierarchy, which solves the conflicts between them" (p. 82).

Arguers and arguer-critics (including audiences) can better understand argumentation and its pertinent values by considering hierarchies. A defender of aid to the Nicaraguan Contras, speaking to a skeptical liberal college audience, might try to create a hierarchy that ties the values the audience holds (e.g., knowledge, struggle, freedom, independence, human rights) to financial support for the Contra cause. Critics can examine hierarchies by considering the hierarchies an arguer intends and by identifying hierarchies a given audience might perceive and accept.

Critical to the understanding of a value hierarchy is the identification of its organizing principle. Wallace (1972) remarks that Perelman's value theory emphasizes "the structuring and ordering of values, and the notion of order in turn underlies what people regard as better or worse, superior or inferior, more or less" (p. 388). Supporters of capital punishment, for example, value life. In the case of capital crimes, though, they invoke a "better or worse" hierarchy that places greater importance on the victim's life and retribution than on the life of the criminal.

Hierarchies may follow an argument principle, such as precedence or presumption. The latter, Perelman (1982a) writes, is associated with "what can be reasonably counted upon" and with "the idea that what happens is normal" (p. 25). Tradition, normalcy, reasonability, and predictability may, as presumptive values, serve as organizing constructs. Defenders of the present system may urge us to "not rock the boat" or proclaim, "if it ain't broke, don't fix it," inferring that we decide a value conflict according to tradition. A university tuition increase, for example, may be accompanied by an argument claiming that such action is inevitable, regular, and necessary.

Hierarchies can order other hierarchies. Arguers may contest values by suggesting their preference of one hierarchy over another. Such a preference might be shown by organizing values according to an undisputed value or hierarchy. A value hierarchy arranged according to the "collective good" could subordinate a group of values organized by "personal success." These "double hierarchies," Perelman and Olbrechts-Tyteca (1969) propose, become justified through discovering "a relationship between the two hierarchies based on reality" (p. 338). Perelman (1955) explains that the double hierarchy "can be used in all cases where there exists a relationship similar to that which we establish between a person and his acts, relationship between a group and its members, between a style and works of art, between an epoch and the events or institutions which characterize it, between the substance and the acts which are its expression'' (p. 801). This commentary implies that hierarchies can be ordered, placing one within another.

The dispute over the use of animals in scientific research illustrates this concept. The controversy involves interdependent, competing hierarchies. Animal rights activists and defenders of animal use in scientific and medical research both value life and shun cruelty. Within a system of values promoting life, each group includes a very different hierarchy. Animal rights activists extend a ''right to life'' to animals, and contend that animal research is cruel and inhumane. Animal experimentation advocates, in their value hierarchy, distinguish human life from animal life, stressing that animal research leads to scientific discoveries that save human lives. For these people, not conducting animal experimentation would be cruel and inhumane to those humans whose lives might be prolonged or sustained through advances in medical research.

The concept of hierarchy does not necessarily provide arguers with a means for resolving value conflicts such as those imbedded in the animal experimentation controversy. Still, hierarchies are important because they help arguers and critics comprehend the relationship of one set of values to other values. Perelman's concept of hierarchy also indicates that, through argument, new hierarchies can appear providing new value arrangements that promote agreement.

The agreement worked out in the spring of 1989 between a Democratic Congress and the Bush Administration on aid to the Contras offers a good example of this resolution. A proposal emerged, agreed to by Republicans and Democrats alike, that provided humanitarian (medicine, food, clothing, etc.) aid to the Contras while working to give the Arias peace plan supported by the central American countries a chance to succeed.

Congress passed a version of this same agreement during Ronald Reagan's presidency, but the Administration never actually accepted the proposal. Instead, it worked through a variety of means to provide illegal military assistance, leading to the Iran-Contra hearings and the trial of Colonel Oliver North. So, the values of humanitarianism, peace, cooperation and negotiation implied by the idea were not accepted by one side. Force and the over-throw of the Sandinista government were still considered essential to America's peace and security. The agreement made in the spring of 1989 supported contingencies of stronger action should the adopted plan fail, but it also represented an agreement by all the parties to a common hierarchy of values.

Loci

In analyzing an argumentative situation, critics will look for the values which explicitly or implicitly support or refute the claim. More than that, they will search out the hierarchy of values implied in the argument and look for the principle by which that hierarchy is organized. Finally, they will seek its evaluative principle. The available evaluative principles Perelman calls "loci." Initially referring to this idea as "schemata," Perelman (1955) proposes that the justification of value judgments "will resort to argumentative schemata," something "no real argument about values can do without" (pp. 800-801). In a refinement of this concept, Perelman (1982a) recasts schemata as loci of the preferable (Aristotle called them topics). He distinguishes between general and specific loci: "General loci are affirmations about what is presumed to be of higher value in any circumstances whatsoever, while special loci concern what is preferable in specific situations" (pp. 29-30).

The concept of loci can be understood by considering how people determine their preferences. Perelman, in a variety of writings, answers by delineating six loci of the preferable. The first locus, quantity, is premised on what is good for the greatest number, what is normative, and what is common to all. According to this locus, arguers base their preferences on how many can benefit the most. The second locus, quality, reflects what is unique, exceptional, original, individual, irreparable, and immediate. If quality is the foundation, the arguer's preferences will correspond to an important attribute or to the degree of "goodness" they perceive. Order, the third locus, mirrors a principle, goal, or cause. It suggests that preferences pertain to the arguer's aspirations. The fourth locus, the existent, prefers the concrete over the possible. Following this locus, the arguer would choose the tangible and real entity over something hypothetical. Essence, the fifth locus, bases preference on the superiority of those who represent the core of the group or class. Preference drawn from the final locus, of the person, considers the superiority of what is related to the dignity and autonomy of the person. In other words, the quality of a person guides the preference (see Cox, 1980, pp. 3-4; Perelman, 1979, pp. 159-63; 1982a, pp. 28-31; Perelman & Olbrechts-Tyteca, 1969, pp. 83-99).

These six bases of preference—quantity, quality, order, existence, essence, and the person—provide principles on which a value hierarchy may be organized. Values identify our preferences, hierarchies organize them, and loci offer us the standards for these preferences. If an arguer values friendship, for example, loci found in the argument could lead a critic of that argument to determine how friendship is being evaluated: by the number of friends or by the strength, vitality, and authenticity of friendships?

Loci aid in the interpretation of the use of societal values in public argument. Cox (1982) remarks that they are the "basis for our interpretation of general values in situated moments of decision and action" (p. 21). Arguers use the loci of preference to choose among values. When deciding, for example, whether or not to support President George Bush's nomination of John Tower as the Secretary of Defense, some opposing Senators argued values tied to quality, determining that Tower's past behavior was irreparable and that his case was unique. Some supporters related salient values to order, believing that Senator Tower best met their goal of strong leadership at the Pentagon.

Values permeate argument, hierarchies organize values, and loci order hierarchies and serve as a basis for choosing among values and hierarchies. Loci become meaningful in an argumentative situation; the situation guides our choices concerning the grounding of preference. One cannot say, for example, whether the greatest good for the most people or the uniqueness of a particular event should become the basis for decisions about values. In Perelman and Olbrechts-Tyteca's (1969) words, "all that pertains to the preferable, that which determines our choices and does not conform to a preexistent reality, will be connected with a specific viewpoint which is necessarily identified with a particular audience, though it may be a large one" (p. 66). The situation dictates the voice of the loci. Perelman and Olbrechts-Tyteca further explain that "the argumentative situation, which is essential for the choice of the loci, embraces both the goal the speaker has set for himself and the arguments he may encounter . . . in some cases it will be clear that the choice is being influenced by the attitude of the opponent; in others, on the contrary, we will clearly see the connection between the choice of the loci and the desired action" (p. 96).

The Pacific Northwest forestry policy dispute over the spotted owl exemplifies the interrelationship among values, hierarchies, and loci. The dispute centers on whether or not the spotted owl, an allegedly endangered species, deserves protection at the possible expense of the timber industry.

There are three fundamental players in the dispute, each with different value systems and preferential bases. The environmentalists' views correspond with a locus of quality. They believe that the spotted owl's ecological value is unique and irreplaceable. Consequently, they value protection, beauty, ecological balance, and the sanctity of each species.

The loggers base their position on the locus of quantity and order. They see protection of a small number of spotted owls as a threat to their livelihood and the economy of the region. The loggers value their jobs, providing for their families, and generating revenues for the communities in which they reside. Logging, they believe, rather than protecting the spotted owl, serves the interests of the greatest number of people.

The U.S. Forest Service, a third player, relies on a locus of existence. The Forest Service, responding to pressure from both environmentalists and loggers, emphasizes the concrete, the factual. Therefore, the Forest Service values research in order to determine the ecological and economic impact of a particular decision. In the abstract, all three parties value the environment, the economy, and endangered species such as the spotted owl. In the argumentative situation, though, different loci and hierarchies lead to contrasting positions and decisions.

How Do The Audience and
The Critic Influence Argument?

The spotted owl controversy, as well as the other examples presented in this discussion of values, hierarchies, and loci, suggests the importance of two other dimensions of Perelman's new rhetoric and theory of values: the audience and the critic's role. Just as values lack meaning in isolation, so, too, do Perelman's notions of values depend on the nature of the audience and the role the critic takes in evaluating the argumentative situation.

The Audience

Values in argumentation have little meaning without consideration of the audience to whom they are addressed. The concept of audience comprises a decisive and fundamental part of Perelman's new rhetoric (Fisher, 1986, p. 87). Regardless of the arguer's message, the audience grants or denies adherence. What characterizes the new rhetoric, Perelman (1968) explains, "is a fundamental concern with the opinions and values of the audience the speaker addresses, and more particularly with the intensity of this audience's adherence to each of the theses invoked by the speaker" (p. 18). The analysis of argument requires an examination of the audience(s) invoked, for in the audience the critic of argument will locate meaningful values. Perelman (1967), in fact, regards values apart from an audience as absolute and not arguable.

From Perelman's perspective, adherence can be sought from a single hearer through dialogue or from an audience of many. Noting the difficulty of gaining adherence from a diverse and varied audience, Perelman (1968) recommends that the arguer "simplify his task by addressing discourse to the type of audience chosen at the outset" (p. 19). Consequently, the audience of many frequently becomes focused as a specialized group. The audience addressed remains most authentic in the mind of the speaker. The nature of the audience addressed "does not depend on the number of persons who hear the speaker, but upon the speaker's intention: does he want the adherence of some or every reasonable being?" (Perelman, 1982a, p. 18). In other words, the speaker may address a particular audience or the universal audience.

The particular audience is real; the universal audience ideal. The particular audience consists of the listeners a speaker intends to address. It may include, in Campbell's (1982) terms, "the empirical audience (those exposed to the rhetorical act), the target audience (the . . . audience at whom the act is aimed), and the agents of change (those who . . . can make changes)" (p. 71).

The universal audience has received considerable scholarly attention (e.g., Anderson, 1972; Beatty, 1983; Croghan, 1988; Ede, 1981; Fisher, 1986; Golden, 1986; McKerrow, 1977; Ray, 1978; Scult, 1976, 1985). This discussion certainly does not replace these analyses. The universal audience includes, in a general sense, "all of humanity, or at least all of those who are competent and reasonable'' (Perelman, 1982a, p. 14). More concisely, the universal audience ''is thought to include all [persons] who are competent with respect to the issues that are being debated'' (Perelman, 1968, p. 21).

The phrase, ''with respect to the issues being debated,'' makes it possible to universalize a particular audience as a type of universal audience. Perelman and Olbrechts-Tyteca (1969) discuss the scientist as an example:

> The scientist addresses himself to certain particularly qualified men, who accept the data of a well-defined system consisting of the science in which they are specialists. Yet, this very limited audience is generally considered by the scientist to be really the universal audience, and not just a particular audience. He supposes that everyone with the same training, qualifications, and information would reach the same conclusion (p. 34).

The concept of the universal audience may appear to be some kind of a mystical entity. It confuses some students of argumentation because Perelman has called it the audience ''that philosophers always claim to be addressing'' (1969, p. 31). But, think about it for a moment. No one can address a particular audience in all its particulars. Imagine a particular audience of forty-seven men and sixteen women. What kinds of men or women? With what politics? Married? Children? etc., etc., etc.? So, the particular audience has to be conceived of in its universal manifestation. The arguer seeks to get adherence from an audience whose values, hierarchies and loci may be understood in an interaction between what is known of the particular audience and what can be surmised about its universal characteristics.

As the Committee on the Nature of Rhetorical Invention concludes (with Perelman's endorsement): ''Most important, the task is not as often assumed, to address either a particular audience or a universal audience, but in the process of persuasion to adjust and then to transform the particularities of an audience to universal dimensions'' (Perelman, 1984a, p. 192). The critic, too, can contemplate the reverse, particular manifestations of the universal audience.

This interpretation of the universal audience is made with the full realization that Perelman has seemed to contradict it (Perelman, 1984a, pp. 192-93). Some argumentation, he asserts, is addressed only to a particular audience. That may be true for a speaker's intent as in Perelman's example of ''a young man [who] . . . tries to persuade a young woman to marry him'' (p. 193). The young man's objectives are particular but there is a complex system of conventions which have characteristics of the universal audience. So, despite Perelman's apparent explanation, the young man in his example could universalize his audience. In preparing to persuade the young woman, he will most likely consider arguments appropriate to all young women, or all young women similar to the one he *intends* to ask. But, even if the young man *intends* to speak to his lover and to her alone, the critic observing the argumentation in a somewhat less passionate frame of mind can see universal characteristics.

In preparing a speech to students that calls for increased student financial support of intercollegiate athletics, the speaker can analyze the particular, immediate audience, perhaps a public speaking class with twenty students in it of different genders, majors, politics, and athletic interests. The speaker can also envision a universal equivalent of that audience, an ideal audience of students, all reasonable hearers competent to decide the issue. The particular audience represents the reality the speaker encounters; the universal audience can serve as an audience the speaker strives for, or under ideal circumstances, hopes to create. Both audiences are sources of values, hierarchies, and loci that must be adapted to if adherence is to be gained. But, even if the speaker does not consider the universal characteristics of audiences, the critic must.

The Critical Role

Whether a person is directly engaged in criticizing the argument of others or seeks to make an argument designed to gain the adherence of others, that person is a critic. To make an argument of maximum adherence, the arguer must look for strengths and weaknesses in the arguments of self and others. So, the critical function is central to argument. It provides the basis upon which values, hierarchies and loci are related to audiences, particular and universal.

The initial step in observation and criticism, says Willard, (1979b), concerns "perspective taking," or the adoption of a particular stance (p. 218). An arguer, either as speaker, listener, or critical observer, adopts a persona or role in relating audience to argument and situation (Campbell, 1982, p. 20). Writes Perelman, (1961), "We often forget that criticism implies some qualification in the critic . . ." (p. 48).

The role a person takes in acting as a critic will reflect that person's view of the values adopted. Although the possible roles are not limited to those Perelman describes, the four he has presented illustrate the idea developed here. They are the roles of judge, arbiter, legislator and philosopher.

The judge decides issues on the basis of community norms. "A judge who is accorded a power of evaluation in performing his duties must not follow his subjective views," Perelman (1979) explains, "but rather try to reflect those shared by the enlightened member of the society in which he lives and by the views and traditions prevailing in his professional milieu" (p. 67). The critic as judge analyzes arguments as they pertain to the values of the community, examining similar cases for guidance.

While the judge considers community values, the arbiter looks to the values in the dispute and of the disputants. According to Perelman (1967), "The ideal arbiter will be he whose sense of equity is guided by the same values, the same principles, and the same procedures as the litigants before him. . . . The desired impartiality is not just an absence of prejudgment; it is an active commitment to common norms and values" (p. 74). The arbiter considers values of a defined community; a community of the disputants and who they may represent (e.g., the constituencies in a labor-management dispute).

Like a judge, the legislator bases decisions on social community values. But in contrast, the legislator's actions may generate new rules and community values. "A just legislator," Perelman (1967) suggests, "looks for rules which, while not favoring a particular side, seek to realize the values and the ends that correspond to the aspirations of the whole community" (p. 75). The legislator assesses values in terms of their future implications.

Lastly, Perelman proposes the critical role of philosopher. The philosopher strives for the adherence of the universal audience (Kluback and Becker, 1979). Perelman (1967) stresses that the philosopher-critic "must look for criteria and principles and formulate values and norms that are capable of winning the adherence of all reasonable men" (pp. 75-76).

Perelman's four roles illustrate how a particular critical perspective influences value decisions. The judge acts according to societal values, rules, and laws. The arbiter bases decisions on the values of the immediate community of disputants. The legislator employs social norms and values to guide the establishment of new rules and policies. The philosopher appraises issues in accordance with the values of a universal community.

No one perspective is best, and others can be imagined. Regardless, people do not enter into argumentative situations as "blank slates." They hold critical orientations that influence their evaluations of audiences, the appropriate system of values, and the preferential bases of judgment. Even Perelman's theory is not value free. When he speaks of society it is a democratic society with justice as a central value (1982a, p. 10; pp. 67-68). So, from starting points to final judgment, argumentation is value oriented.

Conclusion

Values are implied by all the characteristics which Brockriede (1975) identified for argument. Furthermore, values appear at every stage in the argumentation process. They are used by arguers to identify issues and choose claims, serve as any part of an argument, link argument and audience, and offer a means for assessing public argument. In this discussion, we have tried to show how this reality can become operational. It is our view that Perelman's comprehensive theory of values provides the basis for seeing how values actually function in argumentation. Facts, truths, and presumptions are potential starting points of argument but only if they are problematic. In their usual form they are accepted as is and serve, therefore, only as evidence to support claims. When they become controversial, they serve as the starting point of a stated or implied value argument.

To understand what happens in argumentation one must observe what kinds of values are being used. The universal values when adapted to a problematic situation become specific values that are found in abstract and concrete forms. These are organized into hierarchies and identified by a locus (or evaluative principle) to define the anatomy of an argumentative situation.

The argumentation in turn needs to be related to the particular audience and its value structure to understand the potential for adherence. That potential for adherence is located in the particular audience but most frequently realized by the universal audience of persons "competent with respect to the issues that are being debated" (Perelman, 1968, p. 21).

Finally, any analysis of values requires that one consider the critical perspective of the person making the analysis. Thus, from starting points to final judgment, values determine what happens in argumentation. We have, in this chapter, engaged in argumentation. But this argumentation has not only been *about* values. It has been value oriented itself. Those who make arguments and those who criticize them have values at the core of what they do.

Perelman's values framework suggests a variety of interrelated questions central to the analysis of values in public argumentation. Together, they lead us to appreciate the complex argumentative situation. The questions include: What is the nature of our audience? What is the universal equivalent of our particular audience? What is our critical stance? What role will we adopt in relationship to the audience, the speaker, the situation, or the subject? What values does the audience hold? How do these relate to the values we believe important? What value hierarchies appear important to the audience? How do these correspond with our hierarchies? Upon what factors will the listeners likely base their preferences? How do these preferential foundations, or loci, compare with ours?

Answering these questions may not be easy, but using Perelman's concepts of values, hierarchies, loci, audience, and critical role as focal points for analyzing an argumentative situation will help us to understand the nature of public argumentation better. Values and their companion concepts comprise a significant part of any public discussion, whether the issues concern a presidential cabinet nomination, defense policy, animal rights, or increasing tuition. Perelman's ideas illuminate values in public argumentation.

Chapter Eleven

Eisenhower's Farewell
The Epistemic Function
of Argument

Robert L. Scott

I tell you the generations
Of man are a ripple of thin fire burning
Over a meadow, breeding out of itself
Itself, a momentary incandescence
Lasting a long time, and we that blaze
Now, we are not the fire, for it leaves us.
(Archibald MacLeish, "The Pot of Earth,"1925)

We should not simply recognize but celebrate the marvelous ambiguity of "argument." When one has "an argument," one may have (1) a reason for a conclusion, (2) a reason and a conclusion, (3) a process for drawing conclusions generally, (4) an extended communicative interchange with another person or persons, or (5) a relatively brief instance from an extended interchange. If these alternatives were from a multiple choice examination of the familiar sort, we could add quickly "all of the above" to the list since we have arguments within arguments.

Although the phenomenon of ambiguity is common to words in any natural language, we often act as if ambiguity were a defect; that is, we seek to correct it. We circle "offensive" words in a paper and perhaps jot "ambiguous" in the margin. In technical papers, we often stipulate a definition or create an operational definition to stabilize, as it were, the meaning of a term.

Mr. Scott is Professor of Speech Communication at the University of Minnesota, Minneapolis.

We should recognize in activities like stipulating or operationalizing definitions the advantages that ambiguity offer. The invitation to narrow meaning—
that is, counting out some referential possibilities—often allows us to count
on some of the potencies inherent in the more pervasive human responses
to the term. Attention, initial interest, agreement-for-the-sake-of-argument
(as the phrase goes) are all at least momentary advantages that one may gain
in the act of reducing ambiguity.

Suggesting that the senses of argument may be discussed as three: argument
as a creative act, argument as a critical act, and argument as a logical act,
might be accorded agreement with emphatic for-the-sake-of-argument. Anyone
agreeing in that spirit might raise at least two questions: Are they exhaustive?
Are they mutually exclusive? The answer to both questions is "no." All the
senses may be present simultaneously, and one may think of other senses
of "argument." These separable but not separate senses are useful in
understanding argument. This assertion may immediately raise another
question: Useful? On what grounds? Let us hold that question in mind while
proceeding.

In most of its common senses, argument may be taken as a communicative
activity. The most primitive model of communication is that someone says
something to someone with some effect. Putting aside the question of effect,
this primitive model has grown into various representations of a *sender*, a
message, and a *receiver*. With these three elements as basic, modelers of
communication often present as attendant or subsidiary the functions of
channel, *noise*, *feedback*, and *content*.

To study anything we must take a point of view and would do well to
recognize that point of view. Argument could be construed as a creative act
from the point of view of the sender of a message and as a critical act from
the point of view of the receiver of a message. This analysis seems to suggest
that considering the message as such is to take argument as a logical act, thus
completing the three-quasi equations of argument and communication. The
third equation seems to contradict the assumption with which the paragraph
begins, for it posits a point-of-viewless starting place, unless one conceives
a detached observer—someone standing outside the communicative circle.
The detached observer, on the other hand, must in some sense be part of the
communicative situation or would remain ignorant of it, that is, would not
be an observer at all.

The notion of a detached observer is usually taken to mean the point of
view of someone who has no immediate interest in the outcome, in this case
of the outcome of communication. A good deal of weight is thrown onto the
word "immediate" since the observer must have some sort of interest to be
an observer at all. Further, that interest is often taken as privileged, which
is to say that the detached observer is in a better position, a superior position,
to draw conclusions than are more immediately interested observers. Even
if accepting the notion of such an observer, one would be well advised to

take care of the sort of conclusions that the observer would draw and to be aware of the ethos that may be implicitly claimed in this position.

The purpose in this chapter is to throw into question the ways we look at argument and in doing so to reconceptualize arguing as inevitably active communication. We shall pursue the quasi-equation that argument as a critical act equals the point of view of the receiver of communication, but, since the three equations suggested are not independent, we must in some ways involve the other two points of view.

Most emphatically, the point of view of the message itself will insert its power ironically into the critical perspective. The result will be to see the truism of contemporary discussions of communication—"Words do not mean, people mean" as a half truth. People do mean, but so do words.

The claim here is that some of what we call knowledge is created in communicative interaction. The first task of the critic is to understand the arguments that make up knowledge. The second task of the critic is to judge the arguments. The third task of the critic is to change roles, that is, to cease to function as a critic and to function in other ways. Those "other ways" vary, but central to the consideration of argument as epistemic is the role of advocate. As advocates, critics assume constructive roles toward the larger social units of which they are parts, taking responsibility of maintaining the integrity of those units by striving with others to establish the ground for their further development.

In the impetus to switch roles, however, critics recognize the existence of argument as such. Even when willing to modify the reality of the arguments that make up some aspect of the world they engage, critics grant, as it were, an integrity to that world that lies outside themselves.

Perhaps this case study will clarify to some extent the interaction between critic and argument.

If a newly inaugurated President of the United States were to refuse to make a speech upon the occasion, that would be remarkable, although an inaugural address is not required by law. With no oath taken, no president; but the speech is simply a matter of custom. On the other hand, although the first president made a well known "Farewell Address," a tradition of such speeches has not been as fully established as inaugurals.

Nonetheless on the event of his leaving the presidency, Dwight David Eisenhower made a rather remarkable speech. It was televised in the evening of January 17, 1961, in what we now call "prime time." I predict that the televised interview David Brinkley conducted with President Ronald Reagan in December 1988 will not be long remembered even though a farewell interview on television could become something of a postmodern tradition. Eisenhower's speech, on the other hand, gave a fresh sense of reality to a very old observation, that is, some persons profit in the preparation for war. Such an observation enlivened the dramatic conflict in Bernard Shaw's 1905 play *Major Barbara*. In the play, the munitions maker, Sir Andrew Undershaft, pushes the lineage of cooperation between those who make arms and those who make war, or at least prepare for it, back for centuries before the British learned to think of German industrialists as part of a dangerous mix of business and government.

Eisenhower's observation, however, burst onto a startled America as fresh. It gave to successive generations a way of thinking about varied realities they sensed in a new term: the military-industrial complex.

Eisenhower's speech has had a continuing and many faceted life of quotation, analysis, and allusion since January 17, 1961; I shall concentrate on the immediate impact of the speech, on the use of the phrase "military-industrial complex" in enabling many claims during the protests of the Vietnam war and, finally, on the role of the speech in helping to fuel arguments about arms control and especially its recent revival.

I shall not bother with the question of who invented the key phrase, although the struggle for ownership is sometimes amusing and perhaps in itself significant. Nor shall I be concerned with the problem of tracing in Eisenhower's earlier career the thought that inspired the Farewell.

It seems to me that a broad sort of consensus has formed recently among critics of communication. Although they work along different lines and certainly disagree in many details, that argument, although certainly being spoken or written or displayed by individuals, takes on a life of its own not independent of arguers but more than what one would take as the additive value of their statements (Bormann, 1985; Fisher, 1987; McKee, 1980). With Eisenhower's speech, terms with which to think came into being. Our meaningful lives are results of constant interpretations of what we are pleased to call "reality." Eisenhower's speech, with the phrase the "military-industrial complex," simply gives us an especially dramatic example that what we call "argument" at some times and "exposition" at others is the constant effort by individuals to make meaning and, more, that individuals constantly interact with one another, not content that their meaning be wholly private, needing cooperation and verification in the sociality that is as real as individuality.

Just as the bodies in any room produce heat that becomes a part of the atmosphere of the room in which all are living, that atmosphere being as real as any person in the room, arguments produce the residues that are themselves part of the sociality in which people live and interpret themselves and others as real.

What I am saying, again, is that the old half-truth "meaning is in people not in words" is indeed half true. It is useful to remind ourselves that the *proper meaning fallacy* is a fallacy and that we can erect a verbal ritual to exorcise it, but meaning is also in words, and those words often give us lively examples of a constant though changing relationship of existence to experience.

In short, rhetoric is epistemic, even though we shall continue to struggle to interpret that sentence until we become bored with it (Scott, 1967; 1976). But our boredom, though it may quicken our impulses to find different phrases to try to make commensurate with our experiences, will not obviate our constant activity as interpreters and makers of reality.

Let's return to Eisenhower's speech to illustrate the epistemic function of argument. Perhaps I should confess that I was no fan of Dwight D. Eisenhower's when he ran for the presidency in 1952, nor was I in 1961 when his second term ended. I shared the opinion that he had been fundamentally an ineffectual president and shared the jokes about his ineptness. Recently, however, I have found myself with a growing sense of admiration for his leadership. Although one would scarcely describe his style as "confrontational," Eisenhower had a way of laying things out, not neutrally but in intensely persuasive fashion, leaving the question open and inviting participation, even though his position may have been clear. He seemed to work from the premise that not only must agreement be voluntary, but that any issue needed the sort of willing agreement that would engage the abilities of respondents to be active in creating meaningful assent.

I probably attribute too much to him and undoubtedly have signalled to a fair extent my reading of his speech. But I would make two observations. First, faced with a rather constant questioning later about what his farewell speech meant or why he made a farewell speech, Eisenhower rarely commented beyond saying simply that he wanted to say goodbye to the American people as a person who had long served them. The importance of that statement can be too easily waived and was, but I assert that there is a genuine regard and even love in his response and in the broader purpose that I have attributed to him generally. And second, the general conviction that seems to me to animate his public life and his speaking (that open, willing, knowledgeable assent is vital to the life of a democracy) is altogether consistent with the common characterization of his speech as a warning.

It is as a warning that his words have enlivened persistent controversies. As such, the whole is represented by its part, the military-industrial complex:

> In the councils of government, we must guard against the acquisition of unwarranted influence, whether sought or unsought, by the military-industrial complex. The potential for the disastrous rise of misplaced power will persist (*New York Times*, 18 January 1961).

For me the more significant warning came just a few hundred words later when, after speculating that Federal employment could compromise the freedom of the nation's scholars, Eisenhower said,

> Yet, in holding scientific research and discovery in respect, as we should, we must also be alert to the equal and opposite danger that public policy could itself become the captive of a scientific-technological elite (*New York Times*, 18 January 1961).

But it is the former specter that haunts us. As with fears generally, we seem to primp before the idea of a military-industrial complex, bidding it, as Hamlet did his father's shadow, to come forth, make itself known, and confirm our suspicions.

The guises in which it has been known, using somewhat arbitrary divisions, are at least three.

1. The Military-Industrial Complex Lives

Immediately, Eisenhower's speech became a signal for many to take the military-industrial complex as a fact. Although we like to say "the facts speak for themselves," we rarely are content to fall silent having said so (Scott, 1968). Although the dots on the page of a children's book can be taken as facts, lines must be drawn from one to another to show what the face in them only partly revealed "really" looks like. Of course different commentators on "the facts" may connect the dots differently.

In an early, and very well known depiction of the military-industrial complex, Fred J. Cook (1961) heralded the warfare state. Called into being by the Cold War, an American Juggernaut was fueled ideologically by the John Birch Society, whose spokespersons were supported eagerly by industrialists specializing in defense contracts. "And one thing is now certain," Cook wrote, "however bad the situation might have been that seemed threatening to Ike, the future, with many more billions at stake, is almost certain to be infinitely worse" (p. 281).

Another writer for *The Nation*, Jerry Greene (1961), starts with the industrialists but quickly warns that the complex is much more complex than a few, large arms suppliers—the influence of intertwining interests sweeps up workers and local merchants as well. The lobbyists hired by leading companies are all the more powerful because they represent a tight knotting together of interests that can be given a local habitation and name—that is, a diversity of people unified in being constituents of members of Congress.

Greene's main interest was in showing the tightening cooperation among military officers and arms manufacturers. This line of thinking begged for detail, and reporters were quick to supply it publishing lists of retired military officers hired by defense contractors. One could write a headline that would cover a myriad of newspaper columns, magazine articles, and book chapters: From Arms Buyer to Arms Purveyor. The names and numbers attested to the factualness of the military-industrial complex.

Predictably the is-ness of the complex shifted to an ought-ness, or, rather, to an ought-not-ness: the relationships that were detailed in contacts and contracts did not simply exist (how can one have contracts without contacts?) but were of the sort that should not exist; that is, they were unfair, undemocratic, and wasteful. The military-industrial complex is known by its fruit, and its fruit is rotten. These sorts of claims are detailed not so much by the ever present facts-of-the-matter as by appeals to virtue or to the lack of virtue in terms hallowed by American rhetorical history. Decisions should be made openly and honestly, but decisions about arms systems are being made with influence peddlers operating sub-rosa. The public welfare should come first, but what actually comes first is safe and inflated profits for those with privileged connections, the insiders of the MIC club. Indeed, the military-industrial complex was soon frequently cited in such shortened form. The result, rather than dependable means to defend freedom, is waste and perversion.

The theme of perversion strikes me as especially important and, regardless of what Eisenhower did or did not intend, was invited by his tone of warning reinforced by "unwarranted influence" and "disastrous rise" and "misplaced power." The fundamental charge was that democratic process was being perverted and thus the deepest strength of our society to defend itself was being eroded as the nature of that society as a free society, and therefore worthy of defense, became questionable.

A few saw the essential nature of capitalism as well as democracy perverted. Competition became a sham and the profit motive polluted. An interesting instance of the perversion theme is found in the argument of Seymour Melman (1971) that the freedom of American capitalism has been lost as the military-industrial complex has evolved into something even more nefarious than Eisenhower could have envisioned: state management. "No sooner had Dwight Eisenhower warned the American people and his successor against the combination of military and civilian, industrial, technological and scientific institutions than his successor took office and proceeded to make obsolete the very institution against which President Eisenhower had warned" (p. 7). In Melman's scenario, and he was not alone, the Department of Defense, "the largest industrial management in the United States, probably in the world," has invented "Pentagon Capitalism."

Although Melman saw the demise of the MIC in the birth of something at least faintly communistic, others argued that the constant interpretation of the military-industrial complex was fundamentally the fixation of those leftists who, if they did not actively support the Soviet Union, were deep haters of the free enterprise system. These apologists saw Eisenhower's speech as a simple warning to heed. Although there had, of course, been excesses and mistakes, the warning should have been and had been guarded against.

In spite of some rather potent arguments that I have certainly scanted, the dominant interpretation was that the MIC lives, that its appetite aggrandizes the few at the expense of the many and perverts the basic truths of democracy. In an analysis of what he called war and the philosopher's duty, Warren E. Steinkraus (1968) wrote, "A nation may spend billions defending 'freedom' thousands of miles from its shores while its own citizens are not free from harassment because of skin color or free from the encroachments of a military-industrial complex — which regards itself as a 'bulwark of freedom'" (p. 16). Thus he captures the perversion theme and at the same time takes the life of the MIC as a given. He also brings us to war.

2. The Malignant Spirits of the Vietnam War   (+ book?)

Just as the term "Vietnam" helped many in the struggle for the meaning of U.S. involvement in Nicaragua currently, the term "military-industrial complex" helped others define meaning in confronting Vietnam. As a powerful and malignant presence in American government, industry, and armed forces, the sheer citing of the MIC undercut the claims that freedom, commitment, and human dignity were at stake. Portraying Vietnam as a test of American will in preserving democratic ideals was easily seen as a mask for the self-interest of a profit hungry and power mad elite.

An elite usually has its clients, those whose privileges depend rather directly on the beneficence of those they serve. The MIC was consistently so pictured. What arose has been referred to as the M-I-X-C phenomenon: military, industrial, fill-the-blank complex. Often unions and union leaders were scourged as being hand-in-glove with the "power elite"—an earlier term that found renewed life in these controversies. For many of those who protested the American role in southeast Asia, their colleges and universities housed the malign influence that had polluted what should be a life-giving stream with death and dishonor. The military-industrial-educational complex made the war not something remote and evil but immediate, infusing the very moment with corruption. The protesters were in the belly of the beast.

By the time the first flush of outrage at the North Vietnamese and the enthusiasm for standing up to communism had waned for many and protest was clearly established, the potency of the MIC helped idealize the role of anyone who resisted official positions. But even though the MIC was a monolith for most protesters, I discern an interesting bifurcation of interpretations of its nature. The division may be between older and younger protesters, those with a longer personal history and those with a shorter. If so, the younger were dominant. Those with longer histories had more to account for.

The accounting was quickened by President Richard Nixon's propensity to cite a growing but nonetheless consistent presence of this country in preserving if not the liberty at least the possibility of liberty for South Vietnam and therefore for all of Southeast Asia. He was fond of alluding to and often citing directly John F. Kennedy's decisions deepening and extending military intervention. Many of the older protesters found themselves embarrassed by their past commitment to Kennedy as a renewal of the American spirit. Further, if the invidious MIC now entangled us in Vietnam, why had they not identified and resisted it earlier?

One response, of course, was to admit guilt and seek expiation in the cause of resistance, often admitting at least tacitly the moral superiority of youth. The other was to picture the military-industrial-educational complex not as a sinister conspiracy of greed but rather as a sad mistake—the malaise of democracy gone wrong in a technological era. This vision could take military leaders, corporate executives, members of Congress, and even college deans as sincere but duped not by diabolical leaders but by the course of events to which their understanding and will was incommensurate. Those who demurred these descriptions of themselves could be pitied, scorned, and, if necessary, swept aside for their own good as well as the general good.

If there were a slight struggle in interpreting the MIC as either a dreadfully persistent lack of insight into the consequences of the ordinary commitments of thousands of well intentioned people or as a malevolent conspiracy, that struggle took for granted the existence of a structure of power that subordinated genuine expressions of popular will to the purpose of maintaining its own existence.

3. The Guarantor of Nuclear Terror

During what we now call the Vietnam era and persisting with renewed vigor today is the conviction that the MIC is the chief, if not the sole, impetus in the nuclear arms buildup. Building and deploying an anti-ballistic missile system meant huge profits and extending the connections of influence and dependence throughout vast areas of the nation and many sectors of the economy. The MIC, not the nation, benefited.

In 1985, Jerome B. Weisner, former president of MIT, looked back more than twenty years to claim that "Eisenhower's message reflected his frustration with his inability to control the combined pressures from the military, industry, Congress, journalists, and veterans' organizations for procuring more weapons and against his efforts to seek accommodations with the Soviets. [para.] As a member of Eisenhower's Science Advisory Committee, I saw firsthand how individuals from government and military industries collaborated with members of Congress to defeat the president's efforts" (p. 102). A year later, E.P. Thompson (1986) wrote that "the military services are secondary partners in Star Wars. They do not motivate the program, but they have crowded behind the banner of S.D.I. and are rushing it forward in pursuit of a multitude of longstanding strategic and service interests. Their research designs combine perfectly with the second component, which is an authentic motivating force driving Star Wars forward: the capacity of the military-industrial-academic complex" (p. 234).

Just as in trying to understand Vietnam some analyzed the MIC as a tangled web of self-deceit, so in striving to fathom the failure of American policy to come to grips with nuclear disarmament some see the MIC as a manifestation of a deeper malaise of the national body politic. In this vision, the MIC is but the epiphenomenon of genuine virtues that have become skewed and tangled (see, e.g., Tsipis, 1972). But most who decry the MIC see it as Thompson does: an unholy combination of blind zealotry and willful profiteering. The *New York Times* headlined the MIC in 1982 when reporting on Admiral Hyman Rickover's "swan song" in testifying before Congress. Among other things Rickover said that "business executives were abandoning traditional values in their preoccupation with profits, . . . a trend . . . [that] threatened the nation's free enterprise system" (29 January 1982, p. A17).

As did the *New York Times*, the *Rolling Stone* introduced its report of Rickover's congressional testimony featuring the MIC as a menacing presence that made the Admiral's words the denunciation of an enemy within (1 April 1982). One could read ironically these sorts of accounts as being the McCarthyesque red scare retrofitted. Even more to the point, the *Rolling Stone's* headlining of their story as a "warning" calls up the label given immediately to Eisenhower's farewell. The general, from his deep experience, saw that great threat to our way of life; now the admiral, even more pointedly declaring, "I'm not proud of the role I've played," understands the very existence of nuclear weapons as pushing humankind to the edge of oblivion. "I do not believe that nuclear power is worth it if it creates radiation. Then, you might ask me, why do I have nuclear-powered ships? That's a necessary evil. I would sink them all. Have I given you an answer to your question?"

In Rickover's testimony, especially as it was reported and used, the third person not the first person inspirited the MIC. *They* are the polluters of our values; *their* greed and lust for power denies us our legitimate voice and may extinguish all life.

Although this analysis does compete at every juncture in understanding what and how and why the military-industrial complex is, and although generally the pollution and need for expiation to find redemption is felt strongly, the downward way rather than the upward way dominates. In confronting the evils of the Cold War, Vietnam, and nuclear presence, American dissent has favored scapegoating to mortification.

Eisenhower's "Farewell Address" has lived a fascinating rhetorical life. We see it clearly in three circumstances and could, without much imagination, see it in three times three. In classical terms, the speaker's ethos is key: Eisenhower's great authority, all the more powerful because it takes on the aura of reluctant witness, is an attribute dramatically magnified when Admiral Rickover was brought to testify at the end of his naval career.

The metaphor of *complex*, reinforced by the hyphen, invited participation to fix its mysterious depth. It breathed, "There's more here than meets the eye? What is it?" And since we prefer our mysteries to be created, "Who is behind it?" The openness of the concept issued the M-I-X-C invitation: name the co-conspirator who fits the circumstances you are a part of.

But any entity is a mystery. Taken as it is, *it* simply is, as Kenneth Burke (1952, p. 251) taught us long ago. But can we take anything as it is? *As is* we do not take anything at all. Think of the familiar admonition not to take things out of context. How do we take anything without taking it out of context?

Of course the admonition simply cautions us to be aware of a context, to become familiar enough with the context so that when we do take something, we leave it as intact as possible. Regardless, however, we cannot both uproot something and leave it rooted. "Wholism" is a name often given for some experience of something as whole, but the "whole" that we experience will always be a part of some larger entity. What we have here is the opposite of a so-called "infinite regression." We might call it an "infinite progression" that may hypothetically reach some supposed "everything that is" but which is obviously as impossible to conclude as its opposite.

In recognizing human participation in the very notion of experiencing, we do not deny the existence of things outside ourselves. We only note our participation in experiencing them.

As I said near the outset of this essay, the critic must at some point shift roles, and I have done so. Perhaps it has been clear all along that I am an advocate of the "reality" of the military-industrial complex. It is something that people in our time have had to deal with and will continue to deal with. We have created this reality, but that does not make what we have created any less constitutive of the world in which we live. Through our arguments, we do constitute the environments in which we experience whatever each fresh moment brings and what we bring to these moments.

The "things" around us are not things for us until we give them habitations and names. In these last few paragraphs, I have claimed in effect, that arguments as messages are constitutive, thus giving them a name. The name is chosen to help call to mind the other two names I have used on considering argument from a communicative perspective: the creative and the critical. These three functions of argument have been associated with *sender*, *receiver*, and *message*. Although we may focus on any one of these aspects of communication, taken together they constitute an epistemic function of argument.

Chapter Twelve

Naming and Name Calling as Acts of Definition
Political Campaigns and the 1988 Presidential Debates

Jane Blankenship

Since their modern inception in 1960 during the John F. Kennedy-Richard M. Nixon contest, televised debates have been a part of every presidential campaign (except for 1964-72). They help reinforce voter decisions and may help with late decisions. For example, the night before the first 1988 presidential debate, 37 % of the probable electorate had no preference or could switch allegiance. Not only were well over a third of the prospective voters undecided or weak leaners, but a significant number of likely voters (39%) said that the candidate who performed the best would get their votes. This is not dissimilar to a 1984 poll when prospective voters who saw the debates were asked, "How important would you say the debates were in determining how you will vote in the presidential election?" Sixteen percent answered "Very Important" and 32% answered "Fairly Important" (Swerdlow, p. 179).

The debates also help set the agenda for the media as they report the final phases of the general election campaign. Moreover, the way the media talks about who won and who lost occasionally makes a difference in whom the audience perceives to be the winner. For example in 1976, immediately after

Ms. Blankenship is in the Department of Communication, University of Massachusetts, Amherst. An earlier version of this chapter was presented at a symposium on the 1988 Presidential debates held at the University of Massachusetts in December, 1988. She wishes to thank Maureen Susan Williams, Serafin Mendez-Mendez, and Debra Madigan for their valuable help in preparing this essay.

the Ford-Carter debate, many thought Gerald Ford had "won"; after media analysis, however, far more thought Jimmy Carter was "the winner" (Germond and Witcover, 1985, p. 512).

There are a number of ways of examining political campaigns in general and presidential debates in particular. When addressing political campaigns, one can, for example, focus on a particular presidential campaign (Drew, 1985; Germond & Witcover, 1985; Goldman & Fuller, 1985; Henry, 1985); a particular contest within a campaign such as the Iowa caucuses (Winebrenner, 1987) or the New Hampshire primary (Orren & Polsby, 1987); a particular campaigner, e.g., Gary Hart (Chase, 1986); some major aspect of campaigning such as political advertising (Diamond, 1984; Jamieson, 1984; McClure, 1976; Patterson & McClure), and the like. With political debates, one can, for example, focus on the history of the debates and their likely future (Jamieson & Birdsell 1988); the issue of who should sponsor presidential debates (Swerdlow, 1987); the debates themselves (Bitzer & Reuter, 1980; Kraus, 1962; 1979); an "insider" view of the goals, strategies and tactics of particular debaters (Martel, 1983); the primary debates preceding the general election debates (Blankenship, Fine & Davis, 1983), and the like.

In this chapter, I will attempt to answer two questions: (1) How do we tend to characterize (that is, define) the nature of presidential campaigns in general and presidential debates in particular? (2) How did George Bush and Dan Quayle characterize (that is, define) Michael Dukakis in the 1988 debates? I shall argue, first, that we explicitly characterize our presidential campaigns and the general election debates by a few fundamental metaphors that define them and that these metaphors have implications for the way we perceive and, hence, act toward our political process. Then, I shall argue that in the 1988 general election debates Bush and Quayle explicitly characterized Dukakis by two fundamental terms and that these two "terministic screens" (Burke, 1966) suggested powerful implications which successfully "demonized" their opponent. *Both* acts of definitions (namings) decree that we *view* in one way rather than another, and the implication of these namings suggests arguments *why* we should view that way. In this sense, all namings are arguments from definition.

Characterizing (Defining) the Nature of Presidential Campaigns

Marie Nichols (1971) reminds us that language "is not an objective tool; its symbols are not empty but freighted with the experiences of [people] who are its makers and interpreted by [people] who bring to it the feelings and experiences of their existential selves." If "to understand ourselves, we must study our symbolic behavior" (Wallace, 1970), even a brief examination may prod us to ask: "What does the way the media (and the candidates as reported in the media) talk about (construct) a political campaign tell us about how they have come to view that part of our political process?" As consumers of these metaphors, we may want to go beyond that question to another question: "What do our acceptance of and mindless mimicking of the same set of metaphors tell us about *our* selves?" Elsewhere I (1976; Blankenship & Kang, 1990) have examined the fundamental metaphors deeply embedded in the way the media, candidates and candidate staffs characterize (define) presidential campaigns and the debates therein.

Such studies attempt to provide something of a topological map of our political discourse and speculate about the implications of such a linguistic landscape. In brief, my earlier study suggested that several kinds of metaphors shape much of our talk about (construction of) political campaigns.

Metaphors of general violence, even when those referring to war and contact sports are specifically excluded, dominate our political discussions. Those metaphors are closely followed by metaphors of warfare, sports, games, and show business. Existentially, political campaigns seem to be scenes in which violence is the norm rather than the exception. Flaying is the essential activity, whether the candidates direct it at each other or at the issues. The encounters of the candidates with one another and their tactics are generally violent if not specifically warlike. Moreover the violence is multidirectional; it is directed not only at fellow candidates but at constituencies as well; voters are treated much like a people under siege. Small wonder that after more than a year of bruising battle, not only are the candidates bloodied and impotent but their constituencies are as well. In this scene, there is little place for the careful, reflective consideration of issues during a campaign and little will or capacity for it immediately after a campaign.

There is a gamelike nature to all of this. The carnage is both real and unreal. The favorite sports metaphors (horse races, boxing matches, etc.) are gladiatorial in nature. They are, first of all, largely spectator sports. Few players actually get bloodied and many can watch at a safe distance. Fans not only participate vicariously in the fray but by high-stakes gambling on the outcome, they add dimensions of excitement that applause and lip service alone do not generate. Onlookers are one step closer to the fray but still largely unbloodied.

Politics also often appears to be a genre of show biz, again, more to be watched than participated in. The cast is still predominantly male. Some aspirants try out for their roles and occasionally one has the potential at least of stepping into the starring role without trying out for it. The playbill consists more of musicals ("follies" and the like) and situation comedies (for example, the "Odd Couple") than of serious fare. But, Westerns and cloak-and-dagger capers occasionally are available for divertissements. Scenarios prepared by campaign staffs are rewritten or discarded as the drama is played out before audiences. And, in politics as in show business, comebacks are often more easily dreamed of than enacted.

The near obsession for likenesses is clear. Since the roles in the political process are either ill-defined, unconsidered, or disliked, candidates are seen in terms of something else. They are seen as other people—as cheerleaders, doctors meting out medicines, Clark Kent/Superman, or school boys studying for exams. The range is wide indeed, but most typically, people largely stand at either end of the continuum. Even the piano is only played by a Johnny-one-note or a concert pianist. Thus, our political figures seem either smaller than life or larger than life.

Often, indeed, the political scene is inhabited not by candidates but by animals of all varieties, more domestic than wild. Moreover, it is peopled not by a constituency carefully considering the issues but by coveys and flocks who are corralled or herded into their decisions. Thus, if one does not want to go to gladiatorial games or to the theater, one might well go to the zoo— there, again, mostly to look.

All of these proceedings are viewed not as exceptional but as natural. Candidacies blossom as readily as plants. Even in this category, violent imagery persists; for example, drought, washouts, or earthquakes are the fate of many. Still amid all of the avalanches and floods, some greening persists.

If this represents something of the linguistic "architecture" of our political landscape generally, what, in particular, does linguistic construction of our presidential campaign debates look like? Again, by far the most pervasive metaphor used is a kind of undifferentiated aggression. The candidates do not so much debate or discuss issues as *make hamburger* or *hash* of each other. The debaters: *assail, assault,* and *attack* each other. They *beat up, blast, bloody,* and *blow each other away.* They *clean each others' clocks, clip, clobber, cream,* and *cram it down* one another's *throats.* Just as clearly, the debates are viewed as *war zones* where the *combatants* draw *battle lines,* engage in *ambushes,* fire their *heaviest artillery.* Their *lieutenants, troops,* and *firing squads, hit the ground running, helped hold the fort, exercised damage control,* and *cut losses.*

The debates are also sporting events. In 1984, Walter Mondale needed, depending on the commentator, *at least a base on balls, the longball,* or a *home run.* Some judged that he had *hits but no home run* and thus did not win despite Ronald Reagan's *late inning collapse* in the first debate. Boxing metaphors also dominate the press coverage of presidential campaigns. In 1984, in round one, a *gloves off* fight, the *challenger* had the *champion,* who looked like he had gone *too many rounds with Ali, on the ropes.* Still, there was *no knockout* and, according to *the ring judges,* the challenger was *still behind on points.*

Much has been made out of politics as drama (Combs, 1980; Gronbeck, 1984) or at least as dramatic. It is true, of course, that terms such as *actor, performance, script* and *lines* were used, but the debates seemed to be more specifically "constructed" as *a nice little bit of theatre* rather than *a (high stakes) drama*. The likenesses are more typically to TV and movie characters. In 1984, Bush sounded like a *parody of Jimmy Stewart* set to a *tune of John Phillip Sousa*. The line between reel life and real life, between metaphor and the literal became blurred, indeed. When Reagan faltered in the Louisville debate, the score was reported as *Gipper 0—Fritz 1* because the *Gipper cannot play defense*.

In 1984, of course, there was some acknowledgement that one of the debaters was a woman. Geraldine Ferraro's handlers were not inclined to *play Pygmalion at the eleventh hour*; they did not try to *manicure her idiosyncrasies*. The *tricky task of jousting with a woman without beating up on the lady* fell to Bush. Bush and Ferraro took to *squabbling like the falling leaves* during their *turn in the ring*. Whether they judged Ferraro's performance as a slight win, a draw, or a clear loss, there seemed some consensus that the *Fighter from Philly* did not *walk away with her head in her hands*. Still at least one writer seemed somewhat surprised by the female member of the Mondale-Ferraro *tagteam's staying power*; he observed that "Ferraro's political appeal should be as narrow as a bra strap or a false eyelash." Preponderantly, however, the fact that one of the debaters was a woman went largely unnoticed by the metaphor makers.

How did the media characterize (define) the *1988* debates? If we didn't see *debates*, then what *did* we see? Most often, the answer appeared to be a sports event of some kind, mainly a *boxing* match. "The setting was a college chapel in Winston-Salem, N.C. but the blood lust was as acrid in the air at ringside as at a Mike Tyson fight . . . [Dukakis] came at Bush like an Olympic boxer jab-jabbing with padded gloves to make points with the judges when he needed to win by a knockout (*Newsweek*, 1988, November 21, p. 120)." The *Boston Globe*, for example, was so enamored by this view that the headlines for each debate read:

> Round 1: The nation looks on as Bush and Dukakis slug it out (Boston Globe, "Dukakis Slugs It Out," 1988, September 26, p. 1).
>
> Round 2: Bentsen, Quayle Spar; Qualification issue dominates (Boston Globe, "Bentsen, Quayle Spar," 1988, October 6, p. 1).
>
> Round 3: Candidates tone it down (Boston Globe, "Round III," 1988, October 14, p. 1).

Donald Rothberg (1988) refereed: "Bush, Dukakis slug it out with no major gaffes. . . ." Dukakis seemed to disavow the boxing metaphor; he frequently said this race was a marathon, rather than a boxing match. (This metaphor got Dukakis in trouble, even early on when his much-vaunted marathon man image was upset when he crossed the Iowa caucuses' finish line in second place and became a "Tier One" candidate almost immediately.) Dach (1988) even proposed a new format for the debates—"a television game show: Why can't they just have buzzers and podiums like on 'Jeopardy?' Can't you just

see George Bush choosing a category like 'Drug Peddling Dictators for $40?' "
Tom Wicker (1988a) recalled the Western genre when he answered his question
"Who Needs Debates?" with: "A Presidential debate . . . is a high-noon
shoot-out in full view of the nation." Later Wicker (1988b) combined the
worlds of show biz and sports with his piece "No Oscar, No Knockout."

Characterizing (Defining) Michael Dukakis in the 1988 Presidential Debates

The presidential debates of 1988, like the others, were preceded by many
weeks of wrangling between the camps of the candidates over how many
debates there would be, who would sponsor them, and what the format would
be. The last debate was conducted by the two parties without the customary
League of Women Voters' sponsorship.

The Expectations Game. Susan Estrich (Dukakis' campaign manager),
James Baker, III (Bush's campaign manager) and others worked hard before
the debates to *lower* expectations for their candidate and, commensurately,
to raise expectations for their opponent. Victory could then be measured by
whether their candidates *exceeded* such expectations. Thus, Estrich reminded
potential viewers: "Bob Dole is a great debater, and Bush beat him three
times" and Baker pointedly recalled that Dukakis had "participated in many
debates and once ran a TV show" (J. Alter, 1988, p. 16). Indeed, for over
a month Roger Ailes, Bush's media man, openly and continuously denigrated
his candidate's debating capabilities.

With Bush's edge in the polls seemingly solidifying, he needed merely to
protect his lead. Still, might not Dukakis' inadequacies so evidently revealed
in the weeks before the debates make any victory in the debates appear to
be an even bigger one?

Pre-debate Perceptions of Michael Dukakis. When he announced his
candidacy, the media described Dukakis in terms such as "pragmatic,"
"serious," "analytic," "intensely disciplined," "naturally aloof." He
appeared to be definitely "not one of the boys." Terms such as "efficient,"
"reliable," "little style and lots of utility" were used. A "hands on manager"
who "immersed himself in the policy details of governing," Dukakis' ability
to articulate his vision for the future compellingly appeared in question from
the beginning.

Within the Dukakis campaign, there was an ongoing debate over the extent
to which the governor should and could be warmer, more intense. "The Duke"
worked hard to reveal compassion publicly. A governor who had apparently
never put much stock in symbols struggled to show that he knew not only
the "stilted prose" of politics, but its "poetry" as well (Kenney & Turner,
1989, p. 18).

Growing concern arose over the power of impression—the knowledge that nonverbal cues have become very important. Dukakis' attempts to smile more and to be a regular fellow were, by pre-debate time, mercilessly chronicled by friends and foes alike.

Both candidates came to understand that approximately 500 million people throughout the world would be tuning in to watch, trying to find out which man generated more *savoir faire*, more warmth, and more strength in addition to addressing the issues. Dukakis, long used to taking a cerebral approach to public policy, finally faced the presidential debates with growing recognition that a key question for many people watching the debates would be: "Who am I likely to be more comfortable with?" Much advice (Martel, 1988) was given to both debaters that "You win debates on style, not substance" and "people want warmth and feelings rather than an encyclopedia of facts."

Terministic Screen One: The Iceman. After his third place showing in the Iowa caucuses and a tight race with Robert Dole emerging in the New Hampshire primary, Bush was advised to conduct a "see-me, feel-me, touch-me campaign." In addition to running with the theme "Ready from Day One," Bush ran an "I am one of you" campaign.

Very early in Republican circles there emerged a Niceman vs. Iceman strategy—Bush, the kind, caring fellow; Dukakis the cool, aloof, cerebral fellow. This strategy was to be played out in the press long before, during and after the debates. After becoming his own man, during his acceptance speech at the GOP Nominating Convention Bush apparently convinced a large number of people that if he did not, macho-like, stand tall in the saddle, at least he could shake some of the previously designated wimphood and emerge a somewhat more animated and forceful exponent of a "kinder and gentler America" without appearing to be a 90-pound weakling who would have beach sand kicked in his face by other more manly personae. The modern political campaign is largely a contest over definition—definition about who the candidates are and what vision of the future best suits the American public. As pollster and pundit, Pat Caddell (Farrell, 1988, p. B11) has observed: "...if pitching is 75% of baseball, then 75% of election victory revolves around the definition of the campaign. ... He who sets the definition of the campaign usually wins."

In the debates themselves, several key parts of the iceman strategy are played out. In outline they are:

1. explicitly use the label;
2. turn even Dukakis' claim of competency against him;
3. watch the press help you along with the scenario;
4. watch Dukakis himself demonstrate it; and
5. manage, when you can, to relate the "iceman" label to the L-word; that is, "liberal."

Now let us watch the strategy play out in the debates. In the first debate, Bush observes explicitly: "Wouldn't it be nice to be the iceman." Even Dukakis' claim of competency is used against him: "Wouldn't it be nice to be perfect." From that point on, Bush was able to stand back and watch the press help him along with the iceman scenario. For example, in the first debate, Peter Jennings intones: "Governor, one theme that keeps coming up about the way you govern is passionless, technocratic." Dukakis, himself, repeats the charge when he asks: "Passionless?" And for the third time the "cool" word is used when Jennings replies: "Passionless, technocratic, smartest clerk in the world."

In the second presidential debate, the press again points to this perception of Dukakis. Margaret Warner recalls: "Governor, you won the first debate on intellect and yet you lost it on heart. . . . The American public admires your performance but didn't seem to like you much."

Not only could Bush stand back and let the press reiterate his charges, but Dukakis' own way of talking about his life appeared to enhance Bush's answers as personal, Dukakis' as political (Kenney & Turner, 1989, p. 41). If in the first debate Bush referred to Dukakis as the iceman, in the second presidential debate Dukakis appeared to demonstrate the accuracy of that definition. To Bernard Shaw's opening white hot question: "Governor, if Kitty Dukakis were raped and murdered, would you favor an irrevocable death penalty for the killer?" Dukakis gave an "ice cold answer" (Kenney & Turner, 1989, p. 41):

> No I don't, Bernard, and I think you know that I've opposed the death penalty during all of my life. I don't see any evidence that it's a deterrent and I think there are better and more effective ways to deal with violent crime. We've done so in my own state and it's one of the reasons why we have had the biggest drop in crime of any industrial state in America, why we have the lowest murder rate of any industrial state in America.

It was Bush, the nice man, who supplied the human adjectives:

> Well, a lot of what this campaign is about, it seems to me, Bernie, gets to the question of values. . . . You see, I do believe that some crimes are so heinous, so brutal, so outrageous — and I'd say particularly those that result in the death of a police officer — and for those real brutal crimes, I do believe in the death penalty.

As Dukakis' media adviser, Dan Payne, aptly put it, Dukakis "responded to a caveman question with a lawyer's answer. . . ." (Beachy, 1988, p. 139). In his reply, Dukakis did not even mention his wife Kitty's name. As one account summed it up: ". . . even as his political dreams hung in the balance, Dukakis mustered all the emotion of a time-and-temperature recording" (Beckwith, 1988, p. 18).

Still there was one more part to the ''iceman/niceman'' strategy. Tie that demonizing descriptor to the second and perhaps even more damaging negative definition—that of Dukakis as a liberal. The L-word and iceman labels were twinned, thusly, in the second debate:

> I don't think that it's a question of whether or not people like you that make you an effective leader. I think it's whether you share the broad dreams of the American people; whether you have confidence in the people's ability to get things done. Or whether you think it all should be turned over, as many liberals do, to Washington, D.C. See . . . it's a question of values. (*New York Times*, 1988, October 14, p. A14)

Terministic Screen Two: The L-Word. The implications of Dukakis' failure to define *himself* are nowhere more apparent than in Bush's use of the word ''liberal'' to define him still more negatively. Dukakis, in part, won the Democratic primaries because ''the messenger was the message'' (Farrell, 1988, p. B11). He was, as Farrell described him, ''Cool Hand Duke,'' noted by his peers to be ''the most effective governor, master of the post-industrial economy.'' To Dukakis, the election was not about ideology; it was about competence. Still, according to a Dukakis adviser, Tad Devine (Farrell, 1988, p. B10): ''Nobody knew who Dukakis *was*. . . This was a new candidate, whom Bush moved in [on] and defined negatively. A lot of that negative definition stuck and stuck hard.'' Indeed, even before Dukakis was nominated at the Democratic National Convention in Atlanta, Bush was ''busy pinning the liberal moniker on him, in the obvious hope that it [would] send voters . . . fleeing'' from him (Germond, and Witcover, 1988). In a *New York Times/CBS* poll two-thirds of the conservatives polled did not think of Dukakis as a ''liberal.'' Among that group he ran neck-to-neck with Bush, but by September 14, 1988, a *New York Times* headline read: ''Poll shows Bush Setting Agenda for Campaign.'' Among the results the poll reported:

> . . . Mr. Bush's persistent effort to label Mr. Dukakis 'a liberal' is a promising tactic. Only one voter in 10 said they looked favorably on someone who was described as 'liberal.' Three in 10 said they looked less favorably on someone described that way. To be labeled 'a conservative,' on the other hand, was more a political plus than a minus.
>
> The Republican's effort to make 'liberal' a dirty word may be having an even broader impact. In the latest poll, only 15% of those surveyed described themselves as liberals, the lowest recorded since *the Times* & CBS News began polling in 1975. [Dionne, 1988, p. A29]

''Indeed it was eerie,'' said Lee Atwater, Bush's one-time campaign manager, ''like they were allowing us to run both campaigns'' (Farrell, 1988, p. B11).

The slowness of the Dukakis campaign to respond to the L-word was stunning, even with the playing of the black and white Willie Horton commercial:

> As Governor Michael Dukakis vetoed mandatory sentencing for drug dealers,
> he vetoed the death penalty. His revolving door prison policy gave weekend
> furloughs to first degree murderers not eligible for parole. While out, many
> committed other crimes like kidnapping and rape and many are still at large.
> Now, Michael Dukakis wants to do for America what he has done for
> Massachusetts. America can't afford that risk.

Indeed, in Maryland, the husband of a rape victim made a commercial for
the state G.O.P. Committee, telling viewers that Willie Horton, who fled
from his furlough,

> . . . broke into our home and for 12 hours I was beaten, slashed and terrorized.
> My wife was brutally raped. When his liberal experiment failed, Dukakis
> looked away.

Although Dukakis countered with two commercials, one of which pointed
out that the furlough program in Massachusetts was started by a Republican
governor and one which recalled that "George Bush sat by while a federal
furlough program released thousands of prisoners, many of them drug dealers,"
they proved less potent than the G.O.P. commercials. Dukakis' replies were
simply too little, too late. Charlie Brake (Farrell, 1988, p. B11), Dukakis
field director, commented: "It took 3 months for the furlough thing to sink in."
To make absolutely sure the L-word remained in focus, two days before
the first debate, at a Baylor University rally, Reagan pejoratively referred
to "liberalism" or "liberal" 22 times. At one point he said: ". . . the one
issue, the only issue that will matter on Inauguration Day is the issue of
direction. Will we re-elect peace and prosperity? Or will we play 'Truth or
Consequences' with trenchcoat liberals?"
A few days before the second presidential debate, continuing to raise the
specter of a sinister "they," Bush said:

> They're giving me a lot of grief for mentioning that whole question of the
> Pledge of Allegiance, but they're not going to have me stop talking about
> it because I think it's right for teachers to lead the kids in the Pledge to
> Allegiance in this country.

> Liberals hate it. They can't stand it, but I am right, and I am with the American
> people on this and on voluntary prayer in schools, and on a whole bunch
> of things that I consider fundamental values. [In D. Alters, 1988, p. 13]

Just before the first of the presidential debates, Andrew Kohut of the Gallup
Organization pointed squarely to the two fundamental reasons Bush was steadily
gaining in the polls: ". . . Two key reasons for the Bush resurgence are that
his attacks on Dukakis have worked and that he is riding President Reagan's
coattails. . . . Most effective has been his summer-long effort to paint Dukakis
as a liberal" (Lightman, 1988, September 23, A22).
In the general election campaign, the pinning of the label, "liberal," to
Dukakis started as far back as Reagan's farewell speech at the G.O.P.
Convention in New Orleans in August 1988.

Before we begin to look at the L-word as it played out in the debates, it is important to point out that the debates were contexted by frequent and ubiquitous clusters of demonizing terms. David Nyhan (1988) noted the following:

—from George Bush: Dukakis is for "*socialism.*"

—from Roger Ailes (Bush's media man): Dukakis is a "*pacifist.*"

—from Henry Kissinger: The foreign policy of Dukakis springs from "the *radical* movements of the 60s."

—from the Maryland G.O.P. State Committee: Dukakis would "inflict black rapists on unsuspecting white families. . . . You, your spouses, your children, your parents, and your friends can have opportunity [sic] to receive a visit from someone like Willie Horton if Mike Dukakis becomes president."

By now there seemed little doubt about the correct answer to the question posed by Bush: "Why won't [Dukakis] stand up for the Pledge of Allegiance?"

In the debates themselves, the L-word played out in an extraordinarily potent set of equational structures. Below are a few of the most potent (and occasionally amusing) equational structures.

Liberal = ACLU card carrier (Hmm, you remember those *pinkos*.)

ACLU = those who would let Bush's 10-year-old grandchild go to an x-rated movie.

= take tax exemptions away from the Catholic Church.

= want to see kiddie porn laws repealed.

= would have God "come out from our currency."

Liberals = big spenders. Such "big spenders," indeed that they "think the only way to do it [aid the inner cities] is for the Federal Government to do it *all*.

= advocating tax hikes ("tax hike Mike.")

= hanging around with "Harvard buddies" and telling "American farmers to grow Belgium endive."

= being "viscerally anti-military."

= "sneering at common sense." Worse yet, sneering at "common sense advice—midwestern advice from a grandmother to a grandson."

Such a heinous set of equations makes Quayle's final remarks appear tame:

Liberal = bigger government

= higher taxes

= cuts in national defense

= high interest rates

= high inflation and unemployment.

= writing "blank checks." ("I had this talk about a blank check. The American people are pretty smart. They know who writes out the checks.")

= lacking confidence in "the people."

> = *not* understanding the heartbeat of the country nor understanding family values and the importance of the neighborhood.
>
> = wanting "to see the Federal Government licensing grandmothers."

Aside from using the L-word with "card-carrying," "progressive," and "left wing," the pseudo qualifiers *very* liberal, *most* liberal, and *George McGovern* liberal . . . also laced the dialogue.

Recall, again, that the demonizing of Dukakis *twinned* two dominant terministic screens. The twinned terministic screen tells us that Dukakis is not *only* a "liberal," but a "passionless" one at that. Recall Bush's quite remarkable:

> We are going to make some changes and some tough choices before we go to deployment on the Midgetman missile or on the Minutemen, whatever it is. We are going to have to—the MX—we're going to have to do that. It's Christmas. It's Christmas. Wouldn't it be nice to be perfect. Wouldn't it be nice to be the iceman so you never make a mistake. [*New York Times*, 1988, September 26, p. A18]

Conclusion

In this chapter, I have tried (1) to examine briefly the potency of the ways we characterize (define) our political process and construct presidential debates and (2) to examine the way Bush and Quayle worked in the 1988 presidential debates to characterize (define) Dukakis. By their use of two powerful terministic screens "iceman" and "liberal," they came to demonize Dukakis. Dukakis helped *empower* those terministic screens by vividly demonstrating the efficacy of the "iceman" charge and by failing to counter effectively the negative connotations Bush and Quayle attached to the definer "liberal." It was not until *after* the second debate that he accepted the term "liberal." Even then, as one commentator observed, Dukakis' acceptance had the ring of a "confession." If by accepting the label he expected to diffuse the potency of Bush's attack, he was clearly wrong. The focus on the L-word continued and, even in its most virulent form, would not go away.

Try as he might Dukakis' attempts at warmth failed to mitigate his frostbite problem. In one of the most striking recent lapses of political savvy, Dukakis said on October 14 that he had been unfairly labeled: "It's not the label; it's the vision." Neither he nor his staff seem to really appreciate the potency of terministic screens and their defining power.

In some respects "we the people" give little thought to the potency of the terministic screens through which we characterize (define) our political campaign process and our presidential debates and about the name-calling within those debates. Terministic screens both reveal *and* conceal. While we have focused here on what they reveal about the way the candidate and the media talk, we might pause briefly to ask, what do they *conceal* about *us*?

If rhetors (candidates and media script writers) construct audiences, to what extent do *we* construct rhetors by our own duplicity; that is, in our largely silent acceptance of and mindless mimicry of such potent naming exercises. To paraphrase that astute commentator on the argument from definition, Richard Weaver (1953) this is very likely a world in which we get what we want more often and more directly than we sometimes like to think.

Part IV

Arguing in Philosophical and Technical Communities

> The philosophic arguer wants to have only those points of view prevail
> that can do so in the face of the most stringent criticism possible. . . .
> Like the philosopher, the scientist also seeks free assent. . . . [He or she]
> takes pains to give his [or her] claims every chance of being proved wrong
> (Brockriede, 1972, pp. 6 & 8).

The common characteristic of philosophers and scientists, according to
Brockriede, is that they want their arguments to be challenged and refined *[sic !]*
by others in their communities. The arguers in philosophical and technical
communities are insiders with specialized knowledge who have their own
criteria for evaluating the strengths or weaknesses of the arguments they
present. The procedures for getting data, standards for making inferences
and using evidence, and processes for refining arguments apply a rigor different
from the standards used in personal and social communities. The specialized
audiences who respond to arguments in these communities demand a technical
vocabulary that is often not understood by the public.

Students can find arguments in these specialized communities in the papers
presented at technical conferences, in academic journals, in scholarly debates,
in economic discussions, and in technical reports about the environment, safety,
and health of the public.

The chapters in this section of the book are focused on philosophical and
scientific argument in two different ways. John R. Lyne and John Angus
Campbell describe the process of arguing in science. On the other hand,

William R. Brown, Charles Arthur Willard, and Sharon Bailin focus on the philosophy of argumentation.

Lyne, in Chapter 13, notes that argumentation is the process used by scholars who create and evaluate research in the disciplines classified as human sciences. He views scholarly argument as part of the philosophical community. Lyne claims that research in the human sciences is carried on by specialists who make their cases to other specialists about the realities they observe. He recommends that students analyze arguments in this community by reconstructing the arguer, the argument, the audience, the discipline, and the context. The author warns that these arguments are frequently difficult to find because they are disguised in the specialized vocabulary of the professional and academic disciplines for whom they are designed.

In Chapter 14, Brown makes the case that those who study argument should do so considering a new point of view called trialectics. Trialectics, according to Brown, is a way of explaining the complex content of argumentation processes and effects within the discourse of philosophical communities. Trialectics presents a new "frame of reference" that allows observers to analyze arguments holistically without separating the discourse into distinct parts. Trialectics is a perspective for explaining argumentation that is part of moral codes, philosophical debates, or reasoning within complex organizational systems. Trialectics has a different form and different rules than classical or dialectical argument. It avoids some of the logical traps found in classical or dialectical argument. This perspective permits observers to see that everything is related to everything else in a way analogous to a hologram.

Campbell, in Chapter 15, builds a case to support his claim that theoretical knowledge and common sense are united in the scientific process. As evidence for his argument, Campbell shows that Darwin's theory of evolution offended the technical communities of both science and religion. Darwin's theory was persuasive, however, because he used conventional religion and conventional common sense to make his theory appear pious, intelligible, and respectable. Darwin chose the common-sense, religious principles to show that life ultimately came from divine creation and that God was responsible for each adaptation of the species according to general laws of nature. Conscious of the common sense knowledge of his audience, Darwin placed orthodox interpretations on ideas, moved from familiar concepts to those that were unfamiliar, and used familiar analogies so persons would not be offended by the implications of his theory. Campbell explains how an arguer, like Darwin, adapts the arguments from the technical community of science to the public so that the argument is acceptable to those outside of this specialized community.

In Chapter 16, Willard notes the importance of argument among persons who adopt the philosophical premises, concepts, and implications of postmodern critique. Willard defines postmodern critique as the attempt to understand and check the negative effects of modern organizations and institutions. Willard claims that argumentation is essential to the critique because it can restore human control to tyrannical organizations. To make his point, Willard traces epistemology from its concern with absolute and deterministic knowledge to a current view of knowledge as a social creation produced by rhetoric and argumentation.

In Chapter 17, Bailin looks at the epistemological perspective on arguments. Specifically, she views argument criticism as a constructive as well as a creative activity. She finds evidence of this creative process in judgments which identify problems and recognize solutions, interpret and recreate circumstances, and reconcile and mediate judgments. The creative process in argumentation surfaces when arguers supply missing premises, classify fallacies, evaluate analogies, and consider alternative arguments. Bailin emphasizes that this perspective is an important one for teachers and learners to adopt when they study critical thinking and informal logic.

Chapter Thirteen

Argument in the Human Sciences

John Lyne

In the institutional life of American universities, knowledge is commonly categorized as falling within the sciences, the social sciences or the humanities. The notion of a natural science, such as biology or physics, does not pose much of a problem for these broad schemes of classification. But the distinction between humanities and social sciences generates a good deal of debate because there is disagreement about whether a science using methods developed to study planetary movements or the structure of a cell is the appropriate way to study the activities of human beings. The methods of experimentation, hypothesis-testing, and quantification seem to work better for some purposes than for others—better, say, for assessing probabilities within large populations than for helping people to reap the benefits of literature or philosophy. What kind of line can be drawn, and where to draw it, between the scientific approach and so-called humanistic approaches to knowledge of human culture is the subject of ongoing debates. Many communication departments, for instance, harbor a "scientist-humanist split" concerning how best to secure knowledge.

Human Sciences

In recent years, the term "human sciences" has been increasingly used to designate areas of systematic study of human works, culture, behaviors,

Mr. Lyne is in the Department of Communication Studies at the University of Iowa.

and institutions. In some ways, this term cuts across the familiar distinction between a social science and the humanities and perhaps helps in some way to repair the rift that those two categories have produced. The notion gets part of its shape and origin from European sources, most notably the German notions of intellectual sciences (*Geisteswissenschaften*) and sciences of culture (*Kulturwissenschaften*), and the French human sciences (*les sciences humaines*), following recent waves of interest in European scholarship in America. We have found our own ways to define and use this term, and in this case it has a rather broad usage. "Human sciences" weds the notion of being systematic with that of looking at things that are distinctively human — that is, things formed not only by principles of individual or group behavior but by history, politics, and creativity.

So where are the human sciences? A pat answer is difficult to give, as there are no rigid boundaries determining what is within the human sciences. If anything, there is a spirit of rejecting such boundaries in favor of interdisciplinary understanding. It might help to cite the initial editorial in a recently established journal called *History of the Human Sciences*:

> "Human sciences" . . . encompasses a number of different disciplines, including sociology, psychology, anthropology, and linguistics. Unlike "social sciences" it suggests a critical and historical approach which transcends these specialisms and links their interests with those of philosophy, literary criticism history, aesthetics, law, and politics [1(1) (1989), p. 1].

Other disciplines, such as economics, might be added to this list. Human sciences are those that seek systematic knowledge rather than, say, aesthetic appreciation or practical application as a primary objective. Because they are concerned with matters whose significance is largely cultural rather than natural, the human sciences involve a strong interest in questions of interpretation, especially the interpretation of language and texts. They are generally more interested in accounting for things historically rather than predictively (Taylor, 1971).

The natural and social sciences have well-advertised methods for securing knowledge, such as statistics or laboratory procedures, and so it is sometimes forgotten that scientists also need to "make their case" when they write for their peers or for others. They have in common with the human sciences the need to construct arguments. The way that arguments and other means of persuasion occur in the human sciences has become a matter of increasing interest, especially among those who study "rhetoric of inquiry" (Lyne, 1985; Nelson, McCloskey & Megill, 1987; Simons, 1989). The importance of understanding such arguments is underscored by the fact that to a large extent they determine what will be offered as knowledge in the scholarly world, in textbooks, and in popularizations. That is, argument is one of the means by which knowledge claims are advanced, secured, or criticized, and so it has a fundamental role to play in shaping what we know, or think we know.

Locating Arguments

Studying argument in the human sciences presents certain challenges to the student of argument. Academic work ordinarily presumes some specialized knowledge and training, and with it a specialized vocabulary and specialized ways of drawing inferences. This can pose real obstacles to someone coming as an outsider to a specialized field. Unlike politics or public debate where the assumption is that the average citizen should be a part of the audience, arguments in the human sciences are often created for fellow specialists. To be an effective analyst or critic of these arguments, therefore, one must make oneself a competent member of the audience, sometimes by undertaking serious study of the subject matter. Obviously, few will have the time or inclination to follow technical disputes, unless there is something more than casual interest in the issues. Often, however, more than technical questions are at issue. In many ways and in many contexts, the human sciences are forums for great debates about human nature itself (Schwartz, 1986).

There are good reasons from the perspective of liberal education to study this scholarly discourse. A college student is often put in the position of trying to learn from it; without a grasp of how the arguments are functioning, it will be hard to take away much more than a sense of the author's conclusions, rather than the reasoning that produced them. That would mean almost exclusive reliance on the authority of the writer, not on the merits of the case. It would also leave one in the position of having to accept or reject conclusions without really understanding why. As citizens and taxpayers, we all have a stake in the arguments in the human sciences because they have an impact on our social institutions, whether by shaping laws, determining curriculum, or defining the intellectual climate in which we live. A democratic society, if it is to remain one, cannot leave all the important judgments to the "experts" (McGee & Lyne, 1987). Of course, the serious student of argument will not want to neglect this vast domain of evidence and proof which must have a place in a general theory of argument.

Defining Arguments

Many of the argumentative practices in the human sciences are the same general ones used in everyday contexts, meaning that anyone with a good eye for arguments can often detect them and recognize their strengths or weaknesses. Arguments from example, or by analogy, or from authority, for instance, can occur in virtually any discipline. Other practices are particular to the fields involved, meaning that to become a competent member of the audience, one must gain some sense of what "counts" as a proof and as evidence in that field. The amount of evidence deemed sufficient to support a general claim can vary widely from one field to the next. An historian may attempt to generalize about political revolutions from a half dozen cases, for instance, whereas no psychologist would dream of generalizing about human beings based on observing only six people. There are even different conceptions of what constitutes evidence. In the field of economics, for instance, testimony by merchants and manufacturers as to why they buy and sell is almost never considered valid evidence of economic motivation; in law, by contrast, self-reports can be crucial for explaining motive.

Besides the variable standards of evidence, there are also shared beliefs and assumptions of a field which supply different argumentative warrants. These are often represented explicitly in theories, but they are sometimes at work only implicitly, as a result of the arguer's and the audience's socialization and training (Barnes & Edge, 1982). In using the term "warrants," for instance, I am assuming that readers have some familiarity with Toulmin's use of that term and that this mobilizes certain assumptions about what is required to establish a claim. Each intellectual enterprise operates against a backdrop of shared theoretical and, sometimes, ideological assumptions. Arguments in the human sciences depend on the arguer as well as the audience having shared standards and strategies of proof.

Analyzing Arguments

As one moves from the context of face-to-face interactions in everyday life to the sort of arguing that goes on in academic journals, there are certain adjustments that need to be made in how one thinks about arguments. Arguments in the medium of print can engage a wide variety of readers across a great period of time. One can read arguments created long ago, intended for audiences far away. If argument is to remain a two-way affair, this often means entering into dialogue with faceless, perhaps deceased, persons one has never even met. Moreover, the very identity of the arguer is in a sense a social construction. Contributions to the human sciences are made by professionals, and so the voice of the arguer is not the voice of a person exactly, but of someone who has assumed a professional role which will shape and constrain things to be said. An anthropologist might venture any number of personal judgments at a cocktail party but will have to discipline those judgments to meet professional standards when writing up research. In other words, the "self" who is on the line is the professional self, not the whole personality. The immediate context of an argument might be a series of other articles by a variety of people, not just the space of the writer-reader relationship. Someone unfamiliar with the pertinent literature might have the feeling of having just walked into the middle of a conversation with no clear sense of what it is about.

Thus one needs to take some care to understand academic arguments in the special framework in which they occur. To think systematically about this, it helps to have an analytic scheme. The following is one general scheme, intended to help the student of argument provide a well rounded account of how arguments can be located, defined, and analyzed in the human sciences.

It presents general considerations under the general headings of the arguer, the argument, the audience, the discipline, and the context. The assumption behind it is that argument is a situated activity and that the elements of its situation need to be reconstructed in order to grasp the argument as an organic whole.

Elements of Argumentation
in Scholarly Research

The Arguer

The credibility, or ethos, of a scholarly writer is of critical importance to any systematic attempt at knowledge. A great machinery of professional standards helps to assure the credibility of those whose works appear in reputable journals. To succeed in getting articles published, the author has to pass over a number of hurdles designed to keep the less professionally agile from getting through. This may sound elitist, and in a certain sense it is; disciplines police themselves in order to maintain high standards because shoddy work can do damage to the credibility of an entire field. The process is "democratic," however, in the sense that (in principle at least) anyone who meets the requisite standards of a journal has a shot at publication, depending largely on how stiff the competition is for space in that journal. By the time someone's work reaches print in a reputable journal, therefore, there is a presumption that it is accurate in its factual claims, reflects sufficient knowledge of the relevant literature, and is generally compatible with the standards and practices of the fields.

In fact, published articles not meeting these criteria sometimes get past the initial gatekeepers. Although an author's neglect of relevant literature can be fairly easy for expert reviewers to spot, errors of fact are more difficult to screen out, because journal editors and referees generally do not have the time or resources to check them. In time, however, a sufficiently wide readership can bring published errors to the surface, and so there is a self-correcting aspect to work in the human sciences. This points to another significant feature of academic argumentation in general. Judgments are not final as they might be in a competitive debate—any claim stands subject to correction and any argument to reevaluation, as long as it appears in print. The arguer who goes to print, therefore, incurs long term scrutiny. The arguer casts a discourse out for any who may wish to read it. There is a certain one-sidedness in this, in the sense that the author is finite but the audience is in principle infinite. Some readers will likely be those who do not supply the same warrants as the author. Others will be less knowledgeable in the subject—or in some cases more expert in the subject—than the author. The author can be ambushed from any direction.

Thus there is a kind of ongoing, recurrent testing of arguments in the human sciences, and arguers have their sights set on that. Winning the day only to lose credibility over the long run is a risk that few will wish to take because their credibility is their most valued resource. Unlike commercial publication ventures where making money is a leading motivation, academics do not make money directly from published articles (although they may from textbooks). Their earning power, and even their self-worth, usually depends on their standing in the professional community, not on sales. In fact, academic writers who achieve too much success in the general marketplace, are often regarded with suspicion by their academic peers. The relationship of the arguer to the community of fellow academics is thus an important part of what must be "won" in the argument. The ethos at stake is more than just "the person who wrote this article." Arguments that one may encounter in a journal article may be, so to speak, notes in the symphony of someone's career. The deeper and more impressive that career, the more presumption one accords the individual arguments within it. In this sense, "appeal to authority" is not a fallacy or irrelevant to the scientific spirit but, rather, an appeal to a presumption that may or may not be granted.

To win credentials as an expert in a given field, the academic usually has to learn how to "talk like" a member of the profession—to learn the "code," so to speak. There are two general accounts that can be given of this, and each probably captures part of the truth. One account is that the "jargon" of academics is indeed a code; using it is a way of proving one's membership in the relevant community and a means of excluding others. Do lawyers speak "legalese" by necessity, for instance, or do they use that as a way of making it harder for ordinary citizens to handle their own legal affairs, to the benefit of lawyers? Is the capacity to "talk like an economist," or a psychologist, or whatever, the professional equivalent of having a union card? A good case can be made that specialized terminology serves functions of isolating and protecting various professional interests, and of giving experts power in society (Aronowitz, 1988; Gouldner, 1979).

The other story that can be told about specialized language is that it is simply a necessary part of technical and precise thought. A chemist needs a language apart from everyday language that is adequate to the things chemists study—should we not expect something beyond everyday language of specialists in the human sciences? After all, if everything were instantly accessible to anyone, would that not imply that special training is unnecessary? These seem legitimate questions, just as the concerns over professionalization as a self-protective measure seem legitimate concerns. The two stories are often told about academic argument. Perhaps they help academics and their audiences to take a more reflective view of specialized language.

The Argument

Argument within the human sciences can be based on qualitative evidence drawn from observation, historical materials, the written and spoken word, or on quantitative evidence, including statistics. The methods of investigation are generally based in history and interpretation: making predictions is more often, but not exclusively, associated with the "social sciences." In either place, one will find different attitudes toward the sufficiency of qualitative evidence and toward the role of statistics in proving claims. To advocates of the humanistic perspective, journal articles using statistical methods sometimes seem not to argue at all. Rather, they present "findings," statistical outcomes of studies or surveys: people in such-and-such a condition, according to a study, are more likely to do x that y; variable V accounts for more variance in behavior than variable Z. In studies of this sort, the critic might ask, so what? What's the argument? The method may seem to be producing conclusions by pure demonstration, not by argument. But one needs to be careful to understand the broader context of a study before reaching such a conclusion. Often studies are ongoing tests of a more general theory purporting to explain a wide range of behaviors. So the theory is put to the test in many different contexts. In effect, the general theory is a kind of broad hypothesis: "the theory of social discombobulation predicts that when confronted with vexation, people will behave in a discombobulated manner." A variety of studies will test out conditions under which people are confronted with vexation to see if people behave in the manner the theory predicts. If they behave this way repeatedly, then confidence builds that the general theory is correct.

The pattern of reasoning represented here is what philosopher C.S. Peirce called "abduction" (Reilly, 1970). If a given generality were true, the reasoning goes, then many particulars would be expected to turn out a certain way; if those particulars turn out in the predicted way, then the generality *may be* true. As more particular cases turn out in the predicted way, confidence in the general theory builds. An abductive inference may occur on the basis of a single case and this can generate productive insights; but one case is not sufficient to prove a general rule. As one goes on investigating other cases, according to Peirce, one finds that the generalization will apply a certain percentage of the time. By statistical induction, one establishes what that percentage, or probability, is. There are, however, certain hypotheses that are framed in such a way that a single instance which did not go in the predicted direction would disconfirm the theory. Some philosophers believe that all good empirical hypotheses should be framed in this way, so that theories that are wrong can be shown so decisively (Popper, 1963).

In practice, such decisiveness is not very common in the human sciences, however. There are usually ways to "save" a theory in the light of apparently disconfirming results, and these require some argument. The common argumentative strategies include: making a refinement of the theory, arguing that the theory applies differently in different contexts; contending that the case in question failed to test what it was intended to test; or maintaining that the theory operates subject to certain restrictions or exceptions, hence requiring more research to determine how many of these exist. In other words, there are arguments to be made about how the findings are to "count" in light of the theory. It is relatively rare that a single set of findings are regarded as counting in a decisive way, one way or the other.

Indecisive findings may be used and cited by others in a way that makes them appear more decisive than they are, however. For instance, a group of midwestern college sophomores behave in the predicted direction on a particular test and this becomes a "reference" in the literature supporting the claim that people (in general and with no specification of context) seem to behave in this way. The original authors of a study are generally careful to qualify the meaning of their research. From the perspective of argument, it can be profitable to examine the conclusions at the end of a study, which often consider the possible general implications of the findings. These will suggest, if not claim, that light has been shed on something bigger and more general. Given the question of how findings are going to count, the body of a research article may be but a fragment of an argument whose other parts must be found elsewhere. Scientific researchers work within communities of peers, who also contribute to building the "case" for a theory. By placing oneself in such a community through the use of footnotes and references, one signals that there is an ongoing case to be made to which others contribute—the premises of which are not all reproduced in any given article.

The Audience

In a sense, the first audience for work in the human sciences consists of journal editors and referees who assess it, usually suggest revisions, and decide whether it is to be published. The editor of a journal which may publish only twenty or so articles a year will likely have to reject a great many of those submitted. The editor is expected to exercise good judgment in applying the standards of the field, and this usually means consulting with those who specialize in the areas with which an article deals. For fairness, the work is normally reviewed "blindly," meaning that the identity of the author is not supplied to the referees. This also means that the referees are not supposed to take into account the reputation and credibility of the author, except in so far as credibility is established in the work itself. Referees must therefore operate on generic considerations rather than ones specific to the author. As soon as work is published, however, it meets its primary audience who will make judgments about the credibility of the author, in addition to the credibility of the journal itself.

The readers of a widely circulated journal may represent a number of different paradigms of knowledge. Because knowledge is now so specialized, most readers will be highly knowledgeable about only a few of the articles they read in a given journal. For the rest, they are reliant on the expertise of the authors. Despite the appearance that technical or specialized knowledge operates in a closed sphere, it too has a variety of audiences with different levels of understanding. For example, university colleagues may be asked to vote on the tenure or promotion of a colleague whose area of work is not in their specialty. Writers of textbooks covering a whole field will have to rely on specialists within each area to provide knowledge, and so they become a part of the audience, as will the readers of those textbooks. In the process there may be some changes and simplification of the original material, even distortion, over which the original author may have no control. Additionally, writers in one discipline cite work in other disciplines, which leads to a further blurring of the boundaries of the argument's relevance.

The Discipline

This last point leads to an important aspect of argumentation within disciplines. In addition to arguing about particular issues, writers in the various human sciences are often engaged in arguments about the boundaries of their respective fields. Any subject of interest in human society will admit of different perspectives, and so it is not always clear within what disciplinary "jurisdiction" it falls. For instance, argument itself can be looked at as a social process and thus arguably in the purview of the sociologist. On grounds that arguments are processes of inference-making, the psychologist would have a good claim to study them. Because they are forms of communication, students of communication study them. The determination of who "owns" a given problem area is something on which grants and funding, as well as prestige and identity, can depend. It is also a matter of which approach is the most competent and efficient in dealing with questions in which the society takes an interest. Consequently, one finds within each discipline a certain amount of "boundary work" to determine what properly belongs to a field (Gieryn, 1983). Those who write about argument, for instance, will devote attention to why and how argumentation is specifically a communication problem. Recent trends in the human sciences toward the interdisciplinary (as in the above quotation from the new journal) lessen to some degree the importance of boundary work, but do not eliminate it.

Although the various sciences employ a variety of methods and assumptions, one assumption they share is that improvement and correction are possible. Correspondingly, not all opinions are equal; it is possible to be wrong. By open investigation and correction, knowledge advances. Philosophers of science differ as to whether replacement of one paradigm by another entails an advance in knowledge rather than just a change of viewpoint (Lakatos & Musgrave, 1970; Rorty, 1979; Toulmin, 1972). In any case, most scientific thinking occurs within a given paradigm ("normal science") rather than in the context of a paradigm shift (Kuhn, 1970a). Within a given paradigm, knowledge clearly does grow and become refined. The assumption of cumulativity (knowledge grows) plus the assumption of collectivity (many contribute to it) are made in the human sciences as well as in the natural sciences. Fields and disciplines are simply attempts to organize the process.

The function of a discipline is to provide a general logic or set of standards for the conduct of inquiry. Disciplinary boundaries have even been defined in terms of how they establish a particular "argumentation format" for adjudicating knowledge claims (Fuller, 1988, p. 191). Thus one needs to take account of the role and function of the discipline itself in shaping arguments. Some fields enforce regularity of language, style, and format more than others. In some cases, the official style manuals dictate not only the surface features of presentation, but the very form and structure that arguments are allowed to take within a journal (Bazerman, 1988). Instruments such as style manuals reflect the assumptions of cumulativity and collectivity. The degree to which cumulativity may depend on everyone's following the same method is a matter of very different opinions. The human sciences, as a framework and perspective, may place less emphasis on uniformity of method than do the natural sciences and some of the social sciences because they do not usually take the standard model of "the scientific method" as the key to their progress. In part they take their models from the cultural activity that they study: law, not physics, as a model of argument; ritual, not biology, as a source of human solidarity. They seek patterns and structures of explanation at the level of the human activity itself, rather than by reducing explanation to physical or biological laws.

The manner in which knowledge is carved up into specialized disciplines is sometimes criticized as representing a triumph of territoriality over reason. Problems in the world, after all, do not seem to divide themselves neatly along disciplinary lines. The problem of global warming, just to name one, seems to require responses rooted in any number of the natural sciences, plus whatever light the human sciences can shed on human understanding, motivation, and value. If specialized disciplines have gone too far in isolating small parcels of territory, then an appropriate response would be to study the general argumentative topics and strategies that cut across disciplinary boundaries. For the student of argument, the task of finding ways to make knowledge claims from different disciplines interact with each other is both a major and a worthy challenge.

Context

In setting expectations for argument, it is important to take account of the context in which they occur, including the forum and format. The place of publication will often indicate whether the arguments are addressed mainly to peers or to a more general audience. Conference presentations usually follow fewer formal requirements of proof than do journal articles. Arguments responding to attacks, where a direct debate is joined, are controlled by different factors than those that operate in uninterrupted exposition of a theory. Arguments in a book are expected to develop and elaborate fully what could only be sketched in short articles. Speculative essays relax some of the burdens of proof that would otherwise apply on the expectation that this freer play of the mind might generate new insights. These are a few of the important contextual factors to be taken into account.

Another contextual factor is the history and background of the topic. Arguments occur in the context of beliefs, values and assumptions, as well as other arguments, and these can be a changing mosaic. Much scholarship is generated within the context of controversy, that is, a cluster of arguments swirling around a given subject. A number of authors may be participants in the controversy. Picking up a piece of work without knowing that it is intended as a response to someone else's argument would be to miss an important part of the context. Some understanding of these factors is part of what makes one a competent member of the audience.

Arguments are not driven by ideas alone, however. In this era of professionalization, it is important to consider the role of institutions and even economic and political factors in determining the shape of knowledge (McGee & Lyne, 1987). Some work is funded, some is not. Some is published, some is not. Bringing something to print depends on a whole infrastructure, including universities, granting agencies, professional associations, and instruments of communication, such as journals. There is little place for the free lancer. Viewed in this light, knowledge is more than the result of contemplation or observation; it is also a matter of "production." For the scholar trying to secure tenure, scholarship is a question of sufficient output according to the definitions of the discipline and institution of employment. This in turn may mean that something besides intrinsic motivation may drive the arguments. It is well to recognize too that arguers in the human sciences typically have an "investment" in their own theories and beliefs and will argue to protect that investment. This should produce a certain caution in one's understanding of how rationality functions and an awareness that arguments alone do not usually settle things.

Perhaps the argument of a purely intellectual kind, unaffected by self-interest, politics, and so on, has always been a relative rarity. In most cases, arguments are motivated by some concern beyond the argument itself—that, after all, is the pragmatic justification for arguing. Instead of looking to a paradigm of "ideal" argument, unmotivated by circumstances, we might therefor be better advised to take the situated argument as our starting point. Arguments are advanced by people who have ideologies and vested interests, within fields that have commitments, and under the constraints of review, publication, politics, and the like. Rather than ignore those factors in the pursuit of argumentative purity, it would make more sense to see how they shape and constrain arguments. This means a consideration of context in a very broad sense.

The commonalities that argument in the human sciences have with everyday argument are sometimes disguised beneath the veneer of special terminology or the trappings of authority. The differences are largely the result of the programmatic and professional requirements of academic research. Sketching out the elements of the argumentative situation helps to give a fully rounded account of the argument when unfamiliarity with the turf might otherwise lead to a partial perspective or to the mistake of taking a fragment for the entire argument. Using the notions of arguer, argument, audience, discipline, and context as an inventional checklist will help generate a range of questions guiding an investigation of arguments as functional units.

Chapter Fourteen

Classical Argument, Dialectics, and Trialectics

William R. Brown

In a collection of speeches given during the 60s and 70s at the Cooper's Union in New York City, the famed student of mythology, Joseph Campbell, mourned the loss of myths by which to live in Western civilization. In a dialogue depicted at about the same time in *Zen and the Art of Motorcycle Maintenance* the narrator is asked whether he believes in ghosts and he replies that he *does*, while thinking of the law of gravity. The suggestion is clear that for the Western mind, myths by which we live are those taken-for-granted inferences, such as Newton's, that a force named gravity (along with three others) are facts of the "real reality."

If we extend this statement to say that myth is any inference which has been lost sight of as inference, then we should reassure Campbell that we do have myths by which we live, including those connected with argument. Perelman and Olbrechts-Tyteca (1969), in the *New Rhetoric*, argue that philosophers have for too long been living with a myth of human rationality. In exposing that myth, they propose to create a new and living myth, namely that the doing of philosophy is the doing of rhetoric. In this chapter, I propose to scrutinize a myth in the culture of students of practical reasoning. That myth was stated succinctly a few years ago by Wayne Brockriede (1975, 1977, 1985a) when—while discussing other characteristics of argument—he told us that arguers must also share a frame of reference. This chapter will examine

Mr. Brown is in the Department of Communication at Dartmouth College in New Hampshire.

190

that phrase at some length with the following question in mind: At what level do we interpret "shared frame of reference"? What, in other words, can we specify as a shared frame of reference? As part of such a discussion the chapter will also take into account the forms of argument that diverge from or share a frame of reference with each other. Along with that discussion, we shall see the extent to which "shared frame of reference" may be descriptive of shared world views. The following potential uses for the reader should emerge from this chapter: (1) an enhancement of the ability to examine critically one's own arguments, (2) an increased sensitivity in the refutation of others' arguments, and perhaps most importantly, (3) a new appreciation of Brockriede's own ecumenical view of argument and his tolerance for multiple perspectives.

By "shared frame of reference," Brockriede clearly does not mean that there will be an agreement at the level of policy. To say that there must be a shared frame of reference at the level of policy is to suggest that there can be no debate. At the same time, if one says that there must be a shared frame of reference to the effect that persons need to discuss their differences of policy, then one sees immediately that "shared frame of reference" reaches to a higher level of abstraction for the common ground necessary to argument. This common ground becomes the area of investigation for this chapter. For example, why do we conclude that a commitment to reason together is a shared frame of reference? How is it that reasoning and the rules of thought occur in such convincing and compelling ways that we can both assent to them and simultaneously differ in our interpretations of specific questions? Let us begin with what we commonly think of as our usual experience in reasoning.

The Classical Western Shared Frame of Reference for Argument

Forms of Classical Reasoning

As participants in the shared myths of argument in Western culture, we generally experience reality at the taken-for-granted level as follows: the world presents itself to us in categories and in kinds. For our everyday uses, living creatures, inert matter, and events all appear to group themselves into classes which allow us to be familiar with new members of those categories. Meanings themselves seem to be grouped into categories such as freedom, happiness, and individualism—or their opposites. This ability to take for granted the categories of experience is a challenge to the arguer. As long as we understand "shared frame of reference" to mean that our categories of kinds must be shared in order for us to have argument, we shall find Brockriede's prescription difficult to follow. We shall not progress beyond questions of definition.

When we step back from the categories to the act of categorizing per se, we begin to see how there can be a shared frame of reference. Common in our Western way of thinking is that each category will be associated with some defining attribute upon which membership in a given class will depend. As we learn early in our debating experience, the requirement for a clear definition of terms must precede the debate itself. In defining those terms advocates of various points of view may disagree hotly with one another as to what the defining attributes might be, but they will not disagree with the **how** question. For example, there must be crucial distinctions among creatures, among features of the physical environment, and among experiences which place each phenomenon into a category. So fundamental is this taken-for-granted approach to argument that we can extend it to say that policy questions resolve themselves into discussions of the correct categorization of reality along with the carrying out of actions implied by those categories. If, for example, a question of policy can be named as being new-dangerous, then the appropriate action follows—avoid or reject the action if possible. At the same time, if a policy can be categorized as new-safe, then it follows that the appropriate action should be to approach or approve the policy.

In seeing that a given policy recommendation can be named either as new-dangerous or new-safe, we can make explicit the working of the three cardinal axioms for practical reasoning inherited from Western culture. For instance, if we say that a policy has a crucial characteristic making it dangerous, we are saying simply that this is its identity. If we substitute the letter A for that category, we say that A is equal to itself or that A equals A. If we say next that the policy which is new and dangerous is not the same as the policy which is new and safe, we are then saying that A (new-dangerous) does not and cannot, without contradiction, equal B (new-safe). Finally, we are saying that the policy has to be *either* new-dangerous *or* new-safe; this is the axiom of the excluded middle. The policy will be either new and dangerous or new and safe—it cannot be both.

Rules of Classical Reasoning

Given these premises of classification, the arguer will rely on rules of practical reasoning that relate these classes of reality. Early in the history of argumentation theory, those rules were often stated as being the same as the rules for the syllogism. If one can generalize about the behavior or function of a class and if one can show that a new instance belongs to that class, then it follows that the new instance will behave as does the class. It would be a reasonable conclusion to take an ambiguous policy recommendation (ambiguous in the sense that it is uncategorized beyond the fact that it is a policy) and to demonstrate by means of causal reasoning, statement of authority, or literal analogy that since it fits in with other recommendations which are new and dangerous, it too is new and dangerous. Argumentation theorists have since admitted that policies and the persons who make them often do not allow for the unqualified generalization necessary to say that all A's are always A's, that all B's are always B's and that therefore our choices always have to be *either* A or B. Thinkers such as Stephen Toulmin (1958) and his interpreters (Brockriede & Ehninger, 1960; Trent, 1968) have sought to find ways to qualify the generalizations necessary to the syllogistic pattern of argument that itself is a taken-for-granted frame of reference. In the practice of the "syllogism on its side," as Toulmin's layout has been called, the advocate who reasons classically will move linearly (more than interactively or paradoxically) from data taken as reports of real states of affairs, to claims (1) of causes (effect to cause) and (2) of cures (cause to effect). These moves are made by means of "warrants" or accepted premises which, at an acceptable level of probability, justify the conclusions reached.

The importance of such efforts is clear; the ability to retain, as useful departures for practical reasoning, the common-sense experience of categories seems to be the very structure of reality itself. Piaget believed that the maturing human creature has to learn to construct and to manipulate, at both the concrete and abstract levels, the groupings of experiences into "same" or "different." We have, then, an enormous stake in perpetuating this version of reality as being a shared frame of reference itself.

It is a reality of parts. Those parts are relatable by means of classifying them and by means of relating them via cause and effect, part and whole, or symptom and condition. It is, further, a reality in which emphasis falls on a version of knowledge that is based upon the similarity or the differences among entities. These entities, depending as they do upon universal essences for definition, are enduring entities. If they endure, then the concept of time in these conventions of argument is largely arrested; it is a reality of clear structure. When we contemplate these myths comprising a shared framework for argument, we see that it is subject to the criticism that such a structure for reality (as Perelman would call it) does not easily lend itself to conceptions of process. Or, as Tom Scheidel said a few years ago, it is a structure because the process is slowed down.

Traps of Classical Reasoning

In thinking, then, about (1) how to be more reflective and critical of one's own arguments and (2) how to be more sensitive in refuting those of others, we need to remind ourselves as Horn (1984) has done of the blind spots which are built into this set of conventions in the culture of arguing. It is important to remember that these blind spots are the trade-offs we make in return for the powerful help given us by the axioms of identity, non-contradiction, and the excluded middle. For example, when we say that a particular policy A is in fact a member of a class called new-dangerous policies, we make three potential trade-offs for the power of that inference, according to Horn. To say that A is A is to commit willy-nilly to the idea that the policy will forever be new and dangerous. That is what Horn (1984) refers to as the "forever changeless trap" (p. 3). To state that the recommendation is new and dangerous is to run the risk of classifying the recommendation as a thing in the same way that a rock is a thing. We are tempted by our taken-for-granted assumptions of identity to believe that a recommendation involving an unfolding set of occurrences is only a thing. This is what Horn (1984) calls "the process-event trap" (p. 4). To realize that this statement of identity is fundamentally a definition is to tempt us into believing that the question posed by policy alternatives can itself be solved simply by redefinition (Horn, 1984, p. 5). While definition may in this frame of reference be necessary to the solution of a problem, it is not by itself the solution.

When we examine the power that has come from the axiom of non-contradiction (that is, a new-safe policy is not a new-dangerous policy), there are two downside versions. One is related to the identity of advocates as being more independent of and separate from others than may be the case. Horn (1984, p. 6) calls this the independent-self trap. Given the emphasis in this frame of reference on categories building up a whole which is the sum of its parts, it is too easy to see the question raised by the policy as an independent, isolated problem (Horn, 1984, p. 7). That is to say, it appears to be a problem which seems unrelated to many others of which we may be aware.

While the excluded middle axiom is very helpful to us in setting meaningful boundaries to experience, there are, Horn (1984, pp. 8-9) believes, two areas of difficulty. The first relates to the interpretation that problems may be isolated. This one is the single effect trap—that is, the taken-for-granted assumption that adoption or rejection of a policy will have only one main effect. The policy will either remedy or worsen the symptoms associated with the problem. So-called side effects of the action are not easily considered. Secondly, we may assume that there are no areas of overlap between policy recommendations that compete. To say it another way, two policy recommendations are totally exclusive of one another. The reader will have no difficulty in sensing the untenability of that position in view of the frequent use of policy compromise in practical affairs.

So far we have examined the forms of, and the rules for, practical reasoning inherited from our Western culture. We have glimpsed an implied version of reality which emphasizes the division of that reality into entities ranging from persons to physical objects to conceptions. We have also seen how the very idea of an enduring entity precludes the sense of change and flux in reality. Finally, we acknowledged that the trade-off we frequently make for the sense of order conferred upon existence sometimes amounts to blind spots regarding the fact of change, the isolation of persons and problems from one another, and the boundaries that can be uselessly erected between proposals. We also saw clearly that as long as arguers commit to this version of reality and to its forms and rules of procedure—keeping in mind the blind spots associated with these conventions—there exists a shared frame of reference in which arguers can meet.

What happens, however, when different forms and rules for using those forms relate to a conceived reality which seems to be diametrically opposed to that premised on the operation of similarity and differences? Does that approach to argument, while making for a shared frame of reference itself, preclude meaningful interaction with arguers who dwell mentally in this first culture of argument? That becomes the overall point to be considered in the next section of the chapter.

The Dialectical Shared
Frame of Reference for Argument

If the point of view on stable entities and slow change predominates within the classical Western version of argument, it may have been caused by the short lifespan of humans and by their perceptual limitations in discerning steady change in such areas as the drift of continents, the movement of mountains, and the rise and fall of plant and animal species. On the other hand, with the enhanced ability to preserve human knowledge across generations and with the ability to extend our senses via media such as the camera, the telescope, and the computer, we are now aware that even in the most stable-appearing entity, process is the basis of that entity. To refer again to Scheidel, it is now a world of process understandable in the expression that process is structure speeded up.

Forms of Dialectical Reasoning

As was the case with the forms of primitive experience in the classical version of argument, certain experiences present themselves with such clarity in our culture that they take on the dimension of self-evident propositions. For us the concept of growth is self-evident. For example, we see the fertilized egg of a developing organism trap more and more energy until at last there appears a fully-formed organism. Along with this development and transformation, we see that contrary tensions exist within much of that development. Among developing organisms, there is competition for available life-support resources. As the continents drift apart, they sometimes impinge on one another so forcefully that regions of great instability are introduced, as is the case with India and the Himalayas. Our aided senses have revealed that there is a succession of developments in this process-centered, waterfall-like reality that we dwell in. Successions appear to us as resolutions of the contraries which exist in nature.

From these observations, another form of argument premised on "real reality" appears. When we see that creatures develop from eggs to fully-formed animals or when we find in buried ocean trenches the proof that land masses float and are pushed apart until they become different continents, we create the axiom that change occurs by degrees until some rubicon is crossed and a new being or a new continent (or a new economic or political system) has arrived. This is to say: changes in degree can lead to changes in kind. Another axiom for argument appears when we observe the contrary tendencies in the processes of reality. When we see creatures competing for access to resources or when we become aware of the geologic pressures created by the impingement of one part of the earth's crust upon another (or when we see the conflict of interests between owners of capital and producers of labor), we are impressed to the point of certainty that argument must be formed to embody conflict. Finally, when we become cognizant of the conflict-induced mutation from degree to kind, then the succession of processes is seen to culminate in new species (Homosapiens, for example), new ecologies, and new socio-economic systems. This, then, leads to the axiom of synthesis, the resolving of contraries by experiencing them in a new combination.

Rules of Dialectical Reasoning

Given these axioms, the conventions of argument are similar to those of Hegel. They amount to this: within every process, locate the conflicting influences. Then, treat the conflict as the evidence of negation of each other by the polar terms. Finally, negate that negation by moving qualitatively to a new, and presumably higher, synthesis or combination of the conflicting influences. What we see when this happens is argument which fits appropriately the taken-for-granted process of reality itself. This quality in argument has been referred to by Black (1965) as argumentative synthesis. It manifests itself in debate when advocates find details of a controversy taking on a new aspect when conceived at a level of abstraction which subsumes the issues that are dialectically opposed at the preliminary level of the discourse. For example, the dialectical advocate of a policy remedying drug abuse will not conceive of her or his discourse as "argument" but as the action of "arguing"; that arguing, in turn, will be part of—not merely an attempt to reflect—the confrontation of opposites in our culture between hedonism and asceticism, between production and consumption, between power and unpower, and the like. Because the problem of drug abuse in this format of argument is seen in a wide context composed of these contradictions, remedies are seen to depend upon actions taken to resolve them in American culture from a correspondingly wide spectrum (ranging from the neighborhood to the national level). In contrast to the linear mode used by the classical arguer, the dialectical arguer thinks interactively within a world of confronting opposites.

Implicit in these "self-evident" conditions of reality and in their derivative forms of and rules for argument is a vision of the "real reality," a view largely at odds with that of the classical viewpoint as developed earlier. Instead of discrete entities, instead of entities locatable in space and time and related to one another by other entities such as the law of cause and effect, this version of the real reality makes primary the relationships between entities rather than the entities themselves. Instead of specifying boundaries and the relationships that hold among them, this world is what Kvale (1976, p. 90) calls the "stream of behavior." Its rules for category formation are not so much centered on defining attributes, as discussed earlier, as upon actions in the real reality. These actions are seen as flowing from intrinsic relations of contradictions which interact not only with themselves but also with the environment in all of its complexity in order (1) to produce a synthesis of internal and external relations and (2) to make obvious the interdependence not only among internal contradictions but of those contradictions with the environment itself. In this world view that emphasizes the flow of behavior, then, the nature of knowledge is not that of being able to measure changes in and stability of entities locatable in space and time; it is rather the nature of knowledge to be understood by its fruits, that is, the praxis, the concrete knowledge. Furthermore, as distinguished from the starting points of similarity and difference as summarized earlier, the starting point in this world view is that of action in growth and development.

When one wonders whether it is possible for an arguer out of the classical mold to confront and be confronted by one from the dialectical approach, the statement by Brockriede takes on the appearance of a chasm. Not only are differing approaches to categories evidenced, but there also appears to be an unbridgeable value difference between the classical and the dialectical views of argument. The classical, while being able to acknowledge change and to account for it, appears to prefer stability. The dialectical, while being able to account for stability, emphasizes and appears to prefer change. These approaches appear to differ at crucial points on the fundamental nature of reality. The advocate of classical reasoning sees a reality in which analysis is the fundamental operation of discourse. The dialectical advocate sees the polar term as the central quality of reasoning and regards synthesis as the more fundamental role of discourse. Even at the point of these two types of arguers considering what is to be data or evidence, there appears to be a branching of the road between the two. The classical reasoner sees evidence as an entity in its own right, an entity appearing directly in a quantifiable and intersubjective way to the observer who does not alter, create, or influence that evidence — which is of itself unambiguous and non-self contradictory. On the other hand, the emphasis of the dialectical reasoner is upon action (roughly, praxis), and the advocate of this myth conceives of evidence not as being directly presentable, not as being unambiguous, not as being intersubjectively reproducible, and not as being separate from the observer. Rather, evidence lies in the realization within the doer of the consequences of actions. This data is part of and is related not only to the knower but also to the set of interrelating circumstances that make up an ecology of history

(Kvale, 1976). Compared to the classical arguer, the person who argues from the dialectical point of view and the metaphor of action as growth and development is likely to feel that there has been a great gain through practice of the dialectical axioms and formulae. That gain may seem so marked that dialogue with advocates from the classical view can be safely set aside.

Traps of Dialectical Reasoning

Not to be set aside, however, is the recurring principle that all macroscopic versions of argument—depending as they do upon the abstractive functions of language—have omissions leading to gaps or to traps. Again, as in the case of classical practical reasoning, Horn (1984, p. 11) describes some of these traps for the dialectical arguer. First, if we recall the axiom that changes of degree can lead to changes of kind, then we are reminded that error could accumulate by means of the idea that "more" of anything automatically leads to "better" in something. Relatedly, we can be led into the misconception that changes in degree can be forced upon entities, societies, or individuals. We are also more likely to assume that changes of quantity always lead to something qualitatively better. This occurs when the second axiom of dialectic, internal contradictions, says to us that the creative influence in human affairs is always conflict. Since conflict is always present, it is acceptable that there be antagonism between polar influences. Finally, we may be misled by the axiom of synthesis to think that the confrontation of contradictories always has to produce a winner and a loser. As this expected event plays itself out, there is no limit to the transformations (syntheses), which carry the process of development to ever-higher planes.

So far, the advocate is prepared to be more critical of his/her own position, more sensitive in refutation of others, and more appreciative of alternative frames of reference for argument when any particular discourse is traced back (1) to its starting points in a world view, (2) to a key metaphor useful for generating categories, (3) to the forms and rules for argument that accompany such a metaphor, and (4) to the version of the reality that lies behind such moves.

Nothing that has been said so far, however, can lend an insight into the basis for an internally consistent, ecumenical approach to argument (as opposed to confusing eclecticism) embodied in the career of Wayne Brockriede. In internally consistent ways, the classical approach to practical reasoning affirms that choices made by human advocates will be of the "either-or" variety. At the same time, while the dialectic version of practical reasoning contains a strong flavor of the "either-or" choice within the doctrine of contradictions, its emphasis upon synthesis of those contradictions leads to an emphasis on the "both-and" version of choices for human decision makers. If we were to stop here, it would be then a question of whether the relationship between classical reasoning and dialectical reasoning were a choice between (1) "either-or" or (2) "both-and." If reasoners have to use either the classical or the dialectical frame of reference, then one must conclude that no shared frame of reference is present to make possible the practice of argument. It is when we begin to find new levels of common-sense experience that a third alternative for argument becomes possible. A third alternative affirms that since we can have both classical and dialectical modes of argument in the discussion of a public question, there is or at least can be a shared frame of reference entailing the two. That frame of reference is the subject of the next section.

C. The Trialectic Frame of Reference for Argument

Someone has said recently that physics has become the new philosophy. Behind such a statement is the common-sense experience, among physicists at least, of a real reality marked by the paradox that light is both wave and particle. Indeed, some physicists such as David Bohm have gone more deeply into the paradox of modern theoretical physics to see a reality not composed of separate entities nor one composed of processes driven by contradictions, but rather one in which seemingly discrete objects or actions are only patterns of interference between matter and energy. Even matter consists of relatively persistent patterns of energy interference. While physicists may disagree that this is a common sense experience, lay persons will find holograms pointing toward a reality not of entities, nor of events, but of interference patterns. The reality captured on a photographic plate of the holographic image is not only a three-dimensional one but also a reality of partlessness. This partlessness appears convincingly when the holographic image, under certain conditions, is shattered and reveals a coherent picture of the whole in each fragment rather than a jig-saw pattern requiring piecing together to produce a coherent picture.

Forms of Trialectic Reasoning

Impressive as the experience of the hologram is, however, this example does not convey the sense of dynamism present in a reality of interferences among patterns of energy. Physicist David Bohm has a favorite visual analogy for that dynamism. He likes to show a drop of dye contained in a volume of glycerine. When rotated in one direction, the dye is dissipated to the point that it suddenly disappears; when rotated in the opposite direction, the droplet of dye reappears as suddenly as it had disappeared. This is a metaphor, believes Bohm, for the way in which reality moves in cycles from an enfolded, implicate state, to an unfolded, explicate state (Bohm, 1983). Together, then, the hologram and the droplet of dye stand as metaphors for a partless and cyclic reality, one comprising what Bohm (1983) calls the holomovement. These appeals to common sense then of the hologram and the droplet of dye, commit us to the possibility that a new frame of reference for arguing is possible, one with new rules for forming its categories and with new procedures for interrelating them. It is to that issue that I now turn.

In the midst of common-sense experience of a partless and cyclic reality, the basis for deriving categories subsumes those in both classical and dialectical frames of reference. The categories do not depend on defining attributes of entities, nor do they depend upon the consequences of practice; rather, they come from a holistic view of reality—a version of what Warren Weaver has called the conception of organized complexity. These categories, then, have to be derived in a way appropriate to systemic description. As such, they partake both of synthesis (the emphasis in dialectic argument) and of analysis (the emphasis in classical argument). The analysis is subordinate to the synthesis, but it is a necessary step in the constitution of trialectic argument.

The philosophers and practitioners of trialectic tell us that the system of energy capturing, retention, and dissipation depends, as do all systems, on categories of subsystems. One subsystem category is known as the attractive. The attractive subsystem is a nexus for the collection of energy in what we think of as material substance. The attractive subsystem is a synthesis of all of those processes which we habitually think of as growth. Next, the active subsystem is thought of as the energy itself which is being transformed. This subsystem, broadly defined, includes all the forms of energy which have been defined in other views of reality. Thirdly, synthesizing the attractive subsystem and the active subsystem is a functional subsystem. This category is one that we are accustomed to thinking of as any describable process, the function or the process of digestion, for example. Finally, the subsystem "result" in trialectic is the outcome of the first three. In turn, the result or outcome may itself become an active subsystem, an attractive subsystem, or a function. These category rules, then, help to produce an analysis which is based on synthesis. This approach to categorizing fits with a version of the reality that has the whole residing in every part. Within the active subsystem, there is the seed of the attractive subsystem and vice versa. The function and the result as subsystems not only indicate and depend on the attractive and active subsystems but also contain within themselves the seeds of each other. Further, these subsystems as categories of thought help to account for the dynamics of cyclic movement from implicate to explicate orders (as demonstrated by the drop of dye example).

The scheme or prescription for reasoning as initiated by Ichazo (1976, 1982) and as represented by Voorhees follows and is analogous to the modified syllogism for classical argument and to the stream of behavior labeled thesis-antithesis-synthesis in the dialectic mode.

In Figure 1, the patterned energy (Material Manifestation Point or MMP) **attracting** and transforming energy from other MMPs (the **active** subsystem) via a process of **function** (which is *not* an MMP) equals an outcome or **result**.

Figure 1
(After Vorhees)

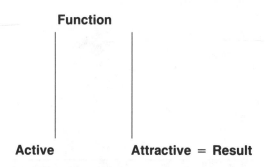

Function

Active   Attractive = Result

A persistent pattern of energy interferences (**Attractive**) transforms energy from other systems (**Active**) via a process (**Function**) with an outcome (**Result**) that may itself become a material manifestation point (MMP).

As Figure 2 makes clear, systems are transformable into each other. The arguer for changes in the moral code of a social group or culture will draw recommendations from (1) the power system (both the "entity" of power as construed by classical arguers and power*making* in the praxis of dialectical reasoners) and (2) the knowledge system (both the "entity" of ideas as construed by classical advocates and the knowledge*making* as enacted by dialectical ones). In turn, when the need system is active (transforming) in support of mutations either in "power" or "knowledge," it will be seen to include both the classicist's *abstracted* need/s and the dialectician's need*making* (Brown, 1978, 1982, 1986, 1987b).

Relatable to the scheme just discussed are the three axioms of trialectics as summarized by Horn (1983b). The first recognizes that reality is composed 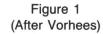 of processes of interference in energy and that when the energy is manifested in a persisting pattern of interferences, it has the capacity to change suddenly, just as the droplet of dye can suddenly appear and disappear. That axiom is, according to Horn, a mutation "from one material manifestation point (MMP) to another material manifestation point." This mutation, according to the meaning of systems, is completed, says Horn, "when internal equilibrium has been achieved" (p. 16). With reference to the outline above, material manifestation points would involve the attractive, that which is attracting energy to itself; the active, those patterns of energy to be transformed; and the result, a mutation. To repeat, the function, while responsible for the transformation, is not itself a material manifestation point. The mutation is completed when internal balance is reached in the new state.

Further light is shed on the nature of the equilibrium by reference to the second axiom. This axiom says that instead of contradictories found internally in all events (as is the case according to dialectic reasoning), there are only

Figure 2
(After Brown)

Function: Motivating

| |

| |

Active: Attractive: =   Result:
Power Systems Need Systems   Moral Code
Knowledge Systems

Function: Relationizing

| |

| |

Active: Attractive: =   Result:
Need System   Power Systems   Power Code
Knowledge Systems

Function: Ideologizing

| |

| |

Active: Attractive: =   Result:
Need Systems   Knowledge   Truth Code
Power Systems Systems

Organismic systems, with each containing the "seed" of others, have the potential of being either **Attractive** or **Active** as functions change.

apparent opposites seeming to foster the exchange of energy internally. Instead of contradictions, these are abstracted opposites which, says Horn, depend "on a balanced circulation of energy" (p. 16). With reference to the scheme above, the seed of opposites (as will be discussed shortly) will appear in all of the MMPs; hence, an MMP that is active will contain within itself a seed of attraction; an MMP that is attractive will contain within itself a seed of the active; and the MMP of result will contain within itself the seed either of the active or attractive.

As all of these possibilities exist in a unified way, the third axiom of trialectic (3) reasoning emerges. Motion from enfolded energy to unfolded energy comes about because of the attraction of energy from one material manifestation point to another. The first axiom, stressing the appearance of change, is that of mutation. The second axiom, stating that energy moves between MMPs and that each MMP contains apparent opposites that circulate energy within itself, is the axiom of circulation. The third axiom, pointing out that movement depends upon the attraction of energy up and down a hierarchy of MMPs, is the axiom of attraction.

Finally, just as classical philosophers gave us the syllogism and its contemporary modifications as macro-strategy for managing argument, and just as Hegelian and post-Hegelian thinkers gave us the macro-strategy of thesis-antithesis-synthesis for managing dialectic argument, Caswell has laid out the procedures for managing trialectic discourse.

Rules for Trialectic Reasoning

Preceding Caswell's injunctions, however, is Horn's (1983b) illustration of the systemic categories of trialectics involved in what he calls a process or a function of reasoning. In this example, the attracting MMP is what Horn calls "X," the feeling of puzzlement (p. 24). The active subsystem is mind, with the result (given the function of reasoning) being a solution or understanding. Nested within that trialectical view of what I call practical reasoning and of what Horn calls psychology, are the injunctions of Caswell (1983). All should be read as describing three different material manifestation points as argument for the process of arguing—an argument for argumentation.

The first injunction is that via the axiom of attraction, the reasoner will look for levels forming a hierarchy of material manifestation points. The reasoner will be aware that movement in the real reality may be from a higher to a lower MMP or vice versa. For instance, the arguer for a comprehensive policy to reduce drug abuse may make human "needs" the superordinate **attractive** subsystem (or MMP) at the top of the hierarchy including human "power" systems and human "knowledge" systems as **active** subsystems (MMPs) to be transformed in service of "needs." Since the attractive contains the seed of the active and vice-versa the advocate could make "knowledge" or "power" systems, respectively, the **attractive** principle in reasoning toward a policy recommendation, while at the same time making a workable choice to limit the potentially inexhaustible relations among "need," "power," and "knowledge" or "attention."

In addition to this injunction to posit systemic hierarchy premised on the axiom of attraction, the reasoner will also attempt to see how within each MMP—regardless of its place in the hierarchy—there are apparent polarities which make possible the circulation within the MMP of energy for the maintenance of the MMP itself. Growing out of this will be the conception not only of cycles *within* an MMP but the possibility of cycles *between* MMPs. For example, within MMPs of "need," "power," and "knowledge" (or attention) systems are apparent polarities. There are individual versus collective versions of need; cooperation vies with competition in providing the basis for human relationships as the locus of power; and anomalous-nonanomalous conceptions fuel the continuation and disruption of truth codes. Cycles *within* MMPs occuring as first one polar term and then the other best describes the system state at a given time. Cycles *between* MMPs occur in the transformation of systems into others and in the patterns of influence among themselves.

The reasoner is cautioned to look beyond the hierarchy and the circulation within and between the hierarchies to the systemic dynamics overall which would include those categories discussed above. What are the stable and the transitional manifestations that account for the sudden jumps or mutations in the unfolded reality? To answer that, as already developed by Voorhees, the attractive variables need to be seen as related to the active variables by means of a function or process which has as output a result, which in turn can become itself the attractive or active or perhaps even a function. For example, the advocate of a policy for remedying drug abuse will see that the overall systemic dynamic is the exchange of energy between deviance-*compensating* and deviance-*amplifying* states of energy. As long as the "need," "power," or "knowledge" MMP is within itself deviance-compensating, there are no sudden jumps or transitions in the overall system. However, when a subsystem of "need," "power," or "knowledge" will be deviance-*amplifying* unless influenced by the others, then this transition makes manifest a mutation.

Such mutability as featured in the worldview of trialectics provides the basis for paradox as generating metaphor (Brown, 1987a) of this worldview. The trialectic advocate, then, thinks not so much linearly, nor so much interactively, as paradoxically. This stands alongside similarity and difference for classical argument, and alongside the act of growth for dialectic argument. In this version of reality, the choices apparent to the arguer are, paradoxically "neither-nor." The choice is neither classical reasoning by itself nor dialectic reasoning by itself but instead is both classical and dialectical in order to arrive at trialectical.

The practitioners of the latter recognize that the more enduring the MMP, the more appropriate is the classical approach to arguing. They also realize that the more fluctuating the MMP, the more appropriate is the dialectical mode of argument. Including, but going beyond, these frames of reference is trialectic which takes as its starting point not the conceptualizing of stable entities, nor the categorizing of conflict, but rather the realization of radical holism. In fact, the subtitle of the work introducing and promoting trialectics is "Toward a Practical Logic of Unity" (Horn, 1983). In this systemic view of reality and argument, everything relates to everything; no single line of influence either in a linearly causal way or in a dynamic of contradiction will account for development in this relatively organismic view of reality. The consequences of dynamics will be neither single in nature nor limited in their awareness of side-effects. The pattern of argument in this third frame of reference promises to open up a human ability to deal not with random complexity (as is the case with statistical inference) but rather with organized complexity.

Traps of Trialectic Reasoning

Powerful as this frame of reference may be as an interesting means for viewing modes of argument as complementary, there are gaps and potential pitfalls awaiting the practitioner. The first and perhaps most basic gap is that in attempting to devise macro-strategies for discourse that is truly holistic, the reasoner may forget that these resolutions are necessarily abstractive. Since any abstraction is not the whole from which it abstracts, the fallacy would be to confuse the abstraction with the whole (Bohm, 1982, p. 63). Horn (1983b, p. 33) has suggested other traps that may await the practitioner of trialectics. One trap which Horn describes is that the arguer will throw out the baby with the bathwater by concluding erroneously that other frames of reference for argument are useless, when in fact they have roles complementary to that of trialectics. Another trap into which advocates might fall is thinking that trialectics—having mistakenly been taken as isomorphic with a partless reality and thereby having eliminated the necessity for either classical or dialectical modes—can be used to coerce auditors into agreement by simply accusing them of not acting trialectically. The use of the "force" of trialectical argument to coerce agreement is a version of the trap in dialectics that the addition of energy can always make, by degrees, a qualitatively better kind. Another gap or trap is that the systemic analysis and synthesis necessary for trialectic argument may be as endless as the interconnectedness of reality itself. To pursue ad infinitum all the interconnections among MMPs and their flows of energy up and down a hierarchy is to carry out a version of the trap in classical argument that definition by itself will solve problems.

The ability that trialecticians have to see how dialectical and classical frames of reference can be manifest within the trialectic mode of argument suggests that the new "logic" has within it a capacity for interrelating, respecting, and using all modes of argument. It is on this ground that the student of argument may find an appreciation of ecumenical approaches to practical reasoning. To be precise, the modes of argument discussed in the chapter may constitute a shared frame of reference in Brockriede's sense which will allow the argument to go forward among advocates of various modes, either explicitly or implicitly. The shared frame is this: given the terms of subordination and superordination, it is possible (1) that the classical mode of argument subordinates the dialectical and the trialectical (classical arguer); (2) that the dialectical mode of argument subordinates the classical and the trialectical (dialectical arguer); and (3) that the trialectical mode of argument subordinates the classical and the dialectical (trialectical arguer). Lest the reader believe that the only place at which this confrontation can occur is on the level of argument about argument, the reader will remember that in a discussion of specific policies whose practicalities lead to the necessity for a decision, those three topics just listed can be brought to bear in a microscopic way as well as in a more macroscopic search. The living myth of a shared frame of reference for argument is nested within our living, taken-for-granted visions of the real reality. Specific policy debates, in turn, entail modes of argument that fit realities of (1) a "classical" world in which the whole is the sum of the parts; (2) a "dialectical" world made whole by action; and (3) a "trialectical" world in which the part contains the whole.

Perhaps the living myth of all myths of argument by which we live is that we shall know our myths and that such knowledge and knowing will make us free.

Chapter Fifteen

Darwin, Thales and the Milkmaid

Scientific Revolution and Argument from Common Beliefs and Common Sense

John Angus Campbell

According to legend, the philosopher Thales, intent upon observing the heavens, fell into a well from which he had to be rescued by a milkmaid. The story symbolizes the gulf separating theoretical knowledge and common sense. The theorist, in order to study what is distant and abstract, must remove himself or herself from the affairs of every day and, in so doing, risks overlooking some gaping practical facts. The person of common sense, totally absorbed with the here and now, cannot help but notice the practical facts but risks missing the larger pattern. The story seems to have two morals: first, common sense must occasionally rescue theory from its disregard of the immediate; and second, if theory is to avoid appearing ridiculous, it must find a way of coming to grips with common sense. No necessity required Thales or the milkmaid to sacrifice one approach to understanding the world in order to develop the other. As Bernard Lonergan (1958, p. 182) points out, Thales might have avoided the well because he was not blind, and the milkmaid might have taken an interest in the stars because she was human. The story suggests that the path of wisdom is to use both: to employ the special insights of theory for dealing with the general and the perspective of common

Mr. Campbell is in the Department of Speech Communication at the University of Washington, Seattle.

207

sense for dealing with the particular. Simple as this principle is to understand, it can be very difficult, or impossible, to apply. The problem is especially perplexing in the case of scientific revolution.

Scientific revolution, by definition, means a major theoretical change in a prior vision of the world (Kuhn, 1970a). Technically, one might suppose that here, if anywhere, theory would be free to speak its own language without resorting to the distorting analogies and metaphors required for theoretical truths to penetrate ordinary minds. Revolutions in science, however, entail a rhetorical "Catch 22." To the extent that an idea is truly revolutionary, it risks being unintelligible, or at the very least ridiculous, both from the standpoint of prior theory and from the standpoint of common sense!

A good example of how common sense must rescue theoretical novelty from the well of abstraction is the Copernican revolution. Copernicus, because he believed that numbers held the key to reality and that he could achieve simpler calculations by a novel assumption, challenged the traditional Aristotelian view that the earth stood still at the center of the cosmos while the sun and planets circled around it. While Aristotle's view was based on the quasi-theoretical notion that each element had a nature—the earth naturally seeking the center, and the heavens naturally tending upward—what supported it in the concrete was ordinary experience. The most obvious objection to Copernicus was that if the earth moved, why could no one perceive it? Copernicus had no cogent response to this objection, and for eighty-eight years after his death (1544) Copernicus' ideas were generally regarded as absurd by all but a handful of astronomers. In his *Dialogue on the Two World Systems*, (1632) Galileo advanced an analogy, which, while certainly less than a proof, proved extremely persuasive. Galileo asked whether when aboard a ship a traveler was aware of whether the vessel was in movement or at rest (Galilei, 1967). The "Galilean theory of relativity," that a moving body communicates its motion to all bodies attached to it, is an ingenious example of "common sense" argument used to remove the imputation of ridiculousness from an abstract theory. So powerfully did Galileo's notion of the earth as a ship in the sea of space appeal to the emerging common sense of an age of expanding commerce and ocean going exploration, that the old common sense of a stable earth seemed less sure than the new analogy! Not until the early 1830s were telescopes powerful enough to observe stellar parallax—the movement of the "fixed stars" which proved the motion of the earth. The decisive battle over Copernicanism had been fought and won two hundred years earlier, not by demonstration, but by a special blend of theoretical and practical argument—a theoretical account to challenge the received cosmology, and a practical one to render a new theory credible (Kuhn, 1959).

From the point of view of theory, this particular story had a happy ending—Copernicanism won. From a practical standpoint the outcome was less unequivocal—Galileo paid for his inventiveness by spending the rest of his life under house arrest where he had been placed by the Inquisition. An issue the Copernican revolution leaves unresolved is the proper role of traditional beliefs, common sense understanding and ordinary language in debates over abstract theoretical questions. Is ordinary language simply a "convenience" for a theorist in a hurry—a kind of "7-Eleven" of the mind—or does the attempt to explain theoretical issues in common terms in some way render revolutionary theory hostage to traditional beliefs? When Thales took hold of the milkmaid's rope, what kind of relationship was he entering?

This chapter will examine the tension between theoretic insight, traditional beliefs and common sense argument in a scientific revolution of the same magnitude as the Copernican, but from a different century and on a different subject: the revolution in biological and popular thought brought about by the publication in 1859 of Charles Darwin's *On the Origin of Species*. Our aim will be to understand how Darwin's presentation of his theory, like Galileo's defense of Copernicus, required not merely theoretic insight, but something quite beyond what we ordinarily think of as proper to "science"— the ability to use informal argument to save theory from ridicule and make abstraction a viable cultural force.

A. Darwin Rediscovers Thales' Well

There are two distinct but inter-related aspects of Darwin's scientific revolution—each of which alone would have rendered it objectionable, and both of which together made it little short of outrageous. The first is the theory of evolution, the second is Darwin's explanatory mechanism—natural selection.

Evolution. Evolution is simply the idea that the present world of plants and animals are the modified descendants of earlier plants and animals. Evolution was certainly not original with Darwin. Six separate thinkers, including his own grandfather Erasmus (1731-1802), introduced one or another version of evolution in the seventy years prior to the publication of the *Origin*. Darwin is important to the history of theories of evolution in general because only after his account did the idea itself become a force in theoretical biology and in popular culture—the world of common sense (Vorzimmer, 1970). The distinctive feature of Darwin's version—the thing for which he is celebrated to this day—is his explanation of the mechanism which drives evolution.

Natural Selection. Natural selection is the application to evolution of Malthus's doctrine of population dynamics. According to Malthus (1766-1834), food supply increases arithmetically while population increases geometrically. The result of this incessant intraspecific competition for scarce resources, is that not as many organisms live as are born. To this thoroughly negative doctrine, Darwin, and later the co-discoverer of natural selection, Alfred Russel Wallace (1823-1913), added two elements which made Malthus' law a positive dynamic force—*variation* and *inheritance*. Darwin and Wallace taught that variation in nature was unlimited and that, while some variations were neutral, others aided the organism in the struggle for life and would be passed on to its descendants. When one combines *variation, inheritance*, and the *struggle for existence*, one is left with *differential reproduction*. Allow differential reproduction to continue over virtually unlimited time in an unlimited variety of changing environments and the result is organic change or evolution (Vorzimmer, 1970). An endless game of biological musical chairs allows one to explain preservation, extinction and novelty. The themes of novelty or origin, preservation, and competition (implying success and extinction), are captured in the full title of Darwin's book: *On the Origin of Species by Means of Natural Selection, or The Preservation of Favoured Races in the Struggle for Life* (Darwin, 1967).

What the Darwin/Wallace theory is not. The Darwin/Wallace theory is not a theory about the origin of life, of variation, or the dynamics of inheritance. Darwin's theory assumes one or a few simple forms of life to have been originally created. He proceeds from there to explain how through the operation of known natural laws, these forms may have become modified and diversified into the abundant and varied life we see. *The Darwin/Wallace theory is not inherently progressive.* According to the Darwin/Wallace theory, complexification will sometimes be an adaptive advantage but not always. Under appropriate circumstances complex organisms would become simpler ("lower") to better adapt to the new conditions. Unlike virtually every other theory of evolution, the Darwin/Wallace theory sees no inherently progressive feature in life itself. The Darwin/Wallace theory does not require evolution to occur but attempts to explain the apparent fact that it has (Vorzimmer, 1981).

Darwin backs into Thales' well. The Thales' well of Darwinism is its abstractness. Though Darwin's theory is extremely simple to explain— (Malthus' law + variation + inheritance = differential reproduction, differential reproduction + time = evolution), it is difficult for the mind to grasp—let alone believe. Proper Victorians regarded the regularities of organic nature as evidence of divine wisdom and creative power. To ask them to see the blossom of a flower or the claws of an eagle as unintended effects of forces as random as those which sculpt the slopes of shifting dunes, was to invite ridicule (Campbell, 1986; Himmelfarb, 1959; Irvine, 1959). Not only was, and is, Darwin's leading idea difficult to imagine (and patently ridiculous to our ordinary ways of thought) but Darwin's vision required a change in the perspective of science. Darwin was saying that species, the pride of the taxonomist, were not permanent entities—not finally real—but temporary breeding populations, eddies in a flowing river of life. Further, he was not resting his argument upon the elegant certainties of Newton's laws but upon messy statistical probabilities of the "all things being equal" variety. Ghiselin (1969) aptly summarizes Darwin's argument "*If* there is variation, *if* the variants differ in fitness, and *if* the variations are inherited, *then*, there is evolutionary change—sometimes" (p. 72). Finally (and especially for Darwin's contemporaries) when one viewed the adaptations of nature not as instances of divine wisdom, design and goodness, but as the result of variation, struggle and death, a shadow came over the world and nature seemed a much less kind and gentle place.

To say that Darwin's deduction of evolution from differential reproduction tumbled him into Thales' well is an understatement. Darwin's theory offended established science, religion, and common sense. The technical features of Darwin's thought made it attractive to an elite group of fellow scientists. The focus of our analysis will be how Darwin used conventional religious beliefs and conventional common sense to make a theory which seemed irreligious, absurd and radical appear pious, intelligible and respectable.

B. Two Strands in the Milkmaid's Rope

Religion

Much as we associate the name of Darwin with a challenge to religious belief, we must remember that he is buried in Westminster Abbey. While this fact is not without irony, one of the most remarkable aspects of Darwin's defense of his theory was his use of religious premises.

While an undergraduate at Cambridge, Darwin had been pursuing a degree in divinity. His career ambition both before and during his around-the-world voyage on the Beagle (1831-1836) was to become a country parson in the Church of England. From his earliest speculations about evolution in the notebooks (1837-1839), Darwin had seen evolution (under one theory or another, and he went through several) as a mode in which the deity operates. While Darwin's development of the theory of natural selection caused him to see that God did not directly intervene in each detail of nature, he held the belief that nature presumed a creator—at least in a general sense—throughout his life (Brent, 1981; Gillespie, 1979; Himmelfarb, 1959).

Science in England, especially since its advent in the seventeenth century, had been closely associated with religious faith. Indeed, one of the aims of the Royal Society was to glorify God as well as to improve humanity's estate (Cope & Jones, 1959). Darwin's *Origin* builds upon the established scientific tradition of finding in nature evidences of God's being, wisdom and power. In the first edition, Darwin's flyleaf contained two citations from works in the tradition of English natural theology, one from William Whewell's *Bridgewater Treatise* (1831) and one from Francis Bacon's *Advancement of Learning* (1605). In the second edition, the first two citations were reinforced by a third from Bishop Butler's *Analogy of Revealed Religion* (1736).

> But with regard to the material world, we can at least go so far as this—we can perceive that events are brought about not by insulated interpositions of Divine power, exerted in each particular case, but by the establishment of general laws.   W. Whewell, *Bridgewater Treatise*

To conclude therefore, let no man out of a weak conceit of sobriety, or an ill-applied moderation, think or maintain, that a man can search too far or be too well studied in the book of God's word or the book of God's works; divinity or philosophy; but rather let me endeavor an endless progress or proficience in both.

Bacon, *Advancement of Learning*

The only distinct meaning of the word 'natural' is *stated*, *fixed*, or *settled*; since what is natural as much requires and presupposes an intelligent agent to render it so, *i.e.*, to effect it continually or at stated times, as what is supernatural or miraculous does to effect it for once.

Butler, *Analogy of Revealed Religion*

In the first edition, the famous final line, which begins "There is grandeur in this view of life," continues "with its several powers, having been originally breathed into a few forms or into one. . . ." Starting in the second edition, the line has been changed to read "breathed by the Creator into a few forms or into one. . . ." (Peckham, 1959, p. 490).

Darwin's use of religious premises was not confined to the beginning and end of his work. Central portions of Darwin's argument turn upon religious premises. At the conclusion of the third chapter, "Struggle for Existence," where Darwin has underscored the fierce competition between and among all living things, he shows how this somber fact reaffirms the conventional view of nature as ultimately kind and benevolent. "When we reflect on this struggle, we may console ourselves with the full belief, that the war of nature is not incessant, that no fear is felt, that death is generally prompt, and that the vigorous, the healthy, and the happy survive and multiply (Darwin, 1967, p. 79). In the fourth chapter, "Natural Selection," the language in which Darwin introduces the scientific alternative to special creation is positively sermonic: "How fleeting are the wishes and efforts of man! How short his time! And consequently how poor will his products be, compared with those accumulated by nature. . . . Can we wonder, then, that nature's productions . . . should plainly bear the stamp of far higher workmanship?" (Darwin, 1967, p. 84).

In the fifth chapter, Darwin argues that either the evidence he has presented indicates evolution is the known law of creation or God is the author of deceit. Having reviewed the evidence of the various species of the horse genus, Darwin argues that the appearance of stripes on colts is evidence of a common ancestor uniting the horse, wild ass, hemionus, quagga and zebra. To assert to the contrary that each of these has been specially created is "to reject a real for an unreal, or at least for an unknown cause," and "makes the works of God a mere mockery and deception" (Darwin, 1967, p. 167). In chapter six, Darwin addresses probably his most difficult case—to explain how the eye could have been formed by natural selection. Here again Darwin argues that assuming that the eye was formed by natural selection is an assumption more pious and deferential to the Creator than the traditional view that the eye was formed by the way man makes optical instruments for himself. Having described how a wide variety of eyes suitable for very different creatures may have been developed from an aboriginal filament sensitive to light, Darwin observes, "Let this process go on for millions on millions of years . . . and may we not believe that a living optical instrument might thus be formed as superior to one of glass, as the works of the Creator are to those of man?" (Darwin, 1967, p. 189).

Darwin also created religious problems for the reader and explained how evolution by natural selection offered a way out of them. Traditional natural theology — at least in one of its versions — affirmed that God was directly responsible for each adaptation of the animal to its environment. At the close of chapter seven, Darwin takes several of nature's ingenious adaptations and underscores the embarrassment they cause to the customary belief in divine goodness. "Finally, it may not be a logical deduction, but to my imagination it is far more satisfactory to look at such instincts as the young cuckoo ejecting its foster-brothers, — ants making slaves, — the larvae of the ichneumonidae feeding within the live bodies of caterpillars, — not as specially endowed or created instincts, but as small consequences of one general law, leading to the advancement of all organic beings (Darwin, 1967, pp. 243-244).

Here the reader is placed in a double bind; if he or she affirms the traditional argument for direct divine creation, God is the author of evil. But with the temptation, Darwin has provided a way of escape — that God works through general laws and these specific laws, not the immediate will of the creator.

The first two years of the *Origin's* reception placed extreme pressure on Darwin to make his theory compatible with traditional views of design. Darwin yielded to this pressure. Perhaps the most striking use of religious argument in the *Origin* appears directly following the table of contents and was added in 1861. The passage reads:

> An admirable . . . review of this work including an able discussion on the Theological bearing of the belief in the descent of species, has now been . . . published by Professor Asa Gray, M.D., Fisher Professor of Natural History in Harvard University. (*Origin*, Variorum text, p. ix.)

The reader of *The Origin* would not know that Darwin himself was responsible for financing publication of Gray's essays in pamphlet form (originally they appeared as unsigned essays in the *Atlantic Monthly*) and until 1867 he would have no way of knowing that Darwin did not believe in the argument they contained. While in private letters Darwin expressed his clear differences with Gray, it was not until 1867 that he publicly rejected Gray's argument in the conclusion to his two volume *Variation in Plants and Animals Under Domestication* (Campbell, 1989; F. Darwin, 1911). No mention of this refutation was ever made in the subsequent two editions of *The Origin* (1869, 1872). Indeed, throughout the body of his book, whether the reader examines Darwin's case for the ancestry of the horse or his account of how natural selection could have formed the eye, Darwin urges his views as more in keeping with proper respect to the ways of Providence than the views of his opponents.

Darwin's use of Gray's pamphlets—and he had them distributed free of charge to various eminent clergy and scientists—is simply the farthest extreme to which he carried what already was a conservative argumentative strategy. Darwin's encouragement to his reader to place a more orthodox interpretation on his book than he personally was able to, underscores the importance Darwin attached to minimizing the religious offense of his theory and to maximizing how intelligible evolution appeared in light of established beliefs and modes of perception.

Common Sense

Equal to the perceptual shock which Darwin's theory administered to conventional religion was the outrage it committed on "common sense." Whether one was an orthodox believer or a hard headed empiricist (or both), random variation seemed a preposterous foundation on which to rest a theory explaining nature's exquisite organic patterns. John Herschel, whose *Preliminary Discourse* had been Darwin's first textbook in scientific method and which in part had inspired him toward a career in science, privately characterized the theory of natural selection (much to Darwin's dismay) as "the law of higgeldy piggeldy" (F. Darwin, 1911, p. 37). Even Thomas Henry Huxley, whose public defenses of Darwin earned him the title of "Darwin's bulldog," seemed not to comprehend fully natural selection. Darwin's private judgment on Huxley's first public lecture on the subject was that it had been a complete failure (F. Darwin, 1903). While a few minds grasped the core of Darwin's principle immediately, throughout the later nineteenth century—and well into the twentieth—skeptics about the principle of natural selection were more plentiful than believers (Bowler, 1985, pp. 641-682). From a rhetorical point of view, Darwin's failure to convince his peers of the truth of his specific theory is largely beside the point. Darwin's skill in setting forth in colloquial language a case for a mechanism plausibly capable of bringing about evolutionary change successfully persuaded many of his readers that one or another naturalistic theory of the origin of species had to be true. The key to Darwin's strategy was to present evolution by natural selection as though it could be seen—indeed, to convince the reader that his theory was not an inference from facts but a fact the reader had witnessed.

Darwin's attempt to align his theory of evolution with concrete observation and to dissociate it from abstract inference begins with the *Origin's* first line. Darwin inaugurates the *Origin* by presenting himself as a passive witness to active facts rather than as a theorist with an active mind. "When on board H.M.S. 'Beagle' as naturalist, I was much struck with certain facts in the distribution of the organic beings inhabiting South America, and in the geological relations of the present to the past inhabitants of that continent.'' Each subsequent sentence in the opening paragraph stresses facts and observation and minimizes theory.

> These facts, as will be seen in the latter chapters of this volume, seemed to throw some light on the origin of species — that mystery of mysteries, as it has been called by one of our greatest philosophers. On my return home, it occurred to me, in 1837, that something might perhaps be made out on this question by patiently accumulating and reflecting on all sorts of facts which could possibly have any bearing on it. After five years' work I allowed myself to speculate on the subject, and drew up some short notes; these I enlarged in 1844 into a sketch of the conclusions, which seemed to me probable: from that period to the present day I have steadily pursued the same object. I hope that I may be excused for entering on these personal details, as I give them to show that I have not been hasty in coming to a decision (Darwin, 1967, p. 1).

Even in the third sentence of the paragraph when the scene shifts to Darwin's personal reflection, his use of the passive construction ''it occurred to me'' and the ambiguous statement ''something might be made out . . .'' keep attention on the facts and away from his role as a theorist. His one reference to theoretical reflection: ''After five years work I allowed myself to speculate on the subject. . . .'' appears to have been an indulgence confined to a single episode. The objective cast of Darwin's paragraph is doubly underscored when, in the final sentence he apologizes for having even troubled the reader by mentioning his role in developing the theory. ''I hope that I may be excused for entering on these personal details, as I give them to show that I have not been hasty in coming to a decision.''

That Darwin's account of his discovery in the first paragraph of the *Origin* is inaccurate, I have dealt with in other essays (Campbell, 1986, 1989). The remarkable feature of the paragraph rhetorically is its description of a major theoretical breakthrough as though it were chiefly the fruit of observation. The pattern foreshadowed in the introduction of the book of leading from fact, with but minimum attention to theory, is recapitulated both in the arrangement and in the style of the subsequent chapters.

By gradual, slow degrees the first four chapters of the *Origin* lead the reader from the familiar ''Variation Under Domestication,'' with its engrossing accounts of the breeder's skill in transforming domestic flocks and herds, to the less familiar ''Variation Under Nature,'' and ''Struggle For Existence,'' to the center of Darwin's theory, ''Natural Selection.'' So subtly does Darwin embed the premises of his theory in apparently straightforward observations, that long before the end of the fourth chapter the reader would feel similarly struck by the facts — as though he or she personally had recapitulated the pattern of discovery described in the *Origin's* opening paragraph.

Chapter four, ''Natural Selection'' is the pivot of Darwin's book — the preceding chapters lead to it, the following chapters rest upon it and extend its implications. Darwin himself described chapter four as "The capstone of my arch." In the *Origin's* fourth chapter, the images of selection, variation, and struggle, introduced in the first three chapters, coalesce into a complex metaphor which occupies a semantic space midway between miracle and mechanism. The root metaphor of the *Origin*, "natural selection," rests upon a complex analogy between nature—the defining characteristics of which (struggle and variation) have been described in chapters two and three—and the breeder whose power both consciously and unconsciously to transform domestic flocks and herds was introduced in chapter one.

The analogy at the heart of "natural selection" is complex because, unlike Galileo's comparison between the earth and a ship, it is not literal. To make the analogy between nature and the breeder make sense, the reader must combine only certain attributes of the breeder and only certain attributes of nature. The analogy is yet more complicated by the fact that each term has been colored by connotations of the other. The narrow ridge of interpretation Darwin must help his reader negotiate is to distinguish the scope and limitation of each half of the analogy while still making heuristic and suasory use of the technically disallowed meanings (Lakoff & Johnson, 1980).

In Darwin's theory, nature is like the breeder in that both in nature and in domestication there is an unstaunchable supply of variation; nature is further like the breeder in that both eliminate certain individuals from their breeding stocks. Nature is not like the breeder in that nature does not consciously choose certain animals or plants to achieve a foreseen end. Thus for Darwin to equate Malthus' laws of population with selection is to use words in a sense that is unusual and technically false. It is Darwin's unusual or misleading use of terms which marks the *Origin* not just as a revolution in theoretical biology but a revolution in common sense. In his metaphor "natural selection" Darwin places conventional language under such pressure as to precipitate a new meaning—an accurate one (or at least a scientifically fruitful one) for a reader well equipped to understand the underlying issues, or an inaccurate (and largely ideological one) for a reader not so happily equipped.

The linguistic and conceptual core of Darwin's case for natural selection rests upon the familiar form of argument known as *a fortiori* or, to the stronger. In its simplest terms, Darwin's claim is that anything humans can do, nature can do better. Yet the extent to which Darwin's terms depart radically from ordinary language emerges only when we observe how Darwin uses the metaphor "natural selection" to create a new category of biological thought and cultural meaning by transferring conventional associations between old categories.

Early in chapter four, Darwin prepares for the introduction of "natural selection" by a lengthy series of contrasts between the breeder and nature. Darwin asks "As man can produce and certainly has produced a great result by his methodical and unconscious means of selection, what may not nature effect?"; and answers: "Man can act only on external and visible characters:

nature cares nothing for appearances, except insofar as they may be useful to any being'' (Darwin, 1967). While most of Darwin's ensuing contrasts stress nature's superior sweep, ''She can act on every internal organ, on every shade of constitutional difference, on the whole machinery of life'' and ruthlessness. Darwin believes that humanity ''does not rigidly destroy all inferior animals, . . .'' and in the end, natural selection not only takes on attributes of the breeder, but attributes of God. In a passage we have examined earlier, Darwin employs language reminiscent of the *Psalms* of the book of *Job*, or of countless sermons on the littleness of humans, to humble the reader before the superior power of a nature redescribed as the breeder writ large.

> How fleeting are the wishes and efforts of man! How short his time! And consequently how poor will his products be, compared with those accumulated by nature during whole geological periods. Can we wonder, then, that nature's productions should be far ''truer'' in character than man's productions; that they should be infinitely better adapted to the most complex conditions of life, and should plainly bear the stamp of far higher workmanship? (Darwin, 1967, p. 84.)

By using the activity of humans as the ground of an analogy with nature, Darwin, in effect, has converted a contrast into a comparison and redescribed nature as a more powerful human. This, of course, is not what the theory of natural selection means, but it is what the theory connotes and the connotation—at variance though it may be with the denotation of random variation and differential reproduction—is what is required to associate the engine of evolution with a world of meaning intelligible to Darwin's audience and to dissociate it from the world of miracles. Having blended the language of animal purposiveness (''struggle''), divine omnipotence (''higher workmanship'') and technology (''selection''), Darwin presents the rhetorical core of his book in the following terms:

> It may be said that natural selection is daily and hourly scrutinizing, throughout the world, every variation, even the slightest; rejecting that which is bad preserving and adding up all that is good; silently and insensibly working; whenever and wherever opportunity offers, at the improvement of each organic being in relation to its organic and inorganic conditions of life. (Darwin, 1967, p. 84.)

The personification of natural selection in this passage completes Darwin's linguistic transfer of the powers of the breeder to nature. Simultaneous with Darwin's redescription of nature as breeder, he has transformed his reader from an outsider—awestruck before nature and without a clue as to how nature develops new species—to a being who understands the origin of species in the same way he or she understands the production of domestic breeds.

The Well, The Rope and The Great Escape
The Price Theory Pays To Common Sense
For Being Understood

As our story of Thales and the milkmaid suggests, the path of wisdom is to employ the insights of theory to address general questions and the perspective of common sense to deal with particular ones. Our study of Darwin and our allusions to Galileo underscore why this principle — so easy to understand — is so difficult to apply.

A novel theoretical insight is difficult to divorce from traditional beliefs and common sense because, in the first place, the emergence of a purely descriptive and technically adequate vocabulary is a historical process. The first expression of a theory will necessarily be allied closely to conventional language and to previous beliefs and understandings. Only gradually will a theoretical vocabulary emerge which significantly transcends the viewpoint of convention. Thales is the first name in the history of physics not because his thought was the most clear, but because his cryptic comment, "All things emerge from water," began a novel symbolism in which speculation about the origin of the world was cast in physical rather than theological terms. Thales also said, "All things are full of gods." While no one knows for certain exactly what he meant by either statement, it is probable — since there was no other vocabulary available — that to indicate the kind of power he was attributing to water, Thales had to relate the term to the accepted creative power attributed to the gods.

Similarly Galileo's analogy between the lack of perceived motion on the earth and the lack of perceived motion on a ship and Darwin's analogy between breeding and evolution enabled each to make use of common sense terms while at the same time to freight those terms with unconventional meanings. In the case of Darwin no less than in the cases of Thales and Galileo, first innovators are rarely conceptual tidiers. Since theory must make use of historically available vocabulary, the initial formulations of a theory will be allied to ordinary language, traditional beliefs and common sense perceptions.

In addition to the historical development required for a technically adequate vocabulary to emerge, the need of conceptual thought for visual images is a second reason common sense and theoretical meanings can be confused. The "point" and the "line" of geometry are accurate primitive terms and no one — geometrician or lay person — can say or think either term without visualizing respectively a " . " or a " _____." Geometrical insight abstracts from these images to grasp the imageless concept of "position without magnitude" or of "the shortest distance between two points." Without the visual images "point" and "line," the theoretical concept would be difficult or impossible to achieve — yet these technically adequate terms mean something other than what they depict (Lonergan, 1958, pp. 7-8).

In the case of evolution as an inference from Malthus, one cannot see evolution happening, for too many variables are involved—Darwin himself described the process as "insensible." Yet both Darwin's technically adequate image of the wedge and his more popular image of "selection" powerfully encourage the reader to think of evolution as something which can be seen. The meaning of an image for an untrained eye and its significance for a technically trained mind must necessarily differ. Not all readers—perhaps very few—will grasp theoretical concepts, but all will think they understand something through the image.

Third, and finally, distinguishing theory and common sense is difficult not only for historical and cognitive reasons, but because scientific theory—both from necessity and design—is rhetorical. Because science must follow culture in order to lead it, the way a theory will be understood—indeed the way theoretical terms invite misunderstanding—can be as important for the social success of a theory as technical accuracy is for its conceptual precision. While a properly trained and receptive reader can certainly extract from Darwin's *Origin*—especially from chapter three—how evolution follows as a corollary from Malthus's laws of population, variation, time and circumstance, Darwin's symbol "natural selection" was more a rhetorical invention than a scientific discovery (Campbell, 1990; Kohn & Kohn, 1985).

The problem natural selection solved was not technical or scientific but persuasive. When, during the six months following his reading of Malthus, Darwin gradually realized that variation was random, and that contrary to his earlier evolutionary thought that the variations were not providentially directed, the extent to which his new ideas were truly revolutionary began to sink in. To convince his colleagues and the public—both of whom believed that animals and plants were specially created—that the being and adaptations of animals and plants were the unintended results of random processes, required Darwin to discover ways to associate his new ideas with beliefs, premises, and images his audience would accept.

Approximately six months after reading Malthus, Darwin made his first comparison between nature and the breeder (Campbell, 1990). By creatively fusing and confusing the goal directed and a theoretical activity of the breeder, the random process of variation, differential reproduction, traditional phrases connoting God's all-seeing providence, and the folk notion of the superiority of nature to human art, Darwin created a powerful illusion that natural selection could be seen. Contrasted to "miracle"—which no one had seen—Darwin's term, "natural selection," tapped the religious and technological imagery of his age and forged a persuasively powerful but conceptually ambiguous image which successfully displaced miracle as a credible account for the development of life.

That Darwin was aware of the rhetorical aspects of natural selection is made clear not only by the evidence of his notebooks and his willingness to finance Gray's design argument (in which he personally did not believe) but by a remarkably candid letter he wrote in response to a letter from Alfred Russel Wallace. Wallace—who had independently applied Malthus' laws of population to the question of organic change—urged Darwin to drop the term "natural selection" as fundamentally misleading. Darwin agreed with most of Wallace's criticisms but he retained the term, not because he believed it was accurate, but because he believed there was a natural selection which also operated on language (F. Darwin, 1986). Darwin believed not only in survival of the fittest organism, but in survival of the culturally fittest term!

One might conclude from our account that Darwin was more interested in persuasive success than in truth. This interpretation is not inevitable. Concern for the social success of a major theoretic insight is one aspect of fidelity to truth. The moral of our tale of Darwin and Thales and the milkmaid is not necessarily that common sense extracts too high a price for its rescue of theory from the well of abstraction, but that common sense and theoretical understanding—while distinct—must be coordinated if conceptual innovation is to persuade. Since common sense and theory can never be equivalent, the price of scientific revolution is the acculturation of scientific theory. Like rays of light passing through deep water, for a scientific revolution to illuminate culture, scientific theory must be defracted from its straight lines. Because an intellectual revolution occurs simultaneously at different levels of abstraction and involves both theoretic and common sense meanings, one among a number of possible conclusions is that a major revolution in ideas may be scientifically true but morally and politically or theologically false, or the other way around. What seems clear is that dependent as is the vocabulary of science upon prior cultural understandings and limited as is its strict application to field specific theoretical concepts, only in a disputable and rhetorical sense can the language of science provide a "foundation" for other fields of inquiry.

Chapter Sixteen

Argumentation and Postmodern Critique

Charles Arthur Willard

This chapter ventures the claim that argument theory is indispensable to a postmodern critique. By *postmodern critique* I mean an attempt to understand the internal workings of modern organizations and institutions. Ours is an age of organizations; almost everything we do occurs inside corporations, government agencies, universities, and social groups. These organizations often have enormous power to affect our lives, so our curiousity about them — often tinged with skepticism or hostility — is a modern survival skill (Berman, 1982; Lyotard, 1984). Postmodern critique thus comes from a keenness to expose the bad effects of modern organizations and institutions and to promote public discussion about them. It seeks to restore human control over tyrannical events and organizations. Argument is essential to this critique, for it is our most reliable method of analyzing and reforming discourses. Organizations are open to change insofar as their practices promote reflective skepticism; and people are open to change when they are able to test their ideas in public argument.

A. Argument and Epistemics

The indispensability of argument theory to postmodern critique is apparent only if one appreciates recent changes in our views of knowledge. Today, most

Mr. Willard is in the Department of Communications at the University of Louisville.

approaches to argument share a concern for the study of knowledge. What is knowledge? How is it acquired, evaluated, used, and changed? How does it vary across disciplinary and community boundaries? How is it imported and exported across boundaries? How is it stored and retrieved in information systems and literatures? How does it affect argument and vice versa?

These are *epistemic* questions. They probe the empirical conditions in which people struggle with problems of knowledge. They are not *epistemological* issues. Epistemology is the branch of philosophy that studies knowledge in the abstract. Its aim is to find a single, universal language to which all particular languages can be reduced. Epistemic studies leave this aim to philosophers and focus instead on how epistemic communities create and change knowledge. Epistemics, as a discipline, aims to clarify problems of reasoning, speaking, and decision making in public life.

Questioning Deterministic Knowledge

This break with epistemology is a recent development. From the late nineteenth century when the first argument textbooks were written through the mid-twentieth century, argumentation theory (as applied logic) was the poor cousin of epistemology—an applied discipline aiming to be as much like epistemology as possible. The ancient Greeks called it "*phronesis*"— practical wisdom—though argumentation's servant-master relation with epistemology was solidified by Kant's distinction between theoretical and practical reason. In that scheme, practical reason gets its ideals from theoretical reason. We confront ordinary affairs with contingent, probable reasoning, but we discipline our reasoning by getting it as close to the ideal as possible.

Argumentation scholars now doubt the ideal—doubt, that is, that practical wisdom should mimic idealized versions of a single universal discourse. First, the search for a single discourse, even as an abstract ideal, has failed. The Vienna Circle, which gave us logical positivism, held that all languages are reducible to the language of physics (thus, for instance, all psychological claims can be reduced to physicalist claims). This reasoning depends on Newtonian intuitions that the world is a deterministic, orderly place. These intuitions were jarred by the idea of relativity and shattered by subsequent developments in quantum mechanics. Physicists *cum* philosophers, such as Nils Bohr and Werner Heisenberg, argued that different stances of observers are not disparate pictures of the same reality but separate realities. Observation is a part of reality. Physics is thus not a single language: nature speaks in a babel of tongues, so humans cannot look to nature for a single language to which all languages may be reduced.

And second, nature's tongues are not equally determinate. Recently, a revolution said to equal the quantum revolution in scope and importance has occurred: *chaos*, once routinely set aside in physical measurements (everyone knew that measurement is approximate, but variations were set aside as trivialities), has taken center stage as a fundamental natural principle. Since Kant, epistemology has seen knowledge as a "mirror of nature" (Rorty, 1979): human knowledge gets its determinacy and order from its reflection of reality—an attractive image if nature is thought to be orderly, but not a pretty picture if, as chaos theory says, the mirror reflects disorderly, unpredictable processes. The metaphors drawn from nature we might now use to describe knowledge are thus relativistic and chaotic (e.g., entropy, extreme sensitivity to starting conditions, uncertainty, relativity). One finds order only on small scales, in particular ecologies.

2. Knowledge and Social Community

The loss of the universal language ideal was accompanied by changes in our thinking about science itself. The idea that science achieves objective certainty has always had critics, prominently Nietzsche and Heidegger. But John Dewey and Ludwig Wittgenstein initiated the debunking discourse most influential today. Dewey launched the tradition of studying the political and rhetorical dynamics of scientific communities. He held that science gets its objectivity from concrete practices, not abstract philosophical principles. Objectivity is thus communicability within a community, not an effect of impersonal technologies. Wittgenstein began his career trying to reduce natural language to logic. He later came to an opposing view emphasizing relativity among language games or "forms of life." One can infer from this view that (1) thought systems are "discursive formations"—hermetically sealed languages with unyielding power to enslave the people caught up in them (Foucault, 1972, 1976, 1977) or (2) communities are ruled by organizing paradigms but still open to critique and reformation (Kuhn, 1970).

If you believe (1)—and many postmodernists do—you will be pessimistic about the possibility of critique. As Foucault says, criticism merely shifts us from one all-determining discursive formation to another. It creates the illusion of control. If you believe (2), you are a more optimistic postmodernist. You are likely to see the study of argument as your point of leverage for understanding different communities. It is now common to see argument described as the means by which knowledge is created, tested, revised, and used. One finds this view in the work of philosophers (Goodman, 1972, 1978, 1983; Rescher, 1973, 1977a, 1977b), psychologists (Weimer, 1979, 1984), economists (McCloskey, 1985), social theorists (Bernstein, 1968, 1983), political scientists (Nelson, 1983), sociologists (Brown, 1987; Goodman, 1962) and argument theorists (Goodnight, 1980, 1982, 1987a, 1987b; Willard, 1983, 1987b, 1987c, 1989a, 1989b). By the late 1980s, the rhetoric of science movement had blossomed (Campbell, 1987; Gross, 1987; Lynn, 1987; McCloskey, 1987; Nelson & Megill, 1986; Nelson, Megill, & McCloskey, 1987). Its proponents see the collapse of positivism as a chance to peek beneath the "masks of methodology" to study the ways scholars in fact make and test claims in all disciplines. To stress the rhetorical nature of how scholars make and test claims is to "replace simple acceptance of their reports with insightful scrutiny of their reasons. Treating each other's claims as arguments rather than as findings, scholars no longer need implausible doctrines of objectivism to defend their contributions to knowledge" (Nelson, Megill, & McCloskey, 1987, p. 4).

Rhetoric, Argument, and Knowledge

This renaissance of rhetoric may seem ominous, for it cuts against two popular views of rationality and science. First, many people distinguish argument from rhetoric on the grounds that the former is logical, the latter illogical. Thus 18th century thought distinguished between beliefs one holds as a result of logical thought ("conviction") and one's beliefs and predispositions which stem from feelings ("persuasion"). At first the study of argumentation was founded on this duality—distinguished from rhetoric by its focus on "primarily logical" thought and speech. The reader who thinks this way may have qualms about the idea that science is rhetorically constituted; the claim seems to assert that science is irrational.

Second, those who search for rationality in the growth of knowledge often distinguish between logical developments in a body of knowledge (one equates a field's growth with the logical progression of ideas in its published works) versus the social facts (the relations, politics, power arrangements, and personal preferences that affect science, but ideally should not). Thus Kuhn's (1970) claim that scientific knowledge depends upon the state of consensus in communities is said to reduce science to "mob psychology."

The first complaint is based on a doubly flimsy view. First, the conviction-persuasion duality is faulty psychology. The brain functions as a unity: thought and emotion are mingled. Our feelings about justice, equality, trust, hope, ambition—indeed our social bonds with others—are indispensible to our success as social animals. These feelings, plus some bad ones, color our reasoning. As Aristotle said, thought and emotion are inseparable; the trick is to identify the right feelings and to keep them under control. Second, why should we think that pristine logic is a worthy ideal? Logic is as easily totalitarian as liberating. Think of the images that haunt the postmodernist— Auschwitz, the arms race, and industries deaf to environmental concerns—a kaleidoscope of horrors. Max Weber (1905, 1946, 1947) called this "the rationalization of society," by which he meant organizations and institutions rationally built upon means-ends reasoning, unchecked by critique, all set dispassionately on calculated courses. Weber was pessimistic about this rationalization, for he saw the possibilities of modernity gone mad alongside the possibility of humans bereft of feeling—people coopted by their organizations. He saw, in other words, the possibility that our organizations might become more powerful than our ability to critique and change them.

The second objection is also doubly defective. Empirical studies of how scientists actually work do not support the "rationalist's" view. Personal preferences and quirks, conventional wisdom, professional politics, and the need for popularization to secure funding all play a part in the puzzles scientists find interesting, the new ideas they are willing to entertain, and the ways their thinking changes. The rational progress one finds in literature has been put there—intentionally—as a field rationalizes its history. These rational appearances may have nothing to do with the ways a field actually solves its puzzles or chooses new ones. Second, when we make a field's activities seem more logical than they are, we are prone to ignore crucial questions. How do people make good decisions (as they sometimes do) when their logic *isn't* pristine? Rationality comes easy in armchairs. But it may not mean much to say that one *should be* free of prejudice, bias, power, and politics. One never is. Should we not wonder, then, how people are able to make good decisions despite their prejudices and politics? Are some modes of public debate better in such conditions than others?

There is a third flaw in these objections to rhetoric's renaissance. Both depend on a single view of rhetoric. The term "rhetoric" has at least three equally useful meanings. First, in common parlance and in journalism, rhetoric is a perjorative term for style and delivery. Thus one might say, "The President's rhetoric is powerful but his arguments are flimsy." Second, rhetoric is the organization and arrangement of ideas in written or spoken discourse; in this sense it is not adornment but integral to ideas. And third, rhetoric is persuasion—Aristotle calls it the art of discovering in any case the available means of persuasion. Persuasion is a cooperative activity: the persuadee actively contributes to the process by which she is persuaded.

Many thinkers focus exclusively on the first meaning—the one behind the objections we are considering here. They see rhetoric as the enemy of philosophy (philosophy being a mirror of nature, rhetoric must be the enemy of truth). Innocent of the other meanings of rhetoric, they assume that their modes of presentation are irrelevant to the substance of their positions—a mistake if the second meaning of rhetoric has merit: one's style and organization are an integral part of one's ideas. To date, only one epistemologist that I know of has made a point of this (Fuller, 1988).

The third sense of rhetoric—as persuasion—has been undervalued by almost everyone—dismissed as an evil necessity or side effect. But the rhetoric of science movement exposes the flaw in this dismissal. Knowledge is rhetorical because it is a public achievement, a cooperative attainment. To get a consensus, I must argue my case. In arguing my case, just as in any process of reasoning, I must depend upon one premise to lead to another. But reasoning is less constrained than communication, for in the latter case *you* must assent to the enabling premise or I cannot proceed. My dependence on your assent makes our cooperative creation of a consensus a rhetorical process. A common label for this view is "consensus theory of truth." A consensus theory abandons the mirror of nature metaphor, so it puts a premium on the quality of a consensus. If we ask how dependable a knowledge claim is, the quality of the consensus vouching for it is a fundamental part of the answer. The search to understand the grounds of a dependable consensus thus becomes a pivotal part of the postmodernist's program.

All three meanings of "rhetoric" come into play when we probe the empirical conditions in which a consensus is produced. We will find glitzy rhetoric$_1$ — "mere rhetoric" — adorning (but subtly changing) methods of exposition (rhetoric$_2$) in persuasive (rhetoric$_3$) contexts. All three meanings tap synergistic dimensions of intellectual life. All three affect the soundness of a consensus.

Argumentation and Postmodern Critique

The centrality of argument to postmodern critique was unforeseen — indeed invisible — until knowledge came to be seen as a social production, an outcome of argumentation. This new connection was dimly seen by many, but most clearly spelled out by Habermas (1970, 1971, 1973, 1979, 1984) who influenced even those who disputed the details of his work. Habermas realized that critique presupposes knowledge and that the degree to which knowledge is trustworthy depends on the quality of the consensus surrounding it. Groups can achieve consensus accidentally (by unreflectively accepting received wisdom), manipulatively (by using brute force), or "rationally" (using argument in which all sides are given equal opportunities to make their cases). A preoccupation with the first two options is one version of postmodernism. For instance, recall Weber's pessimism about organizational rationality (he used the label "instrumental rationality" for the means-end reasoning embodied in organizations). Bureaucracies, for instance, are designed to fulfill purposes. Once in place, they acquire lives of their own. Their policies shape future possibilities. Thus Weber feared the long term effects of organizational rationality; policy momentum and bureaucratic inertia can subjugate critique, making human control a tragic illusion. This pessimism is not unlike Foucault's, though Foucault is less concerned with organizational momentum than with the self-confirming properties of languages. Because a discourse is hermetically sealed from other discourses, criticism may be an illusion.

The possibility of analyzing and changing organizations is Habermas' version of postmodernism. Our lives are bound up in organizations. If we hope to live reflective lives and to control the organizations that affect us, we must examine the ways in which our organizations achieve consensus. This puts a premium on the conditions that promote critique and reconstruction — the conditions that let argument flourish.

The Problem of Authority

What features of organizational life need critique and reconstruction? Though organizations pose many problems, I believe that there is a single problem that stands out from the others as especially urgent and difficult—a problem that befuddles ordinary decision makers as well as actors in the academic disciplines. It is arguably the problem definitive of our century—the problem of authority.

The problem of authority is this: we are dependent on authority; it is presumptively sound to rely on authorities (Haskell, 1984); consulting and trusting experts is what a rational person should do; much of a modern education amounts to disciplining the young to acquiesce to authority (Stich & Nisbett, 1984). The complexity of our society has led to increasing specialization; and specialization—however much we dislike it—increases our reliance on authority. We can't inspect evidence for ourselves in every domain of human activity, so we do the next best thing: we trust properly credentialed experts. Yet reliance on authorities undercuts our control over the critique and reconstruction of modern organizations and institutions. Our reliance is an unavoidable handicap, not a considered trust.

Consider the plight of the legislator who must allocate society's resources for space exploration, nuclear power plants, or welfare programs. Decisions need facts: How much will things cost? How do we calculate the short- and long-term benefits? What about side effects and safety? What things are beyond our control? What is the public opinion relevant to the project? These facts, the legislator learns, do not speak for themselves. They are often ambiguous or incoherent until explained by an expert. Legislation is thus not fueled by facts but by the testimony of experts.

Evaluating Expert Testimony

How does the legislator evaluate expert testimony? If a physicist says that low level radiation from a nuclear plant is "safe," the strength of the claim is in the calculations behind it—which may be incomprehensible to the non-physicist. Expert testimony thus attempts to translate technical facts into a general public language.

"Translation" is a misleading term. Expert testimony rarely "translates" (in the sense that we convert a French word to an English word as if the latter is equivalent to, or close enough to preserve important aspects of the meaning of, the former). But equivalency or resemblance are not always available to link esoteric discourses with popular discourse. Esoteric knowledge, by definition, is mysterious to outsiders. It depends upon background knowledge available or comprehensible only to insiders in an expert community. Popularizations of esoterica may thus not be translations from a complex to a simpler language; there may be no equivalencies, or even partially valid analogies, between (say) one's mathematics and one's policy inferences.

Experts thus create not translations but *conclusions*. Since one wants to influence legislation, one wraps one's conclusions in metaphors and images the legislator is likely to understand and applaud. One is also tempted to put one's position more definitely than one might with other experts. Logical positivism—as a stance toward the self-evidence and trustworthiness of scientific findings—becomes in the public sphere less a philosophy of science than a public relations gimmick. In congressional testimony and grant proposals, hedges become covering laws; one-shot deals become coherent research programs. *Weltanschauungen* theory may play well in academe, but one polishes one's mirror of nature for public testimony. Expert testimony, in sum, is a "rhetorical" enterprise, in all three senses of the term. The legislator can critique neither the facts or the translation, for both presuppose subject matter expertise.

Imagine that I am a City Council member considering whether to approve the creation of a recombinate DNA lab. As in fact happened in Cambridge, Massachusetts, I will find myself weighing competing expert positions—not competing facts. Both sides, rather, have concocted images to sway my thinking. The experts who fear the research ask me to envision scientists who will cross a cancer with the most virulent cold virus (imagine a malignancy as contagious as the common cold). Weighing against that portrait is a probability calculation: given the safety features in the lab, the chances of a killer mutant strain escaping are negligible. I am weighing, in other words, two images backed by expert authority. If this is a standoff, other images may play a role. Proponents of the lab, for instance, will argue that the advancement of human knowledge is worth the risk. If they think I am unpersuaded by the advancement of knowledge for its own sake, they may conjur a different image: the technological advances issuing from the lab will yield concrete benefits to society. Here the experts are imitating the space program, which is rarely defended solely in terms of the advancement of knowledge but is commonly defended in terms of concrete technological benefits. Thus to oppose the lab is to stand in the way of "progress."

As a decision maker, then, I am not examining the evidence and facts. I may pose publicly as a pseudo-expert (much of the decision-making literature recommends the stance of the pseudo-expert), but I am not, and never will be, on an equal epistemic footing with the expert. My incompetence is a pragmatic fact; I deal with a vast array of subjects, from economics to physics to engineering to urban planning—the list might be extended indefinitely. If I am a typical governing elite, I do not have a Ph.D or professional experience in any of these subjects; nor am I likely to possess more than a layman's acquaintance with the disputes that divide the experts. I am a consumer, then, not of facts but of the rhetorical strategies of experts.

3. Arguing by Quoting

This passivity arises in general discourse in the form of a practice we might call arguing-by-quoting: one asserts a claim, then quotes an authority who endorses the claim. X is true because authority Y says X. This practice is pervasive in our pedagogy. In public speaking and argumentation courses, one learns that it isn't enough merely to express one's feelings and opinions to prove one's point. Given constrained speaking time, arguing-by-quoting becomes the method of choice. If one must move rapidly from claim to proof, the temptation to quote is strong. This effect is heightened in academic debate, where arguing-by-quoting often supplants reasoning.

Zarefsky (1980c) argues that debating is a valuable laboratory for studying argument. If Zarefsky is right, the authority-proneness one finds in academic debaters should have parallels in other contexts. Political discourse is a case in point. Political speakers, if they bother to prove their assertions at all, characteristically do so by quoting the conclusions of authorities. Journalists likewise prefer conclusionary quotes from "authorities." Whatever the event, it is common journalistic practice to get reaction quotes from authorities. Short blurbs are preferred, owing to the problem of space (print journalism) and time (electronic journalism).

Scholarly writers also sometimes argue-by-quoting. I have not done a content analysis of every issue of *The Quarterly Journal of Speech*, but I do think that writers in that journal often argue-by-quoting. One asserts X, then quotes Aristotle or Burke or Perelman to prove X. For instance, consider this example from a widely read essay in a communication journal "It cannot be the case that all opinions and beliefs deserve to be elevated to the status of knowledge. The term 'knowledge' is reserved primarily for those claims which we deem to be true and for which sufficient evidence (justification) is marshalled." The footnote reads: "The definition of knowledge as justified true belief is widely accepted by epistemologists. See, for example, Roderick M. Chisholm . . ." (Croasmun & Cherwitz, 1982, p.9). This reasoning will puzzle the reader who knows of a competing (post-Rorty) consensus, or the reader who has objections to Chisholm's reasoning. But consider the plight of the reader who is ignorant of a competing consensus or who has not read Chisholm. If I accept the authors' claim, is my belief in the idea of justified true belief, a justified true belief? The intent of the authors is to say that consensus theories of truth must accommodate the idea of an independently existing reality. But they prove the existence of this reality by quoting a consensus.

Not every case of citing authorities proves my point. Citation is a fundamental part of the structure of scholarly activity. It serves many purposes: to give credit or blame for ideas, to acknowledge allies and kindred spirits, to designate research traditions and schools of thought, or to use names as surrogate labels for whole positions. This last use, however, shades into my point, for we sometimes, from sloppiness or lack of reflection, cite a name to stand for a position, and then take the position for granted as a picture of reality. When this happens, we are arguing-by-quoting.

Aristotle enjoined citizens to know the facts of war, peace, commerce, and government. The defect in his list is not merely that our world is more complex than his, but that specialism and the professionalization of technical mastery have changed the very idea of general knowledge. Our reliance on the specialist is not a convenient option to be dispensed with if need be.

Argument and Public Knowledge

But what, then, *is* public knowledge? How do we train people for public life? Is there a kind of knowledge public decision makers must have? Such questions will, I think, preoccupy argument scholars well into the next century. I can offer here only a rough approximation of where our thinking will go. Public knowledge, I submit, is a package of discourse competencies which equip one for the analysis and appraisal of expert discourse. By appraisal I do not mean deciding whether the experts are right or wrong—that is what experts are for—but deciding how expert testimony will be taken. This suggests that public knowledge consists of knowledge about the sociological dynamics of expertise: how experts are designated and monitored by disciplines, how virtuosity and competence are measured, how status within disciplines is achieved, how disputes among experts are adjudicated, how claims that are disputed within a field get translated into public claims (how disputes are concealed and how they can be brought to public light and understood), and how the experts' ways of insisting upon objectivity may hinder the decision makers' appraisals of expert testimony.

A point of leverage for getting at these questions is provided by a more general question: how do ideas cross field boundaries? This is an interesting question because conceptual innovation within disciplines often requires importing ideas from outside. Communities are organized around the conservation of a body of trusted knowledge; they tend toward conservatism; they resist change *in principle*. Yet they do accept new ideas, even ones that jeopardize old ideas. Their conservatism is overcome when imported ideas offer more attractive puzzles or solve problems which have obstructed progress in the community.

I have argued here that the problem of authority is a pivotal part of the problem of modernity. Certainly there are other problems: inequality of opportunity, unresponsive organizations, reactionary institutions, and the tendency of planners to destroy things of value when they stand in the way of "progress." But I think authority is the more central problem. Skepticism (about society, organizations, or progress) is ineffectual if one works unreflectively within the prevailing authority structure. Critique requires, yet is coopted by, authority. A more thorough critique of authority, therefore, is the the heart of our future agenda.

How do we go about studying and thereby empowering the critique of authority? We should focus, it seems to me, on the one phenomenon that in fact checks authority—argumentation. Thus I have argued that a theory of argumentation is essential to postmodern critique. This thesis very much reflects the intuitions of the Founding Fathers, who built *opposition* into the structure of American government. The separation of powers doctrine is but one version of the idea that institutions and organizations can be checked, reined in, controlled, and reconstructed when opposition flourishes. The problem, of course, is to ensure that opposition flourishes—and *that*, in a nutshell, is the postmodern problem.

Chapter Seventeen

Argument Criticism as Creative

Sharon Bailin

Informal logic has been defined as the normative study of argument (Blair & Johnson, 1980). One central issue which confronts those working in this area concerns how to conceive of argument criticism (Blair & Johnson, 1980). Informal logic's ancestry in formal deductive logic has left, as a legacy, a sense that informal logic is a quasi-mathematical enterprise which involves algorithmic procedures for the correct assessment of arguments. Although a growing number of philosophers recognize the inadequacy of this conception, some theoretical tendencies and pedagogical practices reveal a vestigial trace of this heritage (Blair & Johnson, 1987b). In this chapter, I demonstrate the inadequacy of this conception by showing that criticism has a creative dimension. Argument criticism, although constrained by rules, is not determined by rules but has a generative, imaginative component; it is a constructive enterprise. This chapter elucidates what it means to say that "criticism is creative."

A. Creativity

Viewing criticism as creative may, at first, seem to be paradoxical. A popular perception of creativity is that it involves the unconstrained generation of ideas,

Ms. Balin is on the faculty at the University of Manitoba, Canada.

and thus creative and critical thinking are often set in opposition to one another. This popular perception views creative thinking as a process of free imagination which allows for the breaking of rules, the transcending of frameworks, and the creation of novel products. It defines critical thinking, on the contrary, as an algorithmic process which involves following established rules faithfully in order to arrive at correct solutions within existing parameters. According to this view, creative thinking is necessarily non-critical since criticism must take place according to prevailing standards. Critical thinking is necessarily non-creative since it is essentially a mechanical process.

The opposition of critical and creative thinking is untenable (Bailin, 1987, 1988). In order to make this point, we need to sort out the variety of senses in which the term "creative" is used. Creativity may refer to a person, to a process (as in "creative thinking"), or to a product. Several sources (Bailin, 1988; Gardner, 1988; Nickerson, Perkins, & Smith, 1985), contend that the product sense is primary. A creative product may be thought of as one which exhibits valuable novelty (Bailin, 1988). Given this definition, a creative person would be one who creates creative products, and a creative process would be a mental process or way of thinking which leads to creative products.

The opposition between critical and creative thinking rests on the assumption that there is a distinctive way of thinking involved in the creative process which leads to creative products. It assumes that creative thinking is a nonevaluative mode of thinking. I would argue, however, that evaluation is necessarily involved in the creation of valuable products. Such products are not simply novel but are of value in meeting a need or solving a problem. They must have significance in the context of the domain. Critical judgment is centrally involved in such creative production—in identifying problems, in recognizing inadequacies in existing solutions, in deciding that a new approach is required, in determining directions for investigation, and in recognizing possible solutions. If evaluation were not involved in the very generation of ideas, then the results would be chaos rather than creation. The creative poet does not simply generate a large number of unusual words but rather comes up with appropriate words in specific contexts. Similarly, the scientist does not randomly generate theories and then choose among them but rather comes up with a theory which solves a scientific problem. Both these activities require evaluation in the very process of generation.

The opposition between critical and creative thinking also rests on the assumption that thinking primarily directed to the criticism and evaluation of ideas is strictly analytic, selective, and rule-determined. This position assumes that, given the necessary information from within the relevant framework and the appropriate techniques of reasoning, the process of arriving at a judgment is largely algorithmic. This assumption is unfounded, however. Critical evaluation is not algorithmic; it has a generative, imaginative component. Even in cases which largely involve the application of algorithms, such as solving math problems, people must use some imagination in order to see similarities between current problems and types of problems in order to know which algorithms to apply. As we move from the application of algorithms to the application of evaluative criteria, we interpret circumstances and this involves a degree of imaginative re-creation. The inevitable variability in the circumstances in which the criteria are applied requires imaginative judgment about both their applicability and about the satisfaction of the criteria. Evaluation also involves envisioning potential problems—clearly an imaginative activity. Moreover, assessment often requires a judgment made in the light of possible alternatives; imagining alternatives is a creative enterprise. Finally, arriving at an overall assessment in any complex circumstance requires constructing a view derived from the weighing, reconciling, and integrating of numerous intermediary judgments.

The opposition between critical and creative thinking is ill-founded. In all instances in which serious thinking is required, both the constraints of logic and the inventiveness of imagination come into play showing some degree of creativity in all critical thinking. In some cases, deliberations over what reasonably to believe or do lead one to question presuppositions, to break rules, or to put elements together in new ways—resulting in products which display considerable novelty. Scriven (1976) notes: "Reasoning is a constructive and creative activity that leads us to new knowledge" (p. 35).

B. Informal Logic

This imaginative dimension to criticism is evident in the species of argument criticism which is the domain of informal logic. If the concern of informal logic is the interpretation, evaluation and construction of arguments (Blair & Johnson, 1987b), then imagination is required in each of these aspects and none is totally algorithmic.

Interpretation

Interpretation is the process of analyzing an argument to understand what the argument says. This appears to be a simple and straightforward aspect of the enterprise. Upon examination, it is far from simple. Texts are always incomplete and necessarily so because it is impossible to supply every piece of information and assumption upon which understanding rests. People take these assumptions for granted in communication. Even reading for understanding requires the filling in of information and meaning. Making inferences is central to reading (Phillips & Norris, 1987; Scriven, 1976). We construct an interpretation guided by textual information and background knowledge. Gutteridge (1987) points out that the injunction not to read into a text anything which is not asserted is a vain one. Gutteridge also makes the point that careful reading will not necessarily resolve any problems of interpretation. Sometimes several inferences can be made, and more than one may be plausible given different background knowledge or assumptions. The inference which may seem obvious to some may not be so obvious to others. This point will likely be acknowledged by anyone who has listened to or participated in arguments between students and teachers regarding answers to multiple choice tests.

The fact that arguments are necessarily incomplete means that the receiver of the argument must play an active role in making meaning. Scott (1987) states that the receiver is also, in some sense, the creator of an argument. The receiver must generate possible meanings, and although this generation will be constrained by critical standards, the possibility of differing interpretations remains open.

One circumstance requiring active construction on the part of the assessor occurs when the receiver supplies the missing premises and unstated assumptions to an argument. Considerable debate exists about exactly how to treat such missing elements and how best to go about filling in the premises. A number of principles invoked by various theorists suggest criteria for the filling in of unstated premises, including sufficiency, clarity, preservation, fidelity, plausibility, and testability (Burke, 1985; Ennis, 1982; Hitchcock, 1983; Johnson, 1981). No clear consensus exists, however, regarding precisely which constellation of principles is necessary or which principles take precedence when they conflict. A debate also exists about what persons are doing or should be trying to do by filling in these elements: are they attempting to determine those assumptions which are needed to make the argument a good one (Hitchcock, 1985), or are they attempting to determine those assumptions which were actually used by the creator of the argument (Thomas, 1981)? What seems to be suggested by this difficulty in formalizing the process of supplying missing premises or unstated assumptions is that there are no infallible methods for doing so. Reconstructing an argument is an imaginative activity involving an unavoidable element of judgment informed by principles but also by an understanding of the context in which the argument takes place and by one's background knowledge. In discussing the conflict of principles for interpreting arguments, Berg (1987) makes the point that "such conflicts call for subjective judgment, weighing the relative pull of the various principles along with the grounds for their application and the circumstances under which the argument is being discussed" (p. 15).

With respect to the claim that supplying missing premises is a creative activity, an issue is whether what one is doing is adding something new to the argument or simply discovering what is already there. While the former seems to be an imaginative activity, it may seem that the latter is not. Debate on this issue ranges from a claim, such as Govier's that "the missing premise is a product of the reflective mind" (cited in Gough & Tindale, 1985) to the contention of Gough and Tindale (1985) that "hidden premises . . . are already there, not added to what is there to make something out of what is there." In the former interpretation, supplying missing premises is clearly a creative activity. But even if one accepts the latter interpretation, imagination is not precluded. Finding a premise hidden in an argument is different from finding a toy hidden under the bed. We have to ask in what sense missing premises are thought to be already there, hidden in an argument. Gough and Tindale (1985) make reference to the *Meno*, presumably suggesting that such premises are implicit in the argument in the way that geometric proofs are implicit in the axioms of geometry. Yet, as Scriven (1976) points out, even finding the consequences of the axioms of geometry is partly a creative act. New elements are mentioned in the theorems which do not even appear in the axioms, and extracting them is an enterprise requiring imagination.

If one goes beyond the activity of supplying missing premises to finding more general assumptions, the imaginative dimension becomes even more prominent. Scriven (1976) demonstrates effectively how finding the interesting, illuminating assumptions of an argument, as opposed to the obvious unhelpful ones is not a matter of routine calculation but may require "a good deal of shuffling and rephrasing and a substantial slice of original thinking" (p. 169). He shows, for example, how the argument, "He is a homosexual and so he shouldn't be appointed to this politically sensitive post," rests on the following assumptions: 1) the individual is not already known to be a homosexual, 2) everyone would rather pass up a job of this type than acknowledge homosexuality, and 3) homosexuals run a greater risk of blackmail than heterosexuals. Certainly no algorithms or even reliable methods for uncovering such assumptions exist. The arguments are constructed from our understanding of the logical relationships of stated premises to conclusion but also from our knowledge of people and social and political realities.

Evaluation

This imaginative dimension is also evident in the process of evaluating the types of arguments which are the concern of informal logic. Blair and Johnson (1987a) emphasize that such arguments often involve reasoning which is not strictly deductive. Arguments often contain probable reasoning in which the conclusion goes beyond the evidence and the fit between premises and conclusions is not tight enough to rule out other conclusions. Arguments may contain reasoning in which "the conclusion follows, *ceteris paribus*, or on balance, or in some other qualified way which suggests a more tenuous relationship between premises and conclusion than would be the case with either deductive or inductive reasoning" (p. 43). The play between premises and conclusion makes judgment an unavoidable element in assessing arguments. It is impossible to formalize totally the procedures for evaluating arguments—to create algorithms for assessment. Criteria which govern assessment exist, but although evaluation is constrained by rules, rules do not uniquely determine the outcome of evaluation.

This constructive aspect is exemplified by the process of detecting fallacies. As Blair noted in Chapter 9, fallacies are often categorized into three general kinds: fallacies of relevance, sufficiency and acceptability. The creative dimension is evident for all three types of fallacies. Appealing to a premise which is irrelevant to the conclusion is clearly fallacious, yet relevance is not always easily determined. An argument may be based on missing assumptions which need to be supplied in order to establish relevance, or cases may exist where strong arguments can be given both for and against the relevance of certain considerations. There are certainly guidelines as to appropriate considerations, but they cannot lead infallibly to judgments regarding relevance. As Johnson and Blair (1983) maintain, "relevance is always a judgment call, and there is no reason to think that any algorithmic procedure will come along to change that" (p. 39).

The evaluation is similar with respect to fallacies of sufficiency. Although there are constraints with respect to the adequacy of evidence, (for example, the evidence should be gathered systematically, attention should be paid to a variety of kinds of evidence, and contrary evidence should be acknowledged), no reliable method is available for determining how much evidence is sufficient. Indeed, Johnson and Blair (1983) argue that a charge of insufficiency can be justified only if the critic can cite relevant evidence which has not been considered. In other words, the identification of this fallacy depends not simply on a logical analysis of the structure of the argument, but on bringing in a new element.

Judgments with respect to the acceptability of premises also require imaginative construction. Acceptability is a dialectical matter which must be determined with an imagined audience in mind and in light of the purposes at hand (Johnson & Blair, 1983).

One common device in argument is analogy; an important aspect of argument evaluation involves determining the appropriateness of analogies and the detection of faulty ones. This requires arguers to think of similarities and differences between the cases used and to determine whether they are sufficiently similar in relevant ways. In some cases judgments may be fairly straightforward. For example, in a recent letter to the editor the writer argues that the notion of safe sex is as ludicrous as the notions of safe alcoholism or safe environmental pollution. Here the disanalogies are fairly obvious. For example, alcoholism and pollution are always bad but the same could not be said of sex. Yet even here some knowledge of the world view which sees sex as evil would be necessary to understand the alleged similarities. In more complex analogies, the need for imaginative reconstruction is even more pronounced. An argument cited in Johnson and Blair (1983) is that banning the ownership of firearms would not significantly reduce the number of murders and robberies because banning alcohol did not significantly reduce drinking. Evaluating this analogy requires considerable reconstruction based on under-standing the reasons for the failure of prohibition, projecting causal connections, imagining scenarios to test parallel factors in the firearms case, and judging whether parallels are sufficiently strong. Evaluating analogies is an aspect of argument assessment requiring considerable creative invention.

A powerful tool in testing arguments is the counter-example. Here again, the role of imagination is evident. One might contend that finding counter-examples is not a creative activity in that counter-examples are simply out in the world to be found. Sometimes this does seem to be the case, as in the example of the black swan. Yet one still has to know where to look. One may sometimes need to look in a place no one has thought to look before. Gilligan (1982), for example, discovered in women's moral thinking a counter-example to Kohlberg's generalizations about people's moral thinking, generalizations which had been derived from male samples. Certainly women had been there all along, but a reconceptualization of the situation was required in order to see women's moral thinking as a counter-example which challenged Kohlberg's generalizations. Seeing some phenomenon as a counter-example to a claim arises from the way in which a situation is construed. This process involves recognizing similarities in disparate cases and judging when similarities are sufficient for the phenomenon to count as a case encompassed by the claim.

Assessing an argument forces the evaluator to go beyond the argument itself. One way is to consider alternative arguments. The strength of an argument often cannot be determined in isolation but depends on its plausibility relative to alternative arguments. Scriven (1976) makes this case well with respect to causal explanations, showing that a causal explanation is compelling only if no equally plausible alternative explanations exist. He goes on to say:

> The process of trying to think of alternative explanations of a set of facts . . . is an entirely *creative* process. It is exactly the process which the great original scientist goes through in coming up with a novel theory. There are no precise rules to guide one in such a search, and it requires imagination nurtured by a rich and varied experience to generate the novel hypothesis here. So the very process of criticism necessarily involves the creative activity of generating new theories or hypotheses to explain phenomena that have seemed to other people to admit of only one explanation (p. 36).

Construction

This requirement regarding the consideration of alternatives stems from the dialectical nature of argument. Arguments need to be understood in the context of the process of argumentation which produces them. Two important features of argumentation are (1) arguments take place where there is challenge, controversy, or debate and (2) arguments presuppose two roles, the presenter and the objector (Blair & Johnson, 1987a). The presenter is the one who proposes or creates arguments and the objector is essentially the critic. Each role requires both creation and criticism. An argument must be constructed in conformity with all the critical standards which guide evaluation, and the constructor must see the logical vulnerabilities of the argument as well as anticipate counter-examples and counter-arguments. The role of critic demands imaginative creation in all the ways previously discussed. In the end, the critic must be able to construct a cogent argument to support the proposed critique.

In actual fact, the roles of presenter and objector need not be played by two different individuals. One person may play both. A number of people may share roles or exchange roles. What matters in this regard is not the division of labor within the argument but the epistemological structure of the argumentation situation. Claims are put forth on the basis of reasons; the claims and reasons are challenged and tested, and they may be reformulated or alternative arguments will be proposed. These arguments will be tested and perhaps reformulated, and in the end a judgment is made which may affirm an initial claim, reject it, affirm a contrary claim, accept a modified or qualified claim, or admit indeterminacy on the issue. What is going on is really a process of inquiry in which knowledge claims are put forth and tested. Argumentation is essentially the method whereby knowledge is constructed. In this construction of knowledge, the generative and the evaluative dimensions are both essential and closely intertwined. Evaluation involves imagination in all the ways previously described, and the generation of ideas must conform to critical standards. Moreover new ideas can develop out of criticism which involves an understanding of the weaknesses of previous arguments and a creative synthesis of strong elements. Criticism can be spurred by the introduction of some new element.

C. Pedagogy

What does this analysis mean for the teaching and learning of informal logic, argumentation, and critical thinking? The analysis has shown that knowledge and experience play an important role in criticism. I am not arguing for the discipline-specificity of reasoning nor to deny that there are general criteria and standards. But I do assert that some acts of reasoning such as interpreting arguments, generating counter-examples, proposing alternative explanations, and evaluating the appropriateness of analogies, depend for their effectiveness on arguers having a store of background knowledge from which to draw. Supplying such knowledge is beyond the scope and mandate of argumentation and informal logic courses. Nonetheless, teachers and students of reasoning need to pursue the ideal of a broad liberal education since people cannot reason effectively without it.

This analysis also implies that the creative dimension to criticism needs to be emphasized. Criticism requires considerable judgment and a great deal of practice and experience in dealing with arguments in a variety of different contexts. Assessments are not clear-cut and uncontroversial. There are criteria and principles of assessments, but judgment and imagination are required to make these assessments. Thus discussion and debate are crucial to both the evaluation of arguments and to the construction of arguments to support an assessment. Criticism should not be reduced to the detection of fallacies or faults but must include an emphasis on the generative aspects such as the interpretation of arguments, the generation of counter-examples and the construction of counter-arguments. Critics might, for example, focus not only on detecting faulty analogies but also on the creation of appropriate ones. Moreover, the process of argument evaluation should be portrayed in the context of the larger dialectical process, a process involving the proposal, testing, comparison, and reformulation of claims and ultimately the construction of a view. Students must be involved in this imaginative act of construction but also understand that it is constrained by criteria and principles, that it is characterized by a reciprocal and integrated process of generation and criticism.

The teaching and learning of informal logic are more than training in a technical skill. Students should understand the epistemological grounding of the critical enterprise. The danger in neglecting epistemology is that students may end up with a sense that what they are learning are techniques for arriving at the right answer, at the one correct assessment of an argument. Thus, informal logic instruction might fail to counter anti-critical tendencies in the rest of education and experience and might even end up reinforcing these tendencies. Students should comprehend the nature of the process in which they are engaged so that they understand that it is the basic process of inquiry. In order to foster criticism, informal logic instruction must be grounded in an understanding of the critical and creative nature of the development and assessment of knowledge.

Part V

Arguing in Non-traditional Places

> Argument is also used in a macroscopic sense as an entire and synthesized system of claims that together constitute a rationale for choosing one option rather than another (Brockriede, 1978, p. 34).

Brockriede often told his students that arguments are to be found in the minds of people rather than as part of some objective and verifiable reality. He believed that many unlikely experiences could be conceived as arguments if the persons involved in the argument found the six characteristics (defined in Chapter 1) to be present. This section demonstrates that persons can find arguments in a variety of nontraditional contexts. Each chapter in this section is written by a former student of Brockriede, and each chapter finds arguments in places where many would not expect to find them. Moreover, each of the chapters indicates that arguments can have a variety of consequences not often associated with traditional theories of argumentation. Each essay in this section stresses a different set of consequences—pragmatic, moral, and aesthetic. We hope that readers of this book will identify other places and other consequences that result when persons argue.

In Chapter 18, Karen Rasmussen and Cindi Capaldi identify moral consequences that result when alcoholics share narrative arguments with Alcoholics Anonymous groups. Rasmussen and Capaldi explain that narrative is the rationale or warrant for recovery. These narratives embody the archetype of rebirth and work dialectically to change the consciousness of the alcoholic. The authors identify and explain the stages in the process of recovery that are practiced by members of Alcoholics Anonymous. The narratives of addicts take the form of rebirth archetypes that portray the regenerative process — chaos, death, disintegration of personality, and eventual rebirth through sobriety. These stages of regeneration parallel Burke's explanation of the restoration of order that comes through guilt, mortification, and redemption. Rasmussen and Capaldi argue that the dialectical reasoning of the two stories combine to create an illusionary emancipation with life renewal. This reinterpretation of reality has important social and moral consequences for the addicted person. The authors explain both the intrapersonal or cognitive effects created dialectically by addicts and the responses of the group members who hear their stories.

Ken Chase finds aesthetic consequences for the arguments he discovers in works of art in Chapter 19. This chapter explores the connections between argument and beauty. Chase finds argument when persons attempt to describe the nature of beauty as Edmond Burke and Longinus have done. He finds arguments in the judgments persons make when they evaluate things as beautiful. Since beauty is a perception open to dispute, what is beautiful depends on arguments between people. Beauty also can be an attribute of argument found in an object of art through the unity between its parts, balance and harmony, and pleasing intensity or vividness. Finally, Chase reasons, the beauty of objects of art like poems or painting are themselves arguments. The perspective that art and beauty are related suggests that arguments can be found in music, sculpture, dance, and other artistic activities.

Chapter 20 emphasizes the pragmatic consequences that business arguers envision as they frame public arguments in and outside of the corporation. Janice Schuetz identifies the process of company advocacy, the credentials of advocates, and the arguments that companies make. She develops a typology of four different types of advocacy—economic justification, company storytelling, issues management, and crisis management. Arguments about economic justification give reasons about the products and services as well as the financial assets and liabilities of the company. Company storytelling presents narratives about the experiences and deeds of the company in an attempt to persuade others of company values. A third type of company advocacy, issues management, appears in persuasive messages designed for external publics. This type of advocacy presents policy alternatives to respond to public pressures for changes in company practices. A final type of argument attempts to manage crises. In these cases, companies defend themselves after their practices, products, or services have caused negative consequences for customers. This chapter implies that students can find many examples of arguments with pragmatic consequences in business communities.

Chapter Eighteen

The Narratives of Alcoholics Anonymous
Dialectical "Good Reasons"

Karen Rasmussen and Cindi Capaldi

Founded in 1936, Alcoholics Anonymous has grown from a handful of members to an organization numbering its participants at an estimated one million (Ford, 1989). In its meetings, people attempting to combat their addiction to alcohol gather to "share experience, strength, and hope with each other that they may solve their common problem and help others to recover from alcoholism" (*Alcoholics Anonymous*, 1976). A.A. groups, ranging in size from a few people to several hundred, gather in churches, schools, or rooms rented at A.A. clubs—any place in which facilities are functional and affordable (*Alcoholics Anonymous*, 1976). Successful members typically attend four times weekly and continue doing so throughout their sobriety.

The format and focus of the meetings of Alcoholics Anonymous varies considerably. One prominent variation is the speakers' meeting which begins with reading of A.A. literature and features impromptu testimony by a sober member of the fellowship—a personal story supporting the efficacy of sobriety grounded in the world view of Alcoholics Anonymous. This study addresses the manner in which such stories advance the argument that recovery in Alcoholics Anonymous works. We contend that A.A. narratives warrant recovery **dialectically** by embodying the archetype of **rebirth** within the context of a **rhetorical ritual**. To support that claim we examine the ritualistic *context*

Ms. Rasmussen and Ms. Capaldi are in the Department of Speech Communication, California State University, Long Beach.

of the narratives, detail the way in which their *texts* dramatize the archetype of rebirth, and describe their underlying dialectical *warrants*.

A. Context: Rhetorical Ritual

Investigations addressing the functioning of Alcoholic Anonymous (Gellman, 1964; Griel & Rudy, 1983; Jones, 1970; Kurtz, 1982; Petrunik, 1982) argue that A.A. involves a progress of conversation, that it creates an alternative social reality for the alcoholic, or that it is a rhetorical community characterized by distinctive communicative patterns (Denzin, 1987; Thune, 1977). Central to each perspective is the theme that Alcoholics Anonymous facilitates radical change maintained principally through social action centered around A.A. meetings. Significantly, participants evidence tacit knowledge of the power of the meetings by describing them in ritualistic terms—as "a celebration of life over death," as a commemoration of "resurrection" into a new life (Rasmussen & Capaldi, 1988).

Rituals are "conventionalized joint activities, given to ceremony, endowed with special emotion and often sacred meaning" which are symbolic enactments of processes of change (Denzin, 1987, p. 214). Common rituals include those involving rites of passage, conversion, and reaffirmation. For example, when individuals move from one station in life to another, initiation rituals mark their transition to a different status. Similarly, people embarking on major change pass through the conversion rites of formal ceremonies. Since maintaining an alternative belief system requires energy, ritualistic reaffirmation reinforces adherence to an alternative life style. Because rituals are participative, public acts, they are social activities creating commitment on both individual and social levels. Denzin (1987) describes their role: rituals "legitimize the selves of . . . [participants], . . . give a sense of solidarity and community to . . . group members, . . . [recreate a group's] world view, . . . [and secure] a movement into the future that will be guided by the ritual" (p. 118).

Rituals can degenerate into meaningless routine or retain their life and power by matching a subjective state to an objective display. Such rhetorical rituals are "recurring acts of formalized language and gesture" that embody both the means and ends for achieving psychic balance (Hoban, 1980, p. 276). Objectifying an internal condition while subjectifying an external demonstration validates a meaningful personal experience, makes it memorable to the rhetor and audience, and generates commitment (Berger & Luckman, 1967). Thus, rhetorical rituals are collective, standardized forms of language and action that symbolically maintain, restore, or create a new order (Hoban, 1980, p. 279).

Speaker meetings of Alcoholics Anonymous are rhetorical rituals reaffirming the viability of recovery within A.A. They progress from the greeting to reading the A.A. preamble and other selected literature, to the acknowledging of various lengths of sobriety, to the testimony of speakers, and to the benediction of a closing prayer. This ritual serves three critical functions. First, reading of prayers and literature describing A.A.'s purpose, the nature of alcoholism, and the program of Alcoholics Anonymous reaffirms the organization's collective history and its world view, thus reinforcing a common tradition and perspective (Alcoholics Anonymous, 1953). Second, members' performances of and listening to the ritual create a sense of identification born of active participation. Third, auditors observing the way others speak of their recovery learn the communicative norms of the A.A. community (Denzin, 1987). In other words, taking part in A.A. rituals reinforces a group's orientation, unity, and modes of communication.

The narratives features in speakers' meetings are personal accounts modeled after the stories comprising the second section of the *Big Book* of Alcoholics Anonymous. Most speakers follow that volume's injunction to tell the story of their addiction and sobriety by addressing "what . . . [they] used to be like, what happened, and what . . . [they] are like now (*Alcoholics Anonymous*, 1976). Although some presentations are polished, all are informal and may be disjointed, fragmented, lacking in conventional structure, and marked by dysfluency. Regardless of the degree of refinement, the addresses reaffirm the "plausibility structures" of the life world of Alcoholics Anonymous by "mediating" that world to persons trying to initiate or maintain sobriety (Berger & Luckman, 1967). In essence, they are symbolic manifestations of shared experience and feeling that create the potential for identification between speaker and auditors. Ford (1989) summarizes research addressing the impact of stories told within A.A. by arguing that they "transmit values, present the character of alcoholism, and provide a world view" (p. 3). Thus, the narratives of speakers form the basis for an affective identification among members, publicly dramatize the A.A. orientation and way of life, and function as models instructing members in the art of talking about themselves.

Speakers' meetings of Alcoholics Anonymous, then, are reaffirming rhetorical rituals having the potential to reinforce recovery by enacting a collective orientation, identification, and means of communication. Literature and narrative perpetuate the perspective of Alcoholics Anonymous; personal stories create shared meaning and identification; and both literature and tales of drinking and sobriety function as prototypes guiding the communicative action of recovering alcoholics. Consequently, such rituals "transform the member" into a "talking subject" who is learning and has learned how to speak to his or her experiences of recovery within the ritual structure of A.A. (Denzin, 1987). The showcased talk of speakers' meetings, the personal stories of recovering alcoholics thus draw part of their power from participation in an overarching rhetorical ritual.

B.   # Text: The Archetype of Rebirth

The reaffirming impact of speakers' meetings of Alcoholics Anonymous resides principally in the manner in which A.A. narratives manifest the myth or archetype of rebirth. Campbell (1972) describes myths as "public dreams" that are "vehicles of communication between the conscious and the unconscious, just as dreams are" (p. 50). They function to "provide meaning, identity, a comprehensive understandable image of the world, and to support the social order" (Fisher, 1973, p. 161). Rushing (1989) views myths as "central to the meaning of life," principally because of their "expression of spiritual *meaning*" (p. 2).

The rebirth archetype portrays a regenerative process. It originates in a life in which people find themselves beset by psychic chaos. The experience of chaos is followed by a death characterized by disintegration of the personality. During this period, individual identity deteriorates because of stress created by internal and external disorder (June, 1973, p. 54). Disintegration begins as the person's psychic pain escalates through the loss of sustaining systems and coping mechanisms. Death occurs when deterioration demands escape at any price. In death, personal identity can neither be repaired nor returned to its pre-chaotic condition. Thus, the person must continue to degenerate—to "die" either literally or figuratively—or begin a new way of life through rebirth. By participating in some species of conversion, the individual puts old ways of living behind and experiences a "period of transition or marginality" during which he or she copes with the confusion of change (Hoban, 1980, p. 282). The individual then attains—generally through group support—the strength to become fully reborn and sustain a new existence. Hence, rituals employing the rebirth myth create, maintain, and reaffirm the possibility of regenerative experiences by dramatizing a process of transformation. In essence, they employ a mode of expression which moves "upward and outward, [constituting] an expansion or outburst of activity, a transition toward reintegration and life-renewal" (Bodkin, 1958, p. 53).

Although the content and structure of A.A. narratives vary, to an appreciable degree each dramatizes a precipitate contrast between two versions of the rebirth cycle. The first variation—the drinking story—recounts a damaging series of events beginning with feelings of discontent (life) which are alleviated by escape (rebirth) through use of alcohol and/or other drugs which is followed by disintegration (death) into a negative spiral of deepening destruction. The contrasting variation is the sobriety narrative. It details the attainment of a new life through the "conversion" of separation (rebirth) via total abstinence followed by the maintenance of that abstinence by incorporation (life) of beliefs and actions grounded in the principles of Alcoholics Anonymous.

l. **The Drinking Narrative**

a. <u>*Discontent.*</u>   Speakers generally place comparatively little emphasis on personal background predating their use of alcohol. Those who address this facet of their stories do so in the belief that "what happened to me as a child has a tremendous influence on who and what I am today and [on] so many of those things I'm working on [in sobriety]." Chronicling of their early life reveals divergent personal histories. Individuals come from all economic strata, from various ethnic groups, from both supportive and dysfunctional homes. Many grew up in families already beset by alcoholism and other addiction. The description of one woman is telling:

> The best way I can describe what went on at our house was it was a house — typical alcoholic . . . kind of a house — a house that was full of chaos, struggle, drama, fighting, brawls, and the nightmare that goes on with alcoholism. . . . I never brought home any friends . . . because, see, I didn't want them to see what was goin' on behind those doors and I wanted to act like everything was just fine. . . . We never talked about my father's alcoholism. We never talked about it to each other . . . . We sure didn't talk about it to teachers or anybody on the outside because that would have been disloyal, and I learned not to talk about those feelings and not to face those feelings. It's the way I learned how to survive.

Her account articulates three themes characteristic of stories of persons raised in abusive backgrounds. First, life was chaotic and frightening, plagued by an inherently threatening, arbitrary uncertainty. Second, family members learned to pretend their turbulent existence was normal, thus engaging in denial. Third, because home life was traumatic, individuals did not talk about it; therefore, since they concealed what happened to them, they erected barriers between themselves and other people. This in turn created a threat to "the 'correctness' of the individual's subjective identity" because personal identity "is dependent on relations with significant others" (Berger & Luckman, 1967, p. 105). The result was a painful state of alienation. Chaos, denial, and alienation also are prominent emblems in alcoholic drinking stories.

Other speakers describe less distressing early histories. For example, a middle-aged woman says, "I was raised in a really nice Catholic family. I was taught never to lie, cheat or steal . . . . I had it all as a young woman." Regardless of background, however, alcoholics detail problems coping with the exigencies of living. They speak of being confused about life, of feeling inadequate in comparison with their peers, of being uncomfortable socially and personally. In other words, they portray themselves as beset by feelings of confusion, inadequacy and alienation. Thus, recovering alcoholics indicate a level of discontent, a sense of unease, a sense of tension, a need for relief. That relief was provided by escape through alcohol.

b.   *Escape.*   Kenneth Burke's (1961) "guilt cycle" provides a framework for explaining alcoholics' recounting of their developing addiction. Burke depicts "guilt"—a sense of anxiety, tension, a feeling that things are not as they should be—as an inevitable part of human existence (pp. 294-295). This anxiety, like the alcoholic's expressed discontent, constitutes a state of pollution demanding purification (p. 231). An alcoholic's purification comes from the escape (illusory rebirth) afforded by use and abuse of alcohol. Speakers describe its effects in a manner similar to that of Steven Crites' (1971) explication of what he terms "contracted consciousness": "[people] seek relief and release in the capacity to contract the flow of time, to dwell in . . . a friendly darkness created by feeling and sensation" (p. 309). One speaker relates the effect of alcohol on feeling and function in the following manner:

> [Alcohol] alters my perception of reality. It . . . makes the same things look different. It . . . adjusts my relationship to my environment. It . . . makes me taller and less afraid and [makes], them smaller and less fearful to me. It fills holes that I never knew existed 'til I filled them.

An alcoholic's escape generally took one of two forms. The individual drank either to secure freedom from a painful reality through oblivion or to escape feelings of inadequacy.

Drinking for oblivion was a reprieve from fear, responsibility, and loneliness, or was a retreat into the rush of a high. One man portrays his seeking of oblivion to blot out reality: "I needed to escape . . . any way I could . . . [so] that I didn't have to think about what I was doing or who I was doing it to." Others describe "blacking out"—a period in which the individual appears to be operating normally but one which she or he doesn't remember. A female alcoholic's blackouts mitigated pain: "I would just plain black out. I wouldn't know where I was. I thought everybody blacked out because, see, I drank to get rid of the pain. And I drank to feel okay. So I thought that's how everybody drank, just to black out and erase it all out." Still others describe the pleasure of the high, the "rush" of drinking and using drugs: "I'd walk fast, talk fast, move fast, fall down occasionally, and get back up and go. . . . I guess I felt omnipotent. . . . I felt special and happy and okay."

For many, intoxication combatted feelings of inadequacy. Narrators speak of overcoming alienation through an increased ability to relate to others. A forty-year-old woman tells of the socially lubricating powers of alcohol: "I bought a half pint of vodka . . . and drank half of it down just so I could go back into that office and sit down and talk to those women. And everything seemed to relax and I went in there and I . . . was able to start a conversation." Still others indicate they needed to drink to do their jobs, to interact with family and lovers, to go to the grocery store, to drive freeways, or to perform a myriad of tasks.

Drinking for escape was a way of changing how the individual felt about him or herself. A male alcoholic with thirty years of sobriety recalls his "unusual reaction" to alcohol: "[I]nstead of making me look like a man, it made me *feel* like a man. I took my last drink to feel the way men look—

the same reason I'd taken all the rest of the drinks, to feel the way men look.'' In essence, then, speakers depict their drinking as providing an answer, a solution to problems of tension, anxiety, and dis-ease: ''Alcohol went down inside of me and tore the madness from me. It screamed the screaming madness, the silence that was goin' on inside of me and I was able to be all right, right now.'' This relief, however, quickly became a double-edged sword for addicted people because their behavior had consequences that propelled them toward greater dysfunction.

C. *Disintegration.* The euphoria of consuming alcohol is something speakers report paying extraordinary prices to pursue, prices that increased with their progressive disintegration toward a figurative—and potentially literal—death. Recovering alcoholics recount the loss of families, jobs, homes, friends, and self-respect. They tell of smashed cars, debilitating accidents, physical and psychological abuse of families, trips to jails, prisons, hospitals, and mental institutions. Even though many denied seemingly indefinitely the role alcohol abuse had in escalating their problems, their ''answer'' was illusory because addiction demanded continued abuse of the same drug that generated behaviors producing guilt. Attempts to relieve that guilt, however, were fruitless; therefore, their spiral into the depths of addiction moved inexorably downward.

Burke (1961) argues that purification of guilt requires punishment, either of self or others. Mortification, or self-punishment, involves personal sacrifice. Alcoholics report practicing three modes of mortification. First, they continued behavior causing them pain. Their drinking persisted in the face of hangovers, seizures, and physical deterioration. An elderly Hispanic gentleman sober over thirty years tells of his physical condition and actions toward the end of his drinking:

> I was . . . at a veterans' hospital and after three days I heard them say I wasn't going to make it, so I got up and left . . . . And I had to crawl all the way 'cause I was sick, and I got off on Soto and I had two dollars, less seventy cents. It cost seventy cents for the bus, and I bought four bottles of muscatel wine. Why? . . . I don't know to this day why I drank like I did, but I did, . . . as much as I could as long as I could.

A second form of mortification involved remorse for bad behavior and working hard to make up for actions while drinking. People report working long hours to earn enough money to support their families (and their addiction), begging and buying forgiveness, promising never to drink again. Third, still others describe a conscious attempt or wish to destroy themselves. Some report the desire simply to die or the conviction that their fate was the slow suicide of alcoholism. Talking about her father who did die of acute alcoholism, one woman recalls: ''I would say that after 10 years he stopped talking about coming back to A.A. and he started talking about dying. And it was at this point that he started . . . drinking every single day. . . . He decided to drink himself to death.''

The alternative to mortification is victimage or scapegoating, the transfer of guilt to another (Burke, 1957, 1966). Speakers report use of two varieties of scapegoating. First, they blamed people and situations for their difficulties — "If you had my _____ (wife, children, job, in-laws, problems), you'd drink too." One woman describes her thinking as she sat in a mental hospital: "You see, it was always your fault. It was never . . . [my] fault. It was always his fault, or the situation I was in or somebody else's fault." In a similar vein, a recovering male relates his abusive behavior: "I take and I use and I abuse and when I get through with whatever I'm takin' and abusin' I just cast it aside and go on about my business to somethin' else, with never a thought, never a backward glance." Thus, speakers describe their inability to take responsibility for their own actions. A second form of victimage was to take out frustrations on others. A father tells of his treatment of his child: "I pulled that kid out of the bathtub and I hit him as hard as I could. And, I remember when his head hit the floor . . . [with] his eyes buggin' out of his head. And, I remember the fear in that kid's eyes. And, I remember the fear in my eyes when my Dad would do that to me. And I swore to God I would never be like that and I was."

Death. The alcoholic's use of mortification and victimage provided momentary redemption at best but had another, more important, consistent result: it created greater destruction, humiliation, and pain and therefore a heightened level of dis-ease or guilt. Alcoholics describe the period of highly abusive drinking as a black time, one devoid of hope because if they attempted to quit drinking "the more . . . [they] didn't want to drink, it seemed, the more . . . [they] had to have a drink." They speak of "alcoholic nightmares," of wanting to die, of a sense of worthlessness. Their condition became one in which they "ran out of dreams and aspirations." This state of blackness constituted the phenomenon of "incomprehensible demoralization" described in the book *Alcoholics Anonymous* (1976, p. 59).

Drinking narratives, then, are stories of a descent into death born of discontent, fueled by the illusion of escape, perpetuated by the pain of disintegration. Paradoxically, the desperation of death formed the basis for rebirth into sobriety within the framework of the program of Alcoholics Anonymous. Recovery narratives contrast with those detailing drinking by reaffirming the possibility of regeneration through life renewal.

The Recovery Narrative

Separation. The death or "incomprehensible demoralization" in an alcoholic's life before sobriety became a springboard to recovery, for it established the basis for a *surrender* entailing recognition that life dominated by addiction was intolerable. What the alcoholic experienced is similar to Eliade's description of "initiatory death" as "a recommencement, never an end, . . . [as] a trial indispensable to a regeneration . . . to the beginning of a new life (Eliade, 1964, p. 224). Alcoholics describe the factors correlated with their surrender in three ways.

First, many relate a despair that overpowered their denial of their alcoholism. A Hispanic man describes his surrender at age thirty-two as follows:

> One night . . . I found myself with . . . nowhere to go. I had used up everything and everybody. I was sick and tired of being sick and tired, . . . and a strange thing happened . . . [that] the Book calls 'moment of clarity.' . . . I had to go back to a gal that I dragged through eleven years of nightmare livin' and ask her for a favor. . . . I asked her if she had the phone number to A.A.

Similarly, a female alcoholic recounts her feelings prior to entering a medical facility: "I remember thinking that . . . I had to try and . . . quit living the way I was living. . . . That afternoon . . . I went to . . . [a] hospital and I had myself admitted. . . . And . . . I felt . . . more hopelessness and . . . more loneliness and more fear than I had ever felt in my entire life." Thus, alcoholics indicate that weariness, loneliness, fear, and hopelessness became the basis for their transformation into a new existence.

Second, others portray a traumatic life event as leading to their admission of alcoholism. A young man who had tried staying sober describes the actions he took after retreating to a bar following domestic violence:

> The . . . [bartender] came up and he put a drink in front of me. . . . I don't know why I didn't drink that drink because I wanted to. But the next thought that came to my mind was "maybe the people at A.A. were right." And what I did was I walked across the street to the apartment I just got evicted out of and I called A.A.

For another alcoholic, seeing her family's reactions as she entered a courtroom proved to be the factor preceding surrender: "I couldn't look up at them. . . . How can you look up at the people who love you? I mean, what do you say? . . . [They look at you and ask] 'Why do you do these things? . . . Why do you hurt us so much?' And you don't have an answer." The experience of hurting family members was not new for either individual. What was new was admitting personal culpability. A lawyer who came out of a blackout while defending a client summarizes his reactions: "[I]t was probably the first thing that I'd ever done that I couldn't blame on any person, place, or thing — wife, partner, creditor, conditions, circumstance, or anything outside myself." This recognition of responsibility became critical in overcoming the denial characteristic of alcoholism.

Third, others indicate they experience an inexplicable psychic change that enabled them to stop drinking. They speak of waking up and knowing they could not continue living as they had been; they talk of sudden insight or understanding that life with alcohol was intolerable; they tell of having a "moment of clarity" or a "spiritual awakening" that freed them to seek help. Thus, speakers portray surrender — whether born of despair, admission of responsibility, or insight—as essential to recovery. In other words, they reaffirm the paradox that they "surrendered to win," that defeat was necessary for liberation.

An incongruity expressed by alcoholics is that admitting despair and culpability generated rebirth to a new life grounded in hope and responsibility. The transformation of rebirth, however, was neither immediate nor easy. Alcoholic accounts parallel what Hoban (1980) terms "a period of transition or marginality during which the . . . old and the new are ambiguously and momentarily joined," a period marked by uncertainty, fear, and confusion (p. 281). This state of confusion manifests itself in rhetors' descriptions of dysfunctional attitudes and behaviors.

Attitudinal problems grew out of hostility and alienation. Many alcoholics tell of resentment toward being in Alcoholics Anonymous and antipathy toward others. A successful, sober, businessman summarizes his early problems: "When I came to Alcoholics Anonymous, I did not like it here. And it did not grow on me real fast either. . . . I hated everybody and everything. . . . [P]eople would . . . [ask me] 'Why did . . . [do] you keep coming back?' Because I didn't have anywhere else to go." Others echo this discomfort by relating feelings of guilt, remorse, uniqueness, and unworthiness, all of which led to alienation from others. They speak of isolating themselves, coming to meetings late and leaving early, acting "tough" to ward off others, refusing to ask for help.

Behavioral confusion stemmed from problems giving up previous, harmful activities and from not knowing how to function without alcohol or other drugs. Men and women talk of difficulties forsaking lying, manipulation of others, socializing in bars, and dysfunctional behavioral patterns such as avoiding confrontation and responsibility or insisting on controlling other people. Hence, their stories indicate that becoming physically sober did not right their lives automatically. Significantly, many detail at least one relapse into drinking before finally maintaining a drug-free existence, thus reflecting the particularly precarious nature of early sobriety.

The stage of separation is a story of powerlessness leading to power. It began with a surrender to the idea that the person could not drink successfully followed by a time during which the alcoholic experienced the confusion integral to adopting a new life. This transitory phase was "an uncertain and even . . . frightening period that . . . [was] endured because its completion . . . [promised] a new, more functional . . . [life]" (Hoban, 1980, p. 284). What enabled alcoholics to pass from the trauma of separation into a more useful existence was change in behavior and attitude through adopting the guidelines recommended by others utilizing the program of Alcoholics Anonymous. A male thirty years sober explains the importance of union with others: "[W]hen I became just like you, . . . when I became simple enough to be an alcoholic, . . . then my recovery started. My recovery started when I started to do the things that you have done to recover. When I started to apply those steps to my life, my recovery started." Hence, alcoholics report the pain of transition slowly abating as they came to oneness with others and thus learned more productive ways of living.

b. *Incorporation.* Narrators describe maintenance of sobriety as growing out of incorporation of new principles, behaviors, and attitudes into their lives. One woman talks of seeking stability through balance in her "work," "home," "body," "relationships," and activities in Alcoholics Anonymous. This restoration of balance developed out of a fusion of personal responsibility with involvement in a community and dependence on what Alcoholics Anonymous terms "higher power."

Speakers who emphasize assuming responsibility for their actions generally stress the processes of taking inventory and making amends recommended in A.A.'s twelve steps. Inventorying requires that people survey their lives and come to accept personal responsibility rather than blaming others. The amends process involves making restitution for wrongs committed (*Alcoholics Anonymous*, 1976). One man describes this accepting of responsibility as an extended commitment: "I think it takes every waking moment of my life to heal the scars and to . . . put away the dreams and the nightmares and make amends for the things that I've done . . . to the people I lived in the world with." Others take the position that "nobody's responsible for me but me." Most, however, indicate that their self-examination and restitution to others produced freedom that enriched their lives. Hence, they articulate the paradox that the constraint of responsibility leads to freedom.

The theme of community also is central to incorporation. Narrators talk of maintaining their sobriety by helping others as they had been helped— "you have to give it away to keep it." Others advise their audiences that taking action within Alcoholics Anonymous is a key to sobriety. Rather than isolation, speakers testify that seeking support and sharing with other members was integral to continuing recovery: "Surround yourself by people who are trying, 'cause they will pull you along when you are weak so that you will . . . be strong to pull them along when they are weak." Alcoholics' emphasis on becoming one with others and with an overall community is similar to the requirements for maintaining religious conversion described by Berger and Luckmann (1967): "It is only within the religious community . . . that the conversion can be effectively maintained as plausible. . . . To have a conversion experience is nothing much. The real thing is to be able to keep on taking it seriously; to retain a sense of its plausibility" (p. 158). Membership in a community, then, became essential to the alcoholic's rebirth.

The third theme emphasized by speakers explaining changes incorporated into their lives is faith in a "higher power." Some recount returning to the religion of their childhood. Others tell of a personal faith maintained outside organized religion: "Through the results of the twelve steps, I found me a God. My God. My God of my own understanding. And he's quite a guy. . . . And he's got a hell of a sense of humor, hell of a sense." Narrators talk of learning to trust in God, of turning their lives over to Him, of doing His will, and of their faith enabling them to be "happy, joyous, and free." In essence, they reaffirm the paradox of increased freedom through dependence on a higher power, of gaining strength through reliance on God.

The testimony of recovering alcoholics indicates that to maintain sobriety they have combatted alienation and destructive living patterns by taking responsibility for their own behavior, becoming involved with others and with the community of Alcoholics Anonymous, and placing trust in a higher power. They depict their new way of living, not as a trouble-free existence, but as a life beset by both joys and problems with which they've learned to cope functionally. A cliché used frequently is that "My worst day sober is better than my best day drinking." Many narratives contain direct comparisons indicating that life in sobriety has become the antithesis of life while drinking. A man who talked of his drinking history as a nightmare depicts his sobriety as an awakening into life and living. A woman who emphasized denial of human feeling during abuse explains the actions she is taking to acknowledge and work with such feelings. A man who characterized himself as a taker and abuser describes the ways he gives to others. Hence, the incorporation stage is the culminating action in a continuing process of rebirth that affects a "conversion" resulting in "a second awakening of consciousness" (Crites, 1971, p. 309).

Warrants: Dialectical "Good Reasons"

Stories of recovering alcoholics embedded in a unifying rhetorical ritual merge two contrasting cycles of rebirth—the illusory emancipation of addiction with its attendant disintegration juxtaposed against an awakening into life-renewal through sobriety. These narratives argue that recovery from addiction is possible if individuals maintain abstinence by adhering to the principles of Alcoholics Anonymous. They present accounts of abuse and recovery that make sense of an enigmatic reality by advancing "good reasons" grounded in dialectical relationships.

Walter R. Fisher (1978) defines "good reasons" as "*those elements that provide warrants for accepting or adhering to the advice fostered by any form of communication that can be considered rhetorical*" (p. 378). He defines "warrant" as "that which authorizes, sanctions, or justifies belief, attitude or action" and indicates that argumentation may occur in "all modes of communication, not just those that have clear-cut inferential structures" (p. 378). Within A.A. stories, the forms warranting "belief, attitude . . . [and] action" of the recovering alcoholic are dialectical structures permeating the narratives.

The archetype of rebirth creates dialectical pairings facilitating a functional perspective on the confusing world of the alcoholic. Dialectical relationships involve fusion "in a single figure [of] two incommensurable realities [or] two heterogeneous and asymmetrical terms" to form a unified structure under which opposites, although in tension become comprehensible (Jameson, 1971, p. 6). Rhetors signal their need for understanding, for a way of reconciling seemingly contradictory facets of life and living by speaking of a "great thirst for wholeness," a yearning to be at one with self and others, to find serenity instead of confusion. Dialectical features of the narratives create an acceptance of self and a reinterpretation of reality that makes recovery seem viable and desirable.

Acceptance of Self

For most alcoholics, self esteem is an issue. Individuals speak of being alienated from others and of feelings of inadequacy even prior to becoming addicted to alcohol. Their accounts indicate that these problems escalated during their period of active abuse and continued into sobriety. Hence, an important issue in recovery is self acceptance (Denzin, 1987, pp. 35-39). Narratives of recovering alcoholics warrant self acceptance dialectically in two ways.

First, speakers' stories of drinking and rehabilitation both unite and maintain the tension between pre- and post-recovery personae. Alcoholic accounts pointedly contrast life during drinking with life in sobriety; but rather than denying characteristics and actions while drinking, speaker and audience combat guilt, shame, and humiliation by acknowledging past experience as forming the basis for recovery. Thus, narrating produces a potential union of both selves while reaffirming their differences. Drawing on Carl Jung, Janice Hocker Rushing and Thomas S. Frentz (1980) argue that the facet of personality rejected by an individual, "the shadow"—the persona of the practicing alcoholic—"is a potential source of strength and power" if recognized, confronted, and accepted (p. 384). Alcoholics' narrations of the past and ongoing present facilitate such recognition, a recognition promoting integration of self. Many quote the book *Alcoholics Anonymous* which says that people living sober lives "will not regret the past nor wish to shut the door on it" and indicate that facing the past is the foundation of their recovery (*Alcoholics Anonymous*, 1976, p. 58). Hence, the dialectical contrast and union facilitated by the narratives' juxtaposing the practicing and recovering "selves" creates a oneness acknowledging the totality of the alcoholic's experience which furthers personal acceptance, an acceptance integral to continuing sobriety.

Second, the narratives foster acceptance of self by dramatizing the tension and unity between the individual and the group or community. On the one hand, stories of recovering alcoholics encourage identification. The narratives provide the opportunity for diverse individuals to identify with each other on grounds of shared experience and principle. The telling of stories allows people actively to recognize similarities between themselves and others as they share in the retelling of both events and feelings involved in drinking and recovery. Individuals speak of the impact of hearing others tell their stories and admonish auditors to "listen for the feelings." Participation in this type of identification helps break barriers of alienation and furthers a feeling of oneness with others and ultimately with a community of recovering alcoholics. By embodying the precepts of the program of Alcoholics Anonymous, the narratives also promote identification on the level of principle. People tell of going to meetings to "learn to live," to benefit from the experience of others. Critical advice in the passage containing the twelve steps of Alcoholics Anonymous is that alcoholics need to "practice these principles in all . . . [their] affairs" (*Alcoholics Anonymous*, 1976, p. 58). By hearing others reaffirm A.A. precepts through recounting personal experiences, recovering alcoholics practice an identification potentially leading to both a more functional existence and a feeling of union with a larger community.

Because the process of identifying with others and with a larger community is a participative activity, it creates commitment, thus forming the basis for the narratives functioning as potent tools of socialization. Rhetors juxtapose destructive and creative transformations of identity that align speaker and audience with each other, with the community of Alcoholics Anonymous and with the larger society. By legitimating the beliefs and goals of recovery, the narratives promote stability by strengthening fundamental values. Thus, narratives buttress a shared social order by promoting a state in which "members . . . can . . . conceive of themselves as belonging to a meaningful universe, which was there before they were born and will be there after they die." Interestingly, many speakers tell of "never feeling 'a part of' anything" until they "came to Alcoholics Anonymous."

On the other hand, the way in which identification occurs is through the telling of unique stories. Individuals portray distinctive events in their lives — they relate an abundance of experience singularly their own. Only out of this divergence does identification grow. Persons from different geographical areas, from rural and urban environments, from professional and blue-collar vocations, from disparate ethnic, economic and social backgrounds find their commonality of experience and principle expressed in the inherently different lives of themselves and others. Thus, while proclaiming unity, the telling of individual stories simultaneously asserts the integrity of individual experience. In Burke's (1950) terms, the narratives dramatize the simultaneous union and division of the human condition (p. 21). Hence, the argumentative force of the narratives grows from their dialectically promoting self acceptance by situating individual experience within the context of shared experiences and principles.

Reinterpretation of Reality

Because the narratives embrace the paradoxes of the program of Alcoholics Anonymous, they promote changes in attitudes — "let[ting] go" of "old ideas"

(*Alcoholics Anonymous*, 1976)—necessary for rehabilitation. Alcoholics' reports of separation through surrender and confusion are grounded in the paradox that death was necessary for rebirth into a new life. Their stories are ones of surrendering to win, of despair leading to hope, of defeat becoming the basis for liberation of powerlessness begetting power, of disorder giving way to order. Similarly, their accounts of coming to adopt the A.A. way of life are dominated by the apparent incongruities that the constraint of admitting personal responsibility leads to freedom and that dependence—either on others or on a higher power—results in personal strength. Shore (1981) notes that these and similar paradoxes are implicit in the twelve steps of Alcoholics Anonymous (pp. 12-13).

Denzin describes the alcoholic early in sobriety as having lived "a theory of self that hinged on the denial of alcoholism and the alcoholic pursuit of a fictional 'I'" and as beginning recovery equipped with a "unique personal history" and the conviction that she or he is "unique and special" (Denzin, 1987, pp. 35, 38). He argues that requisite for recovery is the rejection of old beliefs about self and the nature of reality. Reaffirming paradox facilitates such a change in perspective, one akin to that described by Burke (1954) in his treatment of "perspective by incongruity." Burke argues that by finding similarity in the essentially dissimilar, people can escape the bonds of common perception. In addition, uniting or confronting opposites generates the energy requisite for change. Speakers, then, by subscribing to paradox, create order out of confusion and hence generate a more functional view of life and living.

Speakers' meetings of Alcoholics Anonymous are rhetorical rituals enacting a collective orientation, identification, and means of communication. The stories they feature juxtapose two contrasting variations of a rebirth cycle, the drinking narrative and the sobriety narrative, thus reaffirming the possibility of life-renewal in recovery. The narratives' underlying dialectical warrants constitute "good reasons" that produce meaning, identity, understanding and unity. Because they fuse pre- and post-recovery personae, they promote self acceptance by reaffirming the totality of an alcoholic's lived experience. Because they highlight an alcoholic's personal history against a backdrop of common experience and principle, they form a basis for positive identity. Because they embody paradox, they have the capacity to challenge dysfunctional views of the world while creating order out of confusion and thus building a more productive perspective on living. Hence, the power of the narratives flows from dialectical "good reasons" that generate a perspective on self and reality, creating a newly sensible world within the context of a supportive community.

Chapter Nineteen

Argument and Beauty
A Review and Exploration
of Connections

Ken Chase

In late November, 1878, James Abbot McNeill Whistler brought a libel suit against John Ruskin, a prominent art critic. Ruskin had allegedly slandered Whistler in the course of attacking Whistler's impressionist painting of fireworks at night (titled *The Falling Rocket: Nocturne in Black and Gold*). During cross-examination, the defense attorney asked Whistler "What is the peculiar beauty of that picture?" Whistler responded: "It is as impossible for me to explain to you the beauty of that picture as it would be for a musician to explain to you the beauty of a harmony in a particular piece of music if you have no ear for music" (Adams, 1976, p. 21). Whistler resisted defending his judgment of beauty. The resistance is understandable. During the last several centuries, an understanding of beauty has been fostered which is antithetical to the practice of argument. As a consequence of this separation, the discussion about beauty and the discussion about argument have suffered. The discussion about beauty has retreated into a realm of private reflection with the result that the ideal of beauty is excluded from an application to public action and public discussion. Also, the discussion about argument has been deprived of its full extension into the entire range of human influence and response.

In this chapter, I will outline four possible connections between argument and beauty. Despite the brevity of this chapter, a survey of these options will

Mr. Chase is in the Department of Speech at Wabash College, Crawfordsville, Indiana.

illustrate how the artificial and undesirable distinction between beauty and argument may be overcome. Yet before sketching the major connections between the discussions about argument and beauty, a historical review of how this separation developed will provide the background necessary for understanding the problem.

A. The Separation of Argument and Beauty

The connection between argument and beauty is neglected because the two concepts have a modern association with different disciplines. The study of argument, primarily due to its modern connection with logic, has been separated from the practical world of public debate (Perelman, 1970). Beauty, through its connection with aesthetic theory, has been restricted to the individual's own world of subjective perceptions (Dieckmann, 1973). Yet, beauty and argument have not always been separated from the public sphere nor from each other. In the classical writings from the Roman and Medieval periods, the Latin noun *argumentum*, translated as argument, was used to describe both the medieval writer's strategy for producing (beautiful) literature (Kelly, 1987) and as the essence of public persuasive argument (Evans, 1976). Even the Renaissance theorists of the arts—music, painting, and sculpture in particular—relied on the classical traditions of argument (contained in the study of rhetoric) to assist them in their studies (Summers, 1987, pp. 39-40; Vickers, 1988, pp. 340ff).

During the Renaissance era, however, argumentation began to be gradually [Ramus] separated from the study of oratory (rhetoric) and began to be associated exclusively with logic. Rhetoric increasingly became associated with a view of eloquence more closely related to poetry than with public debating. During this late Renaissance and Enlightenment era, the concept of art gradually evolved from a reference to skill and expertise to a reference to the imaginative and creative products of painting, sculpture, music and letters (Williams, 1983). Consequently, later generations now recognize a distinction between artist and artisan; the latter merely one who has particular skills without unusual imaginative, intellectual or creative powers, whereas the former is the one who produces art, those works which are imbued with an aesthetic power.

Coinciding with the development of art as designating a uniquely creative product was the development of aesthetics as a disciplined study of the perceptions associated with the reception of art (Baumgarten, 1735/1954). In the discourse of aesthetics, the work of art was considered as eliciting a particular kind of sensory experience. The concept of beauty was central to the study of aesthetic experience for nearly a century, but continued investigation has both broadened the variety of experience and challenged the priority of beauty (e.g., Goodman, 1976, p. 255).

The rise of aesthetics and the separation of argument from rhetoric led to the eventual exclusion of rhetorical argument from discussions of beauty. Eloquence was usually included within the discussion of beauty, but it was compared, usually unfavorably, with poetry (Kant, 1790/1987; Skopec, 1982). Certainly, the nature of beauty and aesthetic experience were the subjects of much heated debate in the eighteenth century. But as aesthetic experience became increasingly privatized, the study of argument became less important. Consequently, later generations have inherited discourses about argument and beauty which come with a built-in resistance to integration. Of course, the separation between the two discourses is not exclusive; I merely have characterized some dominant strands in this complex historical fabric. Nonetheless, the general tendency to resist the integration of the discourses is evident.

Throughout the last few centuries, many people have called for a return to the study of argument as a means of public disputation rather than as a kind of logical game. Yet the call remains to be fully answered (Conley, 1984). Likewise, the constant battle against the isolation of art (a battle which often has been waged against the ''art for art's sake'' mentality; see K. Burke, 1931/1968; Dewey, 1934/1980; Jenkins, 1973) has not cast serious doubt on the popular conception that the experience of beauty is unique and personal and beyond dispute. I wish to combat both of these anti-public tendencies by identifying the interconnections of argument and beauty.

B. The Connection of Argument and Beauty

Usually those who despair over the separation of art from the public sphere do so by analyzing either aesthetic experience or the nature of art. I will narrow the focus to beauty in order to change the strategy a bit and, frankly, to create a more manageable task. I suggest four possible connections of argument and beauty: (a) arguments about the nature of beauty; (b) arguments about the judgment of beauty; (c) how beauty is a characteristic of argument; and (d) how beauty functions as argument. Although I cannot hope to overturn deeply ingrained presumptions, at least I can raise the issue for inspection. In the process, I hope to expand public thinking concerning both the judgment of beauty and certain conceptions of argument.

1. Arguments about the Nature of Beauty

In this section, I will illustrate an obvious connection, namely, that people argue when they attempt to describe the nature of beauty. While this observation may be mundane, I need to survey some ideas concerning the nature of beauty to assist the reader's understanding of the less obvious connections I draw in the remaining sections of this chapter. I have chosen to examine Edmund

Burke's (1757/1958) classic eighteenth century analysis of beauty and the sublime in order to examine the concept of beauty.

Burke argues for a particular understanding of beauty. Part of his argumentative strategy is to dissociate the beautiful from the the sublime. Burke's argument strategy can be illustrated by contrasting his approach with an alternative examination of beauty and the sublime in *On the Sublime*, a short study of style in language supposedly written by Longinus (3rd century, A.D.). Apparently, Burke wrote his *Enquiry* with Longinus' little book in the back of his mind.

Whereas Burke distinguished between the beautiful and the sublime, Longinus combined them. For instance, Longinus (300 A.D./1906), as he previewed the foundations for success in writing, seemed to combine the "beauties of expression" with "all which is sublime" (p. 10; sec. v). At another point, he referred to those writings which elevate the human spirit as "beautiful and genuine effects of sublimity which please always, and please all" (p. 12; sec. vii). Furthermore, Longinus described the sublime by reference to qualities which many have linked with a description of the beautiful. Longinus offers the following quality as one indication of the sublime: "one factor of sublimity must necessarily be the power of choosing the most vital of the included elements, and of making these, by mutual superposition, form as it were a single body" (p. 22; sec. x). Longinus features a poem of Sappho (c. 600 B.C.) to illustrate how distinct sensuous (romantic-erotic) experiences are combined into an "assemblage of passions." Those who, throughout history, have speculated on the essential qualities of beauty have frequently referred to this quality—the collection of intense images brought into unity—as central.

In contrast to Longinus' collapse of beauty and the sublime, Burke's argument about beauty involves two major steps: he divides human passion into pain and pleasure (Part I); and he associates the sublime with pain and pleasure with beauty (Parts II and III, respectively). Burke believes the qualities of objects can excite the passions of pleasure or pain. So, beautiful objects— those which engender pleasure—are smooth, comparatively small, light, delicate, and clear. Sublime objects, on the contrary, are large, dark and gloomy, rugged, solid, and massive; these objects engender ideas of pain, terror, and astonishment.

Burke's view of beauty proved controversial in that he gave all of the majesty and power to the sublime, whereas that which is beautiful is, in the words of J. T. Boulton, "mere prettiness" (1958, p. lxxv).

I agree with Burke that the nature of the beautiful—that which is central to a judgment of beauty—certainly seems to consist of those qualities like smoothness and clearness and smallness some of the time. But beauty also may consist of darkness and largeness and roughness as well. For instance, many people think of a majestic view of the Swiss Alps as beautiful. Many people also do not hesitate to describe a painting by Renoir as beautiful even though it contains darkly vivid shades of orange and red applied through rough, short brush strokes. Burke is certainly correct to distinguish between the beautiful and the sublime; yet, since many of the qualities which he associates with the sublime are readily associated with the beautiful, the nature of his distinction is highly disputable. Burke's argument for the nature of beauty elicits counter arguments. Yet, the inevitability of arguments about the nature of beauty should not cause one to dismiss arguments about beauty altogether. Instead, arguments about beauty should be recognized as the process of bringing remarkable objects together with remarkable perceptions for the purpose of expanding and enlivening everyday experience.

This brief review of Longinus and Burke is useful not only in illustrating how the analysis of beauty proceeds through argument, but the review also surveys some central characteristics of beauty: a dynamic unity out of diversity, smoothness and clearness, and, perhaps, largeness and roughness. In the following section, I will add to this list in the process of examining another link between argument and beauty.

Arguments about the Judgment of Beauty

Aside from the mundane observation that people argue when they attempt to determine the nature of beauty, the previous section concerning Longinus and Burke also illustrates that people may argue when they judge particular objects as beautiful. This latter observation is significantly more controversial than the former; with this observation, I meet head-on that peculiar resistance of beauty to public disputation. People often claim that a judgment of beauty is personal and cannot be influenced by argument (Kant, 1790/1987). I, on the other hand, claim that people can learn to judge things as beautiful. Since argument is clearly instrumental in learning, then argument can lead to judgments of beauty. Two examples will illustrate this point.

Guy Sircello, in *A New Theory of Beauty* (1975), argues that beauty is a function of particular properties inherent to the observed object. One of these properties is vividness of color. In the course of defending vividness as a sufficient property of beauty, he describes the gold-colored grass of the California coastal mountains in June (pp. 21-29). I was born and raised in California and often enjoyed the beauty of inland mountains in winter or the rugged coastline in the summer, but I do not recall ever thinking of the June grass as particularly beautiful. The grass on the California hills was never quite green enough for my liking, and it never occurred to me that the light brown grass could be seen as golden. Nor did it occur to me that the golden color is uniquely vivid at that time of year, and that the vividness is particularly beautiful.

Yet after examining Sircello's argument for vividness, in which he relies on his experience with the golden grass, I now am intrigued by the possibility of seeing that golden grass as beautiful. Sircello's argument challenges my previously held conceptions of that grass and effectively offers new conceptions more readily associated with the judgment of beauty. I now am certain that, if I ever have the opportunity to return to California in June, I would reconsider the vividness and the goldenness of those grassy hills and, probably, appreciate their beauty.

Laurie Adams (1976) provides another example of how judgments of beauty can be fostered through argument. She describes an art trial in which the judgments of beauty were publicly defended. The matter of dispute was the status of Constantin Brancusi's polished bronze sculpture *Bird in Space* (Figure 1).

In 1926, Edward Steichen purchased the polished bronze sculpture from Constantin Brancusi in Italy and had it shipped to the United States. The U.S. Customs officials failed to see the unusual object as an art piece and, thus, denied it duty-free status. Steichen was forced to pay a tariff of forty percent of the object's value.

The 1927 trial serves as a marvelous record of how judgments of beauty can be defended. Under questioning by the counsel, Steichen responded: "From a technical standpoint, in the first place, it has form and appearance; it is an object created by an artist in three dimensions; it has harmonious proportions, which give me an aesthetic sense, a sense of great beauty. That object has that quality in it. That is the reason I purchased it" (Adams, 1976, p. 43). The beauty of the piece was defended; Steichen provided reasons why his judgment of beauty was reasonable.

Other witnesses provided similar accounts of the object's beauty. Jacob Epstein, an English sculptor, distinguished Brancusi's piece of polished bronze from a polished bronze by a first-rate mechanic: "He [mechanic] can polish it up, but he cannot conceive of the object. That is the whole point. He cannot conceive those particular lines, which give it its individual beauty" (Adams, 1976, p. 52). Frank Crowninshield, the editor of *Vanity Fair*, defended the name of the sculpture by expanding on the analogy with a bird: "It has . . . the suggestion of flight, it suggests grace, aspiration, vigor coupled with speed, in the spirit of strength, potency, beauty, just as a bird does" (Adams, 1976, p. 49). These judgments of beauty were all defended through argument.

Once we can accept that a particular judgment of beauty can be defended or attacked, it is relatively easy to recognize that the mere observation of beauty may be influenced by argument. Those who did not consider the Brancusi sculpture as beautiful, for instance, might see the reasonableness of describing its "beauty" after studying the arguments defending its beauty. The judgment of beauty, therefore, can be learned, and that learning process involves argument.

Of course, people still argue that they are "struck" by beauty; thus, argument has no affect on the existence of their unique perceptual experience. I reply, to the contrary, that the recognition of such experiences are both learned and reinforced through socialization processes in which argument is central. People

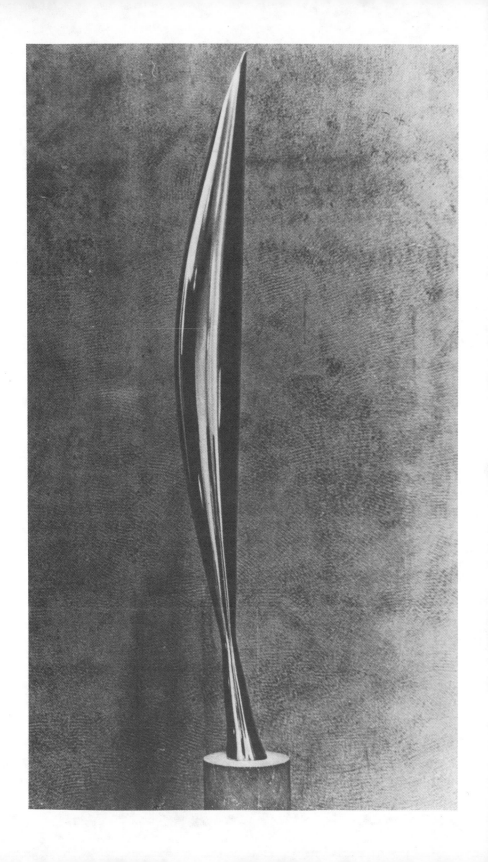

certainly may be struck by unusual perceptual experiences, but whether or not beauty is the desired description of the observation is a result of social convention and dispute. Indeed, even the quality of the experience itself—its uniqueness or unusualness—is open to dispute (notice how, for example, people disagree whether a sunset is beautiful, or whether a particular painting is beautiful).

By recognizing that argument plays a part in the judgment of beauty we can avoid considering beauty as a purely private affair. Argument surrounds the discussion of beauty. The philosophers, the art critics, and the naive California native all can rely on argument to further the observations of beauty. In turn, the judgment of beauty is placed securely within the public realm.

So far I have reviewed two connections between argument and beauty: arguments about the nature of beauty and arguments about judgments of beauty. In these previous sections I have suggested that beauty is mistakenly categorized as uniquely personal and subjective. Instead, beauty is dependent on arguments made between people. In the next two sections, I shift focus slightly and consider how beauty can be central to an expanded understanding of argument. Thus, beauty is useful for expanding the concept of argument.

Beauty is a Characteristic of Argument

Mathematicians, logicians, and scientists often judge certain proofs as beautiful or certain instances of a deductive reasoning pattern as elegant. The question is, however, whether or not informal argument can be similarly judged. This is a crucial issue for the intersection of argument and beauty. If beauty is only applicable to the formal argument of trained practitioners, then the judgment of beauty will merely serve as another standard which can be used to dismiss the vast majority of public arguments as unsuitable for careful consideration. Yet, if beauty is a feature of more ordinary argument, then our appreciation of the common cry of untrained advocates is heightened. By finding beauty in the most common of arguments, we also attribute value to those arguments.

Given the qualities of beauty illustrated in the preceding sections, the nature of a beautiful argument is easily seen. Such an argument will be characterized by the development of unity from separate parts; the argument will produce a certain balance and harmony among those parts; and the argument might be characterized by a pleasing intensity or vividness. To this list I will add the notion of form as developed by Kenneth Burke (1931/1968; Weal, 1985). A beautiful argument has the quality of raising a certain expectation in the respondent and then fulfilling that expectation. This anticipation-resolution pattern intensifies the development of unity and harmony in an argument.

One brief example of a beautiful argument should suffice to illustrate these qualities of beauty. In 1851 at a women's rights convention in Akron, Ohio, the former slave, Sojourner Truth, spoke out in defense of the strength of women. Her short speech followed a series of presentations by ministers who opposed granting freedom to women. When Sojourner rose to speak, the audience knew their beliefs would be powerfully confronted. The entire speech is a model of Burkean form. Her dialect and her vigorous refutation of previous speakers combine to create a uniquely moving and beautifully executed argument. The following is one of the six paragraphs: "Then that little man in black [a minister] there, he says women can't have as much rights as men, 'cause Christ wasn't a woman! Where did your Christ come from? Where did your Christ come from? From God and a woman! Man had nothing to do with Him" (p. 95). The complete speech is required for a fuller appreciation of the place this argument holds; but the beauty of the abstracted paragraph is evident nonetheless. The opening line establishes the expectation of a refutation. The three key terms of the argument—woman, man, Christ—are placed in a relationship which is to be refuted. Sojourner then asks a rhetorical question which heightens the tension by suggesting the relationship among the three terms must be readjusted. She repeats the question to add emphasis and reinforce the expectation that an answer will be forthcoming. The answer is exclaimed and the final sentence completes the reorganization of the terms: Christ and woman are united in God; man is irrelevant. The argument proceeds, then, by breaking apart the position of the opposition and reorganizing the components of that vision into a new framework. The argument is beautiful because it combines intensity with unity and fulfills the expectations created by its opening sentence.

This observation that informal arguments may be beautiful leads suggestively to a larger claim about the nature of argument in general: beauty may be intimately connected with the very production of argument. The connection can be illustrated through reflection on the nature of argument in general.

Perelman and Olbrechts-Tyteca (1958/1969) suggest that all argument is a matter of association and/or dissociation. When arguing using association, the advocate begins with a fact, truth or presumption acceptable to the audience and attempts to unite that starting point with the more controversial end. In the case of dissociation, the advocate attempts to separate an idea or position from that which is acceptable to the audience. Notice that in both cases, argument is conceived as having a beginning and an end; it has coherence and completeness. Thus, an advocate produces arguments by relying on patterns of thinking which share qualities with the production of beauty.

In addition, notice that an argument, according to Perelman and Olbrechts-Tyteca, is dependent on the audience to which the argument is addressed: the success of the association or dissociation depends on the acceptableness of the beginning point and the acceptableness of the connecting move (in which the beginning point is united with the more controversial end). Thus, the production of an argument requires a unity and coherence which extends beyond the mere combination of beginning and ending points to the very integration of advocate and audience.

Therefore, the minimum requirement for the existence of an argument involves those qualities which also often characterize that which we judge to be beautiful. Perhaps an enduring feature of all work on argument—such as analytical diagrams, guidelines for dialectic, or the determination of fallacies—is that an underlying ideal of beauty quietly shapes scholarly thinking.

Beauty Functions as Argument

In the previous section, I claimed that advocates may be guided by the ideal of beauty when they produce arguments, yet in this section I suggest that the beauty in objects is itself an argument. The beauty of, say, a painting challenges the viewer in the same way as an argument challenges a hearer. The beauty itself is an argument.

The sense of this claim can be discerned if we resist the temptation to define argument as a syllogism or an evidence-warrant-claim pattern, or any other kind of propositional structure. In recent years, many theorists have suggested nonpropositional views of argument (Brockriede, 1975; Conley, 1985; Fisher, 1987; Perelman & Olbrechts-Tyteca, 1958/1969; Willard, 1976). My explanation of how beauty "argues" will serve as an additional example in this growing body of literature.

The notion that beauty argues is peculiar and abstract and thus makes the following discussion particularly difficult. I will begin with a familiar connection of beauty and argument and attempt to distinguish between this more familiar view and the view I advocate. In effect, the familiar connection serves a negative purpose: it illustrates what is not meant when I assert that beauty argues.

Argument and beauty are often connected through the assertion that things judged as beautiful—and we usually think of an artistic creation—also provide an argument. We find this connection in such common phrases as "the argument of the painting is . . .," or "the argument of the poem is . . .," or "it seems to me that Beethoven's fifth is his attempt to . . .," etc. In these instances, beautiful objects are caught up in argument. I use the phrase "caught-up" to convey that the beautiful qualities themselves are not *directly* involved in the argument. Beauty, according to this common view, would be only that judgment which draws attention to the argument, in much the same way as we speak of style giving weight or force to content. The beauty of the object, therefore, is virtually irrelevant to the argument itself (see, for example, Fisher, 1987, pp. 158-179; Toulmin, Rieke, & Janik, 1984, pp. 349-367).

This common view, which might be called the interpretive view, is illustrated in the following. I recently had the opportunity to view Mary Cassatt's impressionist painting *Breakfast in Bed* (Figure 2).

I was struck by the skill and insight displayed in this sensitive portrayal of an adult woman and young girl reclining in a bed. The bed sheets, the

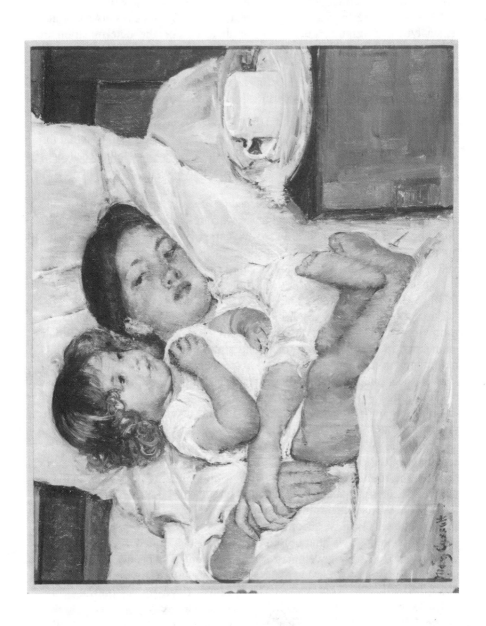

nightgowns and the tea serving are white with blue highlights. The bedboard
and table are in two shades of grey-green. The darker background serves to
deflect attention away from the furnishings and onto the mother/daughter
relationship. Likewise, the dominance of white on and around both figures
establishes the unity of mother and daughter as well as a bright, affirming
context for their relationship.

The action in the painting, however, centers on the faces of the subjects.
The mother is studying the child's profile, yet the mother's head is slightly
turned away from the child and her face reveals a pensive attitude. The mother's
eyes are not directly fixed on the child. The child is looking away from the
mother but does not appear to be looking at anything in particular.

The contrast between the differing gazes is the mystery of the painting.
The faces reveal little, if any, enjoyment of the relationship. Yet the reclining
postures and the physical connection between their bodies indicate affection.
This painting argues for the poignancy of the all-too-human tension between
the buoyancy of life and the weight of deep-seated emotional concern.

Notice that this interpretive claim—the claim concerning the poignancy
and buoyancy of life—is developed without a reference to beauty. A judgment
of beauty is not foreign to this picture, though. Rather, the qualities which
are judged as beautiful bring the painting to the viewer's attention and make
the painting a particularly interesting object for interpretive argument. Beauty
functions to support the meaning of the painting; or, to rephrase it, beauty
is subordinate to the argument of the painting.

The claim that beauty argues is different from the claim of the interpretive
view in which beauty is subordinate to argument. Whereas the interpretive
view understands beauty as a supportive feature of an argument, the competing
claim, which I will label the figurative view, understands beauty as a
constitutive feature of the argument. The beauty of the painting serves to
challenge the viewer's perceptions and experiences; it presents an alternative
perspective on some facet of the viewer's existence. Thus, the argumentative
function of beauty does not lie in its propositional content or its support for
a preferred interpretation of the artwork, but in its offer to reconceptualize
the viewer's everyday existence.

For instance, the beauty of Cassatt's painting provokes a reconceptualization
of color and texture as they appear in the human figure and in a human
relationship. The beauty of the portrayed relationship even provokes a reconceptualization of the relationship I observe between my wife and daughter.
All the beautiful qualities of the painting suggest how a mother-daughter relation
can look: the proportion of the figures in relation to one another and in relation
to the nightstand, the placement of the mother's face in the center of the picture
and the balance of the daughter's placement across that center, the variety
of colors used to create their complexions, the traces of blue marking out
the borders of the linen, the vividness of the white in the daughter's nightgown,
and the intensity of the short, pronounced brushstrokes. The relationship in

the picture is harmonious, intense, full of life and depth. Because the suggestion conveyed by the beauty alone is strong enough to challenge my already existing ways of conceptualizing the female relationships within my family, I even may act with greater sensitivity, understanding and compassion toward the people involved in the relationship.

I have just described the beauty of painting as offering an argumentative challenge to my existing perception of a human relationship. Is this an acceptable understanding of argument, or is argument stretched beyond recognizable applications? Using argument to refer to a perceptual and experiential challenge is not idiosyncratic. The influence of beauty in this case is similar to that provided through the figurative use of language, such as in a metaphor. In the phrase, "Frank is an animal on the court," the speaker indicates how Frank can be reconsidered in terms of the qualities of an animal pertinent to playing his sport. Thus, Frank might be strong, aggressive and easily angered. The metaphor is an argument for seeing Frank as having animal-like qualities (Perelman & Olbrechts-Tyteca, 1958/1969; Ricoeur, 1975/1977). Likewise, the beauty in a painting functions as an argument to see one object, or segment of experience, in terms of another.

Furthermore, a reconsideration of Brancusi's sculpture supports the relationship of figurative argument to abstract art. Unlike the Cassatt painting, the *Bird in Space* has no immediate resemblance to anything in my experience. How can the symmetry, smoothness and balance of that sculpture challenge my existing conceptions when I do not have any conceptions similar enough to be compared? Yet, the interaction between that beautiful object and my everyday observations provides a constructive challenge. As I attend to that art object I grow in my appreciation for those very qualities which make the object beautiful—symmetry, smoothness, balance. My experience with these qualities can awaken my observations of other objects in my existence. I become more sensitive to the smoothness of a polished desk, the roughness of a concrete driveway, or the symmetry and balance of a mature walnut tree. Thus, the beauty of Brancusi's sculpture argues for a certain apprehension of physical objects; it refigures my experience of everyday occurrences.

Furthermore, the title of the sculpture, *Bird in Space*, develops the argument toward refiguring the beauty of a bird. Once the title is considered, the sculpture challenges the viewer to notice the balanced lines and harmonious proportions of a bird as it soars through an uncluttered sky. Of course, a viewer does not need the sculpture in order to observe the beauty of a bird in flight, but the sculpture seems to argue for a particular kind of observation. The beauty itself serves as argument.

These examples illustrate how argument can be conceptualized as something other than a linear sequence of propositions. If this expanded conception of argument is accepted, then the entire notion of advocacy can be expanded accordingly. For instance, the process of advocacy may be usefully compared with the processes of an artist. Instead of using the brush and a canvas, the

advocate may create verbal pictures as a means of influence. One may argue
by developing a view of existence which serves as an offer to refigure, or
reconceptualize, some aspect of an audience's experience. Martin Luther King
Jr.'s "I Have a Dream" speech is the outstanding example of this kind of
argument.

Conclusion

Other possible ways of talking about the intersection of argument and beauty
are possible, but most of them can be placed under the four categories just
surveyed and exemplified. A central purpose of this chapter is to reveal several
promising avenues for further exploration. First, the student of argument may
examine the argumentation of aesthetic theories: what kinds of arguments
predominate, what function does argument serve in the development of aesthetic
knowledge? This activity is similar to a scholarly project which is elsewhere
described as the rhetoric of inquiry (Nelson & Megill, 1986). Second, the
student can examine the nature of art criticism and develop an understanding
of argument as it occurs in aesthetic disputes (see Carrier, 1987). Third, the
student can pursue an aesthetics of argument, in which aesthetic theory is
used to examine the nature of argument and influence (see Burke, 1931/1968,
pp. 123-183). Fourth, the student may pursue figurative argument as a
theoretical concept useful for critical comment on art or as a useful idea for
examining public modes of influence. Michael Osborn's notion of rhetorical
depiction is a valuable reference point for such analysis (1986).

In addition to these four general areas of scholarly investigation, I intend
for this chapter both to assist those who wish to free beauty from its subjectivist
home and to foster an expanded conception of argument. This dual purpose
has an overall practical concern which gains impetus from Wayne Brockriede's
person-centered approach to argument; he has integrated an interpersonal ethic
into the nature of argument in order to encourage advocates to carry on their
disputes with mutual respect and personal integrity (1972).

The connections between argument and beauty are drawn with a similar
encouragement. The discourse of beauty provides an important ideal for the
development of human creative abilities and the governance of human affairs.
The discourse of argument is a remarkable resource for managing disagreement
in human relationships and within human societies. The dialogue between these
two discourses is too important to be ignored. Through argument the ideal
of beauty is brought into the realm of human interaction; through beauty the
resource of argument is infused with a powerfully humane and civilizing ideal.

Thus, the connection between argument and beauty is a further step in
humanizing conflict. Arguers can be artists, bringing the harmony, unity and
symmetry of beauty to bear on the rough edges and fractured relationships
of everyday disputes.

Chapter Twenty

Corporate Advocacy as Argumentation

Janice Schuetz

The importance of corporate advocacy has recently been brought to the attention of the public because of the recurring and dramatic media accounts featuring American companies responding to crisis. For example, Johnson and Johnson had to restore its image after three persons in the Chicago area died from taking poisoned Tylenol in 1982. The poisoning was the result of someone tampering with the medication and putting it back on the shelves. Johnson and Johnson responded by withdrawing Tylenol from stores and by developing a tamper-free product (Leon, 1983). In another case, Union Carbide had to change its policies after government investigators charged the company with negligence resulting in an explosion of one of its plants in Bhopal, India, in 1984, an accident that killed over 2,000 persons. Union Carbide responded to this crisis by introducing new safety equipment at its plants. The company also agreed to provide out-of-court cash settlements to its victims (Winslow, 1985a, 1985b). In still another instance, Continental Airlines had to answer charges from the Federal Aviation Administration implicating its pilots as the cause of two fatal crashes in Colorado. In one case, the pilot had cocaine in his blood stream, and in the other case both pilots lacked experience in flying the aircraft under winter conditions. Continental executives defended the pilots in speeches to the press (McNeil-Lehrer News Hour, 1988, March 17).

Ms. Schuetz is in the Department of Communication at the University of New Mexico, Albuquerque.

These cases, however, are only isolated examples of a far more diverse and complex communicative process called corporate advocacy. The purpose of this chapter is to explain several different approaches to corporate advocacy used by companies to advocate and defend their positions to the public through argumentation. To do this, the essay (1) describes company advocacy, advocates, and arguments, and (2) develops a typology of four different types of advocacy, contrasting each type according to objectives, issues, audiences, structure, and channels.

A. Corporate Advocacy, Advocates, and Argumentation

Corporate advocacy consists of the communicative strategies companies use to advocate and defend their policies, authorize advocates, and produce messages that are centered in reasoned discourse. Advocacy messages are presented in a broad range of forums and mediums including: media advertising, public speeches, brochures, financial reports, and public hearings.

Corporate Advocacy

Specifically, corporate advocacy refers to the discursive means that companies use to manage their images and issues with external publics. In this chapter, the term advocacy is limited to those cases where companies use reasoned discourse to gain adherence to their claims and evidence from an external public audience. This definition excludes oral and written discourse that is not focused on reasoning and excludes advocacy that is directed to employees inside of the company. Corporate refers to any business or company that has the need to manage issues and images. Corporate communicators create, structure, and disseminate argumentative messages to their public audiences. To do this, advocates use arguments ''to create a favorable, reasonable, and informed public opinion which in turn influences institutions' operating environments'' (Heath, 1980, p. 37).

Research about corporate advocacy appears as part of a variety of different subject areas, including corporate advertising, corporate communications, corporate image building, issues management, advocacy advertising, corporate speech making, external company communication, policy management, and company crisis management. Not all of this research fits with the definition presented here, but much of the analysis does deal with a large variety of argumentative messages addressed to external public audiences.

The Advocate

Companies choose spokespersons to act as their official advocates. Bitzer (1979) defines an advocate as someone who represents others by messages and by actions. To be believed by the public, advocates must have the appropriate knowledge and credentials and represent the beliefs, interests, and values of the group that authorizes them to present messages on its behalf (p. 72). Although Bitzer's description applies to public advocates in general, these same characteristics are essential for company communicators because company advocates also must have the appropriate knowledge and job credentials, represent the interests and values of the company, and have legitimate authorization from a company to speak on its behalf. Designated advocates may be single company officials, a group or division within the company, or surrogates.

Advocates, who are individuals representing the company, have credentials because of their positions, roles, and/or job titles. These credentials are often given as part of an introduction to the speaker, a credit in a written document, or as a part of the content of the advocacy message. Several roles or job designations within a company are likely to have responsibilities for creating, structuring, and disseminating advocacy messages. These job descriptions are likely to entail responsibilities for being company advocates: Chief Executive Officers (CEO's), Presidents and Vice-Presidents, Chairs of Boards, Marketing Directors, and Public Relations spokespersons. For example, Chrysler Corporation President, Lee Iacocca, acts as a personal representative of the company when he presents a speech to stockholders promoting a new image of his company as an innovator in the design and sales of recreational vehicles.

Frequently, advocates are groups rather than individuals. These groups create advocacy messages as part of their functions in marketing, advertising, public relations, or issues management. When a group explicitly represents the position of the company, audiences assume that the group has both the knowledge and authorization to do so.

In many companies, one group has the primary responsibility for disseminating statements to the public about new policies, initiating new images, and managing problems for which the company admits responsibility. For example, an oil company uses its public relations director to issue a company response to refute charges that the company is polluting the water supply of the community. In media reports, group advocates are often referred to as "official company spokespersons," and audiences assume that group advocates are knowledgeable, represent the interests of the company, and are authorized on its behalf.

In addition to individuals and groups, companies often use surrogates, particularly in advertising and marketing messages. These surrogates are popular or interesting public personalities who "stand in" for company spokespersons. In fact, the "real" creators of the arguments are likely to be the advertising or marketing divisions of the company. Examples of surrogates are particularly common in mass media advertising. For example, actor Jack Klugman serves as a surrogate when he promotes new products for Canon copiers. Actor James Garner is a surrogate when he attempts to improve the image of beef by urging the public to eat more beef because it is a healthy food. He is an advocate on behalf of the American Beef Council. Clearly the surrogates do not have the special knowledge of the company or its products or services that advocates usually do. The company uses "stand in" advocates as a ploy to attract the attention of the audience to the product or service. Companies assume that the audiences' interest in or respect for the surrogates will result in interest in and respect for the companies' products or services.

Many complicated approaches to advocacy use a variety of different advocates. Companies select advocates for their credibility and rapport with different audiences. For example, the CEO may address stockholders; the public relations director may promote the company to vendors or franchise owners; and surrogates may represent the product or service to the public through the mass media. In most cases the disseminators of the message are individual advocates, but the messages themselves are usually created and structured by groups and committees within the company.

3   Argumentative Messages

Argumentation is reasoned discourse. Arguers advance claims, support them with evidence, make causal connections between evidence and claims, and seek acceptance or adherence to those claims from audiences who act as adjudicators or decision makers. Obviously, not all messages created by companies to reach their external publics are strong arguments. A strong argument must meet the tests that it provides a critical evaluation, has a clear purpose, and presents a reasoned case about disputed issues.

In order for a message to embody strong arguments, the discourse must be centered in reasoning, grounded in evidence, and presented with the purpose of gaining the adherence of the audience to the claims made by the company. Toulmin, Rieke, and Janik (1979) emphasize that "reasoning is a way of testing ideas critically." Argumentation "calls for critical evaluations" of the ideas presented, a willingness "to modify claims in response to criticism," and "a scrutiny" of claims put forward and claims accepted by the audience to whom the argument is addressed (p. 9).

Argumentative messages are purposeful. The reasoned claims presented by advocates seek change in the beliefs and/or behaviors of the audiences addressed. Rybacki and Rybacki (1986) explain that advocates seek to achieve their purposes by confronting "the sensibilities of listeners and readers directly, laying out an analysis of the relevant data upon which the request for an alteration of belief and behavior is based" (p. 3). Company advocates try to gain acceptance of facts, values, or policies. Moreover, the content of their argument centers on disputed issues that relate to company images and issues.

The complexity of the argument differs as the goal and audience changes. Company advocates usually try to get audiences to accept new images, issues, or policies. Arguments contain evidence that justifies claims that lead audiences to accept the goal of the advocate. Some arguments are simple chains of reasons, arguing from a specific case to a conclusion. This type of reasoning is evident, for example, when a company advocate notes that five out of seven divisions of the company increased their sales, and then concludes from these instances that the increases are responsible for large company profits.

Other argumentative messages are complex cases outlining a problem and proposing a new policy to manage the problem. For example, a company may be diversifying its services after deregulation, as the banks did after they were deregulated in the early 1980s. In this case, the banks presented detailed proposals to their stockholders indicating how they planned to expand services to meet new markets. In still other situations, company advocates present arguments in an adversarial arena as they debate about a policy before a group of public decision makers. An example of this type of arguing occurs when a small commuter airline appears before its appointed regulators to get permission to land its small aircraft at a major city airport.

Effective advocacy depends on the knowledge of the advocates as legitimate representatives who are authorized by the company. The company must select advocates who know the facts, issues, and policies of the company and also understand the values and interests of the publics they address. Designated arguers need credentials that certify them as both knowledgeable and representative. Effective advocates present reasoned messages grounded in relevant and sufficient evidence, with an appropriate purpose and in a form that is complete and clear. Company advocacy is unlikely to succeed if the advocate or the message does not meet these standards.

B. Types of Advocacy

Economic justification, company storytelling, issues management, and crisis management represent four types of advocacy that are used by companies. Each of the types of advocacy may be distinguished according to objectives, issues, audience structure, and channels. These types of advocacy represent a continuum ranging from the most simple to the most complex type of argument. These types are not inclusive of every approach that every company uses. Instead, they represent four typical and distinctive approaches of using argumentation in company messages.

Economic Justification

Economic justification is a relatively simple type of argument. The advocate's objective is to give factual accounts about the status of the company in the form of financial statements, descriptions of new innovations in products or services, the volume and efficiency of the business, the economic assets and liabilities, and the status of the company compared with other similar companies.

This type of advocacy deals primarily with issues of fact and often uses financial data to develop these issues. These issues may be controversial because they are previously unknown or because they run counter to the intuitions of the external publics being addressed. To argue these issues of fact, the company advocate (often a financial officer) claims that certain facts do or do not exist and supports these claims with financial evidence. Just as in other contexts of argumentation, claims of fact assert the occurrence or non-occurrence of some action, event, or state of being (Jensen, 1981, p. 47). For example, a company may claim that its revenues doubled in the last five years and support this claim by giving detailed evidence showing the sources of revenue and the rate of expansion. This type of argument also occurs when a company claims that a certain product is selling and provides evidence to show that the inventory has decreased while the production has increased.

Advocates select a target audience for messages of economic justification. The audience has interest primarily in the economic status of this business. Audiences for this type of advocacy are likely to be stockholders, potential investors, bonding companies, or economic analysts. A state or municipality could be interested in the company's economic justification if that company were considering opening a new division or opening a new plant in that area. The general public has access to messages of economic justification but is unlikely to use these arguments for its own decision making.

The structure of the arguments in economic justification is predictable. Company advocates are likely to arrange the arguments either topically according to financial issues or chronologically according to the financial reporting procedures of the company. In most cases, arguments are proactive; that is, the company "monitors, analyzes, and prioritizes issues" prior to the time they are crafted into arguments to be presented to external audiences (Arrington & Sawaya, 1984, p. 149). Advocates can arrange their arguments into different orders depending on their persuasive goals. One effective method for messages of economic justification is simply to list the arguments, with the strongest arguments in the first and last positions and the least important arguments in the middle of the message. Another approach is to structure claims according to a deductive pattern. That is, the advocate puts forth a claim, presents appropriate and sufficient evidence to support the claim, and interprets the meaning of that claim for the audience. For example, an advocate presents a claim in favor of the company's credit worthiness, provides a basis of comparison to its own history or to another similar company, makes the comparison, and concludes by predicting future credit worthiness.

Advocacy that provides economic justification is disseminated through a variety of channels. In face-to-face interactions, such as public speeches, the advocate often uses simple visual aids including handouts, overhead projectors, and posters or charts to emphasize the statistical evidence and to demonstrate the connections between the evidence and the claims. Frequently, economic justification appears in a lengthy form through company status reports, stockholder briefings, and portfolios sent to investors. It can also appear in an abbreviated form in articles in the local newspapers. Numerous examples of the abbreviated economic justification appear in *The Wall Street Journal*, *Business Week*, and in business trade magazines. Televised accounts of economic justification appear on *Nightly Business Report* on public television and on business features of Cable News Network.

The arguments in messages of economic justification belong to a type of argument commonly connected with disputed economic issues and financial facts. Company arguers make claims and support them with data. The arguments are subject to the criticism and scrutiny of the members of the audiences who are likely to make decisions about the need to buy or sell stock, the credit worthiness of the company, or the business' growth potential. Economic justification is a proactive type of advocacy that has a specific and routine method of reasoning, one that appears predictably in quarterly reports, biannual, or annual reports. Economic justifications are subject to criticism or evaluation in several circumstances: when audiences perceive inconsistencies or inadequacies in evidence, when claims are overstated or unqualified, and when predictions are not linked to the evidence.

Company Storytelling

Storytelling differs from economic justification because it centers on issues of value rather than issues of fact. Storytelling works as argument because the stories provide coherent accountings of experiences and deeds that are the grounds for inferences about the values of the company. Fisher (1984) notes that stories work as reasons because the narrative links the experiences and values of audiences with those of the storytellers (pp. 7-9).

The objective of company storytelling is to manage the image by enhancing the reputation of the company with the public in general and its customers in particular. Frequently, the stories told by company advocates center on themes or emphasize the connotative meanings of a company logo. For example, Prudential Insurance Company emphasizes its theme—"If you can dream it, you can do it"—in its advertising. The theme is stated in an advertisement that features the company logo, a large rock prominently featured in an evening setting with a big moon and many stars in the background. To promote the values of the company, the advertisement relates a personal story about how the company helped one of its customers to achieve a dream.

The core of the arguments of company stories are issues of value, such as efficiency, individualism, economy, and personal service. These issues are argued through value claims that make judgments about people, actions, objects, and ideas. Company storytellers support value claims by descriptions (word pictures or actual pictures), by examples or experiences of employees, and by testimonials of customers and employees.

Storytelling is especially suited to audiences who are business allies within the community and to audiences of present and future customers. A typical audience of business allies could be a local Chamber of Commerce, a Rotary Club, or the Better Business Bureau. Corporate advocates reach these audiences by membership and participation in the groups and through formal and informal speeches. Company storytellers attempt to increase the satisfaction of current customers through the communication they share directly with the customer, with a customer appreciation event, or by advertising that emphasizes customer satisfaction.

Company stories used for image management campaigns may have either simple or complex structures. The simple stories feature extended illustrations of the deeds of the company in offering high quality products and services that benefit customers, such as company employees who go out of their way to give quality service to customers. The illustrations are the evidence, and the audience is expected to infer a claim of value from the extended illustrations. These types of stories work in a way similar to a classic enthymeme, an incomplete syllogistic argument in which the audience is expected to give one of the premises. However, in this case, instead of one of the premises being implied, the claim itself must be supplied by the audience. An example of this type of enthymeme is an advertisement by Motel 6, which describes the unfortunate woes of one family who were unable to find an inexpensive place to sleep on their vacation. The ad then gives a contrasting story of a family who found comfortable and inexpensive lodging at Motel 6 and ends by saying "We left the light on for you." Although the storyteller never says "Therefore you should stay at our motel," the premises of the stories point so directly to this claim that the conclusion is inevitable.

In more complex structures, the advocate may present a narrative through a set of specific instances that point to a common theme, such as "Our company makes it right," or "When you talk, we listen." When a health insurance provider promotes its insurance by giving instances of how the plan provided similar care for a frail senior citizen, a young unwed mother, and a technical worker injured on the job, these instances point to a common claim about quality of service. Company storytellers may also offer a very detailed narrative, complete with a graphic depiction of setting, development of good and evil characters, and a plot showing how the company acts as hero to make good prevail over evil. An example of this type of narrative would be a speech by a mining company executive who promotes his company's reputation for reclamation by telling a very detailed story of how the company improved the landscape and helped several families lead better lives through its reclamation programs.

Company storytellers use several different channels to argue their value claims to external publics. One channel is through public presentations—speeches, slide shows, and community discussions. Many public service announcements on radio and television are simple narrative arguments, structured as enthymemes and supportive of the values of the company. Company brochures as well as advertising on television and in newspapers feature narrative as the principle means for justifying value claims about the company.

Storytelling is one of the most prominent forms of argument used by companies to manage their images. Storytelling is an effective way of connecting the needs of the audience with the interests of the company (Heath & Nelson, 1986). For storytelling to work as persuasive argument, the value claims in the messages must connect directly with the understandings and experiences of the audience. Narrative arguments are subject to unfavorable evaluation in several ways: when the story is not realistic and seems contrived, when it is not typical of the experiences of the audiences, when it is not relevant to the goals of the company, or when it is not characteristic of the day-to-day actions of the company. Company advocates are likely to gain adherence to their value claims only when their stories "ring true" (Fisher, 1984) with the experiences of their audiences.

Issues Management

Issues management differs from economic justification and storytelling in that it focuses on policy arguments. Issues managers analyze current policy and try to change that policy to present the company in more positive ways. Arrington and Sawaya (1984) note that the objective of issues managers is to participate in the "shaping and resolution of public issues that impinge on its own operations" (p. 148). Advocates argue issues by clustering together a series of claims to justify a policy. These policy claims support the adoption of new laws, actions, procedures, or practices. Even though policy claims serve as the main arguments, claims of fact and value are also put forth to support policy claims.

Companies use issues management as a strategy for persuading external publics who are both allies and adversaries. This type of advocacy occurs in response to changes in the business environment. For example, companies are likely to offer policy alternatives to respond to public pressures urging increased regulation, new forms of taxation, and changes in products and services needed to meet competition. In some cases, the policy options are presented as proactive strategies to prevent damage to the company. In other cases, the policy is promoted as a reactive strategy to limit the harm that has already occurred.

This type of advocacy is directed to two different selective audiences. One audience consists of the adjudicators, the elected or appointed persons who have the authority to accept, reject, or modify proposals. This audience may be a board, regulatory commission, city or county council, an oversight group, or a state legislature. A second audience consists of opinion leaders who influence the primary adjudicators, including lobbyists, business groups, special interest groups, vendors, or customer advisory boards. Issues managers usually develop a series of different messages that they present to target audiences over a period of time.

The structure of the arguments used by issues managers often follows a problem-solution organizational pattern: problem identification and definition, solution identification and formulation, and a statement of the advantages or benefits to be gained from the proposed plan. Typically, only one major policy proposal is presented in a given message. Often the proposal is developed according to a traditional stock issues analysis that is used in policy debates (Jensen, 1981). Advocates use stock issues by developing a chain of reasons specifying why change is needed, what plan is best able to meet the need, and the details of how the plan will produce advantages to the company and the public. These three modes of justification support the proposal by using a large variety of evidence—statistics, testimony, analogies, illustrations, and precedents.

An example of this type of analysis of a policy argument occurs when an electric utility seeks higher rates from its customers to finance the construction of a new generating plant. The utility company first defines the source of the problem as a decline in revenues and a need for more power. Next, the advocate proposes the solution that the regulatory commission should allow the company to increase rates to each customer for each kilowatt hour the customers use. Finally, the utility company presents reasons why this plan will solve the problem and predicts long term benefits to the customer and the state if the proposal is approved. Because the public utility commission is the authorized decision maker, the utility company designs its arguments for that audience and seeks its adherence to the claims presented.

Issues advocates present their cases through many channels to different audiences. A case evolves in several stages: a detailed written document; a summarized or paraphrased oral presentation; and a sequence of questions or refutations from witnesses, adjudicators, and/or adversaries of the policy change. Usually, policy arguments are reported in brief form as part of a news story. Sometimes the policies are debated in public forums or gatherings. Many of the policy proposals are filed or printed into public documents and disseminated prior to or at the same time as they are presented to decision makers.

Arguments in issues management differ from those in economic justification and storytelling with respect to the amount and intensity of public scrutiny and refutation that the policy arguments undergo before change is accomplished. For example, some states take six to twelve months to decide rate increases for utilities. Some tax legislation affecting corporations takes years. Issue advocates may present the same policy argument for years before they get a decision.

4. Crisis Management

Crisis management is the most complex of the four types of advocacy. This type of advocacy is reactive; that is, the company is forced to defend itself after its practices, products, or services have produced negative effects. A crisis demands immediate action from the company to remedy problems for which the company assumes responsibility. Company arguers respond to crisis in two typical ways; they defend or apologize for the problem, and then they propose solutions to prevent, compensate, and/or remedy the problem. Situations that call for crisis management are common for large corporations. Crises result from a company's liability for its products and practices. This occurs, for example, when a family implicates a product of a toy company as responsible for the death of their child, when medical investigators identify a food product as the source of illness in the community, or when a wholesale petroleum company spills its gas into the water sources of the community. Whatever the crisis is, companies should react immediately so that they can retain their reputations as responsible businesses.

The primary objective of crisis management is to provide "accurate information as quickly as possible" to external publics affected by the crisis (Heath & Nelson, 1986, p. 184). To achieve this objective, Ressler (1982) warns companies to make immediate contact with the media and to announce their finding about a crisis as soon as possible. Additionally, he advises companies to issue progress reports and to develop policy proposals that will prevent similar problems from occurring in the future. Effective crisis management never completely absolves the company from the responsibility for the harm it has created, but it does help to restore the reputation of the company.

Crisis managers both advocate and defend issues of policy. They are obligated to react to the public, to explain the reasons for the harm, and to recommend company policies that will prevent the negligence, accidents, poor services, or inferior products in the future. Although disputed issues of policy are the core of the arguments that crisis managers use for advocacy, companies also must defend themselves against what they consider inaccurate or inappropriate claims of fact and/or of value that are directed toward the company.

To manage a crisis, advocates need to address several audiences. First, the company must react to the persons or businesses who have been harmed directly by the policies or actions of the company. Usually, the advocate admits responsibility and stresses the intent of the company to compensate victims for the damage. Second, the company responds to its stockholders and investors whose economic interests are likely to be affected by the crisis. The company explains to this audience the measures it plans to take to solve the problem and identifies the economic impact the crisis is likely to have on the financial status of the company. Finally, advocates present information to the general public giving the company's definition of the crisis, refuting claims made against the company, and proposing solutions that are likely to be enacted by the company to remedy the problem.

Company arguers respond to crisis by structuring a complex case for their audiences. This case develops in a sequence that resembles the following: (1) describes the crisis and stresses that the company is taking action to manage the crisis; (2) admits culpability by taking responsibility for the company's contribution to the problem; (3) reassures the public that the company is taking appropriate and immediate action to deal with the problem; (4) promotes changes that will limit the likelihood that similar problems will occur in the future; (5) negotiates some procedures for settlement or compensation; and (6) attempts to restore the reputation of the company by proactive image management. The company may also need to develop a defense of its polices, explaining why something occurred, what went wrong, and how the company is responding to the problem.

Company crisis managers are likely to present different stages of this case to different audiences. For example, arguments about company culpability and plans for compensation are directed to persons who have suffered harm from company actions; new policies are presented to regulators or investigative agencies to whom the company is accountable; arguments to enhance image are directed to the general public; and arguments to defend policies are directed to adversaries and detractors. In some cases, companies may advocate new policies and defend old ones in the same message.

The complexity of this type of message demands a variety of channels to reach the different audiences. Initially, the company tries to reach the mass audiences through television, radio, and newspapers to assure them the immediate crisis is over and that the company is cooperating with other agencies to find a quick solution. The company offers specific policy proposals through detailed speeches and policy statements. In some cases, leaders of the company might hold press conferences or host public meetings to discover what all of the issues are prior to the time proposals are presented. Several advocates should be available to deal with the problems. The public expects direct messages from leaders of the company because these messages indicate that the problem is being handled by those with the power to get change.

All events labelled "crisis" are not of equal complexity. Small crises with limited damage are relatively easy to manage. For example, a chemical company can easily manage a problem caused by a small amount of toxic waste that leaks on one landowner's property. Large crises that involve death or disability to persons or significant property losses are very difficult to manage and may end up in long term litigation. For example, a chemical company may spend years trying to recover after its toxic waste leaks into the public water supply and contaminates city wells. Many kinds of crises are likely to result in company messages that outline the reasons for the problem and propose solutions. Heath and Nelson (1986) conclude that a crisis can make companies more aware of the need to prevent problems, to establish credibility with the community, and to make themselves available to the public directly or through the media.

Conclusions

These four types of advocacy represent distinctive approaches in which companies give reasons and seek adherence to the claims they present to their external public audiences. This typology provides a classification of four modes of company advocacy that differ according to the way advocates argue objectives, issues, audience, structure and channel. The chapter does not attempt to identify every kind of advocacy but merely to present four distinctive types that are typical of many companies' methods of arguing. The typology is best interpreted as a continuum with the most common and simple arguments presented in economic justification and the most complex in crisis management.

Readers can use the typology as a starting point for their understanding of advocacy. They can expand the typology by subdividing the four types into subspecies, discover how the types are integrated with a company's plan of external communication, and explain why or how these types of advocacy are delegated to divisions or persons within a company. The typology also offers some type of starting point for analyzing the advocacy messages of large national corporations or of a company with which readers are familiar. Readers can also elaborate the typology so that it includes advocacy that is directed internally to the companies' employees. Clearly, knowledge of argument assists people in understanding how corporate communicators create, structure, and disseminate advocacy messages.

Part VI

The Future of Argumentation

> Let me end where I began. Let us celebrate at this conference twenty-five years of solid achievement in the study of argument. The people and the titles of the papers here represent many of our advances. . . . As we celebrate past renaissance and enjoy present stimulation, we must realize we have not exhausted either our perspectives or uses. We face a lot of hard but interesting work during the next twenty-five years to continue improving our understanding of what argument is, where it applies, and how it works. (Brockriede, 1983, p. 24.)

Brockriede made these comments at a conference in 1983 to signal that the future of argumentation holds a good deal in store for those who will continue to pursue its study. His comments seem equally appropriate here as we end this text by looking toward what the future has to hold. In the final two chapters, Dale Hample and David Zarefsky comment on where argumentation has been and speculate on where its path might lead.

In Chapter Twenty-One, Zarefsky forecasts future directions in argumentation theory while in Chapter Twenty-Two Hample anticipates the development of research practices. Both Zarefsky and Hample anticipate theory and research in argumentation studies to continue developing both in quality and quantity. Zarefsky suggests that scholars will focus the study of argument by searching for a common core of concepts in order to advance argumentation theory. On the other hand, Hample suggests that argumentation will continue

285

to develop in its present pluralistic manner. Hample welcomes pluralism while Zarefsky yearns for a clearer focus. Are focus and pluralism incompatible goals? If so, which is the best direction for argumentation theory and research? These are just a few of the many important questions raised by Hample and Zarefsky. How students of argumentation respond to these and other questions they have raised will significantly affect the future of argumentation studies.

Chapter Twenty-One

Future Directions in Argumentation Theory and Practice

David Zarefsky

The essays in this volume illustrate the great breadth in argumentation studies during the past generation. Unlike an earlier age, in which studies were limited to formal logical structures embodied in formal speaking situations, teachers and researchers investigate written and oral argument, formal and informal argument, discursive and non-discursive argument, interpersonal and public argument, specialized and general argument, creative and critical argument. No domain of knowledge or method of inquiry is precluded. The breadth represented here is also characteristic of the proceedings of the Summer Conference on Argumentation, which has been held biennially since 1979, and of the major journals, *Argumentation* and *Argumentation and Advocacy*.

This trend in the discipline would have pleased Wayne Brockriede. In "Where Is Argument?" (reprinted in this volume) he sought to dispel the notion that argumentation took place only in formal settings. He tried to specify the conditions for argument—conditions which could be widely applied. In his work taken as a whole, he rebelled against narrowly drawn boundaries and he championed interdisciplinary inquiry. It is fitting, then, that this book captures the spirit of his work. The breadth and interdisciplinary reach of argumentation studies during the 1970s and 1980s also forms the context within

Mr. Zarefsky is Dean of the School of Speech and Professor of Communication Studies, Northwestern University.

which to speculate about the future. We can expect theoretical development which builds upon this trend and work which seeks to address problems which it has created.

A. The Future in Argumentation Theory

If the future builds upon the past, it is unlikely that argumentation theory will narrow. Many of the interests which have been opened up in recent years will be pursued in greater depth, and others no doubt will appear. We can expect at least seven major emphases in argumentation theory: attention to the definition of argument itself, search for replacements for the norms of formal logic, study of the arenas in which argumentation occurs, use of the argumentative perspective to study discourse of various types, a growing stress on argumentation as social practice, increased attention to the development of argument over time, and links between argumentation and other disciplines. Each of these emphases will be described briefly.

(1) *Definitions of argument.* As the range of argumentation studies has been extended, it has not always been clear that theorists are examining the same thing. There is the danger of entropy — that argumentation studies will become so diffuse that they have little in common, with the result that there is no central core of theories, topics, or methods characterizing argumentation. If that were to occur, then, rather than being a strong interdisciplinary cluster, argumentation would be little more than a convenient umbrella term. To avert this result, theorists are likely to devote renewed energy to an attempt to capture and clarify the nature of argument itself.

In the existing literature, at least two different basic notions of argument are evident. One regards its primary characteristic as verbal conflict. Naturalistic studies, particularly of interpersonal argument, often take this perspective. They describe situations in which people are in conflict with one another and examine the kinds of verbal statement produced in such situations. On this view, argument is a substitute for physical force as a means of addressing interpersonal problems. Theory development is a matter of identifying the types and the patterns of statements produced and making predictions about how either would be affected by various modifications in the situation.

Another approach defines the central feature of argumentation as reason-giving and focuses on how people seek to justify claims they make on the attitudes, beliefs, values, and actions of others. On this view, the crucial element is not the fact of conflict but the ways in which people authorize or warrant decisions in response to requests made upon them or which they make of others. Theorists in this vein focus on how people determine that a statement is a good reason for believing or doing something, or they seek to improve this process of decision making.

Whether one views argumentation as conflict or as reason-giving, a second ambiguity presents itself. O'Keefe (1977) was the first to identify the confused notions of argument as product and process. Viewed as product, an argument is something people make, through a pattern of statements which are related in some defined way. Viewed as process, an argument is a type of interaction which people have, when they disagree with another person and try to convince that person to change his or her mind. For some time after O'Keefe's essay appeared, scholars engaged in the exercise of trying to determine which sense of the term took priority. That debate has largely been abandoned as pointless. The two concepts can coexist as long as it is clear which is being invoked in any given case. Both senses of the term are important and raise significant questions, but they are often different questions.

Other writers have suggested additional senses of the term "argument," including Wenzel's (1980) emphasis on argument as procedure, Zarefsky's (1980a) suggestion that argumentation is a perspective or point of view, and Hample's (1980) work on argument as cognition. In the coming years, it is likely that theorists will continue to work along all these avenues, but also to ask increasingly how they are related to one another.

Beyond avoiding entropy and diffuseness, there is another reason for trying to focus the definition of argument. Without such a focus, theoretical work may not advance beyond the initial insight that there is argumentation in virtually every domain of human activity and that virtually any human product could be studied from an argumentative perspective. Those are important insights, but they do not take us very far. At some point they become repetitive breast-beating to establish the importance of a discipline rather than real progress in developing more extensive and powerful theories within the discipline. After all, the proof of a discipline's importance ultimately is in the power of the ideas it can produce, not in its self-conscious claims of its importance. In order to avoid these risks, theorists will be likely to focus more on a search for a common core of concepts or elements which characterize argument in all its various manifestations.

(2) *Replacement for formal norms.* A second likely theoretical development will be the continuing search for alternatives to the normative standards of formal logic. As Cox and Willard (1982) explain, for much of its history argumentation relied upon a kind of "applied formalism." It was a normative field, concerned with standards of "good" argument, and it took those standards from the model of formal logic. Several twentieth-century philosophers, however, most notably Toulmin (1958), have noted that formal logic is a very atypical form of reasoning. If it is used as the standard, then whole areas of deliberation must be consigned to the irrational. The unacceptability of that alternative led Toulmin, Perelman and Olbrechts-Tyteca (1969), Booth (1974), and others to search for alternative standards, trying to recover the strength of rhetorical reasoning which was prominent until the

Cartesian revolution in the seventeenth century. Broadly speaking, four general approaches to this problem dominate the recent argumentation literature.

First, some writers have maintained that the discipline should abandon its traditional concern for norms altogether and should study arguments descriptively in order to theorize about how people engage in argumentation. The foremost exponent of this view is Willard (1983, 1989b). His project attempts to abstract a theory of argumentation from the practice of people who find themselves to be advancing what they construe as incompatible statements while in the course of daily life. Studies in interpersonal argument are often of this type, as is illustrated by essays in this volume.

Stressing descriptive studies to the exclusion of normative considerations would change the long-standing commitment of teachers and researchers to improve, as well as to understand, processes of reasoning and decision making. Other writers, therefore, have retained a commitment to norms but sought substitutes for the norms of formal logic. The second general approach is represented by the informal logic movement in philosophy, which seeks to extract norms of sound reasoning when context rather than form relates statements to one another. Their work, represented by Blair and Johnson (1980), gives special attention to the fallacies and suggests that fallacious arguments are not necessarily those which have an error in form, but those which somehow are inappropriate in their contextual setting. Other writers, among them Rescher (for example, 1977b, 1988), have sought to develop quasi-mathematical formulas for determining the soundness of informal statements.

The third major approach to the problem is to regard argument as fundamentally narrative and to develop a logic built around such concepts as the consistency and fidelity of a story. This approach is represented most forcefully in the work of Fisher (1987), who regards narrative as a fundamental paradigm of human communication. This emphasis is an outgrowth of Fisher's earlier work on "the logic of good reasons" and suggests that reasoning should be evaluated according to narrative rather than formal criteria. Adaptations of the narrative paradigm to argumentation have regarded argument structures as stories which advocates tell. Unfortunately, more attention has been devoted to the side issue of whether narrative really ought to be called a paradigm than to theories which use the concept of narrative to deepen and enrich understanding of argument. Future theoretical work may redress this imbalance.

Finally, several writers find standards for argument not in form but in procedure. They share the field's traditional concern with assessing and improving the quality of discourse, but they believe that formal logic is the wrong source of norms. Believing that argumentation is a kind of social action, they look to procedural standards instead. What distinguishes strong arguments, in this approach, is whether they received a rigorous test — whether they were discussed in a context free of prejudice, surprise, or domination; whether advocates were willing to re-examine their own assumptions if questioned; whether everyone involved felt free to speak; whether decisions are made without regard to politics or personality; and so on. The foremost advocate of this approach is Habermas (for example, 1973), whose concept of the "ideal speech situation," though counterfactual, is the standard against which to measure actual argumentative situations. Perelman and Olbrechts-Tyteca's (1969) notion of the "universal audience" is a similar approach to assessing argumentative statements. Arguments will be valid if they would be able to obtain the assent of a hypothetical audience of all reasonable people. These procedural norms are analogous to the concept of validity in formal logic.

Naturalistic studies of argument certainly will continue. It is less likely, however, that theorists will maintain that norms or standards are irrelevant to argumentation studies, for the simple reason that people are uneasy when strong and weak arguments cannot be distinguished on bases other than just their empirical success.

(3) *Arenas of argument.* In establishing the atypical nature of formal logic, Toulmin (1958) suggested that argumentation took place within fields. Originally he was vague about what a field was, saying only that two arguments were in the same field if they were of the same logical type. But at the heart of the idea of fields was that standards of proper argument were not universal but field-dependent. This insight led to a call for mapping a variety of argument fields and determining their field-specific standards. Some theorists, such as Rieke and Sillars (1975, 1984) equated fields with academic disciplines and sought to identify the nature of argument in law, religion, business, politics, and the arts. Others have distinguished fields by situational characteristics, by the audiences addressed, or by the shared purposes of the arguers. The most recent sustained field-specific investigation is that of the Project on Rhetoric of Inquiry at the University of Iowa, which has resulted in a series of books (for instance, Nelson, Megill, and McCloskey, 1987) examining how reasoned deliberation takes place through the use of special topics and methods in a variety of subjects and disciplines.

If "field" was the key term for this sort of investigation during the 1970s, it has been largely replaced during the 1980s by a concern for "spheres." For some writers, sphere is a synonym for field. Others, such as Gronbeck (1989), maintain that spheres are qualitatively different from fields, broader in scope and less definite in their boundaries.

The key work on argument spheres is Goodnight's (1982) study of the personal, technical, and public spheres. Each is distinguished by assumptions about relevant audiences and about appropriate standards for argument, but it is not a settled matter, for any given argument, in what sphere an argument resides. Indeed, Goodnight's later work, and other research spawned by his theory, addresses how advocates attempt to define an issue as residing in one or another of the spheres in order to bring it within the ambit of certain assumptions and to exclude others. Much of this work has been informed by the conviction that the technical sphere is parasitic of the public and by a desire to reinvigorate the public sphere and to encourage active citizen participation in decision making. Others have suggested that certain subjects ought to be regarded as falling within the technical sphere, so that a commonly accepted set of procedures could be invoked. Recently, a number of theorists, including Birdsell (1989), Biesecker (1989), and Vallinger (1989) have called for a creative fusion of the public and technical spheres. The notion of spheres has proven to have great heuristic power in encouraging research and criticism, especially in drawing attention to the size and scope of the relevant audience for argumentation, and it is likely that further theoretical development of these issues will be forthcoming.

(4) *Applications of an argumentative perspective.* One consequence of regarding argumentation as a point of view or a perspective is that a wide range of activities and products—including some not overtly argumentative in nature—can be viewed from that perspective. Movements and campaigns can be studied from the point of view of their arguments, as can foreign policy, jurisprudence, economics, or art. Historical as well as contemporary studies of argument have been undertaken, and more can be expected.

This work is in some ways similar to that on fields or spheres. But it is not claimed that the objects examined have some inherently argumentative characteristics. Indeed, scholars working in this vein may deny that there are any such characteristics. They do not maintain that what they examine "just is" argument; rather, they maintain that their subjects can be illuminated by looking at them from an argumentative perspective. In Burke's (1961) sense, argumentation provides "perspective by incongruity." It offers another way to look at phenomena which may yield unique insights. More such work can be expected. While such studies, particularly critical studies, sometimes say far more about the object of the study than about argumentation itself, nevertheless they do frequently identify principles or implications of more general applicability. For example, the body of literature on specific cases of reasoning in the technical sphere yields insights about the general question of how expertise is privileged and how non-expert discourse is effectively silenced. Likewise, interesting theoretical questions can be suggested by an insightful historical case study. Finally, of course, argumentation can provide a valuable frame of reference for a theory of the particular case itself.

(5) *Argumentation as a social practice.* One of the most significant trends in argumentation studies in the past generation has been the growing emphasis on argument not just as isolated discourse structures but as a social activity. The practice of argument both creates and reflects culture. Studies of particular argument forms, such as conspiracy argument or definitional argument, facilitate understanding of the values of a culture and how they are modified and mirrored in its discourse. Arguing has consequences for social and cultural identity and change. Social practice and political alignments may change as a result of argumentative changes, as when the prochoice side in the abortion

controversy began to argue for their liberal position by invoking the conservative value of limited government, or when the use of the military metaphor in the context of antidrug programs gave rise to corollary arguments as natural progressions. Many of the historical-critical studies in argumentation focus on key events or moments at which society reconfigured argumentative patterns and thereby changed the course of its direction. More work along these lines will likely be forthcoming.

A particular application of argumentation and social practice involves the relationship between discourse and power. Power relationships influence what is said, and yet power is often achieved through discourse. If certain patterns or styles of argument are repeatedly chosen by those without power, or if an argumentative cluster reconfigures the power relationships, then theorists will be able to understand in greater depth how argument is both a source and a resource for power.

In addition to large-scale social and cultural studies, intensified work can be expected which deals with how argumentation is involved in the creation, maintenance, and decay of interpersonal relationships. Whether theories concern marital and family arguments, strategies for interpersonal bargaining, or the relationship between argument skills and the formation of friendships, what is involved is the explanation of a significant kind of social practice.

(6) *Studies over time.* Seldom in public communication are major effects achieved by a single message. It is far more common that the effects of argument are seen over time, as messages interact with one another and with their environments. Accordingly, scholars have begun looking at argument longitudinally—tracing the development and decay of particular argumentative patterns and exploring how these patterns are modified by epochal events. Such study reveals patterns, trends, and repetitions, and may lead to the plotting of a general curve of development for arguments.

For example, Farrell (1982) traced the course of arguments about authority and showed how the appeal of this particular form was modified by the Carter presidency. Campbell (1981) explored the influence on argument of epochal events, and Goodnight currently is involved in a research program examining how the availability of nuclear weapons has affected argumentation about war and peace. Zarefsky (1980b) investigated how the value of "equal opportunity" was modified through redefinition by President Lyndon Johnson, with consequences for the progress and effects of the civil rights movement.

A particularly interesting aspect of longitudinal studies involves the reemergence, often in quite different contexts, of seemingly "lost" argument patterns. The opposition to school integration during the 1950s replayed the states' rights argument that had been developed during the nullification debates of the 1830s. The moral arguments for and against the right to abortion during the 1980s and early 1990s are not unlike those which developed on the slavery controversy before the Civil War.

[argumentative rhetoric]

Longitudinal studies trace the evolution, maturity, decline, mutation, and resurgence of argument patterns. Continued studies along these lines will sharpen knowledge of the trajectories of an argument and will permit prediction of its likely development and appropriate strategies of intervention in the course of an argument, if appropriate. This type of study can make significant contributions to understanding rhetorical history and the history of ideas.

(7) *Interdisciplinary linkages.* Finally, argumentation theorists will be likely to seek increasingly close ties with kindred spirits in other disciplines. This is not just a matter of finding congenial colleagues but also of extending the reach of argumentation theory to enrich understanding of interdisciplinary issues. Although firmly based in the communication discipline, argumentation also has assumed something of the character of an interdisciplinary field. As a result, scholars in argumentation and those in cognate areas have more to say to, and to learn from, each other. For instance, as Hample (1980) demonstrates, argumentation both contributes to and borrows from cognitive psychology with its emphasis on the processing of messages within the individual. Economists such as Galbraith (1955) and McCloskey (1985) are becoming more conscious of habitual argument patterns in their discipline and are calling attention to how economists argue. Studies in political science and sociology increasingly focus on the relationship between argument and ideology, or the social construction of argument, or the uses of argument to develop, maintain, challenge, defend or overturn power. The series of books emerging from the Iowa Project on Rhetoric of Inquiry is tracking the growing self-consciousness by scholars in various disciplines of their own argument practice and of the influence of argument on how they perceive various disciplinary issues.

Like much of the communication discipline, argumentation traditionally has had a one-way relationship with other fields. Argumentation has been a derivative field, borrowing from the literature of other subjects and applying it to practical problems while contributing little in return. As argumentation studies become more sophisticated and cover a wider span, that relationship should change. Argumentation, not bound to a particular subject for its content, can make great contributions to various fields through the analysis and critique of reasoning patterns.

Each of these seven predictions about argumentation theory is basically a straight-line projection from existing experience. Sometimes theory advances in that fashion. But often it is an unexpected event or research finding that reshapes the agenda of a discipline. In retrospect, the influence is clear to see; it is harder to comprehend at the time. Toulmin's (1958) introduction of "field" clearly had such an influence, as did O'Keefe's (1977) distinction between product and process. So, too, are argument studies affected by factors in the external environment, such as the collapse of the Cold War, the emergence of conditions of scarcity or abundance, or the achievement of technological breakthroughs. All this is to suggest that any sound predictions about the future of argumentation theory need to leave room for the unforeseen and unexpected.

ß.   The Future in Argumentation Practice

Argumentation is both a subject for disciplinary study and a practical art, absorbed intuitively or learned formally. Projecting the future requires making assessments of how argumentation will be used as well as studied.

Some predictions can be made with confidence. An underlying premise of the discipline is that arguing is a natural and inherent human activity, whether (as some believe) a substitute for force which makes civilized society possible, or (as others believe) an expression of creativity which liberates the individual, or (as still others believe) the glue which holds society together by linking the separate interests and concerns of otherwise atomized individuals. In any case, it can be predicted safely that people will continue to argue, and that they will do so on an unspecifiably large range of topics in a variety of situations. Moreover, the premises and warrants employed in argumentation will mirror the dominant beliefs and values within a society and will change as society and culture change.

In formal settings in which established conventions and protocols have developed, those structured occasions for arguing likewise will continue. In courtrooms, in legislative hearings, in religious assemblies, and in academic disciplines, people will engage in specialized argumentation. For the most part they will respect the conventions and assumptions of the field about which they speak, although their practice will modify these conventions at least in subtle ways.

Two developments in argument practice bear special watching. One is the resurgence in the United States of debates as an integral part of political campaigns. As Jamieson and Birdsell (1988) chronicle, debates have emerged as the centerpiece of modern political campaigning. There is, however, widespread belief that this form of argument falls short of its promise and that improved argument practice would enable debates to make a greater contribution to civic education. The other development relates to the dramatic changes which have overtaken Eastern Europe and the Soviet Union in the late 1980s and early 1990s. Suddenly people without a tradition of public argument as a means of social decision making find themselves in political situations in which such skills are required. In some ways, their circumstances are not unlike those of ancient Greece, where citizens suddenly found themselves in need of argumentation skills in order to defend their claims to property in courts of law. It will be interesting to see how argumentation practice is both imported to and modified by the culture of Eastern Europe.

What is much less certain is the role that argumentation practice will play in our own public life as citizens in a democracy. Some signs, such as the declining participation in politics, are not encouraging. Recently published critiques of the American educational system also offer cause for concern. On the other hand, the growing movement for educational reform often involves argumentation in major ways. The push for training students in critical thinking skills, for instance, involves the ability to discern sound and unsound arguments and to make appropriate and effective inferences. The push for higher skill levels in writing and oral communication also endorses the belief that training in argumentation is an important step in the development of the ability to communicate effectively.

The stakes are great because democratic ideology always has assumed that citizens are able to make and to evaluate arguments. American political ideology was heavily influenced by the Enlightenment of the eighteenth century and by its belief that reason was the dominant influence on people. Citizens were naturally moved by appeals to their understanding, and their support for public measures could be obtained in that fashion, so government could be based on the assumption of good judgment and good sense. (Whether these assumptions were warranted is an open question, and in any case they actually applied only to the politically relevant audience of white male property owners.)

These optimistic assumptions about the capacity of the people for critical thinking and reflective judgment were challenged by the development of empirical social science in the late nineteenth century, which led to a concern not for how people ought to behave but for how they actually did. Under the added weight of the findings of crowd psychology studies and the Freudian emphasis on unconscious motivation, the assumption of rationality was hard for academics to sustain. The discovery of the significant role of propaganda in World War I seemed the final nail in the coffin.

Walter Lippmann's career illustrates the effect of these forces. Lippmann was an astute and prolific commentator on American society and politics. His first major book appeared in 1913, and his writing career remained active until his death some sixty years later. Influenced by postwar disillusionment, Lippmann wrote *Public Opinion* (1922). The book began with the premise that public opinion had been "disastrously wrong at the critical junctures" and inquired into why that was so. Lippmann concluded that people's opinions were shaped by stereotypes, mental pictures which often were false. Not only were citizens therefore not capable of making intelligent decisions about public issues, but their intellectual laziness caused bad arguments to drive away the good, suggesting that over time the public would become even less competent to regulate its own affairs.

In a subsequent book, *The Phantom Public* (1925), Lippmann was even more pessimistic. He argued that citizens could not be trained or educated to make competent decisions about public matters because education always lagged behind the pace of the issues and decisions. Therefore, Lippmann concluded, there was no alternative but to abandon a commitment to the competent public and leave decision making in the hands of specialized experts.

His judgment that the public must retreat from citizens to spectators anticipated John Dewey's (1927) concern about the eclipse of the public and is akin to more recent harsh critiques about the effect of mass media.

In his later years, Lippmann moderated his position somewhat. He suggested (1955) that the remedy for the problems he earlier cited could lie in the deliberate cultivation of what he called "the public philosophy." By that term he meant a world-view or outlook grounded in an awareness of what Bitzer (1978) has called "public knowledge"—the fund of truths which are based on collective human experience and which are the premises for public judgment. A speaker becomes competent to argue about public issues by knowing what the public knows and being able to speak as the public would speak if it were organized, articulate, and aware of its truths and interests. Speaking for the public involves making claims which are grounded in public knowledge and which are supported to the best of one's ability. Developing and supporting such claims involves training and practice in argumentation.

In other words, it is the cultivation of the skills of argument practice that permits a public to emerge, capable of governing itself and making its own decisions. It is the skill of argument which enables a citizen to understand public issues even if not directly involved in them—and, if involved, to make his or her opinion count. Such a view places argumentation in the role it enjoyed in classical times, when rhetoric was one of the primary liberal arts and argumentative skill was a means of instruction, of persuasion, and even of self-defense. Whether the practice of public argument in American society can achieve that high ideal will in large part determine the quality of our public culture and decision making in the years ahead.

That is a heavy responsibility to place on argumentation practice. Yet it is one Wayne Brockriede would have welcomed. Concerned that argumentation had not become an insular study and committed to the role of argument in personal and public life, he dedicated his career to teaching students to understand, to value, to analyze, and to participate in argument as the best instrument for intelligent decision making that has yet been devised. The essays in this book challenge you to reach for the same high ideals.

Chapter Twenty-Two

Future Directions in Argumentation Research

Dale Hample

This chapter is concerned with research methods and the directions that argumentation research is likely to take in the next decade or so. Since the previous chapters dealt with the development of argumentation theory and practice, I will concentrate here on the practical details of doing scholarship.

The specialty of argumentation has developed rapidly in the last quarter century. Conceptual growth has been accompanied by—and perhaps even stimulated by—parallel development in research methodology. A quarter century ago, we were mostly concerned with practical advice on how to debate (see Cox & Willard, 1982) and were primarily restricted to previous centuries' rhetorics in our efforts to extract some theoretical bases for what we taught (see W. Benoit, 1990, & Sproule, 1986). We have not stopped worrying about the practicalities of arguing today and neither have we quit studying classical rhetorics. In fact, work in those veins has become considerably more sophisticated; Wayne Brockriede's own scholarship is among our best examples of the evolution of argumentation's traditional concerns.

However, the most striking difference between the argumentation research of 1950 and that of 1990 is the new interests we have today. Among the new developments, which are well represented in this book, are studies of inter-personal arguing, marital disputes, scientific communication, and arguments

Mr. Hample is in the Department of Communication Arts and Sciences at Western Illinois University, Macomb. He is grateful to Pamela J. Benoit and Charles A. Willard who commented usefully on earlier drafts of this essay.

in artistic media. In addition to these studies of argument in settings which were not often studied in years past, we have also begun examining new possibilities for explaining the process of arguing. We have found new ways to understand the structure of argument in conversation, in social milieus, and in private thought.

Many of these developments would have been unlikely, if not impossible, without new methodologies. Having a good idea is not enough. A scholar must also know how to test, explore, and expand an idea in order to make a contribution to the discipline. This shows the importance of methodology and explains why a chapter like this one ought to be read by anyone who is beginning a serious study of argumentation.

This chapter is divided into four parts. The first deals with reflection and critical thinking, which are fundamental to good research in any field. The second is more specific to argumentation and discusses how assumptions about the nature of argument affect research strategy. Third, a large number of research methods are briefly discussed. Finally, I will share some of my expectations about what might happen in the field between now and the end of this century.

ⓘ Research and Critical Thinking

Good research proceeds from good thinking. Formal research procedures are nothing more than a codification of the principles of critical thought. The discipline of research, however, requires that certain kinds of criticism be automatic. Research principles are developed in order to ensure that a scholar's work is not susceptible to fatal critique.

Another way of putting this is to say that a good piece of research makes a good argument. Brockriede (1974) himself explained this in reference to rhetorical criticism, but the idea is equally applicable to any kind of scholarship (for example, see Jackson, 1986). A researcher should strive to have a clear thesis, supported by good evidence which is linked to the thesis by means of justified, explicit arguments.

A specific piece of research deals with the concepts, or variables, which are of special interest to the researcher. These concepts must be well integrated with a coherent theory of argument and will often have been derived from such a theory. Now this may give the impression that people get ideas for research from reading theory, and this is often so. Certainly, it is the impression that formal journal articles are designed to give. However, it is also commonly true that the impulse to do research on a topic comes from some less formal source. For instance, a person may be having a recurring and apparently insoluble argument with a romantic partner and therefore get interested in studying arguments in dating relationships. This is fine. However, before actual research can be undertaken, the scholar must translate the idea into theoretical terms. This is necessary for several reasons: (1) theories provide more intellectual depth and detail for such an impulse; (2) research is essentially a public endeavor, which is characterized by public theory rather than private motivation; and (3) previous theory and research often help to refine a substantive question or research design. No study ever stands alone: it acquires much of its significance from what it says about our previous knowledge of argumentation. Each bit of theoretically informed research naturally becomes a voice in the scholarly community's dialectic on the nature of argument.

To make a real contribution, the scholar must offer new and valuable data. Valuable data has certain characteristics. First of all, it must be pertinent to both the theory and the research issue. Evidence about what a person *said* is, at best, only indirectly informative about what that person *thought*; if you are investigating the thinking that produces arguments, you will need more direct indications of cognition. On the other hand, if you are doing research on how people actually argue, you will need to observe them doing so; merely to ask people how (they think) they argue will not get you close enough to the phenomenon you want to examine.

Secondly, your data must be authentic. In the case of textual analysis (perhaps for rhetorical criticism or conversation analysis), you must be sure that the communication you have is actually what was said and done. In many cases, we have inherited flawed versions of speeches; Patrick Henry's *Liberty or Death* address is a particularly clear example. Conversation analysis works in part from transcripts, which are surprisingly hard to produce accurately, and which in any case always omit things the researcher didn't think to consider: nonverbal behaviors are often not included and words may be hard to understand in many passages. You should make a special effort to ensure that your evidence is as authentic as possible; otherwise your conclusions might be influenced by something that didn't occur at all or by your failure to notice that something else did happen.

The idea of authenticity is also applicable to quantitative research, where it takes on the labels of reliability and validity. Both of these terms refer to the quality of your measurements. Reliable measuring instruments produce pretty much the same answer over and over; valid measurements are true ones. A valid measure is always reliable, but a reliable instrument is not necessarily valid. Both reliability and validity can be assessed quantitatively, and a good research report will include evidence on the degree to which both these criteria have been met. The greater the reliability and validity of your measuring instruments, the less likely is the chance that conclusions based on your data will be wrong.

As you surely know by this point in the book, quality of evidence is not the only important feature of a good argument. Whatever premises or ideas your data provide must also be processed, that is, converted to conclusions by means of warrants or other intervening ideas. Much of the point of a formal research methodology (such as analysis of variance) is to provide scholars with "automatic arguments." In other words, given a particular result, the methodology insists that a specific warrant be applied and dictates the conclusion. I will outline a number of specific methodologies in the third section of this chapter. Before doing that, however, we need to consider the different views of argument you might have, and how they might affect what you think is worth researching.

What Is to be Studied?

In order to study arguments, you must be able to recognize them. This is an obvious point, but in the context of argumentation it is a delicate one. There isn't much controversy about what a dog is, and the subjects of canine research are easy to identify. "Argument," however, is a much more ambiguous and elastic term, and different scholars have different understandings of it. Perhaps without realizing it, you have your own assumptions about what an argument is, and your research efforts will naturally be restricted to what you think qualifies as an argument. For example, here is a list of questions to which various scholars quite reasonably give opposite answers: Is a syllogism an argument? Is a claim without a warrant or evidence an argument? Are nonverbal behaviors part of an argument? Can animals argue? If two people agree on a potentially controversial point, did they have an argument? Is the thinking that produces or interprets a message part of the argument? Is arguing logical? These are certainly not the only disputed issues, but they ought to be sufficient to show you that whatever your implicit understanding of an argument is will strongly influence your recognition of one.

Various scholars have tried to guide us through the maze of possible points of view regarding argument's nature. Wenzel's chapter, in the first section of this book, distinguishes three perspectives on argument. From the rhetorical perspective, a scholar wishes to know how effective an argument is and why. Logical criticism is concerned about the validity or strength of an argument. From the dialectical point of view, you might wonder whether an argument reflects all that is known about a topic, and whether the argument has proceeded in a way free enough to permit all reasonable contributions to be properly evaluated. Notice that these are not three kinds of argument; they are three legitimate points of view that may be taken in order to analyze the same argument.

In contrast, O'Keefe (1977; 1982) distinguishes two kinds of argument, two different senses of the word "argument." He says that $argument_1$ refers to something a person makes, such as an essay or a speech. $Argument_2$, on the other hand, is something two people have, such as a dispute over whether to study together. Hample (1985) has suggested a third kind, $argument_0$, which represents the cognitive processing which is necessary for the production of either $argument_1$ or $argument_2$. In contrast to Wenzel's development of three perspectives on the same thing, O'Keefe and Hample have tried to distinguish three different phenomena that can properly be studied under the heading of argument.

These distinctions by O'Keefe and Hample lead us to an important issue of perspective, that of individual versus social (see Jackson, 1983; Klump, this book; LeFevre, 1987). Is an argument fundamentally something an individual produces, something that arises from one or more minds? Or is it controlled by the social rules for coherence, probity, and politeness? Or is it, in some measure, both at once? The question of whether argument is essentially private or public is difficult to decide, and may even be insoluble (see Hample, 1988). However, your instincts about this issue will naturally lead you to see arguments as being individual or social productions and will therefore impel you to look for arguments either in minds or in texts.

The traditional view had been that arguments are individual enterprises, invented by solitary minds and made public though the action of a particular person (see LeFevre, 1987). The attractiveness of conversational analysis, however, gave rise to research which considers that arguments are mutually constructed by conversants and might better be considered emergent than authored. Champions of this perspective take an essentially social view. They often focus on publicly dictated phenomena, such as adjacency pairs (for example, question/answer, request/grant-or-refusal; Jackson & Jacobs, 1980) or speech acts (things done with words, such as promising and perhaps arguing; van Eemeren & Grootendorst, 1984). By identifying social structures that strongly constrain arguers, these scholars place part of the inventional responsibility for an utterance on the shoulders of society.

Besides having (and in fact, needing) a perspective on what an argument is, you may also have a point of view on what counts as good research. Some people respect only findings that can be quantified; others automatically mistrust numbers. Both of these extremes are pretty much rejected today as being parochial. However, at least one issue about the nature of research is now quite current in argumentation: whether scholars should adopt an interpretive approach or what I will call the distanced one.

Interpretive work is designed so that the researcher can stand in the shoes of the people providing data (see Glaser & Strauss, 1967; Trapp, 1986; Trapp & P. Benoit, 1987). The idea is that the scholar needs to interpret people's experience in the same way, in the same terms, as they do. An interpretive researcher does not so much collect data as participate in it, forging an intersubjective bond with informants. These people's understandings become the basic data, and the researcher tries to avoid imposing any foreign concepts. For instance, an interpretive researcher would not start a project with a specific definition of "argument." S/he might ask respondents questions about "argument" (undefined), try to work out from their answers what *they* think "argument" means, and then endorse that answer as the best available one. This sort of work has actually been done by Trapp (1986), and you might wish to examine his article as an example of interpretive work. Those of you who choose to look over Trapp's chapter might be surprised to notice that it uses statistics in order to help make sense of his data.

A contrary research perspective is that of the distanced researcher. Where interpretive scholars try to share the experiences of their respondents, the distanced researcher intentionally tries to stand apart from them. Interpretive and distanced scholarship reverse the priority of two of their main concerns: instead of honoring intersubjective sharing of experience, the distancing scholar puts publicness in first place. The idea is that research must always have an essentially public character—that is, its results cannot depend on special features of the person who does the investigation. Procedures must therefore be formalized, so that the study can be (almost) exactly replicated by any other competent investigator. Distanced research might use standard questionnaires, unvarying interview protocols, and clearly described step-by-step procedures. Distanced researchers do not hesitate to define "argument" in their own way and to instruct subjects to respect this definition. This perspective is the traditional social scientific one, and examples of its use abound. You might want to look at some of Infante's (1981) research on argumentativeness to see whether this point of view matches your own.

Though there is an unavoidable sense in which these two research perspectives are competing, they both seek answers to the same sorts of questions, and scholars from one perspective pay attention to research of the other kind. As with the issues on the nature of argument discussed earlier, you are not required to choose *one* point of view forever; nor are you expected to be able to say whether one or another is "right" to the exclusion of the other. You should choose a research method that suits your talents and your research question. Your main obligation in this regard is to be able to defend your choice—with good arguments, of course.

Your perspectives on what argument is, and how to study it, go a long way toward controlling your recognition of an argument. Interpretive researchers generally permit their respondents to identify arguments for them, but distanced work usually requires that the scholar do the recognizing alone. For this latter group, definitional criteria are needed. One common standard (e.g., Jackson & Jacobs, 1980) is that arguments have a certain *function*: that of disagreement regulation. Any verbal exchange that is/resolves/explores a disagreement is an argument. A more sophisticated version of this idea is that all conversational repairs are arguments, since any break from preferred custom requires justification (Jackson & Jacobs, 1980).

Another approach to the distanced recognition of arguments is to look for a certain *structure*. The history of argumentation can almost be written in terms of the structures which arguments have been thought to have. Some of the candidates have been these: syllogism, enthymeme, epicheireme, stases, Toulmin (1958) layout, fallacies, felicity conditions, and the lists given by Perelman and Olbrechts-Tyteca (1969). If you have read a textbook on argumentation for this course or an earlier one, you might wish to glance back through it to see what sort of structural assumptions it made: Does it have a section on formal logic? Does it use the Toulmin model? Does it list stock issues for policy or value debate? Does it derive the structure of argument from the nature of conversation? Does it give lists of fallacies? Does it classify types of arguments (e.g., definition, testimony, statistics)? The structure of argument has, over the centuries, been a hotly contested topic. Scholars can find objections to all the possibilities listed above but can also make defenses for each of them. The argumentation community's difficulty in settling on one clear structural standard has been frustrating and may have stimulated the use of interpretive and functional criteria. But the feeling that things can be defined structurally is a strong intellectual bias, and so structural efforts continue to be refined. You will need to make up your own mind about this in order to study argument, because otherwise you won't be able to recognize arguments (or, worse, won't be able to defend your "recognitions").

One final recognition issue ought to be mentioned: where does one look for an argument? In many ways, a person's answer to this question depends on how one decides the earlier ones. Although there are exceptions to some of the generalizations I offer here, let us explore some possible choices. You might answer that arguments are to be found in texts; this often implies that you think argument is not essentially cognitive, that it can reasonably be studied in a distanced way, and that you will be able to recognize arguments and distinguish them from non-argumentative text. You might say that arguments are to be found in individual people; here you would presumably believe that arguments are connected thoughts, which might or might not be reflected in texts, and you could study argument interpretively or in a distanced way. You might answer that arguments are in conversations; this would suggest a partly social origin for them and might well commit you to most of the textual assumptions in addition. You could locate arguments in communities; you would then collect texts (but perhaps interpretive materials as well) which display the views of a social movement, or a social class, or a community of some other sort. No doubt there are other defensible locations as well, and you might even wish to restrict your answer to a particular setting—for instance, you might want to examine courtroom or scientific arguing on the grounds that it is somehow purer and therefore easier to study than more commonplace arguments. In any case, the essential scholarly burden is the same as with the other issues discussed in this chapter: that you be self-conscious about your choices, that you make them reflectively, and that you be able to produce good arguments to justify your decisions.

③ Methodologies

A methodology is a formalized set of procedures for doing research. The degree of formalization is quite variable, ranging from the fairly specific list of steps you might encounter for traditional quantitative work to the general admonition that you should think well to do conceptual scholarship. In principle, however, there is no difference in rigor among methodologies. No matter what they look like, all methodologies are specialized restatements of the requirements for good argument. As we discussed earlier in this chapter, you need good evidence, good theory, and good reasoning in order to do research of any kind.

Some methodologies have become quite formalized because they require very similar kinds of thinking for every project, and it has proved convenient to codify procedures so that every new researcher doesn't have to start from scratch. But other methods—philosophical reflection is an example—can be quite different from one project to another, and codification is not helpful for this kind of work. Still other methods are in between: rhetorical criticism, for instance, can be partly structured (by applying a rhetorical theory) but will also be somewhat idiosyncratic (when the critic begins making judgments about the text and the theory).

The most important consideration in selecting a methodology is its appropriateness. As you will soon see, different methods tend to point to different kinds of questions. You must have a method capable of providing a reasonable answer to the question or hypothesis that motivates your research. As a practical matter, your method must also suit your own abilities as well. If you can't do statistics, for instance, you shouldn't try to use a quantitative method, and this in turn implies that there will be certain kinds of questions that you will be unable to investigate.

In this section of the chapter, I want to introduce a range of methods that are useful in the study of argumentation. These are not the only possible methods, but they strike me as being those that are most current and show the most promise for the future. Any one of these methods could be the subject of an entire book, so you certainly should not read these brief treatments as full-length analyses—they are more in the nature of appetizers.

To make the section as concrete as I can, I will discuss two examples whenever convenient. Let me introduce them now.

> *Luther.* On April 18, 1521, Martin Luther, who had already been excommunicated, appeared before the Diet of Worms to say whether he would recant his writings. He refused to do so, saying that he was bound by conscience: "Here I stand; I cannot do otherwise, so help me God!" (Peterson, 1965, pp. 85-89)

> *Watergate.* On September 15, 1972, President Nixon, H.R. Haldeman, and John Dean conferred about Watergate. That morning, seven men had been indicted by a Federal grand jury for breaking into the Democratic National Committee's headquarters in the Watergate complex (*New York Times*, 1974, pp. 57-69).

I'll give you more detail about these two examples as we consider the different research methods.

The methodologies are divided into three categories: philosophical reflection, qualitative methods, and quantitative methods. These are in a crude order from least codified to most, although there is considerable variation within each category.

Philosophical Reflection. This term refers to those methodologies that consist largely in hard, independent thinking, either about argument in general or about a specific argumentative text. I don't mean to imply that the other methods don't involve sophisticated critical thinking, however. What is really distinctive about these methods is the degree to which they are philosophical, that is, their effort to draw conclusions about the nature of humankind, or the nature of social life, or the nature of argumentation. These research projects tend to have the most ambitious aims of all. I will discuss four such methods: epistemology, ethics, social critique, and conceptual analysis.

Epistemology is that branch of philosophy which concerns itself with knowing: What counts as knowledge? What is truth? How do we go about gaining knowledge? Many scholars now argue that truth is intersubjective — that is, it is sustained by general agreement, which is created by means of communication (Scott, 1967, 1976; Cherwitz & Hikins, 1986; Willard, 1983). Thus, communication has an epistemic function. Scholars doing this kind of work try to show how rhetoric functions to create knowledge.

> *Luther.* Luther's speech is interesting in this regard because he discusses what should count as justification and what should not. "Unless I shall be convinced by proofs from Scripture or by evident reason — for I believe neither in popes nor councils, since they have frequently both erred and contradicted themselves — I cannot choose but adhere to the word of God, which has possession of my conscience . . ." (p. 89). Notice a couple of epistemologically interesting things about this passage: the special elevation of Scripture over any other kind of evidence; its apparent equivalence with reason; and that Luther contemplates that one or the other might affect his adherence to (or interpretation of) the word of God. The passage implicitly contrasts conviction and conscience and holds that conviction is the higher force, since it can change the mandates of conscience. This is a strong statement about religious belief: it should be justified by Scripture and reason, and not by the testimony of religious leaders.

A second kind of philosophical reflection concerns itself with ethics. This has been a long-time concern of rhetorical theorists and has roots in Aristotle's concept of *phronesis*, or practical wisdom, and in Quintilian's insistence that a good orator be *vir bonus*, a good man. As Weaver (1953, Ch. 1) showed, every message from one person to another reflects the speaker's ethical orientation to the listener and to the responsibility for saying dialectically justifiable things.

Watergate.   Here is part of the transcript of the conversation between Nixon (P), Haldeman (H), and Dean (D):

P - We are all in it together. This is a war. We take a few shots and it will be over. We will give them a few shots and it will be over. Don't worry. I wouldn't want to be on the other side right now. Would you?

D - Along that line, one of the things I've tried to do, I have begun to keep notes on a lot of people who are emerging as less than our friends because this will be over some day and we shouldn't forget the way some of them have treated us.

P - I want the most comprehensive notes on all those who tried to do us in. They didn't have to do it. If we had had a very close election and they were playing the other side I would understand this. No — they were doing this quite deliberately and they are asking for it and they are going to get it. We have not used the power in this first four years as you know. We have never used it. We have not used the Bureau and we have not used the Justice Department but things are going to change now. And they are either going to do it right or go.

D - What an exciting prospect.

P - Thanks. It has to be done (p. 63).

What 15 years' hindsight makes most striking is that Nixon and Dean thought of Watergate as a political dispute, for which they use a war metaphor, rather than as an issue of ethics, law, or truth. Dean has begun making a list of enemies, and both see the Justice Department as a means of exerting power. They recognize that some people in the FBI and Justice Department may not view themselves that way, but if they don't follow orders, they will have to go. This is to Dean an exciting prospect, and Nixon is pleased at Dean's enthusiasm. We cannot quite tell whether Dean is being sycophantic or is in genuine accord with Nixon here, but in either case it is very clear that neither man is much concerned about the truth. One wins a war with shots that defeat enemies, but one finds truth through open-minded inquiry. Truth is a communicator's ethical obligation; winning at any cost is what a general has to do.

A third kind of philosophical inquiry is social critique, whose purpose is to uncover the hidden sources of power in society and to raise people's consciousness about this power, so that they can be emancipated from it (Burleson & Kline, 1979; Wenzel, 1979). Free communication is the means by which consciousness can be altered, while restricted communication reinforces the elite's position (who else could have restricted discussion, and for what other reason?). From this point of view, arguments are examined for evidence that they are restricted and whether they offer hope for emancipation.

Luther.   After having discussed his books and explained why he would not recant any of them, Luther addresses himself to the effect his writings have had on others: "It must now, I think, be manifest that I have sufficiently examined and weighed, not only the dangers, but the parties and dissensions excited in the world by means of my doctrine, of which I was yesterday so gravely admonished. But I must avow that to me it is of all others the most delightful spectacle to see parties and dissensions growing up on account of the word of God, for such is the progress of God's word, such its ends and object. 'Think not I am come to send peace on earth; I came not to send peace, but a sword. For I am come to set a man at variance against his father, and the daughter against her mother, and the daughter-in-law against her mother-in-law; and a man's foes shall be those of his own household'" (p. 88). This is a celebration of dissent, of open discussion. We have already noticed how Luther has rejected the authority of Church leaders and held up reason and Scripture as the arbiters of conscience. He wishes to reform the Church, to emancipate Christians from the papacy. Notice, however, that this is a limited emancipation: Luther's quotation of Scripture on this point is a concession to its power, and a denial that individual reason ought to be completely free. Luther seeks the progress of God's word, not the emancipation of people from the power of religion.

The final method of philosophical reflection to be mentioned here is conceptual analysis, which consists simply in considering what our concepts really mean. To use words loosely is to think badly. An improvement in our understanding of the concepts we work with should also constitute an improvement in our theories. Rather than offer an example from Luther's speech or the Watergate conversation, I will again mention O'Keefe's (1977) fundamental essay, in which he distinguishes between argument₁ and argument₂. His method was to consider how the word "argument" is used, and he noticed that it is used in two ways: in the first sense, to refer to something one *makes*, and in the second, to refer to something people can *have*. O'Keefe therefore concludes that "argument" is ambiguous, and that scholars must clarify which thing they mean in particular research projects.

Qualitative Methods. The second main category of methodologies is qualitative. Some of these have much in common with the philosophical methods just discussed but differ in that their aims tend to be narrower, more restricted to the discourse under study. Other qualitative methods shade almost imperceptibly into quantitative procedures, and in fact, the distinction between qualitative and quantitative is not a very sharp one.

The first qualitative method is a kind of criticism known as hermeneutics. The term originally described very intensive efforts to understand exactly what Biblical passages mean, but today it has a more general meaning. Hermeneutics is interpretation, which involves expression, explanation, and translation of meaning (Balthrop, 1982). The scholar tries to understand what a text meant in its own mileau, as well as what it says today, but makes a concerted effort to keep these separate. This involves setting aside one's own assumptions and letting the discourse speak. This is as much an attitude as a method, but perhaps I can display a little of it for you.

> *Watergate.* Here is part of the opening of the conversation between Nixon, Haldeman, and Dean. They are discussing the day's indictments and other events.
>
> P - How did MacGregor handle himself?
>
> D - I think very well he had a good statement which said that the Grand Jury had met and that it was now time to realize that some apologies may be due.
>
> H - Fat chance.
>
> D - Get the damn (inaudible)
>
> H - We can't do that.
>
> P - Just remember, all the trouble we're taking, we'll have a chance to get back one day. How are you doing on your other investigations?
>
> H - What has happened on the bug?
>
> P - What bug?
>
> D - The second bug there was a bug found in the telephone of one of the men at the DNC.
>
> P - You don't think it was left over from the other time?
>
> D - Absolutely not, the Bureau has checked and re-checked the whole place after that night. The man had specifically checked and rechecked the telephone and it was not there.
>
> P - What the hell do you think was involved?
>
> D - I think DNC was planted.
>
> P - You think they did it?
>
> D - Uh-huh (pp. 57-58)

We must set aside our own understandings of Watergate, our own memories, whatever we have learned about it, in order to permit the text to speak to us. On September 15, 1972, there was not yet a consensus as to who was right, and the outcome of the scandal was certainly not in sight. The passage above, as well as the one quoted earlier, tell us what "Watergate" meant in the White House. It was a political war, complete with shots and enemies. The enemies are those who are "less than our friends." There are no noncombatants, since people are divided into two classes: friends and not. The most obvious of the latter is the Democratic National Committee, which had been bugged in the first place, and which was now thought to be planting more bugs in an effort to frame the White House. This is a shot from the DNC, perhaps part of the current volley. Shots will have to be fired in return during the war. However, quite a bit of ammunition — including the FBI and the Justice Department — will be left over, to be used when "it will be over," for "we'll have a chance to get back one day." Though legal charges have been made,

Watergate is not really a legal matter. It is to be fought to the end, with a "fat chance" of apologies for past or present conduct.

Traditional rhetorical criticism is another qualitative method (Brockriede, 1974; Nichols, 1963; Parrish, 1954). Here the scholar examines a rhetorical text and explores its essential nature. The objects of such inquiry are: first, to make a judgment about the text's rhetorical quality and second, to improve our rhetorical theory.

> *Luther.* I do not wish to quote the whole first half of Luther's speech here, but let me summarize it, paragraph by paragraph (pp. 86-87):
>
> (1) I am obedient, but humble. If I fail to address the nobles properly, "I entreat you to pardon me as one not conversant with courts, but rather with the cells of monks, and claiming no other merit than that of having spoken and written with the simplicity of mind which regards nothing but the glory of God and the pure instruction of the people of Christ." (2) I will not recant my books, of which there are three kinds. The first treats "the piety of faith and morals with simplicity so evangelical that my very adversaries" regard them as appropriate reading. The condemnation of these is "a monstrous perversity of judgment." (3) The second kind inveighs against the papacy, which is tyrannical and has tortured the consciences of good Christians. (4) To recant these books would lend strength to oppression, impiety, wickedness, and despotism. (5) The third kind involves attacks on individuals, and I regret that "I have written with more bitterness than was becoming either my religion or my profession." Nonetheless, through my retraction "despotism and impiety would reign under my patronage."
>
> In these paragraphs, even in summary, we can see an effective use of traditional rhetorical principles. The opening display of humility and piety is conciliatory and offers a favorable opportunity for his audience to identify with him in spirit if not in station. The three types of books are handled separately, with what is clearly his strongest argument first, his next best argument (including the self-deprecating apology) in the final position, and his weakest argument sandwiched in between. This ordering is in accord with the recommendations of classical authors. Luther has intelligently given the most prominence to his best arguments and has tried to paint himself in colors attractive to the Diet.

A third qualitative methodology is conversation analysis. This phrase is often used synonymously with discourse analysis, but I will follow Hopper, Koch, and Mandlebaum (1986) in considering that conversation analysis tries to discover new features of discourse, while discourse analysis makes quantitative statements about relations among previously established categories of analysis. A pertinent example of conversation analysis is Jackson and Jacobs (1980), who examine the function of arguments in conversation and conclude that all arguments are conversational repairs. That is, arguments are used to justify, point out, or otherwise deal with departures from preferred conversational practices. Here is an instance.

> Watergate. Nixon, Haldeman, and Dean are discussing an audit of campaign finances being conducted by the General Accounting Office. Dean has just reported that the GAO audit was initiated at the request of the Speaker of the House.

> H - That is the kind of thing that, you know, we really ought to do is call the Speaker and say, "I regret to say your calling the GAO down here because of what it is going to cause us to do to you."

> P - Why don't you see if Harlow will tell him that?

> D - Because he wouldn't do it—he would just be pleasant and call him Mr. Speaker (p. 64).

When Nixon expresses his request, he frames it as a question. This is more polite than a command, and the politeness is accentuated by his phrasing, which invites an explanation of why the request should be refused. The conversationally preferred response to a request (especially a polite one) is acceptance, but Dean does not cooperate. Dean's refusal is a violation of conversational norms, and must therefore be repaired, and Dean does so. Notice that his turn at talk is in fact an enthymematic argument—he gives reasons for his refusal but leaves the refusal itself unstated. The argument is an effort to justify his lack of cooperation, and hence functions as a repair. This is an illustration of what Jackson and Jacobs discovered, and displays some of the reasons for their novel conclusion that arguments are repair devices.

Other qualitative techniques include ethnography and participant observation. These require that the scholar participate in a language community and study it from the inside out. Ethnography is even less structured than conversation analysis because conversation analysts hold their texts at arms' length, whereas ethnographers immerse themselves in a culture and may even produce some of the discourse they study. I cannot illustrate these methods with either Luther or Watergate (for the simple reason that I can't go back into time to experience those speech communities), and the methods have only rarely been used in argumentation research (e.g., Hollihan, Riley & Freadhoff, 1986). There is no good reason for this limited use, however, for this approach would seem to be quite compatible with the interpretive view of research. Philipsen (1975) has done ethnographic, participant observation work on communication in a blue collar neighborhood he calls Teamsterville, and the volume edited by Bauman and Sherzer (1974) contains many more examples.

Quantitative Methods. Quantitative methods are the third kind discussed here. As their name indicates, they make use of numbers and statistics to justify conclusions. This requires that concepts be operationalized, or measured.

Instead of working with a concept (e.g., "strong argument"), the scholar uses an operationalized variable (e.g., "any argument rated at 5 or above on a 7 point strength scale"). Statistical procedures and inferences are the most codified of any methods discussed here. The inference rules, however, are not simply about numbers; they also prescribe certain formal research designs, which are used to collect the data in the first place. I will describe two quantitative methods here: discourse analysis and variable-analytic research.

Discourse analysis, as I mentioned earlier, is quite similar to conversation analysis. The difference is that conversation analysts create many of their own concepts to reflect social reality, while discourse analysts use pre-established categories, measure or count them, and make quantitative conclusions (Hopper, Koch & Mandlebaum, 1986). The goal of conversation analysis is to discover something about the nature or possibilities of human conversation, while discourse analysis seeks discoveries about the behavior of humans while conversing. You might review the example of conversation analysis given above before considering the following example of discourse analysis.

> *Watergate.* As the Watergate scandal went on, pressures mounted almost day by day. What had originally seemed to be just another political embarrassment began to threaten the continuation of Nixon's Presidency and the jobs and personal freedom of his aides. Based on a variety of theories (Gibb, 1961; Brehm, 1966) we might therefore predict that the White House would become increasingly defensive as time went on. Defensiveness and perceived threat cause people to pay more attention to their own "faces," that is, to be more sensitive to face threats and more involved in doing "face work." We might therefore hypothesize that face work takes an increasing proportion of conversants' time in the Watergate transcripts as time goes on. We could test this hypothesis by going through each transcript and classifying each turn at talk according to whether it involved face work or not (perhaps using the work of Brown & Levinson, 1987, to operationalize face threatening acts and repairs). We would then calculate the proportion of face work turns to total turns for each conversation and plot those proportions against time. An upward sloping graph would support the hypothesis. Notice that this study would tell us something about how people respond to threat but would not say anything new about the nature of conversation.

The second quantitative methodology is variable-analytic research. This sort of work involves discovering the relationships among variables involved in arguing. Researchers must have theoretical grounds for believing that certain variables are important to the process of arguing and that they will be related. Then the variables are operationalized and measured, and statistical techniques are used to analyze the variables' associations with one another. Principles of research design and descriptions of statistical methods are explained in many textbooks, and these topics are far too complex for me even to sketch them here. But perhaps an example will convey the general idea.

> *Luther.* A traditional concern in argumentation is to say what arguing practices are most effective. As we noticed earlier, Luther used the classically-recommended order for his arguments about the three types of books he had written. Was this really the best available ordering for him? Was he right to put his strongest argument first, his next strongest last, and his weakest in the middle? We could design a study to test the hypothesis that the most effective ordering is first-third-second. Our dependent variable would be the degree of the audience's agreement with Luther's position. This is our criterion for "most effective": the one that produces the most agreement. We would have to rate Luther's arguments for their strength, and might do this by giving each of his arguments to a different group of people, and asking them to rate the argument's strength from 1 (very weak) to 7 (very strong). The average ratings would tell us how strong the arguments were individually. Our independent variable would be ordering, and we might test six orderings, 1-2-3, 2-3-1, 3-1-2, 3-2-1, 2-1-3, and 1-3-2, where 1 represents the strongest argument, 2 the second strongest, and 3 the weakest. We would then prepare six versions of Luther's speech (one using each ordering) and ask about 30 people each to read one version, using 180 subjects in all. After reading the speech, people would then indicate the degree to which they agreed with Luther on a scale from 1 (completely disagree) to 7 (completely agree). We would conclude that the order that produced the highest average agreement score is the most effective, and this would permit us to say whether Luther's 1-3-2 order was best. This study would only allow us to draw a conclusion about Luther's ordering in that particular speech. To generalize about ordering in general, we would have to expand the study to include arguments from other speeches.

This part of the chapter has reviewed a variety of useful methodologies for the study of argument. Whatever method you choose, you ought to be able to justify by reference to your research question. And it may well be worthwhile to approach a single research question with several distinct methodologies; this is called triangulation, and it is highly recommended (P. Benoit, 1988).

The Prospects for Argumentation Research

Judging from the recent past, a safe prediction is that argumentation research will continue to grow in quantity, quality, and variety. The last few years have seen the appearance of several new and significant outlets for research: the new international journal *Argumentation*, the proceedings of the argumentation conferences held every other summer in Alta, Utah, and the proceedings of the Amsterdam meeting held every four years. The character of *Argumentation and Advocacy* (formerly the *Journal of the American Forensic Association*) has also been changing: its former primary focus on forensics has evolved into its present emphasis on broader issues of argumentation theory.

The argumentation community uses many research methods, of which I have mentioned the chief ones here. This pluralism is welcomed on all sides and has resulted in a rich interplay of scholars and research programs which begin with very different assumptions. Argumentation is forging stronger links with its parent discipline, speech communication. Our best scholars are consistently able to publish argumentation research in general interest journals, and many of the best mainstream scholars have been doing argumentation work as well. Argumentation courses are appearing with greater frequency in doctoral curricula, and the next generation of speech communication scholars will surely know more about argumentation than earlier groups. In decades past, the argumentation community was largely defined by its members' association with intercollegiate debate, but this relationship is already perceptibly weakening.

In short, argumentation research is increasing in sophistication and perceived relevance. This progress is due mostly to the research done in the past two or three decades. Wayne Brockriede was an important figure in this develop-ment, partly because of his own research, and partly because of the esteem in which he was held by both the argumentation and speech communication communities. I am optimistic about continued progress into the next century, but a great part of argumentation's prospects depends on the people reading this book today.

Bibliography

Adams, L. (1976). *Art on trial: From Whistler to Rothko*. New York: Walker and Company.

Alcoholics Anonymous (1953). *Twelve steps and twelve traditions*. New York: Alcoholics Anonymous World Services.

———. (1976). *Alcoholics Anonymous*. New York: Alcoholics Anonymous World Services.

Alter, J., et al. (1988, July 4). How liberal is Dukakis? *Newsweek*, p. 14.

———. (1988, September 26). The expectations game. *Newsweek*, pp. 16-18.

Altman, I. & Taylor, D. (1973). *Social penetration*. New York: Holt, Rinehart and Winston.

Alters, D. (1988, October 2). Bush retools his image for heartland. *The Boston Sunday Globe*, p. 13.

Anderson, B. (1983). *Imagined communities: Reflections on the origin and spread of nationalism*. London: Verso.

Anderson, J. R. (1972). The audience as a concept in the philosophic rhetoric of Perelman, Johnstone, and Natanson. *Southern Speech Communication Journal*, *38*, 39-50.

Aristotle. (1941) *Topica* (Book II, *Rhetoric*). In R. McKeon (Ed.), *The Basic Works of Aristotle*. New York: Random House.

Aronowitz, S. (1988). *Science as power: Discourse and ideology in modern society*. Minneapolis: University of Minnesota Press.

Arrington, C. & Sawaya, R. N. (1984). Managing public affairs: Issues management in an uncertain environment. *California Management Review, 26*, 148-60.

Atkinson, J. & Heritage, J. (Eds.) (1984). *Structures of social action*. Cambridge: Cambridge University Press.

Bailin, S. (1987). Critical and creative thinking. *Informal Logic, 9*, 23-30.

———. (1988). *Achieving extraordinary ends: An essay on creativity*. Dordrecht, Holland: Kluwer.

Bales, R. F. (1944). The therapeutic role of Alcoholics Anonymous as seen by a sociologist. *Quarterly Journal of Studies on Alcohol, 9*, 226-78.

315

Balthrop, V. W. (1982). Argumentation and the critical stance: A methodological approach. In J. R. Cox & C. A. Willard (Eds.), *Advances in argumentation research*, pp. 238-58. Carbondale: Southern Illinois University Press.

Barnes, B. & Edge, D. (Eds.) (1982). *Science in context*. Cambridge, MA: MIT Press.

Barrett, L. I. (1988, September). Shifting mist: Pit-bull politics and weak voter convictions make the polls bounce. *Time*, pp. 20-21.

Bauman, R. & Sherzer, J. (Eds.) (1974). *Explorations in the ethnography of speaking*. Cambridge: Cambridge University Press.

Baumgarten, A. G. (1954). *Reflections on poetry*, (K. Aschenbrenner and W. B. Holther, Trans.). Berkeley: University of California Press (original work published 1931).

Baxter, L. A. (1986). Gender differences in the heterosexual relationship rules in break-up accounts. *Journal of Social and Personal Relationships, 3*, 289-306.

Bazerman, C. (1988). *Shaping written knowledge: The genre and activity of the experimental article in science*. Madison: University of Wisconsin Press.

Beachy, L., et al. (1988, November 21). The inside story of campaign '88: The keys to the White House. *Newsweek*, pp. 120, 139.

Beatty, J. (1983). The new rhetoric, practical reason, and justification: The communicative relativism of Chaim Perelman. *Journal of Value Inquiry, 17*, 325-34.

Beckwith, D. (1988, October 24). Bush scores a warm win. *Time*, p. 18.

Benoit, P. J. (1982). The naive social actor's concept of argument. Paper presented at the Speech Communication Association, Louisville, KY.

_____. (1987). Orientation to face in everyday argument. In F. H. van Eemeren, R. Grootendorst, J. A. Blair & C. A. Willard (Eds.), *Argumentation: Perspectives and appproaches*, pp. 144-52. Dordrecht, Holland: Foris.

_____. (1988). A case for triangulation in argument research. *Argumentation and Advocacy, 25*, 31-42.

Benoit, W. L. (In press). Traditional conceptions of argument. In W. L. Benoit, D. Hample & P. J. Benoit (Eds.), *Readings in argumentation*. Dordrecht, Holland: Foris.

Benoit, W. L. & Benoit, P. J. (1987). Everyday argument practices of naive social actors. In J. W. Wenzel (Ed.), *Argument and critical practices*, pp. 465-74. Annandale, VA: Speech Communication Association.

Benoit, W. L., Hample, D. & Benoit, P. J. (Eds.) (In press). *Readings in argumentation*. Dordrecht, Holland: Foris.

Berg, J. (1987). Interpreting arguments. *Informal Logic, 9*, 15.

Berger, C. & Chaffe, S. (Eds.) (1987). *Handbook of communication science*. Beverly Hills, CA: Sage.

Berger, P. L. & Luckman, T. (1967). *The social construction of reality*. Garden City, NJ: Doubleday.

Berlo, D. (1960). *The process of communication*. New York: Holt, Rinehart and Winston.

Berman, M. (1982). *All that is solid melts into air*. New York: Simon and Schuster.

Bernstein, R. J. (1968). *The restructuring of social and political theory*. Berkeley: University of California Press.

Bernstein, R. J. (1983). *Beyond objectivism and relativism*. University Park: University of Pennsylvania Press.

Bettinghaus, E.D. (1972). *The nature of proof* (2nd ed.). Indianapolis: Bobbs-Merrill.

Biesecker, B. (1989). Recalculating the relation of the public and technical spheres. In B. E. Gronbeck (Ed.), *Spheres of argument: Proceedings of the sixth SCA/AFA conference on argumentation*, pp. 66-70. Annandale, VA: Speech Communication Association.

Birdsell, D. S. (1989). Critics and technocrats. In B.E. Gronbeck (Ed.), *Spheres of argument: Proceedings of the sixth SCA/AFA conference on argumentation*, pp. 16-19. Annandale, VA: Speech Communication Association.

Bitzer, L. F. (1979). Rhetoric and public knowledge. In D. M. Burks (Ed.), *Philosophy, rhetoric and literature*, (pp. 67-94). Lafayette, IN: Purdue University Press.

_____. (1980). *Carter vs. Ford: The counterfeit debates of 1976*. Madison: University of Wisconsin Press.

Black, E. (1965). *Rhetorical criticism: A study in method*. New York: The Macmillan Company.

Blair, J. A. & Johnson, R. H. (Eds.), (1980). *Informal logic: The first international symposium*. Inverness, CA: Edgepress.

_____. (1987a). Argumentation as dialectical. *Argumentation, 1*, 41-56.

_____. (1987b). The current state of informal logic. *Informal Logic, 9*, 147-51.

Blankenship, J. (1976). The search for the 1972 Democratic nomination: A metaphorical perspective. In J. Blankenship & H. Stelzner (Eds.), *Rhetoric and communication*, pp. 236-60. Urbana: University of Illinois Press.

Blankenship, J., Fine, M. G. & Davis, L. (1983). The Republican primary debates: The transformation of actor to scene. *Quarterly Journal of Speech, 69*, 25-36.

Blankenship, J. & Kang, J. G., (1990). The 1984 presidential and vice presidential debates: The printed press and construction by metaphor. *Presidential Studies Quarterly* (In press).

Blankenship, J. & Stelzner, H. (Eds.) (1976). *Rhetoric and communication*. Urbana: University of Illinois Press.

Bochner, A. P., Kaminski, E. P. & Fitzpatrick, M. A. (1977). The conceptual domain of interpersonal communication behavior. *Human Communication Research, 3*, 291-302.

Bochner, A. P., Krueger, D. L., & Chmielewski, T. L. (1982). Interpersonal perceptions and marital adjustment. *Journal of Communication, 32*, 135-47.

Bodkin, M. (1958). *Archetypal patterns in poetry: Psychological studies of imagination*. London: Oxford University Press.

Bohm, D. (1982). The enfolding-unfolding universe: A conversation with David Bohm. In K. Wilbur (Ed.), *The holographic paradigm and other paradoxes*, pp. 44-64. Boulder, CO: Shambhala Publications.

_____. (1983) *Wholeness and the implicate order*. London: Routledge and Kegan Paul.

Booth, W. C. (1974). *Modern dogma and the rhetoric of assent*. Notre Dame: University of Notre Dame Press.

Bormann, E. G. (1973). *The force of fantasy: Restoring the American dream*. Carbondale, IL: Southern Illinois University Press.

Bostrom, R. N. (Ed.) (1983). *Communication yearbook 7*. Newbury Park, CA: Sage.

Boulton, J. T. (1958). Editor's introduction. In E. Burke, *A philosophical enquiry into the origin of our ideas of the sublime and beautiful*, pp. iii-ix. London: Routledge and Kegan Paul (original work published in 1757).

Bowler, P. J. (1984). *Evolution: The history of an idea*. Berkeley: University of California Press.

Braet, A. (1987). The classical doctrine of status and the rhetorical theory of argumentation. *Philosophy and Rhetoric, 5*, 1-11.

Brehm, J. W. (1966). *A theory of psychological reactance*. New York: Academic Press.

Brenders, D. A. (1987). Perceived control: Foundations and directions for communication research. In M. L. McLaughlin (Ed.), *Communication yearbook 10*, pp. 86-116. Newbury Park, CA: Sage.

Brent, P. (1981). *Charles Darwin*. New York: Harper & Row.

Brockriede, W. (1972). Arguers as lovers. *Philosophy and Rhetoric, 5*, 1-11.

_____. (1974). Rhetorical criticism as argument. *Quarterly Journal of Speech, 40*, 165-74.

_____. (1975). Where is argument? *Journal of the American Forensic Association, 11*, 179-82.

_____. (1977). Characteristics of arguments and arguing, *Journal of the American Forensic Association, 13*, 129-32.

_____. (1980). Argument as epistemological method. In D.A. Thomas (Ed.), *Argumentation as a way of knowing*, pp. 128-34. Falls Church, VA: Speech Communication Association.

_____. (1982). Arguing about human understanding. *Communication Monographs, 49*, 137-47.

_____. (1983). The contemporary renaissance in the study of argument. In D. Zarefsky, M. O. Sillars & J. Rhodes (Eds.), *Argument in transition*, pp. 17-26. Annandale, VA: Speech Communication Association.

_____. (1985a). Constructs, experience and argument. *Quarterly Journal of Speech, 71*, 151-63.

_____. (1985b). Who is an arguer? A Conversation with Brockriede. In J. R. Cox, M. O. Sillars & G. B. Walker (Eds.), *Argument and social practice*, pp. 35-39. Annandale, VA: Speech Communication Association.

_____. (1986). Arguing: The art of being human. In J. L. Golden & J. J. Pilotta (Eds.), *Practical reasoning in human affairs*, pp. 53-67. Dordrecht, Holland: D. Riedel.

Brockriede, W. & Ehninger, D. (1960). Toulmin on argument: An examination and application. *Quarterly Journal of Speech, 46*, 44-53.

Brossmann, B. G. & Canary, D. J. (1990). An observational analysis of argument structures: The case of Nightline. *Argumentation, 3* (In press).

Brown, P. & Levinson, S. (1978). Universal in language usage: Politeness phenomena. In E. N. Goody (Ed.), *Questions and politeness: Strategies in social interaction*, pp. 256-310. London: Cambridge.

_____. (1987). *Politeness: Some universals in language usage*. Cambridge: Cambridge University Press.

Brown, R. H. (1987). *Society as text*. Chicago: University of Chicago Press.

Brown, W. (1978). Ideology as communication process. *Quarterly Journal of Speech, 64*, 123-40.

_____. (1982). Attention and the rhetoric of social intervention. *Quarterly Journal of Speech, 68*, 17-27.

Brown, W. (1986). Power and the rhetoric of social intervention. *Communication Monographs, 53*, 180-99.

_____. (1987a). The holographic view of argument. *Argumentation, 1*, 89-102.

_____. (1987b). *Need and the rhetoric of social intervention*. Unpublished paper, Ohio State University.

Brutain, G. A. (1979). On philosophical argumentation. *Philosophy and Rhetoric, 12*, 77-90.

Bugental, D. P., Henker, B. & Whalen, C. K. (1976). Attributional antecedents of verbal and vocal assertiveness. *Journal of Personality and Social Psychology, 34*, 105-11.

Burggraf, C. S. & Sillars, A. L. (1987). A critical examination of sex differences in marital communication. *Communication Monographs, 54*, 276-94.

Burke, E. (1958). *A philosophical enquiry into the origin of our ideas of the sublime and beautiful*. London: Routledge and Kegan Paul (original work published in 1757).

Burke, K. (1950). *A rhetoric of motives*. New York: Prentice-Hall.

_____. (1952). A dramatistic view of the origins of language: Part one. *Quarterly Journal of Speech, 38*, 251-64.

_____. (1957). *The philosophy of literary form*. New York: Vintage Press.

_____. (1961). *Attitudes toward history*. Boston: Beacon Press.

_____. (1965). *Permanence and change*. New York: Bobbs-Merrill.

_____. (1966). *Language as symbolic action: Essays on life, literature, and method*. Berkeley: University of California Press.

_____. (1968). *Counter-statement*. Berkeley: University of California Press (original work published in 1931).

_____. (1969). *A rhetoric of motives*. Berkeley: University of California Press.

_____. (1978). (Nonsymbolic) Motion/ (symbolic) action. *Critical Inquiry, 4*, 809-22.

_____. (1970). *The rhetoric of religion*. Berkeley: University of California Press.

Burke, M. (1985). Unstated premises. *Informal Logic, 7*, 107-18.

Burks, D. M. (Ed.) (1979). *Philosophy, rhetoric and literature*. Lafayette, IN: Purdue University Press.

Burleson, B. R. (1979). On the analysis and criticism of arguments: Some theoretical and methodological considerations. *Journal of the American Forensic Association, 15*, 137-47.

Burleson, B. R. & Kline, S. L. (1979). Habermas' theory of communication: A critical explication. *Quarterly Journal of Speech, 65*, 412-28.

Caddell, P. (1988, November 13). In J. A. Farrell, The electronic election. *The Boston Sunday Globe*, B, 11.

Campbell, J. A. (1981). Historical reason: Field as consciousness. In G. Ziegelmueller and J. Rhodes, *Dimensions of Argument*, pp. 101-13. Annandale, VA: Speech Communication Association.

_____. (1986). Scientific revolution and the grammar of culture: The case of Darwin's origin. *Quarterly Journal of Speech, 72*, 351-76.

Campbell, J. A. (1987). Poetry, science, and argument: Erasmus Darwin as Baconian subversive. In J. W. Wenzel (Ed.), *Argument and critical practices*, pp. 499-506. Annandale, VA: Speech Communication Association.

Campbell, J. A. (1989). The invisible rhetorician: Charles Darwin's 'third party' strategy. *Rhetorica, 7.* (In press).

———. (In press). Scientific discovery and rhetorical invention: The path to Darwin's 'Origin.' In H. W. Simons (Ed.), *The rhetorical turn.* Chicago: University of Chicago Press.

Campbell, K. K. (1972). *Critiques of contemporary rhetoric.* Belmont, CA: Wadsworth.

———. (1982). *The rhetorical act.* Belmont, CA: Wadsworth.

Canary, D. J. (1989). Manual for coding conversational arguments. Unpublished manuscript, California State University, Fullerton.

Canary, D. J., Brossmann, B. G. & Seibold, D. R. (1987). Argument structures in decision-making groups. *Southern Speech Communication Journal, 53,* 18-38.

Canary, D. J., Brossmann, B. G., Sillars, A. L., & LoVette, S. (1987). Argumentative structures in marital dyads: A comparison of satisfied and dissatisfied couples. In J. W. Wenzel (Ed.), *Argument and critical practices,* pp. 475-84. Annandale, VA: Speech Communication Association.

Canary, D. J., Cody, M. J. & Marston, P. (1986). Goal types, compliance-gaining, and locus of control. *Journal of Language and Social Psychology, 5,* 249-69.

Canary, D. J., Cunningham, E. M. & Cody, M. J. (1988). Goal types, gender, and locus of control in managing interpersonal conflict. *Communication Research, 15,* 426-46.

Canary, D. J. & Spitzberg, B. H. (1989). A model of the perceived competence of conflict strategies. *Human Communication Research, 15,* 630-49.

Carrier, D. (1987). *Artwriting.* Amherst: University of Massachusetts Press.

Castoriadis, C. (1987). *The imaginary institutions of society* (K. Blamey, Trans.). Cambridge, MA: MIT Press.

Caswell, H. (1983). An injunctive form of the axioms of trialectics. In R. Horn (Ed.), *Trialectics: Toward a practical logic of unity,* pp. 41-46. Lexington, MA: Information Resources, Inc.

Charland, M. (1987). Constitutive rhetoric: The case of *Peuple Quebeçois. Quarterly Journal of Speech, 73,* 133-50.

Chase, S. B. (1986). *Hart and soul: Gary Hart's New Hampshire odyssey—and beyond.* Concord, NH: NHI press.

Cherwitz, R. A. & Hikins, J. W. (1986). *Communication and knowledge: An investigation in rhetorical epistemology.* Columbia, SC: University of South Carolina Press.

Clark, R. A. & Delia, J. G. (1979). Topoi and rhetorical competence. *Quarterly Journal of Speech, 65,* 187-206.

Clarke, G. (1972, January 17). The need for new myths. *Time,* p. 50.

Clevenger, T., Jr. (1966). *Audience analysis.* Indianapolis: Bobbs-Merrill.

Combs, J. E. (1980). *Dimensions of political drama.* Santa Monica, CA: Goodyear Publishing Company.

Conley, T. M. (1984). The enthymeme in perspective. *Quarterly Journal of Speech, 70,* 168-87.

Conley, T. M. (1985). The beauty of lists: *Copia* and argument. *Journal of the American Forensic Association, 22,* 96-103.

Cook, F. J. (1961). Juggernaut: The warfare state. *Nation, 193,* 111.

Cope, J. I. & Jones, H. W. (Eds.) (1959). *History of the Royal Society.* St. Louis: Washington University Press.

Courtright, J. A., Millar, F. E. & Rogers-Millar, L. E. (1979). Domineeringness and dominance: Replication and extension. *Communication Monographs, 46,* 179-92.

Cox, J. R. (1980). Loci communes and Thoreau's arguments for wilderness in "Walking." *Southern Speech Communication Journal, 46,* 1-16.

————. (1982). The die is cast: Topical and ontological dimensions of the locus of the irreparable. *Quarterly Journal of Speech, 68,* 227-39.

Cox, J. R., Sillars, M. O. & Walker, G. B. (Eds.) (1985). *Argument and social practice.* Annandale, VA: Speech Communication Association.

Cox, J. R. & Willard, C. A. (Eds.) (1982). *Advances in argumentation research.* Carbondale: Southern Illinois University Press.

Crites, S. (1971). The narrative quality of experience. *Journal of the American Academy of Religion, 29,* 291-311.

Croghan, V.C. (1987). Perelman's universal audience as a critical tool. *Journal of the American Forensic Association, 23,* 147-57.

Dach, L. (1988, September 12). But before two contestants take a stand, they figure just how to stand. *New York Times,* p. A,19.

Daly, J. & Wiemann, J. (Eds.) (In press). *Communicating strategically: Strategies in interpersonal communication.* Hillsdale, NJ: Erlbaum.

Darnell, D. & Brockriede, W. (1976). *Persons communicating.* Englewood Cliffs, NJ: Prentice-Hall.

Darwin, C. (1967). *On the origin of species, a facsimile of the first edition.* New York: Atheneum (original work published in 1859).

Darwin, F. (Ed.) (1903). *More letters of Charles Darwin.* London: John Murray.

————. (Ed.) (1911). *The life and letters of Charles Darwin.* New York: D. Appleton and Co.

Dearin, R. D. (1969). The philosophical basis of Chaim Perelman's theory of rhetoric. *Quarterly Journal of Speech, 55,* 213-24.

Denzin, N. K. (1987). *The recovering alcoholic.* Newbury Park, CA: Sage.

————. (1988). The alcoholic self: Communication, ritual and identity transformation. In D. R. Maines & C. J. Couch (Eds.), *Communication and social structure,* pp. 59-74. Springfield: Charles C. Thomas.

Dervin, B. & Vight, M. J. (Eds.) (1982). *Progress in communication sciences* (Vol. 3). Norwood, NJ: Ablex.

Dewey, J. (1927). *The public and its problems.* New York: Holt.

————. (1980). *Art as experience.* New York: Wideview/Perigee (original work published in 1934).

Diamond, E. (1984). *The spot: The rise of political advertising on television.* Cambridge: MIT Press.

Dieckmann, H. (1973). Theories of beauty to the mid-nineteenth century. In P. P. Wiener (Ed.), *Dictionary of the history of ideas* (Vol. 1), 195-206. New York: Charles Scribner's Sons.

Dillard, J. P., Sergin, C. & Harden, J. M. (1989). Primary and secondary goals in the production of interpersonal influence messages. *Communication Monographs, 56,* 19-38.

Dionne, E. J., Jr. (1988, September 14). Polls show Bush setting agenda for campaign, *The New York Times*, A,29.

Doherty, W. J. (1982). Attributional style and negative problem solving in marriage. *Family Relations, 31*, 201-05.

Doherty, W. J. & Ryder, R. G. (1979). Locus of control, interpersonal trust, and assertive behavior among newlyweds. *Journal of Personality and Social Psychology, 37*, 2212-20.

Drew, E. (1985). *Campaign journal: The political events of 1983-1984*. New York: Macmillan Publishing Company.

Duck, S. & Gilmour, R. (Eds.) (1981). *Personal relationships 2: Developing personal relationships*. London: Academic.

Ede, L.S. (1981). Rhetoric versus philosophy: The role of the universal audience in Chaim Perelman's *The New Rhetoric*. *Central States Speech Journal, 32*, 118-25.

Edwards, P. (Ed.) (1967). *The encyclopedia of philosophy*, pp. 169-79. New York: Macmillan Publishing Company, Inc. and The Free Press.

Eemeren, F. H. van. (1986). Dialectical analysis as a normative reconstruction of argumentative discourse, *Text, 6*, 1-16.

_____. (1987a). Argumentation studies' five estates. In J.W. Wenzel (Ed.), *Argument and critical practices*, pp. 9-24. Annandale, VA: Speech Communication Association.

_____. (1987b). For reason's sake: Maximal argumentative analysis of discourse. In F. H. van Eemeren, R. Grootendorst, J. A. Blair & C. A. Willard (Eds.), *Argumentation: Perspectives and approaches, pp. 201-15. Dordrecht, Holland: Foris*.

_____. *(1988). The role of argument in the creation and maintenance of community*. Paper presented at the Conference on Argument and Community, Venice, Italy.

Eemeren, F. H. van & Grootendorst, R. (1984). *Speech acts in argumentative discussions*. Dordrecht, Holland: Foris.

_____. (1987). Fallacies in pragma-dialectical perspective. *Argumentation, 1*, 283-301.

Eemeren, F. H. van, Grootendorst, R., Blair, J. A. & Willard, C. A. (Eds.) (1987a). *Argumentation: Across the lines of discipline*. Dordrecht, Holland: Foris.

_____. (Eds.) (1987b). *Argumentation: Perspectives and approaches*. Dordrecht, Holland: Foris.

Ehninger, D. (1968). Validity as moral obligation. *Southern Speech Journal, 33*, 215-22.

_____. (1970). Argument as method: Its nature, its limitations, and its uses. *Speech Monographs, 37*, 101-10.

Ehninger, D. & Brockriede, W. (1963). *Decision by debate*. New York: Dodd, Mead & Company.

_____. (1978). *Decision by debate* (2nd ed.). New York: Harper & Row.

Ellis, D. G. and Donohue, W. A. (Eds.) (1986). *Contemporary issues in language and discourse processes*. Hillsdale, NJ: Erlbaum.

Ennis, R. (1982). Identifying implicit assumptions. *Synthese, 8*, 61-86.

Eubanks, R. T. (1986). An axiological analysis of Chaim Perelman's theory of practical reasoning. In J.L. Golden & J.J. Pilotta (Eds.), *Practical reasoning in human affairs*, pp. 69-84. Dordrecht, Holland: D. Riedel.

Evans, G. R. (1976). *Argumentum* and *argumentatio*: The development of a technical terminology up to c. 1150. *Classical Folia, 30*, 81-93.

Farrell, J. A. (1988, November 13). The electronic election, *The Boston Sunday Globe*, B, 1-12.

Farrell, T. B. (1982). Knowledge in time: Toward an extension of rhetorical form. In J. R. Cox & C. A. Willard (Eds.), *Advances in argumentation research*, pp. 123-53. Carbondale: Southern Illinois University Press.

Farrell, T. B. & Goodnight, G. T. (1981). Accidental rhetoric: The root metaphors of Three Mile Island. *Communication Monographs, 48*, 271-300.

Felmlee, D., Sprecher, S. & Bassin, E. (1988, July). *The dissolution of intimate relationships: A survival analysis*. Paper presented at the Third International Conference on Personal Relationships, Vancouver, Canada.

Finch, P. (Ed.) (1975). *Philosophical explorations*. Morristown, NJ: General Learning Press.

Fincham, L. (1985). Attribution processes in distressed and nondistressed couples 2: Responsibility for marital problems. *Journal of Abnormal Psychology, 94*, 183-90.

Fisher, W. R. (1973). Reaffirmation and subversion of the American dream. *Quarterly Journal of Speech, 59*, 160-67.

_____. (1978). Toward a logic of good reasons. *Quarterly Journal of Speech, 64*, 376-84.

_____. (1980). Rationality and the logic of good reasons. *Philosophy and Rhetoric, 13*, 121-30.

_____. (1984). Narration as human communication paradigm: The case of public moral argument. *Communication Monographs, 51*, 1-22.

_____. (1986). Judging the quality of audiences and narrative rationality. In J. L. Golden & J. J. Pilotta (Eds.), *Practical reasoning in human affairs*, pp. 85-104. Dordrecht, Holland: D. Riedel.

_____. (1987). *Human communication as narration: Toward a philosophy of reason, value, and action*. Columbia, SC: South Carolina University Press.

_____. (1989). Clarifying the narrative paradigm. *Communication Monographs, 56*, 55-58.

Fitzpatrick, M. A. (1988). *Between husbands and wives: Communication in marriage*. Newbury Park, CA: Sage.

Fitzpatrick, M. A. & Best, P. (1979). Dyadic adjustment in relational types: Consensus, cohesion, affectional expression, and satisfaction in enduring relationships. *Communication Monographs, 46*, 165-78.

Fitzpatrick, M. A., Fallis, S. & Vance, L. (1982). Multifunctional coding of conflict resolution strategies in marital dyads. *Family Relations, 31*, 611-70.

Ford, L. A. (1989). Fetching Good out of evil in AA: A Bormannean fantasy theme analysis of the Big Book of Alcoholics Anonymous. *Communication Quarterly, 37*, 1-15.

Foucault, M. (1972). *The archaeology of knowledge*. London: Tavistock.

_____. (1976). *The history of sexuality*. New York: Pantheon.

_____. (1977). *Discipline and punish*. New York: Random House.

Freeman, W. H. (Ed.) (1983). *Close relationships*. New York: W. H. Freeman.

Fuller, S. (1988). *Social epistemology*. Bloomington and Indianapolis: University of Indiana Press.

Galbraith, J. K. (1955). *Economics and the art of controversy*. New Brunswick, NJ: Rutgers University Press.

Galilei, G. (1967). *Dialogue concerning the two chief world systems*. (S. Drake, Trans.) Berkeley: University of California Press.

Garcia Marquez, G. (1988). *Love in the time of cholera*. New York: Alfred A. Knopf.

Gardner, H. (1988). Creativity: An interdisciplinary perspective. *Creativity Research Journal, 1*, 8-26.

Gellman, P. (1964). *The sober alcoholic*. New Haven: College and University Press.

Germond, J. W. & Witcover, J. (1985). *Wake us up when its over: Presidential politics 1984*. New York: Macmillan Publishing Company.

_____. (1988, June 11). The liberal-bashing of Dukakis. *The Boston Globe*, 15.

Ghiselin, M. T. (1969). *The triumph of the Darwinian method*. Berkeley: University of California Press.

Gibb, J. R. (1961). Defensive communication. *Journal of Communication, 11*, 141-48.

Gieryn, T. (1983). Boundary-work and the demarcation of science from non-science: Strains and interests in the professional ideologies of scientists. *American Sociological Review, 48*, 781-95.

Gillespie, N. C. (1979). *Charles Darwin and the problem of creation*. Chicago: University of Chicago Press.

Gilligan, C. (1982). *In a different voice*. Cambridge, MA: Harvard University Press.

Ginsberg, R. (Ed.) (1969). *The critique of war*. Chicago: Henry Regnery.

Glaser, B. G. & Strauss, A. L. (1967). *The discovery of grounded theory: Strategies for qualitative research*. New York: Aldine.

Golden, J. L. (1986). The universal audience revisited. In J. L. Golden & J. J. Pilotta (Eds.), *Practical reasoning in human affairs*, pp. 287-304. Dordrecht, Holland: D. Riedel.

Golden, J. L., Berquist, G. F. & Coleman, W. E. (Eds.) (1989). *The rhetoric of western thought* (4th ed.). Dubuque, IA: Kendall/Hunt.

Golden, J. L. & Pilotta, J. J. (Eds.) (1986). *Practical reasoning in human affairs*. Dordrecht, Holland: D. Riedel.

Goldman, P. & Fuller, T. (1985). *The quest for the presidency 1984*. New York: Bantam Books.

Goodman, N. (1972). *Problems and projects*. Indianapolis: Bobbs-Merrill.

_____. (1976). *Languages of art*. Indianapolis: Hackett.

_____. (1978). *Ways of worldmaking*. Indianapolis: Hackett.

_____. (1983). *Fact, fiction and forecast* (4th ed.). Cambridge, MA: Harvard University Press.

Goodman, P. (1962). *The community of scholars*. New York: Random House.

Goodnight, G. T. (1980). The liberal and conservative presumptions: On political philosophy and the foundation of public argument. In J. Rhodes & S. Newell (Eds.), *Proceedings of the Summer Conference on Argumentation*, pp. 304-37. Washington, DC: Speech Communication Association.

Goodnight, G. T. (1982). The personal, technical, and public spheres of argument: A speculative inquiry into the art of public deliberation. *Journal of the American Forensic Association, 18*, 214-27.

Goodnight, G. T. (1987a). Argumentation, criticism, and rhetoric: A comparison of modern and post modern stances toward humanistic inquiry. In J. W. Wenzel (Ed.), *Argument and critical practices*, pp. 61-68. Annandale, VA: Speech Comunication Association.

————. (1987b). Generational argument. In F. H. van Eemeren, R. Grootendorst, J. A. Blair & C. A. Willard (Eds.), *Argumentation: Across the lines of discipline*, pp. 129-44. Dordrecht, Holland: Foris.

————. (1987c). Public discourse. *Critical Studies in Mass Communication, 4*, 428-32.

————. (1988). *Communities of argument in time: When being reasonable is not enough*. Paper presented at the Conference on Argument and Community, Venice, Italy.

Goody, E. N. (Ed.) (1978). *Questions and politeness: Strategies in social interaction*. London: Cambridge University Press.

Gottman, J. M. (1979). *Marital interaction: Experimental investigations*. New York: Academic Press.

————. (1982). Emotional responsiveness in marital conversations. *Journal of Communication, 32*, 108-20.

Gottman, J. M. & Krokoff, L. J. (1989). Marital interaction: A longitudinal view. *Journal of Counseling and Clinical Psychology, 57*, 47-52.

Gough, J. & Tindale, C. (1985). "Hidden" or "missing" premises. *Informal Logic, 7*, 99.

Gouldner, A. (1983). *The future of intellectuals and the rise of the new class*. New York: Seabury Press.

Govier, T. (1988). *A practical study of argument* (2nd ed). Belmont, CA: Wadsworth.

Greene, J. (1961). Munitions: A way of life. *Nation, 193*, 187.

Griel, A. L. & Rudy, D. R. (1983). Conversion to the world view of alcoholics anonymous: A refinement of conversion theory. *Qualitative Sociology, 6*, 5-28.

Gronbeck, B. E. (1984). Functional and dramaturgical theories of presidential campaigning. *Presidential Studies Quarterly, 14*, 486-99.

————. (Ed.) (1989). *Spheres of argument: Proceedings of the sixth SCA/AFA conference on argumentation*. Annandale, VA: Speech Communication Association.

Gross, A. G. (1987). A tale twice told: The rhetoric of discovery in the case of DNA. In J.W. Wenzel (Ed.), *Argument and critical practices*, pp. 491-98. Annandale, VA: Speech Communication Association.

Gutteridge, M. (1987). First sit down and play the piano beautifully: Reading well is thinking well. *Informal Logic, 9*, 81-91.

Habermas, J. (1970). *Toward a rational society*. Boston: Beacon.

————. (1971). *Knowledge and practice*. Boston: Beacon.

————. (1973). *Theory and practice*. Boston: Beacon.

————. (1975). *Legitimation crises*. Boston: Beacon.

————. (1979). *Communication and the evolution of society*. (T. McCarthy, Trans.). Boston: Beacon.

Habermas, J. (1984). *The theory of communicative action, I: Reason and the rationalization of society*. (T. McCarthy, Trans.). Boston: Beacon.

Hamblin, C. L. (1970). *Fallacies*. London: Methuen.

Hample, D. (1980). A cognitive view of argument. *Journal of the American Forensic Association, 16*, 151-58.

———. (1985). A third perspective on argument. *Philosophy and Rhetoric, 18*, 1-22.

———. (1988). Argument: Public and private, social and cognitive. *Argumentation and Advocacy, 25*, 13-19.

Hample, D. & Dallinger, J. (1987). Individual differences in cognitive editing standards. *Human Communication Research, 14*, 123-44.

Hare, R. M. (1975). Philosophy at Oxford. In P. Finch (Ed.), *Philosophical Explorations*, pp. 730-40. Morristown, NJ: General Learning Press.

Haskell, T. L. (Ed.) (1984). *The authority of experts*. Bloomington: Indiana University Press.

Heath, R. L. (1980). Corporate advocacy: An application of speech communication perspectives and skills—and more. *Communication Education, 29*, 370-77.

Heath, R. L. & Nelson, R. A. (1986). *Issues Management*. Beverly Hills, CA: Sage.

Henry, W. A. (1985). *Visions of America: How we saw the 1984 election*. Boston: The Atlantic Monthly Press.

Himmelfarb, G. (1959). *Darwin and the Darwinian revolution*. New York: Doubleday.

Hitchcock, D. (1983). *Critical thinking: A guide to evaluating information*. Toronto: Methuen.

———. (1985). Enthymematic arguments. *Informal Logic, 7*, 89.

Hoban, J. L. (1980). Rhetorical rituals of rebirth. *Quarterly Journal of Speech, 66*, 275-88.

Hocker, J. H. & Wilmot, W. W. (1985). *Interpersonal conflict* (2nd ed.). Dubuque, IA: Wm. C. Brown.

Hollihan, T. A., Riley, P. & Freadhoff, K. (1986). Arguing for justice: An analysis of arguing in small claims court. *Journal of the American Forensic Association, 22*, 187-95.

Hopper, R., Koch, S. & Mandelbaum, J. (1986). Conversation analysis methods. In D. G. Ellis & W. A. Donohue (Eds.), *Contemporary issues in language and discourse processes*, pp. 169-88. Hillsdale, NJ: Erlbaum.

Horn, R. (Ed.) (1983a). *Trialectics: Toward a practical logic of unity*. Lexington, MA.: Information Resources, Inc.

———. (1983b). An overview of trialectics with applications to psychology and public policy. In R. Horn (Ed.), *Trialectics: Toward a practical logic of unity*, pp. 1-38. Lexington, MA: Information Resources, Inc.

———. (1984). Traps of traditional logic and dialectics: What they are and how to avoid them, pp. 41-76. Lexington, MA: Lexington Institute Monograph 84-102. pp. 41-76.

Huston, T. L., Surra, C. A., Fitzgerald, N. M. & Cate, R. M. (1981). From courtship to marriage: Mate selection as an interpersonal process. In S. Duck & R. Gilmour (Eds.), *Personal relationships 2: Developing personal relationships*, pp. 53-88. London: Academic.

Hynes, T. (1988). *U. S. Supreme Court notions of the military as community: Argument defined as subversive*. Paper presented at the Conference on Argument and Community, Venice, Italy.

Ichazo, O. (1976). *The human process for enlightenment and freedom*. New York: The Arica Institute.

Ichazo, O. (1982). *Between metaphysics and protoanalysis*. New York: The Arica Institute.

Infante, D. A. (1981). Trait argumentativeness as a predictor of communicative behavior in situations requiring argument. *Central States Speech Journal, 32,* 265-72.

_____. (1988). *Arguing constructively*. Prospect Heights, IL: Waveland Press, Inc.

Infante, D. A. & Rancer, A. S. (1982). A conceptualization and measure of argumentativeness. *Journal of Personality Assessment, 46,* 72-80.

Infante, D. A. & Wigley, C. J. (1986). Verbal aggressiveness: An interpersonal model and measure. *Communication Monographs, 53,* 61-69.

Irvine, W. (1959). *Apes, angels, and victorians*. New York: Meridian Books.

Jackson, S. (1983). The arguer in interpersonal argument: Pros and cons of individual-level analysis. In D. Zarefsky, M. O. Sillars & J. Rhodes (Eds.), *Argument in Transition*, pp. 631-37. Annandale, VA: Speech Communication Association.

_____. (1986). Building a case for claims about discourse structure. In D. G. Ellis & W. A. Donohue (Eds.), *Contemporary issues in language and discourse processes*, pp. 129-48. Hillsdale, NJ: Erlbaum.

_____. (1987). Rational and pragmatic aspects of argument. In F. H. van Eemeren, R. Grootendorst, J. A. Blair & C. A. Willard (Eds.), *Argumentation: Across the lines of discipline*, pp. 217-28. Dordrecht, Holland: Foris.

Jackson, S. & Jacobs, S. (1980). Structure of conversational argument: Pragmatic bases for the enthymeme. *Quarterly Journal of Speech, 66,* 251-65.

Jacobs, S. (1987). The management of disagreement in conversation. In F.H. van Eemeren, R. Grootendorst, J.A. Blair & C.A. Willard (Eds.), *Argumentation: Across the lines of discipline*, pp. 229-39. Dordrecht, Holland: Foris.

Jacobs, S. & Jackson, S. (1982). *Conversational argument: A discourse analytic approach*. In J. R. Cox & C. A. Willard (Eds.), pp. 205-37. Carbondale: Southern Illinois University Press.

_____. (1983). Strategy and structure in conversational influence attempts. *Communication Monographs, 50,* 285-04.

Jameson, F. (1971). *Marxism and form: Twentieth century dialectical theories of literature*. Princeton: Princeton University Press.

Jamieson, K. H. (1984). *Packaging the presidency*. New York: Oxford University Press.

Jamieson, K. H. & Birdsell, D. S. (1988). *Presidential debates: The challenge of creating an informed electorate*. New York: Oxford University Press.

Jenkins, I. (1973). Art for art's sake. In P. P. Wiener (Ed.), *Dictionary of the history of ideas* (Vol.1), pp. 108-11. New York: Charles Scribner's Sons.

Jensen, J.V. (1981). *Argumentation: Reasoning in communication*. New York: D. Van Nostrand.

Johnson, R. H. (1981). Charity begins at home. *Informal Logic, 7,* 4-9.

Johnson, R. H. & Blair, J. A. (1983). *Logical self-defense* (2nd ed). Toronto: McGraw-Hill Ryerson.

Johnstone, H. W., Jr. (1978). *Validity and rhetoric in philosophical argument*. University Park, PA: Pennsylvania State University Press.

Johnstone, H. W., Jr. (1982). Bilaterality in argument and communication. In J. R. Cox & C. A. Willard (Eds.), *Advances in argumentation research*, pp. 95-102. Carbondale: Southern Illinois University Press.

Jones, R. K. (1970). Sectarian characteristics of alcoholics anonymous. *Sociology, 4*, 181-84.

Jung, C. G. (1973). *Four archetypes* (R.F.C. Hull Trans.). Princeton: Princeton University Press.

Kahane, H. (1984). *Logic and contemporary rhetoric: The use of reason in everyday life* (4th ed.). Belmont, CA: Wadsworth.

Kant, I. (1987). *Critique of judgment* (Werner S. Pluhar, Trans.). Indianapolis: Hackett (original work published in 1790).

Kelly, C., Huston, T. L. & Cate, B. M. (1985). Premarital relationship correlates of the erosion of satisfaction in marriage. *Journal of Social and Personal Relationships, 2*, 167-78.

Kelly, D. (1987). The imitation of models and the uses of *argumenta* in topical invention. *Argumentation, 1*, 365-77.

Kenney, C. & Turner, R. L. (1989, January 8). The iceman cometh. *The Boston Sunday Globe Magazine*, 17-19, 41-47.

Kluback, W. (1980). The new rhetoric as a philosophical system. *Journal of the American Forensic Association, 17*, 73-79.

Kluback, W. & Becker, M. (1979). The significance of Chaim Perelman's philosophy of rhetoric. *Revue Internationale De Philosophie, 127-28*, 33-46.

Kraus, S. (Ed.) (1962). *The great debates: Background, perspective, effects.* Bloomington: Indiana University Press.

_____. (Ed.) (1979). *The great debates: Carter vs. Ford, 1976.* Bloomington: Indiana University Press.

Krueger, D. L. & Smith, R. (1982). Decision-making patterns of couples: A sequential analysis. *Journal of Communication, 32*, 121-34.

Kuhn, T. S. (1959). *The copernican revolution.* New York: Vintage Books.

_____. (1970a). *The structure of scientific revolutions.* Chicago: University of Chicago Press.

_____. (1970b). Reflections on my critics. In I. Lakatos & A. Musgrave (Eds.), *Criticism and the growth of knowledge*, pp. 231-78. Cambridge University Press.

_____. (1977). *The essential tension.* Chicago: University of Chicago Press.

Kurtz, E. (1982). When A. A. works: The intellectual significance of alcoholics anonymous. *Journal of Studies on Alcohol, 43*, 38-80.

Kvale, S. (1976). Facts and dialectics. In J. Rychlak (Ed.), *Dialectic: Humanistic rationale for behavior and development*, pp. 87-106. Basel, Switzerland: Karger.

Lakatos, I. & Musgrave, A. (Eds.) (1970). *Criticism and the growth of knowledge.* Cambridge: Cambridge University Press.

Lake, R. & Keough, C. M., (1985). Exploring the boundaries of technical and social knowledge: A case study in arbitration arguments. In J. R. Cox, M. O. Sillars & G. B. Walker (Eds.), *Argument and social practice*, pp. 483-96. Annandale, VA: Speech Communication Association.

Lakoff, G. & Johnson, M. (1980). *Metaphors we live by.* Chicago: University of Chicago Press.

Lash, Mike. *Serial arguments.* Unpublished manuscript. University of Northern Colorado.

LeFevre, K. B. (1987). *Invention as a social act.* Carbondale, IL: Southern Illinois University Press.

Leon, R. (1983). Tylenol fights back. *Public Relations Journal, 39*, 10-14.

Lightman, D. (1988, September 23). Democrat is hurt by liberal tag. *Hartford Courant*, 1-A22.

Lippmann, W. (1922). *Public opinion*. New York: Harcourt, Brace.

———. (1925). *The phantom public*. New York: Macmillan.

———. (1955). *Essays in the public philosophy*. Boston: Little, Brown.

Lonergan, J. F. (1958). *Insight*. New York: Harper & Row.

Longinus. (1906). *On the sublime* (A. O. Prickard, Trans.). London: Oxford University Press (originally published in 1907).

Lyne, J. (1985). Rhetorics of inquiry. *Quarterly Journal of Speech, 71*, 65-73.

Lynn, J. (1987). Learning the lessons of Lysenko: Biology, politics, and rhetoric in historical controversy.'' In J. W. Wenzel (Ed.), *Argument and critical practices*, pp. 507-12. Annandale, VA: Speech Communication Association.

Lyotard, J. F. (1984). *The postmodern condition*. Minneapolis: University of Minnesota Press.

Mackie, J. L. (1967). Fallacies. In P. Edwards (Ed.),*The encyclopedia of philosophy* (Vol. 3), pp. 169-79. New York: Macmillan Publishing Company, Inc. and The Free Press.

Maines, D. R. & Couch, C. J. (Eds.) (1988). *Communication and Social Structure*. Springfield: Charles C. Thomas.

Mannheim, K. (1936). *Ideology and utopia*. (L. Wirth & E. Shils, Trans.). New York: Harcourt, Brace and World.

Martin, R. W. & Scheerhorn, D.R. (1985). What are conversational arguments? Toward a natural language user's perspective. In J. R. Cox, M. O. Sillars & G. B. Walker (Eds.), *Argument and social practice*, pp. 705-22. Annandale, VA: Speech Communication Association.

Martel, M. (1983). *Political campaign debates: Images, strategies, and tactics*. New York: Longman.

Marvin, W. (1988, November 14-20). "It's Willie Horton" cartoon. *Washington Post National Weekly*.

McCann, C. D. & Higgins, E. T. (1987). *Goals and orientations in interpersonal relations: How intrapersonal discrepancies produce a negative affect*. Unpublished paper, York University.

McCloskey, D. N. (1985). *The rhetoric of economics*. Madison: University of Wisconsin Press.

———. (1987). Rhetoric within the Citadel. In J. W. Wenzel (Ed.), *Argument and critical practices*, pp. 485-90. Annandale, VA: Speech Communication Association.

McGee, M. C. (1975). In search of the "people": A rhetorical alternative. *Quarterly Journal of Speech, 61*, 235-49.

McGee, M. C. (1978). "Not men but measures": The origins and import of an ideological principle. *Quarterly Journal of Speech, 64*, 141-54.

———. (1980). The "ideograph": The link between rhetoric and ideology. *Quarterly Journal of Speech, 66*, 1-16.

McGee, M. C. & Lyne, J. (1987). What are nice folks like you doing in a place like this? Some entailments of treating knowledge claims rhetorically. In J. Nelson, A. Megill & D. McCloskey (Eds.), *The rhetoric of the human sciences*, pp. 381-406. Madison: University of Wisconsin Press.

McKay, M., Davis, M. & Fanning P. (1983). *Messages: The communication book.*
Oakland, CA: New Harbinger.

McKeon, R. (Ed.) (1941). *The basic works of Aristotle.* New York: Random House.

McKerrow, R. (1977). Rhetorical validity: An analysis of three perspectives on the
justification of rhetorical argument. *Journal of the American Forensic Association,
13*, 133-41.

––––––. (1980). Argument communities: A quest for distinctions. In J. Rhodes &
S. Newell (Eds.), *Proceedings at the Summer Conference on Argumentation,*
pp. 214-27. Washington, DC: Speech Communication Association.

––––––. (Ed.) (1982). *Explorations in rhetoric: Studies in honor of Douglas Ehninger.*
Glenview, IL: Scott, Foresman.

––––––. (1988). *Argument and the creation of a nationalist identity.* Paper presented
at the Conference on Argument and Community, Venice, Italy.

McLaughlin, M. L. (1984). *Conversation: How talk is organized.* Beverly Hills, CA:
Sage.

––––––. (Ed.) (1987). *Communication yearbook 10.* Newbury Park, CA: Sage.

McNeil-Lehrer News Hour (1988, March 17). Public Broadcasting System.

Meier, R. (Ed.) (1989). *Norms in argumentation.* Dordrecht, Holland: Foris.

Melman, S. (1971). After the military-industrial complex? *Bulletin of the Atomic
Scientists, 21*, 7.

Meyers, R. A. & Seibold, D. R. (1987). Interactional and noninteractional perspectives
on interpersonal argument: Implications for the study of group decision-making.
In F. H. van Eemeren, R. Grootendorst, J. A. Blair & C. A. Willard (Eds.),
Argumentation: Perspectives and approaches, pp. 205-14. Dordrecht, Holland:
Foris.

Miller, G. R. (Ed.) (1976). *Explorations in interpersonal communication.* Beverly
Hills, CA: Sage.

Miller, P. C., Lefcourt, H. M., Holmes, J. G., Ware, E. E. & Saleh, N. E. (1986).
Marital locus of control and marital problem solving. *Journal of Personality and
Social Psychology, 51*, 161-69.

Morton, T. C., Alexander, J. F. & Altman, I. (1976). Communication and relationship
definition. In G. R. Miller (Ed.), *Explorations in interpersonal communication*,
pp. 105-26. Beverly Hills, CA: Sage.

Nelson, J. S. (1983). Models, statistics, and other tropes of politics: Or, whatever
happened to argumentation in political science? In D. Zarefsky, M. O. Sillars
& J. Rhodes (Eds.), *Argument in transition*, pp. 213-29. Annandale, VA: Speech
Communication Association.

Nelson, J. S. & Megill, A. (1986). Rhetoric of inquiry: Projects and prospects.
Quarterly Journal of Speech, 72, 20-37.

Nelson, J., Megill, A. & McCloskey, D. (Eds.) (1987). *The rhetoric of the human
sciences.* Madison: University of Wisconsin Press.

New York Times (1974). *The White House transcripts.* New York: Bantam.

––––––. (1988, September 26). Transcript of the first TV debate between Bush and
Dukakis. p. A, 18.

––––––. (1988, October 14). Transcript of the second debate between Bush and
Dukakis. p. A, 14.

Newell, S. E. & Stutman, R. K. (1982). *A qualitative approach to social confrontation: Identifying constraints and facilitators*. Paper presented at the annual meeting of the Speech Communication Association.

Newman, R. (1970). Under the veneer: Nixon's Vietnam speech of November 3, 1969. *Quarterly Journal of Speech, 56*, 168-78.

Nichols, M. H. (1963). *Rhetoric and Criticism*. Baton Rouge: Louisiana State University Press.

_____. (1971). Rhetoric and style. In J. Strekla (Ed.), *Patterns of literary style*. University Park: The Pennsylvania State University Press.

Nickerson, R. S., Perkins, D. N. & Smith, E. E. (1985). *The teaching of thinking*. Hillsdale, NJ: Erlbaum.

Nyhan, D. (1988, November 1). The demonizing of Dukakis. *Boston Globe*, p. 13.

O'Keefe, B. J. (1988). The logic of message design: Individual differences in reasoning about communication. *Communication Monographs, 55*, 80-103.

O'Keefe, D. J. (1977). Two concepts of argument. *Journal of the American Forensic Association, 13*, 121-28.

_____. (1982). The concepts of argument and arguing. In J. R. Cox & C. A. Willard (Eds.), *Advances in argumentation research*, pp. 3-23. Carbondale: Southern Illinois University Press.

Orren, G. R. & Polsby, N.W. (1987). *Media and momentum: The New Hampshire primary and nomination politics*. Chatham, NJ: Chatham House Publishers, Inc.

Osborn, M. (1986). Rhetorical depiction. In H.W. Simons & A.A. Aghazarian (Eds.), *Form, genre, and the study of political discourse*, pp. 79-107. Columbia: University of South Carolina Press.

Parrish, W. M. (1954). The study of speeches. In W.M. Parrish & M. Hochmuth (Eds.), *American speeches*, pp. 1-20. New York: Longmans, Green.

Parrish, W. M. & Hochmuth, M. (Eds.) (1954). *American speeches*. New York: Longmans, Green.

Patterson, T. E. & McClure, R. D. (1976). *The unseeing eye: The myth of television power in national politics*. New York: G.P. Putnam.

Peckham, M. (Ed.) (1959). *Charles Darwin, the origin of species: A variorum text*. Philadelphia: University of Pennslvania Press.

Pepper, S. C. (1942). *World hypotheses*. Berkeley: University of California Press.

Perelman, Ch. (1955). How do we apply reason to values? *Journal of Philosophy, 52*, 797-802.

_____. (1961). Value judgments, justifications, and argumentation. *Revue Internationale De Philosophie, 58*, 327-35.

_____. (1963). *The idea of justice and the problem of argument*. London: Routledge and Kegan Paul.

_____. (1967). *Justice*. New York: Random House.

_____. (1968). Rhetoric and philosophy. *Philosophy and Rhetoric, 1*, 15-24.

_____. (1970). The new rhetoric: A theory of practical reasoning (E. Griffin-Collart & O. Bird, Trans.). In R. Hutchins & M. Adler (Eds.), *Great Ideas Today*, pp. 272-312. Chicago: Encyclopedia Britannica.

_____. (1979). *The new rhetoric and the humanities: Essays on rhetoric and its applications*. Dordrecht, Holland: D. Riedel.

_____. (1980). *Justice, law, and argument: Essays on moral and legal reasoning*. Dordrecht, Holland: D. Riedel.

Perelman, Ch. (1982a). *The realm of rhetoric*. Notre Dame, IN: University of Notre Dame Press.

———. (1982b). Philosophy and Rhetoric. In J. R. Cox & C. A. Willard (Eds.), *Advances in argument research*, p. 287-97. Carbondale: Southern Illinois University Press.

———. (1984a). The new rhetoric and the rhetoricians: Remembrances and comments. *Quarterly Journal of Speech, 70,* 188-96.

———. (1984b). Rhetoric and politics. *Philosophy and Rhetoric, 17,* 129-34.

Perelman, Ch. & Olbrechts-Tyteca, L. M. (1969). *The new rhetoric: A treatise on argument* (J. Wilkinson and P. Weaver, Trans.). Notre Dame, IN: University of Notre Dame Press (original work published in 1958).

Perlman, D. & Duck, S. (Eds.) (1987). *Intimate relationships: Development, dynamics, and deterioration*. Newbury Park, CA: Sage.

Peterson, D. R. (1983). Conflict. In W. H. Freeman (Ed.), *Close relationships*, pp. 360-96. New York: W. H. Freeman.

Peterson, H. (Ed.) (1965). *A treasury of the world's great speeches*. New York: Simon and Schuster.

Petrunik, M. G. (1972). Seeing the light: A study of conversion to alcoholics anonymous. *Journal of Voluntary Action Research, 1,* 30-38.

Philipsen, G. (1975). Speaking "like a man" in Teamsterville: Culture patterns of role enactment in an urban neighborhood. *Quarterly Journal of Speech, 61,* 13-22.

Phillips, L. & Norris, S. (1987). Reading well is thinking well. In N. Burbules (Ed.), *Philosophy of education, 1986,* pp. 187-97. Normal, IL: Philosophy of Education Society.

Pomerantz, A. (1984). Agreeing and disagreeing with assessments: Some features of preferred/dispreferred turn shapes. In J. Atkinson & J. Heritage (Eds.), *Structures of social action*, pp. 57-101. Cambridge: Cambridge University Press.

Popper, K. (1963). *Conjectures and refutations*. New York: Harper & Row.

Rasmussen, K. (1974). *Implication of argumentation for aesthetic experience: A transactional perspective*. Unpublished Ph.D. dissertation, University of Colorado at Boulder.

Rasmussen, K. & Capaldi, C. (1988). *Transcriptions of sixteen speakers made at regular meetings of A.A. in Los Angeles and Orange County, California* (available from the authors located at California State University: Long Beach).

Raush, M. L., Barry, W. A., Mertel, W. A. & Swain, M. A. (1974). *Communication, conflict, and marriage*. San Francisco: Jossey-Bass.

Ray, J. W. (1978). Perelman's universal audience. *Quarterly Journal of Speech, 64,* 361-75.

Reilly, F. E. (1970). *Charles Peirce's theory of scientific method*. New York: Fordham University Press.

Rescher, N. (1973). *The primacy of practice*. Oxford: Oxford University Press.

———. (1977a). *Methodological pragmatism*. Oxford: Oxford University Press.

———. (1977b). *Dialectics*. Albany: State University of New York Press.

———. (1985). *The strife of systems: An essay on the grounds and implications of philosophical diversity*. Pittsburgh, PA: University of Pennsylvania Press.

———. (1988). *Rationality: A philosophical inquiry into the nature and the rationale of reason*. New York: Oxford University Press.

Ressler, J. A. (1982). Crisis communications. *Public Relations Quarterly, 27*, 8-10.

Rhodes, J. & Newell, S. (Eds.) (1980). *Proceedings of the Summer Conference on Argumentation*. Washington, DC: Speech Communication Association.

Ricoeur, P. (1977). *The rule of metaphor: Multi-disciplinary studies in the creation of language* (Robert Czerny, K. McLaughlin & J. Costello, Trans.). Toronto: University of Toronto Press (original work published in 1975).

Rieke, R. D. & Sillars, M. O. (1984). *Argumentation and the decision making process*. Glenview, IL: Scott Foresman.

Robert, M. (1982). *Managing conflict from the inside out*. Austin, TX: Learning Concepts.

Rokeach, M. (1970). *Beliefs, attitudes, and values*. San Francisco: Jossey-Bass.

Roloff, M. E. (1987). Communication and conflict. In C. Berger & S. Chaffe (Eds.), *Handbook of communication science*, pp. 484-534. Beverly Hills, CA: Sage.

Rorty, R. (1982). Philosophy and the mirror of nature. Princeton, NJ: Princeton University Press.

Rothberg, D. (1988, September 26). Dukakis slugs it out. *The Huntington* [W. VA.] *Herald Dispatch*, p. 1.

Rowland, R. (1982). The influence of purpose on fields of argument, *Journal of the American Forensic Association, 18*, 228-45.

Rusbult, C. E. (1987). Responses to dissatisfaction in close relationships: The exit-voice-loyalty-neglect model. In D. Perlman & S. Duck (Eds.), *Intimate relationships: Development, dynamics and deterioration*, pp. 209-37. Newbury Park, CA: Sage.

Rusbult, C. E., Johnson, D. J. & Morrow, G. D. (1986). Impact of couple patterns of problem-solving on distress and nondistress in dating relationships. *Journal of Personality and Social Psychology, 50*, 744-53.

Rushing, J. (1989). Evolution of the "the new frontier" in Alien and Aliens: Patriarchal co-option of the feminine archetype. *Quarterly Journal of Speech, 75*, 1-24.

Rushing, J. & Frentz, T. (1980). *The Deer Hunter:* Rhetoric of the warrior. *Quarterly Journal of Speech, 66*, 392-06.

Rychlak, J. (Ed.) (1976). *Dialectic: Humanistic Rationale for Behavior and Development*. Basel, Switzerland: Karger.

Rybacki, K. C. & Rybacki, D.J. (1986). *Advocacy and opposition*. Englewood Cliffs, NJ: Prentice-Hall, Inc.

Ryle, G. (1971). *Collected papers* (Vol. 2). London: Hutchinson.

Schneir, M. (Ed.) (1972). *Feminism: The essential historical writings*. New York: Random House.

Schouls, P. A. (1969). Communication, argumentation, and presupposition in philosophy. *Philosophy and Rhetoric, 2*, 183-99.

Schuetz, J. (1986). Dimensions of teaching: The methods, relationships, and ideas of Wayne Brockriede. *Communication Quarterly, 34*, 357-64.

Schwartz, B. (1986). *The battle for human nature*. New York: W. W. Norton and Company.

Scott, R. L. (1967). On viewing rhetoric as epistemic. *Central States Speech Journal, 18*, 9-17.

————. (1968). A rhetoric of facts: Arthur Larson as a persuader. *Speech Monographs, 35*, 109-21.

Scott, R. L. (1976). On viewing rhetoric as epistemic: Ten years later. *Central States Speech Journal, 27,* 258-66.

———. (1987). Argument as a critical art: Re-forming understanding. *Argumentation, 1,* 57-71.

Scriven, M. (1976). *Reasoning.* New York: McGraw-Hill.

Scult, A. (1976). Perelman's universal audience: One perspective. *Central States Speech Journal, 27,* 176-80.

———. (1985). A note on the range and utility of the universal audience. *Journal of the American Forensic Association, 22,* 83-87.

Seibold, D. R. & Spitzberg, B. H. (1982). Attribution theory and research: Review and implications for communication. In B. Dervin & M. J. Vight (Eds.), *Progress in communication sciences* (Vol. 3), pp. 85-125. Norwood, NJ: Ablex.

Shore, J. (1981). Use of paradox in the treatment of alcoholism. *Health and Social Work, 6,* 12-13.

Sillars, A. L. (1986). *Procedures for coding interpersonal conflict* (revised). Unpublished manuscript, University of Montana.

Sillars, A. L., Pike, G. R., Jones, T. S. & Redmon, K. (1983). Communication and conflict in marriage. In R. N. Bostrom (Ed.), *Communication Yearbook 7,* pp. 414-29. Newbury Park, CA: Sage.

Sillars, A. L., Weisberg, J., Burgraff, C. S. & Zietlow, P. H. (1989). *Communication and understanding revisited: Married couples' understanding and recall of conversation.* Unpublished paper, University of Montana.

Sillars, A. L., Wilmot, W. W. & Hocker, J. C. (In press). Communication strategies in conflict and mediation. In J. Daly & J. Wiemann (Eds.), *Communicating strategically: Styrategies in interpersonal communication.* Hillsdale, NJ: Erlbaum.

Sillars, M. O. (1973). Audiences, social values, and the analysis of argument. *Speech Teacher, 22,* 291-303.

———. (1985). *Chaim Perelman, rhetoric and values.* Paper presented at the annual meeting of the Speech Communication Association, Denver, CO.

Sillars, M. O. & Ganer, P. (1982). *Values and beliefs: A systematic basis for argumentation.* In J.R. Cox & C.A. Willard (Eds.), *Advances in argumentation research,* pp. 184-201. Carbondale: Southern Illinois University Press.

Simons, H. W. (Ed.) (1989). *Rhetoric in the human sciences.* Newbury Park, CA: Sage.

———. (Ed.) (In press). *The rhetorical turn.* Chicago: University of Chicago Press.

Simons, H. W. & Aghazarian, A. A. (Eds.) (1986). *Form, genre, and the study of political discourse.* Columbia: University of South Carolina Press.

Sircello, G. (1975). *A new theory of beauty.* Princeton, NJ: Princeton University Press.

Skopec, E. Wm. (1982). The theory of expression in selected eighteenth-century rhetorics. In R. McKerrow (Ed.), *Explorations in Rhetoric: Studies in honor of Douglas Ehninger,* pp. 119-36. Dallas: Scott, Foresman.

Sloane, T. O. (1985). *Donne, Milton, and the end of humanistic rhetoric.* Berkeley: University of California Press.

Sproule, J. M. (1986). The roots of American argumentation theory: A review of landmark works, 1978-1932. *Journal of the American Forensic Association, 23,* 110-15.

Stafford, L., Burggraf, C. S. & Yost, S. (1988). *Short term and long term conversational memory: A comparison of stranger and marital dyads*. Paper presented at the Speech Communication Association convention, New Orleans, LA.

Steele, E. D. (1962). Social values, the enthymeme, and speech criticism. *Western Speech, 26*, 70-75.

Steinkraus, W. E. (1969). War and the philosopher's duty. In R. Ginsberg (Ed.), *The critique of war*, pp. 3-29. Chicago: Henry Regnery.

Stich, S. & Nisbett, R. (1984). Expertise, justification, and the psychology of inductive reasoning. In T. L. Haskell (Ed.), *The authority of experts*, pp. 226-241. Bloomington: Indiana University Press.

Strekla, J. (Ed.) (1971). *Patterns of literary style*. University Park: The Pennsylvania State University Press.

Summers, D. (1987). *The judgment of sense: Renaissance naturalism and the rise of aesthetics*. Cambridge: Cambridge University Press.

Swerdlow, J. (Ed.) (1987). *Presidential debates: 1988 and beyond*. Washington, DC: Congressional Quarterly Press.

Taylor, C. (1971). Interpretation and the sciences of man. *Review of Metaphysics, 25*, 1-45.

Therborne, G. (1980). *The ideology of power and the power of ideology*. London: Verso.

Thomas, D. A. (Ed.) (1980). *Argumentation as a way of knowing*. Falls Church, VA: Speech Communication Association.

Thomas, S. (1981). *Practical reasoning in natural language* (2nd ed.). Englewood Cliffs, NJ: Prentice-Hall.

Thompson, E. P. (1986, March 1). Look who's really behind star wars. *Nation, 242*(8), 233.

Thune, C. E. (1977). Alcoholism and archetypal past. *Journal of Studies on Alcohol, 38*, 74-88.

Ting-Toomey, S. (1983). An analysis of verbal communication patterns in high and low marital adjustment groups. *Human Communication Research, 9*, 306-19.

Toulmin S. (1958). *The uses of argument*. Cambridge: Cambridge University Press.

_____. (1989). Logic and the criticism of arguments. In J. L. Golden, G. F. Berquist & W. E. Coleman (Eds.), *The rhetoric of western thought* (4th ed.), pp. 374-88. Dubuque, IA: Kendall/Hunt.

Toulmin, S. E., Rieke, R. & Janik, A. (1984). *An introduction to reasoning* (2nd Ed.). New York: Macmillan.

Trapp, R. (1981). Special report on argumentation: Introduction. *Western Journal of Speech Communication, 45*, 111-17.

Trapp, R. (1983). Generic characteristics of argumentation in everyday discourse. In D. Zarefsky, M. O. Sillars & J. Rhodes (Eds.), *Argument in transition*, pp. 516-38. Annandale, VA: Speech Communication Association.

_____. (1986). The role of disagreement in interactional argument. *Journal of the American Forensic Association, 23*, 23-41.

Trapp, R. & Benoit, P. J. (1987). An interpretive perspective on argumentation: A research editorial. *Western Journal of Speech Communication, 51*, 417-30.

Trapp, R. & Hoff, N. (1985). A model of serial argument in interpersonal relationships. *Journal of the American Forensic Association, 22*, 1-11.

Trapp, R., Hoff, N. & Chandler, K. (1987). *Argument in interpersonal communication*. Paper presented at the Speech Communication Association convention, Boston, MA.

Trapp, R., Yingling, J. & Wanner, J. (1987). Measuring argumentative competence. In F. H. van Eemeren, R. Grootendorst, J.A. Blair & C. A. Willard (Eds.), *Argumentation: Across the lines of discipline*, pp. 253-61. Dordrecht, Holland: Foris.

Truth, S. (1972). Ain't I a woman. In M. Schneir (Ed.), *Feminism: The essential historical writings*, pp. 94-95. New York: Random House.

Trent, J. (1968). Toulmin's model of argument: An examination and extension. *Quarterly Journal of Speech, 54*, 252-59.

Tsipis, K. (1972). Hiding behind the military-industrial complex. *Bulletin of the Atomic Scientists, 22*, 20.

Vickers, B. (1988). *In defense of rhetoric*. Oxford: Clarendon.

Voorhees, B. (1986). Trialectical critique of constructivist epistemology. In J. Dillon, *Mental images, values, and reality: Proceedings of the International Society for General Systems Research*, pp. 47-67.

Vorzimmer, P. J. (1970). *Charles Darwin: The years of controversy*. Philadelphia: Temple University Press.

———. (1981). *The development of Darwin's theory*. Cambridge: Cambridge University Press.

Walker, G. B. (1984). *Perelman's theory of values and its critical implications*. Paper presented at the annual meeting of the Speech Communication Association, Chicago, IL.

Wallace, K. R. (1963). The substance of rhetoric: Good reasons. *Quarterly Journal of Speech, 49*, 239-49.

———. (1970). *Understanding discourse*. Baton Rouge: Louisiana State University Press.

Wallinger, M. (1985). Argumentation in utility rate hearings: Public participation in a hybrid field. In J. R. Cox, M. O. Sillars & G. B. Walker (Eds.), *Argument and social practice*, pp. 497-510. Annandale, VA: Speech Communication Association.

———. (1989). Regulatory rhetoric: Argument in the nexus of public and technical spheres. In B. E. Gronbeck, *Spheres of argument: Proceedings of the sixth SCA/AFA conference on argumentation*, pp. 71-80. Annandale, VA: Speech Communication Association.

Walton, Douglas N. (1987). *Informal fallacies: Towards a theory of argument criticism*. Amsterdam: John Benjamins.

Watzlawick, P., Beavin, J. H. & Jackson, D. D. (1967). *Pragmatics of human communication*. New York: W. W. Norton.

Weal, B. W. (1985). The force of narrative in the public sphere of argument. *Journal of the American Forensic Association, 22*, 104-14.

Weaver, R. M. (1953). *The ethics of rhetoric*. New York: Regnery/Gateway.

Weber, M. (1905). *The protestant ethic and the spirit of capitalism*. New York: Scribners.

———. (1946). *Essays in sociology*. Oxford: Oxford University Press.

———. (1947). *The theory of social and economic organization*. Glencoe, IL: Free Press.

Weimer, W. B. (1979). *Notes on the methodology of scientific Research.* Hillsdale, NJ: Erlbaum.

_____. (1984). Why all knowing is rhetorical. *Journal of the American Forensic Association, 20,* 63-71.

Weisner, J. B. (1985). A militarized society. *Bulletin of the Atomic Scientists, 35,* 102.

Wenzel, J. W. (1977). Toward a rationale for value-centered argument. *Journal of the American Forensic Association, 13,* 150-58.

_____. (1979). Jürgen Habermas and the dialectical perspective on argumentation. *Journal of the American Forensic Association, 16,* 83-94.

_____. (1980). Perspectives on argument. In J. Rhodes & S. Newell (Eds.), *Proceedings of the Summer Conference on Argumentation,* pp. 112-33. Washington, DC: Speech Communication Association.

_____. (Ed.) (1987a). *Argument and critical practices.* Annandale, VA: Speech Communication Association.

_____. (1987b). The rhetorical perspective on argument. In F. H. van Eemeren, R. Grootendorst, J. A. Blair & C. A. Willard (Eds.), *Argumentation: Across the lines of discipline,* pp. 101-9. Dordrecht, Holland: Foris.

Whitteman, H. & Fitzpatrick, M. A. (1986). Compliance-gaining in marital interaction: Power bases, processes, and outcomes. *Communication Monographs, 53,* 130-43.

Wicker, T. (1988a, September 6). Who needs debates? *The New York Times,* A, 23.

_____. (1988b, October 7). No oscar, no knockout. *The New York Times,* A, 35.

Wiener, P. P. (Ed.) (1973). *Dictionary of the history of ideas* (Vol. 1). New York: Charles Scribner's Sons.

Wilbur, K. (Ed.) (1982). *The holographic paradigm and other paradoxes.* Boulder, CO: Shambhala Publications.

Willard, C. A. (1976). On the utility of descriptive diagrams for the analysis and criticism of arguments. *Communication Monographs, 43,* 308-19.

_____. (1979a). *The better part of valor: How arguments "simmer down" and arguers beat retreats.* Paper presented at the meeting of the Speech Communication Association, Minneapolis, MN.

_____. (1979b). The epistemic functions of argument: Reasoning and decision-making from a constructivist/interactionist point of view — Part II. *Journal of the American Forensic Association, 15,* 211-19.

_____. (1983). *Argumentation and the social grounds of knowledge.* University, AL: University of Alabama Press.

_____. (1985). Cassandra's heirs. In J. R. Cox, M. O. Sillars & G. B. Walker (Eds.), *Argument and social practice,* pp. 16-34. Annandale, VA: Speech Communication Association.

_____. (1987a, July). *The language of individualism.* Northwestern University Conference on Argumentation and Public Discourse, Evanston, IL.

_____. (1987b). *L'Argumentation et les Principes Sociales de la Connaissance.* Centre Culturel International de Cerisy-La-Salle, Cerisy-La-Salle, France.

_____. (1987c). Valuing dissensus. In F. H. van Eemeren, R. Grootendorst, J. A. Blair & C. A. Willard (Eds.), *Argumentation: Across the lines of discipline,* pp. 145-58. Dordrecht, Holland: Foris.

Willard, C. A. (1989a). Argument as a social enterprise. In R. Meier (Ed.), *Norms in argumentation*, pp. 161-77. Dordrecht, Holland: Foris.

———. (1989b). *A theory of argumentation*. Tuscaloosa: University of Alabama Press.

Williams, R. (1983). *Keywords: A vocabulary of culture and society*. New York: Oxford.

Williamson, R. N. & Fitzpatrick, M. A. (1985). Two approaches to marital interaction: Relational control patterns in marital types. *Communication Monographs, 52*, 236-52.

Wilmot, W. W. (1979). *Dyadic Communication* (2nd ed.). Reading, MA: Addison-Wesley.

Winebrenner, H. (1987). *The Iowa precinct caucuses: The making of a media event*. Ames: Iowa State University Press.

Winslow, R. (1985a, January 28). Union Carbide moved to bar accident at U.S. plant before Bhopal tragedy. *Wall Street Journal*, p. 6.

———. (1985b, February 13). Union Carbide plan to resume making methyl isocynanate at its U. S. facility. *Wall Street Journal*, p. 10.

Woods, J. & Walton, D. (1982). *Argument: The logic of the fallacies*. Toronto: McGraw-Hill Ryerson.

Zarefsky, D. (1980a). Product, process or point of view? In J. Rhodes & S. Newell (Eds.), *Proceedings of the Summer Conference on Argumentation*, pp. 228-38. Washington, DC: Speech Communication Association.

———. (1980b). Lyndon Johnson redefines "equal opportunity": The beginnings of affirmative action. *Central States Speech Journal, 31*, 85-94.

———. (1980c). Argument and forensics. In J. Rhodes & S. Newell (Eds.), *Proceedings of the Summer Conference on Argumentation*, pp. 20-25. Washington, DC: Speech Communication Association.

Zarefsky, D., Sillars, M. O. & Rhodes, J. (Eds.) (1983). *Argument in transition*. Annandale, VA: Speech Communication Association.

Ziegelmueller, G. & Rhodes, J. (Eds.) (1981). *Dimensions of Argument*. Annandale, VA. Speech Communication Association.

Zietlow, P. H. & Sillars, A. L. (1988). Life stage differences in communication during marital conflicts. *Journal of Social and Personal Relationships, 5*, 223-45.